PRAISE FOR *BLACK CHAMBER*

"As always, [Stirling] comes up with inventive twists that keep your mind racing and the pages turning. Bravo!"
—Robert J. Sawyer, Hugo Award–winning author of *Quantum Night*

"The nice thing about getting a Steve Stirling book in the mail is that you know for a few hours you can fly on dreams of wonder, traveling to a world so much *more* than this angry reality."
—John Ringo, author of *Under a Graveyard Sky*

"It's a great feeling being in the hands of an alternate history master, who knows his material and crafts an utterly plausible world. Stirling gives us Teddy Roosevelt's USA and a Cuban-Irish-American secret agent who's more than a match for an airship full of James Bonds."
—Django Wexler, author of *The Infernal Battalion*

"Imagine that World War One began in Europe with the activist Teddy Roosevelt in the White House instead of the academic Woodrow Wilson. You've got a dandy steampunk setting for a slam-bang spy thriller with an engaging female protagonist." —David Drake, author of *Death's Bright Day*

"One of the most intriguing and entertaining adventures to come along in years." —Diana L. Paxson, author of *Sword of Avalon*

"Serves us a World War One America under a Theodore Roosevelt presidency, spiced with all the possibilities, good and bad, that Stirling's ever-ambitious imagination and meticulous approach to historical can cook up."
—A. M. Dellamonica, author of *The Nature of a Pirate*

"This is a sheer joy of an alternative history. . . . If you can put this book down once you've picked it up, I'll eat my bowler hat."
—Patricia Finney, author of *Gloriana's Torch*

"One mighty fine read—sexy, action-filled adventure in a thoughtful alternate history." —Lawrence Watt-Evans, author of the Obsidian Chronicles

"This novel provides a desperately needed infusion of courage and originality. How appropriate that Penguin, publisher of the James Bond novels, launches a hard-edged new spy series with Stirling. How appropriate that Ace, famous for classic science fiction, is on board for the adventure."
—Brad Linaweaver, Prometheus Award–winning author of *Moon of Ice*

TITLES BY S. M. STIRLING

Novels of an Alternate World War I

Black Chamber
Theater of Spies

Novels of the Change

Island in the Sea of Time
Against the Tide of Years
On the Oceans of Eternity

Dies the Fire
The Protector's War
A Meeting at Corvallis

The Sunrise Lands
The Scourge of God
The Sword of the Lady
The High King of Montival
The Tears of the Sun
Lord of Mountains
The Given Sacrifice
The Golden Princess
The Desert and the Blade
Prince of Outcasts
The Sea Peoples

Novels of the Shadowspawn

A Taint in the Blood
The Council of Shadows
Shadows of Falling Night

Other Novels by S. M. Stirling

The Peshawar Lancers
Conquistador

THEATER
OF SPIES

S. M. STIRLING

ACE
New York

ACE
Published by Berkley
An imprint of Penguin Random House LLC
1745 Broadway, New York, NY 10019

Library of Congress Cataloging-in-Publication Data

Names: Stirling, S. M., author.
Title: Theater of spies / S.M. Stirling.
Description: First edition. | New York: Ace, 2019. |
Series: A novel of an alternate world war; 2
Identifiers: LCCN 2018045381| ISBN 9780399586255 (paperback) |
ISBN 9780399586262 (ebook)
Subjects: | BISAC: FICTION / Alternative History. | FICTION /
Science Fiction / Adventure. | FICTION / Espionage. |
GSAFD: Alternative histories (Fiction) | Spy stories.
Classification: LCC PS3569.T543 T48 2019 | DDC 813/.54—dc23
LC record available at https://lccn.loc.gov/2018045381

First Edition: May 2019

Printed in the United States of America
1   3   5   7   9   10   8   6   4   2

Cover art by Shutterstock
Book design by Laura K. Corless

To Victor Milán, good writer and good friend.
We'll miss you, dammit, Vic.

ACKNOWLEDGMENTS

To Kier Salmon, longtime close friend and valued advisor, whose help with things in Spanish and about Mexico—she lived there into adulthood—has been very, very helpful with this series, as well as her general advice to which I have always listened carefully. My mother grew up speaking Spanish too (in Lima, Peru), but alas she and my aunt used it as a secret code the children couldn't understand, and Kier has been invaluable to fill in those lacunae, as well as being a fine editor (and promising writer) in her own right.

To Markus Baur, for help with the German language and as a first reader.

To Dave Drake, for help with the Latin bits and a deep knowledge of firearms acquired in several different ways. Also, collaborating with him taught me how to outline.

To Alyx Dellamonica, for advice, native-guide work, and just generally being cool. Her wife, Kelly Robson, is cool too and an extremely talented writer now winning implausible numbers of awards. An asteroid would have to strike Toronto to seriously dent the awesomeness of this pair. Soon Alyx will have another book out and it is great; I say this with smug certainty, since I got to read it in manuscript. Fortunately, writing is one of those fields where you have colleagues, not competitors.

To my first readers: Steve Brady, Pete Sartucci, Brenda Sutton, Lucienne Brown, Markus Baur, Ara Ogle, and Scott Palter.

To Patricia Finney (aka P. F. Chisholm), for friendship and her own wonderful books, starting with *A Shadow of Gulls* (which she wrote when she was in her teens, at which point I was still doing Edgar Rice Burroughs pastiche fanfic) and going on from there. One of the best historical novelists of our generation!

And to: Walter Jon Williams, Emily Mah, John Miller, Vic Milán (still present in spirit), Jan Stirling, Matt Reiten, Lauren Teffeau, S. E. Burr, Sarena Ulibarri, and Rebecca Roanhorse of Critical Mass, our writer's group, for constant help and advice.

And to Joe's Diner (joesdining.com) and Ecco Gelato & Espresso (eccogelato.com) here in Santa Fe, for putting up with my interminable presence and my habit of making faces and muttering dialogue as I write.

"It is not the critic who counts; not the man who points out how the strong man stumbles, or where the doer of deeds could have done them better. The credit belongs to the man who is actually in the arena, whose face is marred by dust and sweat and blood; who strives valiantly; who errs, who comes short again and again, because there is no effort without error and shortcoming; but who does actually strive to do the deeds; who knows great enthusiasms, the great devotions; who spends himself in a worthy cause; who at the best knows in the end the triumph of high achievement, and who at the worst, if he fails, at least fails while daring greatly, so that his place shall never be with those cold and timid souls who neither know victory nor defeat."

—THEODORE ROOSEVELT

PROLOGUE

Washington, D.C.
Iron House
(Consolidated War Department–Navy Department Headquarters)
Situation and Maps Room
NOVEMBER 6TH, AD 1916, 1916(B)
Point of Departure plus 4 Years

President Theodore Roosevelt stood with his feet braced and one hand gripping the lapel of his morning jacket, the other thrust into a pocket and clenched into a fist, looking at the maps that showed the Great War's fronts and alliances and disasters, scowling through his pince-nez with his mustache bristling. It was an expression as formidable as his more famous tooth-baring fighting grin. Officers of the Army, Navy, and Marine Corps—and a few from the Coast Guard—bustled quietly amid a clack of keys and murmur of telephones, updating the maps on the walls or directing the WAC girls in their crisp uniforms who used long pool-cue-like sticks to push markers on the big horizontal map-tables that showed the movements of friendly and enemy units and who manned . . .

Or perhaps staffed *is the right word*, he thought.

. . . the coding machines and Teletypes that linked the room to the far-flung legions of the Republic.

The thought came with the relief of a brief moment's whimsy as he gave a fond, proud glance at their patriotic youthful earnestness. And if they were doing soldiers' work, why shouldn't they be in uniform—albeit with skirts a mildly shocking three inches above the ankle—and get the same pay and ranks? He'd plucked Helen Varick Boswell from the Women's Bureau of the Party to organize the Women's Auxiliary Corps for the Army . . . and anyone who didn't like her being *General* Boswell now could just go and do that other thing.

Roosevelt and his aides and personal secretary and Secret Service bodyguards attracted a few glances, despite the disciplined intensity of the work. It suddenly occurred to him that the national vote would be tomorrow . . . and that he hadn't thought about it in days . . . which must be a first for a president standing for reelection, much less for a unique fourth term.

Fourth if you count taking over for McKinley after the assassination in '01, which I do, since the amiable old duffer had all the backbone of a chocolate éclair and never actually did *anything in all his born days, bless him. Not without a push, usually from me.*

Against his usual custom, this time he hadn't even ridden a special train from city to city and town to town, giving whistle-stop speeches to impromptu crowds; events had kept him pinned to Washington.

Not that it matters, the result's even more of a foregone conclusion than it was in 1912, and that was never in doubt after poor Taft's heart attack. How long ago that seems!

A horrible thought occurred to him: *God have mercy on us, if Taft had lived Woodrow Woodenhead* Wilson *might be president now and facing this!*

He shook his head as if to shed the image, though the news was bad enough to inspire any number of morbid fantasies. God or fate or destiny had spared the United States *that* at least. He'd swept back into office on an unprecedented wave of support, the strongest mandate since George Washington's, a vote for his plans to seize the dawning century for America and the New Nationalism.

One of the things he'd done since was take the nation by the scruff and make it face up to the fact that it was a dangerous world now and that you had to be *prepared.*

Getting elected *is only important because of what you* do *once you are. These maps are more important than electioneering.*

There were three on the section of wall he was staring at, showing Paris, London, and Bordeaux—where the top echelon of the French government had retreated after the first airborne gas attack on Paris in

May, which had seemed so terrible at the time but had *only* contained conventional phosgene and *only* killed thousands.

All three maps had broad, shaded marks on them, shaped roughly like an overlapping series of blobby elongated teardrops. That showed where the German super-Zeppelin bombers had dropped fifty to a hundred tons of the *Vernichtungsgas* on each city.

The enemy were calling it that, *Annihilation Gas*, though he preferred the popular coinage of *horror-gas*. The scientists termed it *organo-methylphosphonothioate nerve agent X* and claimed it wasn't even a gas at normal temperatures, strictly speaking, and more importantly they'd found that a single liter of it—two pints—held a hundred thousand lethal doses if perfectly distributed. The half-ton canisters of horror-gas had burst at a thousand feet, or sometimes wherever burning airships had exploded under attack by fighting-scout aeroplanes. Then the winds had carried the finely divided aerosol of drops over square miles of city as they settled. Most of the zeppelins had died over their targets or crashed on their way back, but they had taken three cities with them.

Below the maps were slots where estimates from Military Intelligence and the Black Chamber—and the allied governments, or what was left of them—were updated daily. Paris and London each showed over six hundred thousand dead and climbing fast; Bordeaux much less, but if anything a higher proportion of its smaller population. Nobody had any idea how many more civilians had been crippled or driven mad by marginal doses on the fringes of the killing zones; the gas was so persistent, especially in cold weather or sheltered spots or soaked into skin and cloth and hair and wood, that you couldn't go near the contaminated areas except in something like a deep-sea diver's rubber suit.

And nobody has any idea of how many have just run for their lives and are starving in ditches. The Kaiser's plot . . . or Hindenburg and Ludendorff's plot . . . cut the heads off two great nations at a stroke, he thought with throttled rage. *And came within a hair of wrecking us, if the Chamber hadn't stopped it. When we win this war, everyone involved will hang.*

One of his military aides cleared his throat and took a brief glance at his newfangled wristwatch. Roosevelt nodded brusquely and followed horse-faced young Bradley's jug ears down an arch-roofed corridor toward the meeting room. Two motionless Marine guards with Thompson guns on assault slings across their bellies and faces like carved wood under their turtle-shaped steel helmets flanked the door, snapping to attention for an instant and then returning to their watchfulness.

The president walked past them and sat at the head of the big oval table, nodding to the respectful greetings and salutes. There was a general rustle as files were opened and pads made ready. There were maps here too, set up on easels or hanging before the walls, mostly of Europe and North Africa, some of Asia.

And none showing things I wanted to see.

With the Chiefs of Staff was Director Wilkie, head of the Secret Service and more importantly of the—until recently—officially non-existent subsection that had grown to utterly overshadow it, the Black Chamber. Whose motto was *Ex umbris, acies*: From the shadows, steel.

Though they think I don't know that the unofficial *Chamber motto is* Non Theodorum parvis concitares ne perturbatus sit, *which means "Don't bother Teddy with the details, it'll just upset him"!*

"Right, gentlemen. We're here to appraise the general situation and make sure we're all . . . reading from the same page, as it were."

That phrase was his own coinage, and he thought it was rather pithy.

"And there are some political developments . . . integrating Canada, for instance . . . that will give you enough extra work to keep you from the temptations of idleness and dissipation."

He grinned at that, and there were tired chuckles; none of the men in the room looked as if they were getting enough sleep, and he *knew* he wasn't. He could barely squeeze in an hour or two a day swimming and wrestling and working the punching bag.

"Tell me some bad news, Leonard," Roosevelt said to the head of the General Staff. "Start with the bad, at least, and work your way up to the unthinkably terrible. We can do a world tour; it's a world war now that we're officially in it at last."

"Mr. President, other resources may be short, but of bad news in all flavors we can give you any amount," Leonard Wood said in his soft New England accent.

His long craggy Yankee face was professionally impassive and his voice calm, but they'd been friends for decades and had commanded the Rough Riders together. Roosevelt could tell grimness when it spoke.

"Apart from the fact that the Mexican Protectorate is finally quiet ... fairly quiet ... bad news is about all we have on the menu."

Roosevelt's lips tightened beneath his bushy mustache as he listened to the catalog of disasters that followed. The United States had been forced into a war where Germany stood triumphant. From the ruins and chaos of Russia, through the mass flight of the French to North Africa and on to the desperate heroism of the British rearguards, dying where they stood under hammer-storms of steel and poisoned fire to shelter the improvised evacuation from Dunkirk and Calais. That was an epic that might breed a legend for the future, but right now it was another defeat.

It wasn't war as he'd known it as colonel of the Rough Riders or dreamed of even in nightmares ... nobody had but H. G. Wells, whose *The War in the Air* was starting to look horribly prophetic in this day of the breaking of nations ... but there was no denying that it *worked*. His only consolation was that this time, for once in the history of the United States, he'd ensured that America was more or less ready for a fight at the *start* of a conflict. Against the Germans there wasn't much margin for error or time to learn on the job.

When the litany of blood and destruction was finished, Roosevelt set his palms on the reddish-brown Cuban mahogany of the table and spoke:

"Thank you, General Wood. There you have it, gentlemen. Our course is clear for the immediate future. There remains one matter of very serious import, which Director Wilkie and Admiral Sims will now outline."

Wilkie of the Black Chamber took his cue. "The Imperial German Navy is making serious preparations to sortie sometime in the next few months; we have that by the reports of agents who saw Wilhelmshaven in person, and it's confirmed by our cryptographic work and that of the Royal Navy. Which makes no sense, which means we're all missing something. Something crucial, something that could bite us on ... in a sensitive place."

Admiral Sims stroked his short-clipped white-shot beard. "Naval Intelligence agrees. We and the Royal Navy together have overwhelming superiority, and the short days and bad weather at this time of year mean that such an action would be a close-in slugging match, which adds to our advantage of numbers and weight of metal . . . and they can do the arithmetic too. They have some ace up their sleeve. A surprise."

"The world has lost far too much to far too many German surprises already," Roosevelt agreed. "Director Wilkie, finding out what they have planned is now your absolute priority. If we lose control of the North Sea, Britain goes with it, and Berlin will rule everything from Ireland to the Urals. God may know how we'd come back from that, but I do not."

"Mr. President, we're on it."

The Black Chamber's director looked quietly confident. Everyone else in the room was looking at him with respect at the least, shading up into hero worship from some of the younger officers.

The details were deeply secret, but it was generally known that the Germans had tried to wreck the main American port cities on the Atlantic with horror-gas attacks from specially built U-boats even before the declaration of war. That would have slaughtered millions . . . and killed any chance of thwarting the mad dream of a German-dominated world.

But the Black Chamber *had* thoroughly thwarted it—only the one in Savannah had struck, and there had been enough warning that the city had been evacuated first.

"I'm putting my best field operatives on it, Mr. President," Wilkie said.

Their eyes met. Roosevelt knew who he meant . . . and what the cost might be to someone who'd romped as a child with his own sons and daughters, whose father had gone up San Juan Hill with him, and whom he'd held as she wept over her murdered parents. His own four sons were in the Army, even young Quentin who was only a lad of nineteen and heedlessly eager to be a man. All the boys were in fighting units—including the new Air Corps—by their own wish and doing well by their own merits. He feared for them every day, but it would have broken his heart if any of them had tried to avoid frontline service.

Black Chamber operative Luz O'Malley and that charming, eccentric young Boston girl Ciara Whelan had saved the nation from the German horror-gas plot with cold cunning and high courage . . . but a great nation needed a great deal of saving in this terrible new age, and they were willing and ready to run the risks again, risks worse than going over the top in the face of Maxim guns and mustard gas.

We do not exist for ourselves alone, none of us do. That's why I went to Cuba even though Edith was so very sick and our children so young, though I felt as if I were torn in two. We are the tools of something greater than any of us, and if the tool breaks beneath the strain . . . then another steps forward and the greater purpose goes on. The lines of blood. And beyond that, the nation that is the embodiment and bloodline of all our people.

Roosevelt nodded to the Black Chamber's director, a slight crisp gesture to affirm his choice. Wilkie returned it and went on:

"My very best operatives, Mr. President—and there aren't any better in the world."

ONE

"Now that was a strange and lovely dinner, my darling, and fine people," Ciara Whelan said dreamily from behind the wheel of the auto. "Though it's good to be home, too."

"Glad you enjoyed yourself, *querida*," Black Chamber operative Luz O'Malley Aróstegui said over her shoulder as she swung the wrought-iron gates closed behind them and shot the bolt with a clank.

And speaking of joy, it's finally *here*, she thought as she fished a small package out of the mailbox built into the thickness of the wall beside the gate and slipped it into the pocket of her skirt.

"I had fun too," she added sincerely.

Warmed *sake* was insidious, but neither of them was more than slightly elevated, and very pleasantly satisfied but not full. Their hosts had laid on the full seven-course splendor of a *kaiseki-ryori*, but Japanese cooking at that level hewed to an austere and elegant restraint. The Taguchis couldn't have afforded a feast like that back in Hiroshima Prefecture—Mrs. Taguchi had learned the art working as an assistant cook at a *ryokan* inn, and her husband had been the fourth son on a little peasant farm—but they'd done very well for themselves here with their nursery-gardening-landscaping business after years of toil and grit and thrift.

"And the hair glued across the lock wasn't broken?" Ciara asked.

"Intact!" Luz said.

She'd set three: at the gate, at the front door, and on the light switch just inside it, and she'd been conscious of the FN automatic in her jacket and the six-inch *navaja,* her folding knife, in its special pocket in her skirt as she checked the marker just now. The likelihood of some surviving Mexican *revolucionario* or an inquisitive Abteilung IIIb agent finding out where a Black Chamber operative lived was quite low . . . but low wasn't zero and she didn't intend to die of stupid.

"If they're all still in place, it's pretty certain no one came through the gate or the front door," she continued. "Two intact would be suspicious. One would be *very* suspicious, and three gone definitely means enemy action."

Ciara nodded. She was picking up tradecraft on the job the way most in the Chamber did, though she'd torn through the manuals with ferocious concentration; there were regular training courses now, but still not enough time to put everyone through them first. She'd already noted how all the exterior doors and windows in Luz's home could be fastened from the inside with unpickable bolts.

"But you've got to be careful with the spirit gum or it's obvious," Luz went on. "Just a touch on your pinkie from the tinfoil tube when you apply it, or better still draw the hair *through* it. The main problem is that even a . . . hair-fine . . . hair is visible on a pale surface, and mine's black so it shows up worse even in low light. Sometimes I carry a spool of light-colored thread . . . or I could just pull out one of yours, now, I suppose, sweetie."

"Warn me first, so I don't give us away by shrieking!" Ciara chuckled.

Then she frowned. It was the expression Luz had come to know meant she was deep in something technical and about to display the fruits of natural talent and a lifelong project of self-education, though that life had seen barely twenty-one years so far.

Witness her happy squeals going through Papá's old project plans. Every time she says: Oh, Luz, this is so clever *or* Your da did this so elegantly! *that makes me feel proud of Papá . . . and her . . . all over again.*

"You know, I could do a . . . a hidden counting system . . . adapting a factory punch clock, maybe . . . for all the gates and doors and windows," Ciara said. "And a master switch to set it all going when you leave."

"Excelente!" Luz said. "Hmmm ... probably we could get the Chamber to pay for it, too. And the design would look good in your record jacket, Junior Field Operative Whelan! Very ... *progressive!"*

She leaned into the driver's side for a brief soft kiss that tasted of *sake* and ginger-infused pear, walked around the hood, laid a hand on the side, and swung into the passenger seat with a lithe hop. The low-slung, open-top Cole 4-40 roadster slid forward with a burble of throttled-down engine and a pop and crunch of gravel beneath the wheels. The electric headlamps cut two yellow tunnels in the darkness, showing white crushed stone, and now and then the flutter of a pink tiger moth or a glimpse through groves and gardens.

"And how kind it was of the Taguchis to invite us both to dinner!" Ciara added.

"I thought it was about time to introduce you to some family friends, *mi amor.* And the Taguchis are about the oldest friends my parents had here in Santa Barbara."

She thought Ciara's nod and smile in return had an element of relief. They'd been together just long enough to start thinking seriously about the future, and being madly in love didn't mean you completely knew someone—not when they'd only met in September. If you were smart you realized that, and while Ciara was naïve in some ways and had no natural talent for dealing with people ...

She is as smart as they come. And I'm relieved she's *relieved.*

Luz let her head fall against the back of her seat and the pleasantly cool wind of Southern California's November night play through her bobbed raven-black hair as they drove, looking up at the bright Pacific stars flickering through the leaves of the live oaks that lined the long curving driveway. The air carried the scent of cut grass, flowers, and the sea, and the hiss of surf on the beach southward was just audible.

It took a little time to reach the Casa de los Amantes, as the yellow stucco walls and Roman-tile roof loomed through the trees. It wasn't particularly large by the standards of Montecito, as this neighborhood was known, but the grounds *were* big, with small groves of oranges and olives, figs and peaches, and a little vineyard around a big kitchen garden as well as lawns and flower beds between winding paths, live oak and poplar and cypress, and scattered tall palms. Her father had taken this land as payment for his first big local commission; here she'd played and roamed as a girl, amid brightly colored dreams of adventure and formless longings for she-knew-not-what.

Enjoy every moment, Luz thought, with a mixture of pleasure and sadness. *The Great War isn't going to leave us alone forever.*

She was a little surprised the Director had waited this long to throw them back into the stewpot . . .

Which means I *can't wait any longer to say what I'm planning on saying. But am I reluctant for scruples' sake . . . she is very young . . . or is it sheer cowardice that's giving me palpitations? Scruples were never something I was afflicted with before, any more than I was with pimples, but I've never been in love before either, not like this.*

"It's been a while since I went to a family dinner party," Ciara added.

And then in a voice less happy as her hands clenched on the wheel:

"Not since I let that foolish wicked man Sean McDuffy talk me into going to Germany for him like a fool myself, and believed him when he said that it was for Ireland."

Ciara had wanted to do something dreadful to the British to avenge the brother who'd died on the barricades in Dublin in the Easter Rising . . . though not enough to go along when she realized *how* dreadful the plan was, or that it was meant for America too.

"I'm glad you did go to Germany, or we'd never have met!" Luz said.

And it was revenge on Villa and his men for my mima *and* papá *that sent* me *into the Chamber.*

Aloud she went on: "Also I'd have been dead without you to confirm my cover to Colonel Nicolai and warn me about his alarm system before I went in to crack his files. Dead and very lonely, if that makes any sense! Everyone makes mistakes; it's turning them around that's important, and you certainly did that."

Ciara laughed, and Luz could see her shoulders relax in the dim light. She brought the two-seat roadster to a halt in the converted carriage house with skilled panache, hardly needing to use the brake at all, though she'd never even been a *passenger* in an auto before she left Boston a few months ago as a clandestine courier for the Irish Republican Brotherhood.

Going straight from the violently illegal IRB to the Black Chamber—jocularly known in government and Party circles as "*el jefe's* brass knuks"—was a first, too. But then the Chamber prided itself on putting function ahead of formality, and its ever-growing rolls were full of adventurers, eccentrics, buccaneering soldiers of fortune, genteel university-educated thugs, old cowboy Rough Riders, the odd Indian, and the just plain odd . . . like one Luz O'Malley Aróstegui.

Sometimes the borderline mad, like the head of the Technical Section, Nicolai Tesla.

Hot metal ticked in the engine as they picked up the coats they might have needed on a Santa Barbara November night but hadn't, and walked back to the house hand in hand and up the four semicircular steps of white limestone to the front door, breathing in the scent of the banks of purple-blossomed Mexicali Rose planted around the cream-stucco walls.

Then she unlocked the solid outer doors, twin arched leaves of carved oak set with pyramidal iron studs, and checked that the hair was in place across the inward-swinging inner ones of wrought iron and hammered brass in the shape of peacocks. They had the sixteen-room building to themselves; Luz hadn't kept any live-in staff since she pensioned off the last old retainers when she went into the Chamber. A cleaning and maintenance service did well enough, when she was away so much, and was easy to get in this area of vacation homes. Taguchi Gardens saw to the grounds.

"And the front door and light-switch markers are intact too," she said, swinging the doors shut behind them, locking them and turning on the lights; the chandelier high overhead glowed, turning cavernous gloom to brightness.

"*¡Ay!* That flower scent always takes me back to my childhood. Mima planted those right after Papá built the first part of this house for her, the south wing. They reminded her of her home in Cuba."

Though hopefully not of how her own father tried to have them both killed the night they eloped, she added to herself; she'd told Ciara about that, but few others.

Ciara nodded, then returned to her thought: "I didn't know if . . . well, if we could do that. You know, visit with people . . . together."

"As a couple? With discretion, yes, and depending on the circles you move in," Luz said. "More discretion with some people than others, of course, and absolute discretion with many, alas for the world's idiocy. But even people who disapprove in theory will often make an exception for you in practice if they know and like you as an individual . . . consistency is for fanatics, after all. Your aunties did well enough in South Boston, didn't they?"

"Well, yes, bless them!"

Bless them indeed, Luz thought.

Not for the first time, either. Without Ciara's aunt Colleen and her life-companion, honorary Auntie Treinel, and their good example, things would have been . . .

Much more complicated.

"Yes, they're very well-liked in the neighborhood, for that they've always been ready to lend a hand when there's bad luck or strong need—marketing done or a meal cooked for someone who has to sit up with a sick child, letters written or accounts cast up for those who haven't the knack, help at a wedding or funeral, things like that. So there's a smile and nod and many a stop to pass on gossip when they pass by, but nobody knew that they were—"

Ciara stopped, thought for a moment, then went on:

"No, I think . . . looking back, and knowing what I know now . . . I think a lot of people *did* know about Auntie Colleen and Auntie Treinel, or suspected, but they just didn't *say* anything where I could hear it. So I didn't realize it myself until I started thinking about how I felt about you and it all went *click* in my head, even though they raised me and Colm nearly as much as Da did. To be sure, someone said *Boston marriage* once . . . but that's . . ."

"Ambiguous," Luz said. "Though not as ambiguous as it was in our parents' time. Still, it's not what people know is true that's usually important, it's what they'll *pretend* to believe is true by unspoken mutual consent because it's easier all 'round."

"Did the Taguchis . . . ummm . . ." Ciara said.

"Know we were lovers? Well, nothing was said aloud on either side, but I'm pretty sure they did. I'm *absolutely* sure that Fumiko and Midori did. We were like sisters as little girls and we're still very good friends and keep in touch, and from the smiles and nods and thumbs-up they gave when nobody was looking I know *they* thoroughly liked you. They'd have been polite to you even if they hadn't, but . . ."

And I appreciate the gesture, Luz thought fondly as Ciara gave her a glowing grin that lit her turquoise eyes and snub-nosed, freckled round face for a moment. *The whole Taguchi family always did have exquisite manners*, Dios los bendiga.

Luz grinned herself and trailed her fingers on the balustrade as they linked hands and walked slowly up the curving stairs to the second-story landing, their footsteps going *click* on the iron-hard, black-streaked maroon *curupay* wood of the risers, louder for the silence of the house.

"When I was a little girl I used to love to slide down the banister here. Mima scolded me . . . *¡Ay, mi nena, pero que chamaca mas traviesa eres!* she'd say . . . but her heart wasn't in it, and Papá smiled. Sometimes he'd do it himself, with me in his lap! He always liked it when I did things like that, or climbed trees or rode my pony fast."

"It's quite the tomboy you were, then! And you so . . . so smooth and elegant a lady now!"

"No reason you can't like both. It depends on the circumstances. Once when I was eight and Tommy Deveraux yanked on my pigtails from behind in class hard enough to make my eyes show tears . . . and not for the first time, I might add—"

"The miserable bully!" Ciara said sympathetically; there weren't many schoolgirls who hadn't had *that* experience. "I hope someone gave him a taste of his own medicine someday!"

Luz grinned. "One Luz O'Malley turned around and gave him a black eye then and there, and he punched me back and we went tumbling around the floor knocking things over and screeching and bellowing. Well, I screeched; he tried to bellow and he was built like a little blond bullock, but at eight . . ."

Ciara stopped and clapped her hands in delight. "And how did that end?"

"With me sitting on his chest barking my knuckles on his face and screaming like a banshee while he bawled for mercy and his mother, until the teacher pushed through and pulled me off and carried me bodily out of the room in a hissing fury, wiggling and kicking like a mad ferret, and then they sent for my father. This was back right after the war with Spain started, just before he left for the Rough Rider camp in Texas with a telegram from Uncle Teddy in his hand telling him to make haste if he wanted a commission."

Ciara winced. "Oh, I hope he wasn't too angry!"

Luz shook her head, a fond expression on her face. "Papá? He came into the principal's office with the teacher pouring the tale of it in his ear, and saw me sitting and pouting with my blouse ripped, my hair like a haystack, and my face like a thundercloud, and Tommy whimpering through a cloth full of ice on the other side of the room . . ."

"I can see it as if I were there! He *wasn't* angry?"

"He laughed and said: *Well, and here's the tail end of a shindy I'd have paid good money to see, and no mistake, eh?*"

"And your father wouldn't by any chance have had the blood of Erin's warriors in his veins, would he, Miss O'Malley?"

"Oh, perhaps *solo un poco.*"

"More! Tell me what happened next!"

Luz chuckled; they were still at the stage where they were trying to swallow each other's pasts at a gulp. She marshaled her memories:

"He came over and felt my hands gently; they were all bloody, and skinned in places, and the left one had started to swell. I winced a bit because I'd popped a knuckle . . . you can feel it, here, see, the second on the left hand, it's still a little bit bigger . . ."

"Oh, you poor thing!" Ciara said, and kissed it. "That must have hurt!"

Luz chuckled agreement and touched the finger to Ciara's snub nose.

"By then? It hurt like it was dipped in fire, and the memory's yet green! Papá's eyebrows went up as he felt it—he knew brawler's injuries. Well, he'd been bossing countryside construction projects for years."

"Rough men?"

"Rough men, away from home, many with no family and good reason to keep moving from job to job. And a love of the jug. So that meant thumping beefy quarrelsome drunks now and then to teach them respect, or helping patch up enough of them on Sunday morning to get the project going again come dawn on Monday. And he said:

"We'll need some ice over here too, please, and I think a strip of bandage and a sling . . . does it hurt when I touch the knuckle here, a stóirín, *my darling little treasure?"*

Luz smiled at the memory of his face. "I said: *A bit, Papá, just since I stopped."*

"It didn't hurt right away?" Ciara asked curiously.

"No . . . no, when you're in a fight you're . . . transported, changed, taken beyond the everyday, so things like that don't matter. It's like sharing love, or like flying in dreams. Or at least it is for me, sometimes. And he whistled and said:

"You kept right on punching him hard as you could with that, *didn't you, my little Miss Spitfire O'Malley?*

"To which I replied: *It didn't hurt when I was hitting him, Papá, I was too busy."*

Ciara snorted at that, and Luz squeezed her hand as she continued: "Then he whistled again and shook his head when he put my hands down—gently—and said, as if to himself or to Mima:

"Jesus, Mary, and Joseph but we've bred us a wild one, Luciana darling!

"And then to me: *Your mother will have a word or two to say when she sees you!"*

"And what did *you* have to say to that?" Ciara asked. "It would have had me quaking, I'll tell you!"

"I said with a smugness only an eight-year-old could muster that Tommy's mother would *cry,* when she saw *him."*

"Did she?"

"Like a gardener's watering can . . . only much louder. Papá looked over and they'd just taken down the cloth with the ice so the nurse could have a look at Tommy—she was clucking, but luckily not finding anything that wouldn't heal—and he whistled again and said:

"Faith! His face looks like the beefsteak he'll be putting on that fine shiner you gave him! and I smiled . . . though that hurt too; I had a split lip dribbling down my chin onto my blouse . . . and I said:

"Well, that'll *teach him to pull on an O'Malley's braids!"*

Ciara gave a peal of delighted laughter.

"Good for you! And good for your da!" she said. "A fine man he was! And was it all worth the switching you got from the principal?"

"*Absolutely* worth sitting down carefully for a while. Doubly so when Tommy got the cane too for starting it and he walked out of the principal's office blubbing and I didn't."

"Oh, foolish of him! Knowing children . . ."

Luz's catlike expression was one Tommy Deveraux would have recognized and flinched from.

"The other boys would go *boooo-hoooo* at him on the playground and the girls whispered behind their hands and giggled and he'd turn red as a boiled beet every time. It was *wonderful* . . . and he never pulled another girl's braids."

"That sounds like you, my heart!" Ciara said. "Now, sneaking out of bed to read at night was *my* naughtiness, if I couldn't bear to stop where I was in the story."

Luz smiled and leaned over to kiss the top of her head. "Why am I not surprised? Raised in a bookstore, Ciara Whelan was, the sorrow and pity of it . . . oh, don't throw me in the briar patch, Br'er Fox! So you burned the midnight oil, eh?"

Ciara stuck out her tongue before she continued: "Downstairs in the shop where the streetlamp came through the window, and I'd sit wrapped in the quilt in the big armchair. Da said I'd ruin my eyes and stunt my growth when he caught me at it or saw me yawning too much at breakfast, but never gave me more than a little smack on the fanny, and sometimes he'd come read me a bit until I fell asleep, *The Field of Boliauns* or *The Children of Lir*. He never did take the belt to Colm much, either, for all that he was wild enough as a boy. I think he saw our ma in us. From her picture she looked a little like me, and I inherited her hair—"

She touched her piled locks, a yellow halfway to copper-red.

"—Da's was brown."

She sighed; her mother had died of childbed fever not long after she was born. Then her white, slightly irregular teeth showed in a broad grin full of crackling energy as they came to the top of the stairs. She tugged at Luz's hand and said:

"Let's go swim!"

That was another thing Ciara had never had much chance to do in Boston and had taken to with enormous enthusiasm here. They helped each other unhook their semiformal afternoon dresses when they reached the master bedroom—you didn't do an evening gown for a small family dinner party, not at the O'Malley-Taguchi level of society and not in these more casual modern times. It was a much less complicated process than it would have been a few years ago. As well as being . . .

Luz leaned forward and whispered in Ciara's ear: "It's Christmas early this year, and I'm unwrapping the world's most beautiful present."

Then she kissed her between the shoulder blades.

A happy: "Oh, you!" in reply came with a poke in the ribs. And: "These dresses! They're so comfortable!"

Women's clothing *had* changed drastically even in the five years since she was Ciara's age, and in ways she heartily approved; Coco Chanel's latest continued the trend.

But hobble skirts . . . hobble skirts were an evil plot against half the human race.

They hung the clothes and tossed the underthings in a hamper in the walk-in cupboard. Then Luz stretched on tiptoe with her fingers linked above her head before going down on one knee to light the paper-and-kindling fire set beneath stacked driftwood ready in the bedroom's hearth.

We'll want this blazing when we're through in the pool, even if my love is part polar bear.

She felt Ciara's eyes on her as she tossed the splint into the flames, and winked.

"It's not fair!" Ciara laughed, putting her hands on her hips. "You can put me to the blush so much more easily than I can you!"

That was true enough even discounting experience, since Luz's complexion was a clear olive that tanned readily to a warm light honey-golden-brown; she took after her mother that way, along with full lips and high cheekbones, though the narrow blue streaks near the pupils of her dark eyes were her father's, and so was her long-limbed build. Hair the almost iridescent black of a raven's wing could have been from either. By contrast Ciara's skin had a translucent paleness that showed blue traceries of vein and didn't take the sun at all. She was also fuller-figured than Luz's leopardess build, two inches shorter at five-four but weighing about the same.

She *did* blush now at Luz's frank appreciation, a flush spreading down from face to bosom.

"So, swim!" she said, extending a hand.

Half an hour later Luz was glad of the loose djellabas of striped wool she and Ciara were both wearing as they climbed back to the terrace outside the bedchamber. A friend had brought a dozen of them back from a mission in Oran in French North Africa and given them to her last Christmas, and they were amazingly, softly comfortable, one-size-fits-all, and just warm enough.

I'm glad I got Julie something nice for this *Christmas,* Luz thought, distracted for an instant—or perhaps taking refuge in an irrelevant thought. *She and Bob will love those matching Purdey .338 side-by-sides. And there won't be any more, since Purdey & Sons had their shop right in Mayfair.*

Ciara didn't notice cold nearly as much, but then this was fine June weather, by Massachusetts standards. Perhaps she felt the chill in Luz's fingers.

"There's that lovely alpaca-skin rug before the fire," she said as they came to the top of the stairs, her voice sweet with promise. "That would be all toasty by now for my delicate hibiscus-blossom beloved..."

"*Una inspiración maravillosa,* but wait just a moment, my heart, *mi amor,*" Luz said.

And my goose bumps aren't all from the chill, she thought before continuing aloud:

"There's something worth seeing from here."

They stood by the railing, arms around each other's waists and Ciara's head on her shoulder. Luz leaned her own cheek against her lover's damp locks, looking out from the terrace toward the blue-black line of the ocean just west of due south from here. The sky was cloudless and a blaze of stars from horizon to horizon; she'd switched off the exterior lights, and Santa Barbara was neither close enough nor large enough nor bright enough at nearly midnight to wash out the sky. The Milky Way reared in an arch of white diamond dust above them.

Gibbous and hugely yellow-gold, the moon hung over the waters to the south and east. A long path glittered from it over the foam-flecked waves, leading beyond the world.

Ciara made a wordless sighing sound, and her arm tightened on Luz's waist.

"Oh, thank you, my darling!" she said, watching the moon hang over the Pacific. "That is . . . marvelous!"

Luz swallowed; her throat was a little dry and tight. She turned and faced Ciara. The younger woman's eyes searched hers gravely, matching the sudden seriousness she sensed.

"*Mi amor . . . mi corazón* . . . these weeks together have been the happiest in my life. Not just fun, but . . . happy."

So happy I feel very slightly guilty, feeling so absolutely happy amid the wreck of the world . . . but life goes on for people. It has to, and it would do nobody good to sit and mope po-faced.

"For me too, my darling one," Ciara said earnestly. "I love you so much, and I want more of this . . . more than anything. I want *you*, for my very own, always."

"And I you, beloved," Luz said.

She reached into the pocket of her robe, and her fingers closed around the little box that had arrived while they were out.

"If it weren't for the war, I'd . . . I might have waited a little, for your sake, my heart, so that we could have gotten to know each other better, more deeply. But we don't have all the time in the world before the world visits us again."

And quite possibly kills us, she thought, and knew the thought was shared. *Probably, even.*

Ciara smiled a little. "If it weren't for the war, we wouldn't have met at all! I know how it says *hurry*. So don't keep me in suspense!"

Luz braced herself and opened the box, setting it on the balustrade railing between them. Ciara gave a soft gasp. Within the velvet padding were two *Claddagh*, Irish pledge rings with bezels in the shape of two linked hands clasping across a crowned heart, done in gold, silver, diamonds, and ruby chips that glittered softly by the light of moon and stars. The form had been used among the Gael for centuries, in pledging loyalty or troth.

"Ciara . . . will you stay with me, and be my love?" Luz said, taking up one ring. "Shall we be comrades and partners through life?"

A tear glistened at the corner of one of Ciara's turquoise-green eyes.

"I . . . yes, Luz. Oh, yes."

TWO

Casa de los Amantes
Santa Barbara, California
November 18th, 1916(b)

Just after noon the next day the doorbell rang in a series of chimes, as they sat over the remains of a very late breakfast in the patio courtyard. Luz and Ciara started, froze, looked at each other, and burst into laughter at the same moment.

"Hold that thought," Luz said as she rose from the big chair they'd been sharing while they fed each other spoonfuls of fresh berries and cream and the rest of their breakfast.

As she walked through the arched door of the courtyard and into the entrance hall of the *Casa* she felt her armor slipping into place, a cold catlike awareness that radiated out like an invisible psychic shell. It had grown stronger every day since her parents died while she hid in the wardrobe a few feet away. The good thing was that now she knew she *could* take it off. By the time she'd reached the front door, Ciara was back . . . with a billhook from a storage closet, a heavy curved blade on a long pole used for trimming shrubbery. Or inconvenient people, if you knew your medieval history.

Luz gave her a quick smile of approval; she'd seen first-hand that her partner didn't lose her nerve in a tight place. Not that she expected a fight now, but you never knew; that was why she had the Browning automatic and her knife, the Andalusian *navaja*, in her pockets. Which was something of a judgment on the life that fate or her own choices had handed her, but you couldn't run things back and see how they might have turned out differently.

"Glad to have you with me, *querida* . . . but let's not terrify an innocent deliveryman too much as he stands outside with a box of oysters on ice, *sí*? People might talk."

Ciara nodded and put the billhook behind a tall ornamental vase, where she could lunge for it if she had to. Then she stepped sideways and glanced through the edge of one of the big grillework-barred windows that flanked the entrance.

"It *isn't* a deliveryman, unless Diehl's Grocery has gotten a canary-yellow Cadillac Type 53 Roadster with black trim to replace their Model T truck since last week. Very nice, the one with their high-compression seventy-seven-horsepower V-8 engine. It's probably as fast as your lovely, lovely Cole 4-40!"

Luz used the fish-eye lens concealed in one of the door studs. The man outside was three years older than her twenty-five, and wore a lightweight sack suit and matching waistcoat of a pale fawn sharkskin silk-worsted mixture, beautifully cut to conceal the shoulder holster under his armpit and the stiletto in a forearm sheath.

"It's someone I know, another senior field operative," she said, and slid her hand out of her pocket . . . without the gun.

"Though come to think of it, I outrank him now. Damn the man! But this is Black Chamber business.

"Hello, James," she added as she pulled the outer door open.

The Chamber's discipline wasn't as obvious as the Army's, but it was stronger if anything.

James Cheine had six slim feet of height and a long bony face with the weathered tan of an Anglo-Saxon who spent much time in the open air; a thin three-inch-long vertical scar marked his right cheek, and there was something very cruel about his blue-gray eyes and rather curved lips. A comma of hair nearly as black as Luz's own Polaire-style bob fell on his forehead.

"Do come in, briefly," Luz told him. *"Mi casa . . . no es su casa."*

He doffed his gray homburg politely, though he used the left hand that also held an attaché case, in a practiced reflex that kept his right free at all times. Document courier was far below his usual pay grade, which meant it was something of the highest priority . . .

"Good to see you, too, Luz," he said.

The case wasn't handcuffed to his wrist, but doing *that* just put up a flag reading: *Something you really want to see here! Kill me and cut it off!* The sort of thing you expected the Federal Bureau of Security or the Heinz 57 varieties of Military Intelligence to do.

But perhaps it's better that way, because they're *mostly so dim it might just slip their mind that they put that pesky case full of Utterly Secret documents down on the seat in the streetcar and then walked off and left it* . . .

"Or should I say *Executive Field Operative* Luz now?"

Like hers, his palm was hard, callused, and dry as they shook hands.

"That's *your exalted and most high mightiness* emperatriz omnipotente *Executive Field Operative O'Malley, ma'am,* James," Luz said dryly. "But don't let your humble awe and the oppressive knowledge that you are as worms and dirt beneath my jeweled sandals make you over-formal."

"And this charming young lady, your Omnipotent Imperial Executive Highness?" he said, inclining his head and smiling.

"My friend Ciara Whelan, now a junior field operative herself," Luz said.

She pronounced it properly as *Keera,* and with a slight sigh; the outside world was crashing back into weeks of golden dream.

"Ciara, this is Senior Field Operative . . ."

"Cheine," he said, accepting her brief firm shake too. "James Cheine."

"Pleased to make your acquaintance, Mr. Cheine," she said warily, unconsciously stepping closer to Luz for reassurance.

"Enchanted, Miss Whelan; I'm very glad you're here, as my instructions from headquarters involve you too.

"And what a lovely home!" he added.

He looked around at the high airy tile-and-plaster splendors of the hallway and the double stairs curling upward toward the landing. Through the archway between them the dappled shade of the courtyard showed, and the glitter and tinkle of the fountain.

"The New Californian school, but built before that became so very fashionable, I should think, from the state of the gardens. Which are beautiful even by Californian standards."

"Cuban style, actually, but that's water from the same Spanish

Colonial well," Luz said; it could have been the *casa grande* of a hacienda in any land where Spain's flag had once flown. "Papá wanted something that would make my mother feel at home."

His voice had a Groton-School-and-Harvard-Yard patrician accent of an East Coast variety much like Uncle Teddy's. The Black Chamber was infested with recent Ivy League graduates of the more adventurous sort, and of course the president had been a Harvard man himself. They included a scattering of Bryn Mawr alumni like Luz, and a few from Wellesley and Smith and Vassar and the others. She'd been accepted as a field operative back in the Chamber's beginnings and the example had stuck; things had been fluid then, despite which it had taken all her powers of persuasion and moral blackmail at the presidential level and blunt just-shut-up-and-make-it-happen orders from Uncle Teddy thereafter.

"She laid out the gardens. The house had all the modern conveniences right from the start, though, and under the stucco it's earthquake-proof."

"Cast mass-concrete with galvanized-steel reinforcing bars," Ciara said impulsively. "One of the very earliest examples! With integral ducting for electrical lines and pipes."

She blushed and subsided, but Luz smiled at her and added:

"That's it. Papá was a progressive long before the Party; he knew the twentieth century was coming soon."

"Unlike some of *my* relatives even now," Cheine replied ruefully, hanging his hat on the mahogany rack. "For whom it's always the blessed eternal noon of 1899, Queen Victoria's still alive, J. P. Morgan and J. D. Rockefeller allow the president to cut ribbons and kiss babies while they run the country, and all's well with the world."

The older generation of the Upper Ten Thousand mostly thought Uncle Teddy a traitor to his class, a would-be Caesar Augustus, or both, and the whole New Nationalist movement a grubby upstart affair of wild-eyed middle-class radicals. But plenty of younger scions like James had embraced the Progressive Republican Party's new order; the *strenuous life* was *much* less boring than old-style politics had been, or sitting and biting your thumb in grumpy isolation like your parents while the world went elsewhere.

"Do please step on through to the patio and join us, Mr. Cheine," Ciara said carefully.

Watching her accent, too, Luz thought with a feeling of protective annoyance directed at the man as they walked through the hallway and around the ascending glazed shells of the fountain.

She knew it was irrational, since James was just talking in the way he did when he wasn't putting on something else. The plummy tones nevertheless activated Ciara's hardscrabble Boston Irish defensive hackles, and that made Luz bristle for her in turn.

Ciara hadn't finished high school—few people did, and even fewer girls in not particularly affluent families who weren't aiming to be schoolteachers—but she had an excellent vocabulary and her grammar was very good, since she'd grown up a voracious reader who lived above a bookstore. Her vowels did tend to be long and a bit nasal, though; she usually said *Baahst'n* when she referred to her native town, and beneath it ran a brogue as green as a shamrock and broad as her Dublin-born father's that she could bring out when she wanted to or that crept out under stress.

Cheine's blue-gray eyes flicked between them, and Luz saw him noting the identical robes they were wearing, Ciara's instinctive half step closer to Luz's side, and then the pledge rings and mentally going: *Aha, I might have known!*

"No, James, that wasn't the reason," Luz said pleasantly, denying him the salve for his vanity. "It's just that I never liked you that much."

Ciara choked slightly as she realized *that wasn't the reason* included an unspoken final phrase *why I wouldn't sleep with you,* flushed pink as she realized what Cheine had picked up effortlessly about *her,* then coughed to cover it and the shocked giggle that might have followed.

Cheine held Ciara's chair with gentlemanly *politesse* and waited for Luz to sit before taking another himself across the granite-slab table beneath an arbor overgrown by Queen's Wreath and its long drooping panicles of purple blossom. The gentle splashing of the fountain sounded in the background, and hummingbirds buzzed by.

"Coffee, Mr. Cheine? Sugar? Cream?" Ciara asked.

"That's very kind of you, Miss Whelan, and I would love a cup. Black will do nicely. So sorry to have interrupted your luncheon."

Luz fought down a startled laugh of her own with a strong but practiced effort of will that left her slight polite smile intact.

Ten more minutes . . .

Ciara poured, though with a very slight twitch at the same thought, and he took an appreciative sniff and sipped.

"Ah, thank you! Jamaica Blue Mountain, I think?"

Ciara nodded. "Diehl's Grocery in town stocks it, Mr. Cheine. They have a very wide selection of coffees . . . of everything, really."

"They should, in this sybaritic nest of plutocrats at play. Blue Mountain is my favorite; the very nectar of the gods, compared to the weak burnt Harvey House muck from Brazil on the trains, though I admit they serve a decent steak. *If* you stand over the cook with a pistol to his head to make sure it's done really rare, but that applies to restaurants all too often. *Certainly* to the one where I stopped for lunch."

"You had steak for lunch?" Luz said. "You're looking a little peaked, James, if you don't mind me saying so."

He'd always been leanly strong and moved with the fluency that told an expert observer that he could be very fast indeed, but now he was slightly gaunt in the way you got if you were putting out everything you had and not eating all that well.

"I've been away from the land of the free and home of the sirloin; the steak helps, and the bacon-wrapped grilled oysters. I'm having steak three times a day for a while. Steak and eggs for breakfast today, steak and potato au gratin for lunch at the Claremont here, and I'm planning on steak au poivre with *frites* for dinner with a nice zinfandel and a green salad, and peach Melba to follow at the Potter tonight. Besides, I hear Food Director Hoover is going to be decreeing meatless days for the war effort and I'm doing my best before the dreaded nut cutlet arrives, smothered in scientifically enriched puréed green-bean burgoo."

He went on with a wry smile:

"And here I see the inside of your beautiful home for the first time and then you wound my sensitive, delicate feelings on the very doorstep, Luz. And I always thought we worked together so well! We saved each other's lives that time the Zapatistas inconsiderately overran the safe house at three in the morning."

"Of course we did, James," she said.

A flash of memory went through her, her skin prickling a little at the visceral impact of it, though her face retained its calm.

The darkened house in Cuautla, waking at a draft from the door opening, air across skin wet with the tropical heat of the *tierra caliente*. The smell alerting her as much as anything, tobacco and marijuana and rank sweat soaked into coarse cotton rarely washed. The distinctive body odor of men who worked in the hot sun of the cane-fields and lived on corn tortillas and *frijoles refritos* and chilies and cheap flavored spirits, overlain with the musky harshness of anger and fear. And beyond that, fresh blood—not very close, but somewhere in the house, and a lot of it.

A board creaked under a huarache sandal.

Sliding out a hand and picking up the little FN automatic from the side table, nothing else moving, doing it smooth, fast but without the jerk or gasp that might draw attention. She kept the pistol cocked at night and relied on the grip safety, and the door was only twelve feet away. Her black Chinese-style silk pajamas made the motion invisible in the dark and they were perfect for action, which was why she didn't sleep naked or in a nightie anywhere she didn't consider very, very safe.

Aiming was like pointing a finger but the angle was awkward . . .

Ptak! Ptak! Ptak! Ptak! Ptak!

The light .380 cartridges made a sharp sound more like a little dog's shrill yapping than a bang, and the small rounded weapon bucked in her hand. Five shots at the half-seen black silhouette of a man outlined against the low dim glimmer like a target at a range; the corridor outside was open to the inner patio of the building on that side. Brief flashes showing red and giving grotesque strobing images, a bushy black mustache in a round brown face, eyes wide with shock and black dots punched into the breastbone of his dingy off-white shirt.

The second one tripping over the falling body as he tried to rush in behind the first, a hand thrown out for balance gripping the hilt of a Morelos-style machete like a broad point-heavy sword, and stumbling frantically forward trying to recover his footing so that the muzzle of the automatic was almost pressed to the bridge of his nose as their eyes met.

Ptak! Ptak!

No time to reload, though she snatched up the spare magazine and stuffed it into a pocket while she flipped the gun into her left hand.

A near-shriek from the corridor: *"¡Carlos! ¡Miguel! ¿tan bien?"*

Strip the *navaja* out from under the pillow, snap it open in the same motion. Out into the corridor, out from darkness into dimness, ducking smoothly down into a low crouch as she stepped toward the one who'd conveniently pinpointed himself by yelling. And who couldn't see a thing . . .

You can look from darkness into light; but not from light into darkness. Darkness is my old friend.

The third man's machete flashed over her head, a whisk of motion close enough to leave a tiny cooling draft on the back of her neck as she uncoiled forward and it banged into the plaster wall. Legs like springs pushing her up as she spun in a blur with the blade sweeping rightward, *knowing* in her gut and muscle where the neck had to be from glimpses and motions.

Then an instant's tug as the sharp steel ripped hard across taut skin and sliced deep, with the unmistakable crisp shearing feeling of striking the cartilage of a windpipe, like cutting through a cardboard tube. An incredulous choked gurgling grunt followed it, and salty drops landed across her face.

"Carlos y Miguel están jodidos, igual que tú, cabrón," she snarled under her breath in belated answer to his question as relief washed over her skin like stepping into a warm bath.

She continued the spin until she was facing back toward the stairwell at the end of the corridor, and the graceful spray of blood from the Toledo blade was liquid geometry for an instant on the pale stucco of the wall where it had followed the curve of the *arrebato* cut to the jugular. The body thumping to the tiles behind her, amid that hot salt iodine stink that was like seawater and meat. A rustle through the leaves of the banana trees in the courtyard, and the scent of night jasmine under the blood and powder-gas.

And slurred peasant voices on the stair ahead of her shrieking: *"¡Viva Zapata! ¡Muerte a la Cámara Negra! ¡Viva Mexic—"*

Cheine burst out of his own room, mother-naked and barefoot. Two steps and he was at the head of the stairs in the classic edge-on stance with his left hand down by his side holding two spare magazines and the big Colt automatic in his outstretched right.

CRACK! and a half-second pause as he brought it back down to firing position.

Then six more at the same metronome intervals: *CRACK! CRACK! CRACK! CRACK! CRACK! CRACK!*

Stunning-loud as he emptied the weapon, using the crimson stab of each muzzle flash to aim the next shot; the attackers were trying to do this quietly to get in and out before a reaction force from the garrison arrived, but for the Americans the more noise the better. Flashes of light on the white eyes and teeth and the honed edges of the machetes as the campesino guerillas stormed upward to kill the hated gringo spies . . .

He'd started with the man in the rear and then moved his aim forward in a ripple of death, so that the leaders would think he was missing and not stop or take time to think about shooting instead of chopping. Seven shots for eight men, seven massive 230-grain chunks of lead moving a thousand feet a second as the shooter grinned like a death's-head. The second-to-last had fallen backward from six feet away as the .45 slug put a blue hole in the top of his forehead and exited in a gout of bone fragments and gluey pink brain and blood that was red-black in the dimness.

That left the one in the lead, raising his machete with a shriek of rage. Luz had snaked her left hand around James's body.

Ptack!

A flutter of cloth as she fired close enough that the muzzle blast singed the *machetero*'s long cotton shirt. He started to fold as the bullet hit in the pit of his stomach, and then he flipped backward in a crackling tumble all the way to the bottom of the stone staircase as Cheine kicked him in the face with his heel.

Then they'd leapt down from stair to stair, careful to avoid the bodies, some still prattling like pithed frogs from the head shots. They reloaded on the move. She'd had the knife in her teeth as she did, and the blood had tasted as metallic as the steel . . .

Luz shook her head as she returned across years and miles to the house her parents had built. When she spoke her voice was light:

"And we picked leeches off each other's backs in that *pinche selva* in Quintana Roo, James. I have the highest *professional* regard for you, *mi camarada*."

Professional, because there's also the fact that you're a bit of a bully sometimes when you get the chance, Luz thought behind her smile.

Secret-agent work tended to attract the type, for some reason. There were women who found that attractive, though not as many as men thought, but it wasn't a fantasy she'd ever had the slightest interest in accommodating.

I actually do *quite like you, James, just not as much or in the way you think is your due.*

"No accounting for tastes," he said. "I understand from catching up on the Chamber rumor mill that *professional* congratulations are in order for your promotion and to both you ladies for a job well done . . . whatever the job was. Getting the *corona obsidionalis* without dying . . . Not many have managed that."

"Precisely two," Luz corrected. "Us."

"True. And without even being crippled for life first! No details, I don't need to know! But add my envious congratulations to the pile, for what they're worth."

"Thank you. Yes, the mission did go rather well," she said, and gave Ciara a fond glance and half wink. "Though Miss Whelan and I ended up saving each other's lives any number of times."

Cheine had almost certainly figured out that they'd been involved in foiling the horror-gas plot somehow, since nobody had ever said he was a fool and there weren't many alternative explanations. But what wasn't explicitly said didn't have to be acknowledged *or* denied. Silence could be a wonderful thing, both tool and weapon.

"And you've been . . . where, James?"

"Congratulating myself, of late, on being among the non-decomposing minority of humankind," he said nonspecifically.

There was a newish purple scar on the back of his right hand; it looked very much like the Cyrillic letter Ш, cut in with a knife, which would stand for the initial *s* in шпион, the Russian word *Shpion* . . . spy.

"You had a bad time in Russia?" she said, and added: "If that's not a redundant adjective these days."

The Czar's inept Ruritanian autocracy had started its circling swirl around the porcelain bowl at Tannenberg and the Masurian Lakes in August 1914, when the Great War was young and where Generals Hindenburg and Ludendorff had made their names while obliterating two invading Russian armies. Then last year more armies millions strong had vanished into the iron jaws of the German *Kesselschlachten* one after another, at obscure hamlets whose names were now written on history in letters of fire and blood—Gorlice-Tarnow and Grodno, Białystok and Brest-Litovsk. This summer and fall had seen the final gurgling flush of collapse, abdication, and abject surrender to the status of German puppet, with the ex-Czar's first cousin once removed Grand Duke Nicolai as theoretical regent for the sickly Czarevitch and actual glove on Ludendorff's iron Prussian fist.

"Right in one, Luz," Cheine said, and rubbed ruefully at the healing wound.

"It must have been *strenuous*."

"It's . . . even worse there now than the papers say," he said, and added: "You never did miss much."

"Russian is one of your languages, and with that scar . . . not much doubt about which particular pot of boiling sewage the Director dropped you in."

"Yes, I'm going to have to have some cosmetic work done on this," he said, touching the back of his hand.

Luz nodded with cheerful ruthlessness. "The Chamber should get *something* out of the surgeons we keep on retainer."

Cheine snorted. "When I . . . finished what I was doing . . ."

She would have been shocked if he'd been more specific.

". . . I made it out of Moscow just before Colonel Nikolai's men—"

Ciara stiffened for a moment at the mention of the name of the head of Abteilung IIIb, then relaxed as Luz touched her on the shoulder briefly and gently. There was nothing like that knife-edge threat of death and torture to make memory stand out with cut-crystal clarity afterward, and the feelings came back with the images.

That can be bad, Luz thought. *It's worse when they come back in your dreams.*

"—arrived to extract my name from the Okhrana and then extract my toenails to make me talkative. I jumped onto the very last through train on the Trans-Siberian before they stopped even trying to run them. Which was a relief."

He rubbed the scar again. "Only then Baron von Ungern-Sternberg's cavalry hijacked the train east of Lake Baikal in the name of the new Yekhe Khagan of Greater Mongolia and gave me this when they realized I wasn't Russian."

"Ungern-Sternberg? Is that a Russian name, Mr. Cheine?" Ciara asked; she sounded a little more sympathetic now, probably because of the reminder of their common enemy. "It sounds more German."

"It *was* German, a very long time ago, Miss Whelan, in the Crusades against the Baltic heathen; a lot of officers in the Russian army are from the Baltic-German nobility. Von Ungern-Sternberg was, until he decided he'd rather be a bloody-handed Mongolian warlord. A fair number of troops followed him when the Russian army collapsed, and he decided to take over Mongolia with them, chase out the Chinese, and declare himself Kha Khan. And he's become a very odd variety of Buddhist."

"Odd?" Luz said.

She knew a little about Sōtō-Zen but not much of the faith in general, except that it had even more distinct flavors than Christianity did, which was saying something.

"As in *reincarnation of Genghis Khan* and *avatar of the war goddess Jamsaran*. And he's quite sincere, too."

"He must be crazy!" Ciara blurted.

"Mad as a hatter, Miss Whelan, and looks it—a demented stare with one bulging eye bigger than the other, and his face twitches and this damned great scar on his forehead flushes purple just before he starts the random killing. Well, usually there's burning and flaying and impaling first."

Luz's brows went up at something she caught beneath his casual tone of ironic amusement. She'd learned by personal experience that Cheine had strong nerves even by the Chamber's exacting standards, but if you knew him well he sounded a little . . .

Disturbed. This bloody baron must be very bloody indeed.

"He has a whole carnival freak show of desperados and lunatics and assorted maniacal butchering horrors in his train complete with heads on spears and necklaces of ears and teeth and drinking fermented mare's milk out of cups made from human skulls lined with gold. I suspected they had more of the ever-popular game of Carve the Yankee in mind—"

"Or possibly a new skull goblet . . . what's fermented mare's milk like?" Luz said.

"Vile, as you'd expect, but not quite as vile as you *would* expect. So I abjured their hospitality, stole a string of Mongol ponies, and made my way east. Then I got out of Vladivostok on a Peruvian-flagged freighter bound for the U.S. just moments before our new and dearly beloved Japanese allies in the struggle against the evils of Prussian militarism arrived with their Tokko-Kempeitai."

"Special secret section of the Japanese military police," Luz translated for Ciara. "They do what we do, more or less. A very unpleasant lot."

She turned to Cheine: "Under our great and good new friend General Akashi Motojiro?"

"I heard rumors to the effect it was to be that very same nasty and far too clever piece of work, with Sado Araki and the Black Dragon Society in tow," Cheine said.

Luz nodded; the Black Dragons were a secret society of fanatics who believed Japan destined to rule all East Asia, and operated through propaganda, subversion, and assassination. Araki was one of Japan's best secret agents and had a network of spies and sympathizers that stretched all the way to Central Asia.

Cheine went on: "Since what's left of Russia is a German puppet these days, we can't even really object to the Japanese taking it over . . . and they'll keep going until they and the Germans meet up somewhere around Lake Baikal in Siberia, is my guess."

"Akashi is their best Russian specialist," Luz clarified for Ciara. "He's half the reason Russia had a revolution in 1905, while they were fighting Japan."

Ciara frowned. "I thought that was because the Japanese sank their navy and beat the stuffing out of their army?"

"That was the *other* half, Miss Whelan," Cheine said with a raised eyebrow at the naïve but acute analysis. "I was sure Rikugun-Shōshō Akashi would be just as glad as Herr Oberst Nicolai to have a long friendly chat with me, but luckily my humble, rusty, wheezing, guano-scented but beautiful *Santa Rosa de Lima* escaped attention as we sailed out past a gigantic convoy of Japanese troop transports and warships impressively inbound and headed by *Fusō* and *Yamashiro*."

"Their latest big battleships," Ciara said, with an absentminded look that Luz knew marked her consulting the reference library in her head. "Just under thirty thousand tons displacement. Brown-Curtis direct-drive steam turbines, water-tube boilers, mixed oil-coal firing, forty thousand shaft horsepower, twenty-three knots. They must have hurried *Yamashiro* through her sea-trials."

"Yes, Miss Whelan," Cheine said, with a well-hidden look of surprise.

Luz didn't bother to hide a smile, or her pride. Ciara wasn't particularly interested in warships as such. Big complex modern machines with turbines, on the other hand . . .

"That sounds like the sort of close call that's much more fun in retrospect," Luz said. "Because then you *know* how it turned out."

Cheine nodded. "There was already panic in Vladivostok; not to mention drunken despair, arson, looting and rioting, and stampedes trying to get on departing ships . . . a bit of the *strenuous life* and no mistake. Not that I blame the locals for being a trifle put out at the change of management. They know the Nips well in that part of the world, and the Russki love the little yellow devils not, a feeling which is very much mutual."

"It all sounds very . . . exciting, Mr. Cheine," Ciara said.

Luz glanced at Cheine and pursed her mouth slightly. In their line of work *exciting* also meant something had gone spectacularly wrong, since ideally the enemy never knew what you'd found out until what they *didn't* know about what you *did* know about *them* hurt them very badly.

Which ideal Ciara and I just about brought off, except for the very last bit in Boston and that was too late to do the Germans any good. Though James does seem to have recovered with style.

It also sounded very much as if relations between the United States and the Dai Nippon Teikoku were going into the toilet too, rounding out the round world's agonies as the Great War spread like cancer, or filaments of mold in bread. If you knew how to look between the lines . . .

Our very nominal new allies in Tokyo are going to grab with both hands while the grabbing is good and the Western powers are wrecked or fighting for bare survival, she thought; they'd already taken over the Dutch East Indies and French Indochina, theoretically . . . very theoretically . . . to keep the Germans out. *And now we can't stop them putting the knuckle on China either, the way we did when they tried with their Twenty-One Demands last year.*

It didn't surprise her, and this certainly wasn't one of the very rare occasions she felt moral outrage either: Empires were empires and people were people and they both did what they did. Getting your knickers in a twist about it put you on the wrong side of the way she *did* usually divide the world, apart from the obvious, eternal and elemental one of Us and Them, and cutting across it: not into good or bad, but into smart people on the one hand, and on the other . . .

Fools. But on a personal level I really must get the whole Taguchi family on the protected-contact list without delay just in case. It could get unpleasant here for people with Japanese names if things go badly toes-up. Even with that cabrón *William Also-Ran-dolph Hearst, the Wizard of Ooze, retired to his ranch.*

In 1907 the Boss had called Hearst *the most potent influence for evil in American life*, and their longstanding mutual loathing had gone even further downhill from there. The last straw driving *el jefe* into one of his rare but impressive rages had been an editorial comparing the American troops in Mexico to the Germans in Belgium and hoping the *revolucionario* guerillas would drive them out. The subsequent visit to Mr. Hearst by the Chamber had included James Cheine to do the talking, and one Luz O'Malley Aróstegui being persuasive by standing in the background smiling a sinister Latin smile and rolling her open *navaja* across her knuckles. When he'd blustered about whether the president had authorized this *outrage*, she'd smiled again and said softly, glancing down at the moving glitter on the edge of the Toledo steel:

"Not in so many words, Mr. Hearst. But . . . there *was* something that with enough deliberate ill will might have been interpreted as: *Will no one rid me of this meddlesome priest?*"

At which Hearst looked as if he'd bitten into a lemon, not fancying Thomas à Becket's martyr's crown one little bit. James had raised a patrician eyebrow, and quoted the Chamber's unofficial motto:

"Non Theodorum parvis concitares ne perturbatus sit."

Then he'd smiled with genial, cruel contempt and added: "You are a detail, sir. And one way or another, you *will* cease to bother."

That had finally pierced the narcissist's armor with the realization that the rules had well and truly changed; whereupon Hearst had decided to lead a quiet rural life on his enormous coastal ranch near Paso Robles, and sold his papers at quite fair prices to designated buyers to finance a mansion and art collection there. These days those rags weren't indulging in their former specialty of trying to whip up feeling against Japanese immigrants and "Orientals" in general . . . or against the Party and Uncle Teddy . . . or the Intervention policy in Mexico . . . or in favor of Germany . . . or spreading atrocity stories recycled from the Philippine Insurrection days either.

"Better you than me when it comes to last-minute escapes, James," she said aloud, and wrote a brief note on a pad. "Hand this on to Station Chief Reiter when you get back to San Francisco, would you? And tell him I need a minor favor from him, sub rosa. I want those people put on the shelter list, just in case."

Reiter would normally do any valued operative a small favor like this as a matter of courtesy as long as it wasn't counter-mission or financially smelly; and still more so for *her*, now that she was in the Director's extremely good graces.

And he'd be able to call on her for some equally moderate return in the future. Luz prided herself on never forgetting a debt, for good or ill. As a bonus, Ciara smiled with delight when she realized what Luz meant.

"Certainly," Cheine said, glancing at the note before putting it into one of his waistcoat's slash pockets. "Friends of yours?"

"Yes. Personally, and old family friends too; there are debts of honor involved."

"I don't think the Boss or the rest of the Party leadership will let the State government go too far, unless there's actual war with Japan . . . and that won't happen soon if ever. Teddy admires the Nips because they're hard workers and tough fighters. And clever little devils too, and because they're disciplined enough to make Prussians look like anarchists."

"He thinks the ones we have here are national assets," Luz agreed. "But not everybody's as sensible as *el jefe*. And the elder Taguchis are still Japanese subjects, which might matter—though their children are American citizens, of course. You easterners don't appreciate how strong that feeling is on this coast."

"I do remember how *el jefe* had to take the mayor of San Francisco to the White House woodshed in '07 and give him a sound spanking over trying to force Japanese children out of the local schools."

"That whole idiotic episode cost us goodwill with Japan we'll have to pay for with blood someday," Luz said grimly. "I can't stop the California state legislature from being hysterical buffoons, but I can hold out an umbrella for a few people if it starts to rain stupid."

"I'll ask Reiter to get right on it."

"*Gracias*, James."

"Think nothing of it."

"We'll pay you back with a Hangtown fry dinner and a bottle of Inglenook at the Tadich Grill next time we're all in Fogtown at once, while you entertain us with the grisly Gothic details of your *trabajos patrióticos* in Outer Mongolia."

"It was all epically hellish and bloody *cold* even a few weeks ago, and my getting out was an epic too, of dash and grit and good old Yankee ingenuity. What a pity the report will languish in the Class A Secret files! Unless Teddy reads it for a little light entertainment."

Luz chuckled. "He does do that, you know he does—says it has Richard Harding Davis's adventure stories beat all hollow, or even this new English author he's so fond of, Buchan—you know, *Prester John* and *The Thirty-Nine Steps*."

"John Buchan?" Cheine said, and surprised her a little by laying a finger beside his nose. "Just between me and thee, Buchan actually *is* in British Intelligence now . . . military intelligence. If he's still alive, that is. He was on Haig's staff in France when I met him for a little quiet liaison work back in the spring, when we were still neutral . . . officially . . . and before everything went to hell. Haig *is* dead, by the way."

"The horror-gas got him when they shelled his HQ?" Luz asked, and Cheine nodded.

"Plumer has his job now, poor chap. Talk about inheriting a poisoned chalice!"

"You'd never know Buchan's really in the trade from his books," Luz said. "Outrageous coincidences *como pulgas sobre un perro.*"

"I wouldn't know about either the fleas on the dog or the coincidences in the books," Cheine said loftily; speaking Spanish well was a common accomplishment in the Chamber. "*I* never read that pulp trash myself."

"Liar," Luz said amiably.

"Spy," Cheine replied with a shrug.

"Glad you agree with my analysis of your character, James. And I think Uncle Teddy likes to imagine himself a dashing secret agent, *Dios lo bendiga.* But then as Alice put it, he'd like to be the bride at every wedding, the corpse at every funeral, *and* the baby at every christening."

Cheine barked a startled laugh. "*Did* she? Tongue like a viper, that girl."

"You can get away with it if you're the president's eldest."

"And if it's true enough to cut."

Luz nodded agreement. "Speaking of weddings . . . did I ever tell you my parents and I were at his niece Eleanor's wedding to her cousin Franklin . . . fifth cousin, wasn't it? You were at Groton School with him, I think?"

"Franklin Delano Roosevelt of the Hyde Park Roosevelts? Yes, though only as lowly first-year dirt beneath his exalted senior-year feet. I missed the wedding, but the papers were all over it because of Teddy—they hardly mentioned the bride, and Franklin only in passing. I think he's doing something administrative in the Navy Department now, and he and Eleanor have a swarm of little Roosevelts, which must put that prig Davenport in seventh heaven."

Dr. Charles Benedict Davenport, secretary of the new Department of Public Health and Eugenics, was indeed a frigid, ruthless, fanatic prig of a man. Not too different from his long line of Calvinistic Puritan ancestors, if you substituted *genetic defectives* for *sinners* and *witches*.

"What was the wedding like?" Cheine added with interest.

"Apart from the Ancient Order of Inebriated Hibernians—"

Ciara chuckled, though she might not have if Luz hadn't been Catholic and surnamed O'Malley.

"—bellowing 'The Wearing of the Green' outside because it was St. Patrick's eve? The wedding was . . . a very genteel political rally. Teddy gave her away, slapped the groom on the back after the kiss-the-bride, boomed out a hearty 'Well, Franklin, there's nothing like keeping the name in the family!' with every tooth showing in that grin of his, and made a beeline for the dining room and the buffet with Aunt Edith sighing and rolling her eyes in his wake."

Cheine grinned. "And all the guests followed him?"

"Like ducklings waddling after their *mamacita*, leaving Franklin and Eleanor standing there alone listening to the crowd laughing at his stories in the other room."

"Oh, poor Franklin!" Cheine said, with an unsympathetic chuckle.

"*El jefe* didn't *mean* any harm by it . . . but I stayed with them for a bit anyway."

Out of the corner of her eye she saw Ciara giving her a nod and a slow smile for the minor kindness. Luz felt a slight stab of guilt at taking the credit. She'd done it out of vicarious embarrassment for Teddy and Edith, whom she adored, as much as anything. Your elders embarrassed you so easily when you were fourteen, and her father had just said that if he'd followed the colonel up San Juan Hill he wasn't going to object to following him to the punch bowl.

Cheine slapped a hand on the table in delight. "That's the Boss, all right! He'd be a complete blowhard and jackass, if it weren't that every bit of it is the real thing, in spades and all the way down. And he'll enjoy my report—full of manly, masterly understatement about my exploits. Though I was sorely tempted to throw in a knife fight with a snow leopard in a Mongolian forest, just for him."

Luz and Cheine both laughed aloud at that; on a hunt in 1901 Roosevelt had famously leapt on a cougar and stabbed it to death.

"So you can see the temptation to throw a huge evil cat into my report, Miss Whelan," he said. "And then, alas sans hand-to-hand battle with a leopard in a snowbank . . ."

"Cliff, James," Luz interrupted. "You could have rolled off a cliff *into* a snowbank, locked in a death grapple with the beast."

"And torn its throat out with my teeth?"

"Broken its neck with a full nelson, the way Burroughs's wild man does to African lions."

"*And then*, in prose rather than poetry, I debriefed at the San Francisco station and Reiter gave me this paperwork from HQ for you, Luz. He added a verbal message from the Director: that he's sorry to interrupt the vacation, but it's time you two got the standard reward for good work."

Luz laughed again, without much humor this time, and added to Ciara: "The reward for good work is more work, of course."

Cheine nodded. "I expect to go right back into the soup myself, with a bandage on my hand. We're stretched a bit thin and San Francisco was a madhouse, everyone running around waving handfuls of paper in the air and talking on the telephone at the same time. You and the fair Miss Whelan must have really *shone* to get this much of a holiday."

"Like diamonds in the noonday sun, James," she said, and winked at Ciara. "Like onyx and gold."

He put the attaché case on the table, where it *thunked* on the stone surface with an authority that revealed the lining of armor-grade alloy-steel plate, and worked the little inset combination lock before snapping the catches. Inside was a shortened Colt .45 automatic pistol in a concealed integral holster that made it very convenient for drawing and shooting someone who was forcing you to open the case and thought you'd been disarmed, and a thick set of heavy legal-sized envelopes sealed with cord and wax and nothing on their outside except letter-number combinations.

Cheine handed Luz one of two identical lists, and they ceremoniously checked them and exchanged signatures that the envelopes had been delivered, listing their numbers and attesting that they were fully sealed at the time of transfer. Most of them felt as if they held briefing files, false passports, and similar tools of the trade, but one . . . she felt her brows rise as Ciara solemnly signed for one of the lighter ones herself.

"This is for you, Ciara," she said, and handed it to her.

Ciara opened it, and her rather broad mouth turned into an O of surprise as she read the letter inside.

"Oh, my goodness!" she said excitedly, in what was almost a breathy squeal. "*Tesla* agrees with me! The thing I saw on the big ships in—"

"No! No!"

The words blurred as Cheine's voice overlapped with Luz's saying the same thing.

"I don't need to know, Miss Whelan," he said, smiling to take the sting out of it. "And therefore I shouldn't. Particularly if the Mad God of the Technical Section is involved. Believe me, that's best all 'round."

He always did have good manners . . . most of the time, Luz thought, as he clicked the attaché case shut and gave a half bow to them both.

"Good afternoon, Luz, Miss Whelan. I'll see myself out," he said.

Ciara waited until she heard the door close. "Luz . . ." she said. "*Leeches?* On your *back?*"

THREE

American National Railways *Coastal Express*
Southern California
NOVEMBER 19TH, 1916(B)

S aints, what's that?" Ciara said.
Or literally: *"¡Por los santos! ¿Qué es eso?"*

Their prospective cover identities in Europe were Spanish-speaking until they got to Germany, and it was never too early for Ciara to practice the language. Luz stretched, yawned with a hand over her mouth, and put aside a newspaper with yet another article on Canada: the very orphaned Dominion's very shell-shocked parliament had reacted to the destruction of London by voting to join the United States last week, each province—plus Newfoundland—to be a state, with the unhappy but sincere approbation of Lord Protector Milner over in Britain.

Instead of reading more—there was an interesting article in the *Times* on how former Princess Mary, the sole survivor of her family due to a lucky visit to Bristol and now Queen-Empress Victoria, was planning an "indefinite" stay in New Delhi—she turned her eyes out the compartment window to follow Ciara's finger as the *Coastal Express* halted at one of the level crossings that had survived the rebuilding so far.

"Por todos *los santos,"* she corrected automatically as she did.

Luz had ridden this line from Santa Barbara to Los Angeles all her life, and the stuffy warmth had made her drowsy despite the new-build smell of paint and varnish in this side-corridor compartment car. Fresh air came through a narrow crack of open window with the oily petroleum stink of the locomotive's smoke, though that was a lot better than the hot cinders and clinging smeary soot of the old coal-burners that were now rare west of the Rockies.

The younger woman hadn't traveled much at all until recently, though. This time what Ciara was staring at with bright-eyed wonder was another train sitting on a siding next to the main track. There were five heavy-duty fifty-by-ten flatcars behind the big new 4-8-4 ANR Goliath-class superheated fast freight loco, followed by an ordinary freight wagon and then a passenger car and the caboose. Four of the flatcars had identical rectangular *somethings* under tied-down tarpaulins of Army drab, which meant a military cargo, and the *somethings* were themselves chained to the frames of the flatbeds with massive links held tight by eyebolts.

"Those must be armored cars, Lynx battle autos—" Luz began, and stopped as she realized she was wrong.

The silhouettes under the canvas didn't look quite right. And an ANR flatcar like the ones in this train could hold *two* Lynxes. And they wouldn't put covers on them. Successive models had been around for a couple of years now and weren't any sort of secret; there were thousands of them and they featured in parades often enough.

The fifth flatcar had the same thing with the tarpaulin peeled back, and a group of wrench-wielding men in blue-almost-black military fatigue overalls were swarming around an open compartment in the rear of . . .

"No, that's definitely *not* a Lynx," Luz said, keenly interested herself now.

Whatever-it-was had the same general sort of slab-sided angular hull of riveted armor plate as the American cavalry's standard war-auto, liberally splashed with mud as you usually saw them when they weren't inches deep in khaki-colored Mexican dust. The unit insignia was familiar too, the 2nd Cavalry's palmetto leaf and eight-pointed shield with *Toujours Pret* blazoned on it.

But it had the eye-baffling quality of something new; it was bigger, with what looked like a six-pounder cannon rather than a pom-pom in the turret besides a machine gun. And instead of having three evenly spaced rubber wheels four feet high on each side like the Lynx armored war-autos she'd seen so often, this had six much smaller metal wheels in pairs resting on . . .

"That's endless metal treads, like a Holt tractor," Ciara said. "I saw an article on them in a copy of *American Mechanical Engineer* I picked up a few years ago while I was helping Colm at the machine shop where he was working. I'd bring him his dinner from home and then work on the lathe while he was eating."

"A Holt crawler . . . *¡Ay!* Now I see!"

Her mind snapped the pieces together. Luz had seen Holt crawler-tractors in the delta country west of Sacramento, where they were used on the deep soft soils reclaimed from the marshy islands. And on major construction projects the last couple of years too, like the Colorado Valley Authority dams and canals, or the huge road program and the Yaqui Valley irrigation settlements down in the Protectorate.

"Caterpillar treads, they're called—a belt to reduce the ground pressure," Ciara said. "The power is transmitted with that sprocket at the rear, and the driver sits at the front—see the little folding windows and slits in the steel?"

"So they've taken an armored battle-car, made it bigger, and put it on top of a Holt crawler-tractor . . . though the Holts don't have those little wheels and the things they're attached to?"

"The ones paired on the . . . what's the Spanish for *suspension?*"

"*Suspensión.*"

"And they're connected to the body by that bell crank and the horizontal volute spring, see? What's that in Spanish?"

Luz opened her mouth, hesitated, and thought for a moment before she spoke.

"Ah . . . springs are *muelles*. Horizontal is *horizontales*, of course. *Volute* . . . that sounds like a Latin loan in English, so it's probably *voluta* or something like it. Bell crank . . . I *think* that's *palanca acodada*. Say . . . *suspensión con muelles de voluta horizontales y una palanca acodada?* A Spanish speaker would certainly understand it, but I've no idea if a Spanish-speaking engineer would use the phrase just that way. Or if there is a phrase for that in Spanish . . . yet."

"That's the first time you've had problems with a translation!"

"I didn't. It's not my Spanish that's the problem, it's my . . . my engineer-ish. I couldn't have come up with that in *English* either, not to save my life. Fortunately, I have an expert with me!"

Ciara repeated the Spanish phrase to fix it in her memory, then continued: "The springs and cranks would be to help reduce battering at higher speeds. Holt tractors don't go faster than walking pace, so they don't need it. But how clever it all is! They've put together a lot of known things into something that's just . . . new. How very, very clever!"

Luz blinked; *clever* wasn't a word Ciara used lightly, and she was frighteningly sharp in the broad areas of her special interest.

"Why? Wouldn't it still be slow?" she said. "Holt tractors crawl, but a Lynx can really zip along, top speed all day and faster than a horse over any sort of firm open ground. They're extremely useful."

Ciara looked at her as if she'd asked why railroads didn't use mules instead of bothering with locomotives.

"But . . . Luz . . . mud! And crossing trenches and shell holes! And you'd make nothing of barbed wire driving *that* machine, you could just crush it and rip it up. And shell and shoot up machine gun nests, even in concrete pillboxes."

Something went *click* in Luz's mind; Ciara was describing the conditions that had kept the European war deadlocked until just lately *and* a method of neutralizing them. The Germans had developed their *Stoßtruppen* and then the *Vernichtungsgas* to do that. This might be another way.

"Well, when you're right, *querida*, you're right," she said thoughtfully.

And Ciara got it from one glimpse of the machines, what she knew about crawler-tractors, what she knew about the Western Front from newspapers and magazines, and what she deduced from that. I think I've gone and fallen in love with the smartest person I've ever met . . . and I've met people like Uncle Teddy and Nicolai Tesla.

"Ah, the Armored Water Tank Project," she said, and at Ciara's questioning expression continued: "I heard we were doing something with that code designation, but it was supposedly about supplying outposts with Holt pulling wagons. There are a lot of secret projects these days. Uncle Teddy does love his gadgets."

Ciara clapped her hands in admiration, still staring back at the war machine as the *Coastal Express* picked up speed and started to earn its name again.

"*So* clever," she said wistfully. "I wonder if they use a purpose-designed engine? Or . . . I *do* so wish I could stop and talk to them about it!"

Luz chuckled. "Yes, but after they showed you everything they'd have to shoot you, *mi querida*. Then I'd have to kill *them*, and it would all end in tears."

Ciara chuckled and stuck out her tongue and settled back in to watch the passing countryside.

They could talk freely since they had the train compartment to themselves by some freak of scheduling that probably wouldn't happen again for years. They couldn't speak all that *quickly* because they were speaking Spanish. Ciara had studied the language in desultory fashion for several years off and on—more or less on a whim, and because the government had offered free correspondence courses wholesale during the Intervention to increase the pool of interpreters. She didn't have a natural gift for languages, but her excellent memory and almost intimidating capacity for focused hard work were expanding her vocabulary quickly. The accent and grammar, on the other hand . . .

Needs work, Luz thought. *Needs quite a lot of work. Speaking it all the time has already helped a bit, though.*

And Germans rarely learned Spanish as a second language anyway—French was their first choice, English next, Italian after that, and even Polish or Russian would be more common—so those able to notice that Ciara's Spanish was still rough would be few.

And there are times when English is a little dull. In bed with a lover, for example, she thought. *You feel as if you should be screaming: Oh, my goodness gracious, what a* jolly *sensation! Please do go on with that perfectly* splendid *thing you're doing, dearie . . . if it's not too much trouble.*

Then, after a thought tickled at her for a moment she snapped her fingers:

"*¡Dios mío!* That's what Ted meant! That was the Second Cavalry's insignia on the . . . whatever it was."

"Ted?" Ciara said.

"Theodore Jr., Uncle Teddy's oldest son. We've been friends since the Rough Riders came back from Cuba—I was just eight, then, and he was eleven going on twelve—and we worked together in Mexico later. I drop in on him and his family now and then, and their *niños* are little darlings who love Auntie Luz to death."

"What's he like?" Ciara asked curiously. "I've seen his name in the papers. There was the battle in that Durango place where he got the Medal of Honor, for a start."

"He's smart as a whip, though not as brilliant as Uncle Teddy is or as given to playing with ideas. Charming in a way too—but don't get *in* his way, if you know what I mean, and his men would follow him anywhere. Ambitious, and young for a full colonel even these days. I wouldn't be surprised if he was president someday, or Chief of the General Staff, or both."

"And he knew something about those . . . those water tank things?"

Luz nodded. "Ted's been with the Second since the Intervention got going, and they got the first model of the Lynx at the beginning of 1914. He wrote me back in February when he got his colonel's oak-leaves and regimental command, saying they were getting *something new* and that it would be a *big surprise*. I thought it was improved armored cars, which in a way . . . so this is going to be the *big surprise*. With the Germans being surprised, for a change."

"About time!"

"*¡Ciertamente!* So until then it has to be deeply secret."

"Oh! I hadn't thought of that. I suppose I should have."

"It takes a while to learn to think like a spy," Luz said, and reached over to pat her knee. "So you didn't see a revolutionary new armored fighting vehicle, you just saw some . . . water tanks."

"Tanks it is!" Ciara said.

And those Army idiots are going to get a very unpleasant rocket up the fundament after I turn in my report on this, Luz thought with momentary grimness at the lapse in security. *I'll give Ted a heads-up first, but I'm sure it's not his fault; he must have been losing a lot of experienced enlisted men combed out as cadre for new units and getting green recruits in their place. In fact, he's probably on his way to Europe with the first wave right now.* Malditos confianzudos!

"But you're learning security much faster than *I* could learn what *you* know, you brilliant beautiful pinnacle of American womanhood, you!"

Ciara laughed and flushed; she still hadn't entirely gotten used to not being thought odd and unfeminine for her technical interests, still less to being praised or appreciated for them.

"After the war," Luz said thoughtfully, "what we should do is get *you* into Stanford, like Josh . . . Yoshi . . . Taguchi. It's a fine school and close to home, I don't think you'd have any problems with the entrance exams, and it's coeducational."

The engineering school is technically *coeducational,* Luz thought, punning silently. *But Food Director Hoover's wife got a BA in geology there back around the turn of the century, which was a precedent.*

The look on Ciara's face was like the sun rising, and Luz grinned in delight herself. When you felt that much pleasure from pleasing someone . . .

"Oh my darling one, do you think I could? It was always a dream for me, to go to university and study engineering, but . . ."

Luz nodded understanding. For a Boston-Irish shopkeeper's daughter, a university technical degree was still very nearly as far-fetched as marrying the king of England, for all the tweaking and scolding by Secretary of Education Jane Addams.

Though give her time . . . she thought, and went on aloud:

"It's certainly *possible.* The money's no problem. And for any other . . . impediments . . . well, my *papá* put in a word for Josh Taguchi when someone complained how many *nisei* students there were—he said Josh had talent and to spare—and since he'd made donations to their engineering department . . . and since Papá's friends are still there . . ."

Ciara jumped across the compartment and landed on Luz with a hurricane-style hug. Then Ciara sat back and pulled the letter Tesla had sent her with the briefing papers out of a pocket in the light jacket of her shirtwaist outfit and began ripping it up into very small pieces.

Luz waggled an admonishing finger at her. This line of work required relentless attention to detail.

"Tsk!" Luz said aloud as Ciara looked sheepish. "You should have thrown it in the fire with the rest of the papers this morning! Tsk! Naughty! Naughty spy!"

For the same job-related reason Luz was also doing her best to sound like a Chilean, using idiosyncratic vocabulary like calling skirts *polleras* and dragging the final syllable of each word out.

"It's terrible that I can't keep the letter from Mr. T . . . from *N*! He said that I showed *great perspicuity* in deducing what the Germans may have done with Hülsmeyer's Telemobiloscope! He . . . he thought *I* gave him a *valuable insight* and saved him *much research time* on how to tell distance by wave reflections! He promised to show me the records of the experiments he plans, and to explain everything. Oh, Luz, I may actually get to visit his laboratory!"

Her face was glowing with hero worship and it wasn't the first time she'd rehashed the letter. Luz *had* visited that solitary fortress in upstate New York, and had been ignored once she stated her requirements— she didn't have the technical education necessary to make Tesla notice her, and he was deeply in love anyway.

With a pigeon, she thought. *And blue flames talk to him and he talks back to them . . . floating, speaking blue flames invisible to anyone else, that is. But he and his accomplices . . . what they do may be* mad *science, but it works. Maybe the floating blue flames are real too!*

"*Querida*, remember that there will be a copy in the files. Later . . . much later, when it's not deeply secret anymore . . . you can get one for yourself and frame it. And have him sign it for you, and an autographed photograph of him saying, *Well Done, Operative Ciara Whelan*."

"I will do that!" Soberly: "And . . . it's really an honor that he thinks I can assemble the device in Berlin and operate it."

I suppose it is. If we don't get the specs on the Telemobiloscope, apparently the German Navy will be able to target ships accurately in fog and darkness, both of which are abundant in the North Sea.

"Even with all the parts and plans . . ." Ciara mused, evidently running over the job in her head.

Even with all the parts and plans if things go according to plan, Luz thought. *I don't like that. It's a complex plan, and there are far too many single points of failure. And it's rushed, you can feel it's rushed.*

Luz took the fragments and carefully wrapped them in a handkerchief. When they got to the station she'd flush them down the ladies' toilet, which was just as good as burning and often less conspicuous.

Ciara had the papers verbatim at first reading, and they'd stick. Luz could memorize text like that too, but she'd had to work much harder at developing the knack, which seemed to be almost effortless for her partner. Uncle Teddy had the same uncanny ability. He could quote whole chapters of anything he read years later . . . and he read several books a *day* most of the time.

"And here we are in Des Moines by the sea, also known as Los Angeles," Luz added dryly, as the *Coastal Express* left the truck farms and half-built suburbs behind and slowed into the built-up area. "And to think it's in the same state as San Francisco."

Ciara raised her brows: "I thought San Francisco was very pretty when my aunties and I visited last year for the Exposition—though we stayed at the Inside Inn on the grounds because of Auntie Colleen's foot; the hills would have been too hard for her. You don't like Los Angeles?"

"San Francisco is a real city, a port with folk from all the world, wonderful restaurants, good art and music and *two* first-class universities. *This* place is full of midwestern farmers living among orange groves and palms and patios and wondering why it doesn't make them happy. Then they take up weird religions and crazy politics."

She shrugged. "And in San Francisco we could go out dancing if we wanted to."

Ciara frowned. "Not that I don't love dancing with you, darling; you dance so beautifully, you're graceful as a cat, and it would be lovely with a good live orchestra, I could do that for hours and hours. But wouldn't people think that was . . . odd? I mean, nobody thinks anything of it if women dance together when there's no men, or not enough of them they know well enough to dance with, but you mean a *thé dansant?*"

Luz chuckled. "Odd? Not in the place I had in mind. Most nights we'd be some of the least odd people there, and that's *counting* the musicians. Ah, well, we're leaving immediately anyway."

"And we'll go to San Francisco when we get back and have some time to ourselves," Ciara said with stout-spirited cheerfulness.

A moment, and she went on with a wry smile: "And are you being a little bit of a snob there, my love? Because you sound very like someone from Boston talking about New Yorkers being all money-grubbing and vulgar, with a sniff, so to speak."

"*¿Verdaderamente?*"

"*¡Verdad!*"

"Ouch," she said in acknowledgment. "But I'm being a very *Californian* variety of snob. California is a dualist religion in which San Francisco doesn't believe in Los—"

"*Los Angeles!*" a voice cried from the corridor; it was the conductor—the conductress, actually—striding by and looking at her pocket watch and blowing a whistle. "*Los Angeles!* All out for Los Angeles Grand Central Station, please!"

"—and vice versa," she finished.

Los Angeles's very new Grand Central Station was very big for a medium-sized city, and extremely grand; the builders had looked to the future with what Luz *hoped* was demented optimism. And it was not particularly central, being located in the Echo Park district away from the sporadically flooding Los Angeles River.

Or at least not central yet, she thought. *Despite the way they're actually implementing their new plan, rather than just talking about it like most places.*

The train station, the new City Hall, combined State Police and LAPD and FBS headquarters, museums and courthouse and central public library and Federal Building and opera house and sundry others were grouped about a huge new plaza modeled on the Prato della Valle in Padua, complete with ornamental canal around the central garden, but bigger and with more in the way of fountains and statuary and flowers and young trees of modest size but some promise. All the buildings around it were in an instantly recognizable Californian sub-variety of the style called American Imperial these days, one that Luz thought of as *Half-Finished Panama-Pacific Exposition Monumental*, a Mediterranean-Italo-Hispanic-Moorish accented variation on Beaux-Arts neoclassical.

A square, vaguely Alhambra-esque tower covered in geometric Mozarabic tile was the centerpiece of the station. There had been scaffolding all over it in the spring, the last time she'd been through, but the whole edifice shone with bright new-out-of-the-box completion now.

They stood and pulled down their coach bags from the overhead racks as the train came to a halt with a *chuff-chuff-chuff* and a lurch and screech of steel.

"There's no train shed!" Ciara said, peering with interest out the corridor window; most stations this size had a giant glassed-in area over the tracks, like a titanic greenhouse.

"It doesn't get cold enough here to make that worthwhile," Luz said.

Instead the passenger areas between each set of double tracks were sheltered from the occasional winter rain by arched glazed covers borne on tall slender white-marble columns rising from the colorful tile pavement of the platforms.

"Efficient," Ciara said approvingly. "Much easier to allow natural ventilation if you can."

The rumble of sound in the background turned to a roar as the doors of their car swung back, and Luz could see out over a sea of heads as she paused on the little two-step folding stair. Most of the noise was coming from the departures section, as a troop train full of local reservists prepared to pull out amid a waving of hats and flags and handkerchiefs, returned from the windows of the cars with billed alpine-style Army caps and grinning male faces. Outstretched hands— of mothers, fathers, wives, and sweethearts—were clasped and then released as the long train began to move. Small children were held up for last-minute kisses.

The roar resolved into song. Movement stilled in a ripple as the crowds farther away and on the other platforms paused in their pursuits and joined in. She caught:

"Glory, glory hallelujah!"

Luz and Ciara stopped themselves and performed the Bellamy salute that children made to the flag during the Pledge of Allegiance, and which more and more adult civilians used on general patriotic occasions these days: the right hand brought to the heart and then the arm stiffly outstretched, palm up, like the old Roman salute in reverse. A whole host of arms were raised as they all sang "The Battle Hymn of the Republic," which Uncle Teddy loved and had made the official national anthem. The vast mass of tracks and trains and sidings rang with thousands of voices roaring out the last two verses:

"For I have read a fiery gospel
Writ in burnished rows of steel:
'As ye deal with my contemners,
So with you my grace shall deal';
Let the Hero, born of woman
Crush the serpent with his heel,
Since God is marching on!
Glory, glory, hallelujah!
Since God is marching on!

He is coming like the glory
Of the morning on the wave;
He is Wisdom to the mighty,
He is Honor to the brave!
So the world shall be His footstool
And the soul of Time His slave,
Our God is marching on!
Glory, glory, hallelujah!
Our God is marching on!"

The vast space shook as the crowd gave the last chorus everything they had, then dissolved in cheers and the shrieking hoot of the train's whistle, and they stepped down into the mass on the platform. Getting through it was something more suited to an eel slathered in olive oil, but they managed with a bit of discreet shoving and hitting with their cases, helped a little because the crowd was mostly male.

"Faith"—Ciara said, or literally *por mi fé*—"but it's beautiful!"

That was as they emerged from the platforms section into a long rectangle of flower-decked garden patio with a pavement of colorful twining patterns in hydraulic tile, and a central fountain bearing water-spouting bronze lion heads around its top; ten great arched doorways rimmed in Tiffany favrile-glass mosaic murals of (highly romanticized and distinctly cleaned-up) scenes from Californian history led into the main concourse.

The crowd thickened again inside and slowed them down to a crawl once more. A harried-looking redcap porter who was obviously of Mexican birth put their gear on a wheeled dolly at the baggage station, giving Luz a grateful look at the dime tip and dutifully falling in behind them at her call of:

"Gracias, maestro. ¡Por favor sígame!"

"Gee, but it's fine!" Ciara said again, looking up at the gilded rosettes on the barrel-arched coffered ceiling far above.

"But so crowded!" she added, nudging someone with her bag who'd been about to step on her toes as he was pushed back by someone in front of *him*. "The Boston subway has nothing on this."

The areas around the entrances to the ticket booths, restaurants, and concession stands and the restrooms were packed solid, with an occasional cry of *make way for the kid!* and stir in the mob as mothers with young children were let through to the head of the line, which was a new custom the Eugenics people had spread. Luz mentally decided to dispose of the minutely torn-up letter from Tesla at the airship haven instead, and was glad that she didn't need the toilet for the usual purpose.

It's not fair! Even when there are as many ladies' rooms as there are for the men, which there aren't anywhere I've been, women still have to wait in line to pee half the time.

"These will mostly be the local reservists or men on leave, so the crowding's the war," she said, with a smile of State pride at her partner's enthusiasm for the building.

There's less history here than out east to get in the way of what we're doing. We're making the history.

"We're lucky the new training camps on the coast have their own sidings, though," she added.

The dominant note in the mob was young men with the Army's billed caps on their bristle-cropped heads and the infinitely drab baggy multi-pocket modern field uniforms, or the slightly different Marine versions. Knots of Navy personnel making the same slow halting progress stood out vividly in their blue sailor-suits and beribboned white saucer hats.

Sergeants and officers looking harried and waving clipboards shouted the names of companies and battalions; MPs and shore patrollers with armbands and white belts and truncheons checked the transit papers of those not moving as units. She saw them pounce on one man staggering around singing a bawdy tune about "Big Hips Sally" with a mostly empty bottle in his hand, administer a brief brisk flurry of whacks to the elbows and collarbones, and drag him off, but there was less friction than she'd have anticipated.

Uncle Teddy and his band of brothers built well, she thought, proud again.

This time she was proud of the Party and the way it had gotten the country ready to fight. The usual American way to start a conflict was a shambolic ill-equipped volunteer rush of enthusiastic chaos, along with spending the first year or two getting the country's collective face kicked in if the other side wasn't a pushover.

Compared to the state we were in fifty years ago in the Civil War or Uncle Teddy's scuffle with Spain when I was a little girl, it's a miracle . . . and miracles are what we need. We're not fighting Indians or Mexicans or each other or grabbing off the tag ends of a played-out dying empire this time. The Deutsche Kaiserreich *has beaten the snot out of every Great Power on Earth except we our glorious selves and our very theoretical ally Japan.*

There were farewells here in the waiting hall too, and the YMCA/YWCA had teams—mostly of matrons or teenage girls or Scouts—handing out coffee and soda and juice, sandwiches and donuts to the troops, and packages with little luxuries, spare toothbrushes and socks and free-stamped forms for writing letters home and improving magazines or books and board games. Some of the military transients were waiting by stretching out in corners and snoring with their heads on their duffels or seabags, utterly heedless of the crowds and clamor. Luz grinned reminiscently at the sight.

"What's funny, darling?" Ciara asked, leaning close to be heard under the echoing roar that made the conversation fairly private.

"It reminds me of working with the Army down in the Protectorate when I first joined the Chamber," she said. "Soldiers . . . and people working with them . . . pick up the habit of eating wherever there's food and sleeping whenever they get the chance. You regret it later if you don't."

Most of the traffic was departures eastbound; when a burst of several hundred moving as a group detrained from the westbound arrival tracks and moved into the concourse all at once, it blocked Luz's and

Ciara's passage. And then the newcomers blocked their own, halting and peering around in bewilderment in the middle of the bustling crowd and getting in everyone's way and clutching battered-looking bags often held together with old belts or bits of string. Luz and Ciara stopped abruptly to avoid plowing into a small column of toddlers walking hand in hand, and the porter nearly trod on *their* heels.

"*Póngalo en la parada de taxis y espérenos por favor, maestro,*" Luz said to him, and waved him forward; his uniform and experience would clear a path to the taxi stand a good deal faster than trying to do it as a group.

"English refugees," she murmured to Ciara. "And that poor minder there has probably been stuck with them on a slow train all the way from the East Coast."

An obvious American civil servant type in charge of the English sank onto her own suitcase, dropped her bespectacled face into her hands, and quietly wept with relief. Apart from her the group *all* looked pallid and shabby and grubby and most had spectacularly bad teeth, and smelled frowsty or of long-unchanged babies; they were small and skinny and subtly non-American, down to the shapeless flat cloth caps or battered bowlers the men wore, and the clotted adenoidal accents.

"And from the East End slums, at that. The edge of the killing zone."

The little ones looked appealing . . . and also dirty and snot-nosed enough that you didn't want to express your sympathy at close range unless you had to. Ciara smiled at them, and winked and crouched for a moment to make silly faces at a towheaded four-year-old in a ragged too-large straw boater and cut-down pink dress, until the little girl giggled helplessly and put both hands over her eyes, peeking between her fingers and giggling again before the others dragged her off looking backward and smiling. Luz gave the proto-Morlocks a final once-over.

"Not the most impressive specimens of Anglo-Saxondom, but they've certainly got reason to move," she observed.

The horror-gas only killed every six or seventh person in London. But it killed the city, too. A head shot is a small wound, but the corpse won't walk; with no Parliament or King or Bank of England or ships or trade, what's the reason for London? They can't even go in for the bodies, and the stench of a million unburied dead must be apocalyptic. Nobody who was close to that wants to wait for more of the same from the Gotha bombers, either.

So the convoys that bore warriors and supplies to Britain were coming back over the ocean crammed to the gunwales with people, to be shoved right onto the trains from the insanely overcrowded docks without wasting time on formalities and dispersed over the continent just as fast as was physically possible without severely endangering their lives.

As she watched, a group of Party volunteer activists—you could tell them by their American-flag armbands—started chivvying the crowd out of the way of the refugees and setting up sawhorse-and-rope barricades on the tile floor to give them some space.

The Party was *good* at organization, and that revealed a set of tres-tle tables with military-issue tin cups and plates and cutlery, urns of coffee and tea, jugs of chilled water or cold milk or fresh-squeezed lemonade with drops of condensation running down them, more heaps of sugar-dusted donuts and things like cold cuts and cheese and sardines and sliced buttered bread and fruit, the latter mostly boxed oranges, something Southern California wasn't going to be short of anytime soon.

The refugees hesitated for a moment, broke into excited smiles as they realized it was all for them, and headed for the food and drink with concentrated zeal as the activists kept order. Some of the soldiers in transit and bystanders spontaneously pitched in to help, and soon all the children were clutching glasses of milk in one grubby hand and cookies or other treats in the other, while their parents fell on the sandwich makings and drinks. One or two were actually crying at the taste of the tea as they diluted it with milk and shoveled in sugar, as if all three were things they hadn't had for a while and missed sorely, the taste of a lost home and time.

"Oh, a cuppa," one of them said between sobs. "A luverly luverly cuppa!"

A big sign went up behind the tables: *AMERICA WELCOMES OUR ENGLISH COUSINS!* and *A GOLDEN FUTURE IN THE GOLDEN STATE!* with crossed flagstaffs holding Old Glory and the Union Jack, or the British flag and the dumpy, grumpy-looking grizzly bear on California's state banner.

Other tables held stacks of forms in front of seated clerks, and smaller signs reading *Housing* and *Employment* and *Food and Clothing Ra-tion Books* and *Collect Your Temporary Stipend*—all under a bigger *You Must Register Here Now!* notice.

A further table had a quick photo booth set up next to the sign reading *National Health Insurance Agency*, with a white-coated elderly doctor and nurses in those odd-looking folded white caps behind it ready to administer the compulsory course of vaccinations. Heaps of clean diapers and trash cans with tight-sealed lids beside a table with a rubber cloth and buckets of disinfectant-laced water showed that some-one had been thinking ahead, and there were some Department of Public Health and Eugenics bureaucrats as well.

Probably itching to get calipers on the Cockneys' Anglo-Saxon heads. Though I'd delouse them first!

FOUR

Grand Central Station/General Wheeler Airship Haven
American National Railways/American National Airways
Los Angeles, Southern California
NOVEMBER 19TH, 1916(B)

Luz and Ciara walked quickly toward the great exit doors in the wake of their baggage like pilot fish behind a whale, anonymously upper-middle-class in their plain good *tailleur* shirtwaist outfits, slightly flared calf-length skirts, and moderately broad-brimmed round hats, each with a single pheasant feather in the band above the right ear. They came out into the brightness and mild warmth of the great curved loggia in front of the station, amid a spill of purple and crimson bougainvillea planted in man-tall ceramic vases between the soaring marble height of the Corinthian columns that burst into clusters of gilded acanthus leaves at their summits.

"There'll be plenty of jobs for the Cockneys; right now, there's work for anyone breathing," Luz went on. "And we're not short on food or clothes either, *¡gracias a Dios!* Though with the way Los Angeles has been growing they may have to put them in prefab barracks or even Army tents for a while. No hardship in this climate, but I hope they've got better quarters ready for the ones they're sending to Chicago or Minneapolis."

"The unfortunate Sassenach can get work building houses to live in, then, the way our folk did in Boston, Luz," Ciara said a little tartly.

She'd been utterly horrified by the Annihilation Gas attacks and risked everything to stop Germany's Projekt Loki . . . but that didn't mean Ciara liked the British Empire any better than she had. Ancestral grievance still spoke:

"There wasn't anything like this on hand when *our* folk came off the coffin ships back in the famine years. Crawled off or were dragged off by the feet, often enough. And the signs *they* saw were likely to read *No Irish Need Apply.*"

It speaks loudest when she's not looking at actual toddlers rather than theoretical enemies, Luz thought fondly. *The* niños *turn her from Avenging Goddess of the Gael into a smiling puddle of goo making funny faces.* ¡Dios mío! *but she's better than I deserve!*

"I take the point and that's gospel true, *mi amor*," Luz said aloud. "But this is a better way to treat immigrants, and progress is what being a Progressive is about, isn't it? They'll be Americans soon enough, more sausage in the stewpot like all the rest of us. Besides—"

Luz nodded to a poster. This one showed Uncle Teddy, scowling through his pince-nez with his left forefinger stabbing forward and his right hand clenched into a fist—it was a print taken from a famous photograph of one of his speeches, and one that had always made her imagine he was about to jump on a miscreant and beat him senseless the way he had that drunken gunman in Nolan's Saloon when he was ranching in the Dakota badlands.

Underneath was a familiar Party slogan: *100% Americanism! Vote Progressive Republican!*

That was a little redundant given the results of Tuesday before last. The papers were still trying to come up with superlatives strong enough, since *landslide* and *avalanche* were plainly inadequate. The Party—and Uncle Teddy—believed in driving arguments home with jackhammer repetition; subtle boiled no potatoes. They knew you had to make people *feel* as well as think, feel like a tribe on the warpath or a pack howling in unison behind Wolf . . . or Bull Moose . . . Number One.

Half an hour of suffering through Woodrow Wilson droning abstractions and subclauses through his Princetonian nose is enough to illustrate the difference.

She went on: "Their children . . . like that little girl you had giggling . . . will be one hundred percent and then some. You won't be able to tell that their ancestors didn't help row Miles Standish ashore from the *Mayflower* at Plymouth Rock, or that they aren't descended from Pocahontas like all those First Families of Virginia people."

"Well, yes," the younger woman said. "Still . . . oh, you're right, darling, and half of the Cockneys probably have an Irishman in the woodpile, come to that. Plenty went east in the hunger time, to build railroads in England, and mine coal and load ships and work the looms."

Other posters showed Uncle Teddy in his Rough Riders uniform, unmistakable though considerably younger and slimmer, with:

Leading the charge of Progress then and now! above, and two lines of print below:

The New Nationalism—Prosperity!—Unity!—Strength!

They maneuvered around a Four Minute Man standing on a box and holding forth to a small crowd, using another poster behind him as backdrop for a quick rundown on why the German Empire was, indeed, a *very bad thing.*

This one showed a snarling gorilla in a German uniform and obsolete spiked helmet dancing across a wrecked house amid the dead bodies of women and children with a blazing torch in one hand and a blood-dripping knife in the other.

You couldn't even say it's all that inaccurate, which must be a first for wartime propaganda. Germans just have no sense of public relations at all; no wonder they ended up fighting the whole world!

Uncounted American Schmidts and Bauers and Meiers were making quick visits to registry offices and emerging as Smiths and Farmers and Stewards, while the clatter of German-language newspapers and schools shutting their doors resounded all the way from Texas to Wisconsin.

Though of course . . .

The problem is that so far they're beating the whole world, too, one enemy at a time.

Luz stopped at a newspaper kiosk and passed the disabled veteran who ran it one of the handsome new Walking Liberty half-dollars for copies of the *New York Times*, the *L.A. Times*, the *San Francisco Chronicle*, and the *Atlantic Monthly*. Plus the *All-Story Weekly* for Edgar Rice Burroughs's latest pulp adventure, "Wings of Death," which involved evil

Prussians with a flying U-boat in Lake Superior that shot invisible death rays capable of wiping out cities. And a kidnapped heiress surnamed Lehmann in revolt against her questionably patriotic parents; she sabotaged the devilish German plots while maintaining her virtue with the aid of a spy from a carefully unnamed agency undoubtedly meant to be the Black Chamber who'd infiltrated the crew.

The death rays were a lot more credible than they would have been a few months ago.

Plus the November issue of Croly's rag, the *New Republic*, to brush up on what the Party leadership was thinking or at least wanted people to think they were thinking . . . *that* set of wheels within wheels got more wheels within it with every passing month, not even counting factions.

Ciara suddenly remembered she didn't need to skimp anymore by buying her magazines a month late and used, and contributed a coin for *Scientific American*, *Modern Electrics and Mechanics*, and the *Technology Review*.

"No change, sir," Luz said to the man, who took the money awkwardly with a stiff left hand.

Then, stepping back and dropping back into Spanish, speaking softly because the man had probably acquired some south of the border: "All right, a lesson. How would we detect a tail here?"

Ciara nodded tautly; she always took work seriously.

"Look in that mirror above the booth?" she said.

"Yes; but be careful not to be too obvious about it. Windows are good for that too, especially shop windows; or you can stop and turn to look at your watch as cover. But always just a glance; staring alerts people faster than anything else. Keep your eyes moving, tracking across things."

She tucked the newspapers and magazines under her arm, then turned and pointed at an aeroplane flying by, a much more frequent sight than it had been a year or two earlier but still rare enough to attract attention. Unless you were a New Yorker, but *they* probably wouldn't let themselves show anything but jaded boredom even if giant apes climbed the Woolworth Building to be shot down by fighting scouts or if fire-breathing dinosaurs crawled out of the sea onto the Brooklyn Bridge.

"Or anything else it's natural to look at. Scan the crowd quickly as your eyes drop from the sky. It's hard to act completely natural when you're tailing someone; you focus, and that's detectable—it changes the way you walk and hold yourself. Most give themselves away without realizing it. They stiffen when you look at them, for example. You need to train your intuition to spot them, to see what's giving you that *hunted* feeling."

Ciara nodded as she gave the crowd behind them a quick glance, and they walked on. Luz continued:

"Now, when you check behind yourself again, you look for something familiar—hats and clothes are easier to spot than faces at any distance, but faces too."

"I'm not very good at faces," Ciara admitted.

"It's just a matter of paying attention."

Ciara pouted slightly: "But I don't pay attention to people that much unless they have something interesting about them! Well, except you. I mean, you're *always* interesting."

"Flatterer. Don't try to memorize the whole face, as if you were getting to know someone socially. Look for something out of the ordinary and mark that down."

"And if I think I've spotted someone who's following me? How do I make sure?"

"There are giveaways; we call them *tells* in the trade. That's a gambler's term originally."

It's interesting how much of the Chamber's vocabulary comes from . . . irregular . . . sources, Luz thought. *Clandestine work and crime have a lot in common.* She went on:

"If someone stops every time you do, that's an obvious tell, so you stop and start unpredictably; but a tail is most effective if it's done by a team, the bigger the better so they can hand off. Even with only two, one walks by when the subject stops so it's not always the same person behind you halting in unison. I don't think anyone's trying now, but you never know. When we get into the cab, notice if anyone else hurries to flag another one right after us; if they do, keep an eye in the rearview mirror for that cab. It's easy since they have to have the license number on the front and rear bumper plates these days."

Ciara smiled. "I will. Though I've never actually taken a taxicab before. Or *any* auto before I left Boston!"

"See how our friendship is bringing you *all sorts* of new experiences?"

"Oh, you!" Ciara said happily, and gave her an elbow nudge.

"Taxicabs are a wonderful institution from a spy's point of view," Luz went on. "We can wait here for a second and see if anyone stops without a good reason."

Most of the disembarking passengers were walking three lanes out along brick paths through the asphalt of the roads and standing on the island there to take one of the ranks of big yellow-painted Greater Los Angeles Transportation Authority trolley cars; these days the GLATA could zip you all over the basin for a nickel or two, though Luz intended to use a cab. The trolleys pulled up, climbing from the underground section, filled up, and pulled away in endless succession with a rumble and an occasional ozone-smelling spark from the overhead lines.

"Now, if you're using the trolley, you can get on, wait for a tail to get on too, then step off at the very last moment just as the doors close. That's also good for identifying them—they tend to try to follow you and get caught in the doors, or glare through the windows. Give them a sweet smile and a wave and they're more likely to do that."

"And you can go through stores or restaurants and come out the back, you said?" Ciara said.

"Yes, but you have to be careful about that—if it's a team, some of them may have whipped around to the alley at the back when you went in the front. Alleys are a good spot to do a snatch without being noticed, and you can just bundle the subject into an auto with a threat from a gun under the coat over your arm, and drive off, provided they don't have the nerve to run for it, which is very irritating of them because then you do have to shoot them. Or you can sap them with a cosh and pretend they're drunk or in a fainting spell, though that's always very risky."

"Chloroform?" Ciara asked, and rubbed the side of her head where Horst von Dückler had pistol-whipped her in that warehouse in Boston. "Hitting a head . . . it's like hitting a teapot full of jelly."

"A mixture of chloroform and ether works—but that takes a long time, several minutes, despite what the adventure stories would have you believe. The subject has time to . . . object forcefully. A cosh is quick at least, but if you hit hard enough to be sure . . . you're absolutely right about that, it's risking death or idiocy. Practice helps, but people's heads just have a lot of variation. Now, knockout drops in a drink actually *can* work, but there's rarely any privacy, so it's better to make them woozy rather than try for a lights-out dose and have some kindhearted *imbécil* call for a doctor."

She looked around at the crowds. "Thank God they got the station and the trolley lines finished before the declaration of war. It would be an even more complete zoo otherwise with this much traffic."

Ciara took a glance too. "They'd have finished it anyway as a war priority if they had any sense," she said. "You'd lose more resources on increased transport costs than you spent. Assuming the war lasts more than a few months, but then, has *anyone* expected the Great War to be over by Christmas since December twenty-fifth of 1914?"

Luz thought for a moment; it was an excellent point . . . though believing the war was going to last forever meant falling off the other side of the same horse, even if it was emotionally easier now.

"True, if they're rational about it. But a lot of other projects are going to be slowed down or put in mothballs. *Desvestir a un santo para vestir a otro.*"

"Taking the clothes off one saint to clothe another . . . Oh, I see!" Ciara said, and shifted back to English for a phrase: *"Robbing Peter to pay Paul."*

"Yes, *robbing Peter to pay Paul.* They'll be keeping on with the things like dams and roads that have a definite payoff, and leaving the pretty buildings for later," Luz said, and sighed. "It's a real pity, we had so much planned."

The porter had spotted them and waved; Luz nodded to him and raised a hand toward the rank of waiting cabs. A plain Model T Ford type with open sides slid forward. That was common here since this climate rarely needed more, even in winter.

She gave the delighted redcap an additional dime, and was taken a little aback when she saw that the driver, while in the blue porterlike uniform of the local Metro Cabdriver's Cooperative, a sub-branch of the GLATA, was a tired-looking woman of about thirty with mousy brown hair pushed up under her billed cap.

"General Wheeler Airship Haven, thank you," Luz said, as Ciara slid into the rear seat.

A female cabbie would have been very unlikely four years ago, and uncommon even last year; Luz thought of herself as flexible, but the pace of change in the modern era could make you dizzy sometimes. The cabbie didn't touch the taximeter's lever to start it ticking, either.

"Do ya one buck flat an' no tip, miss?" she said, turning to look at them; her accent was purest quick nasal working-class New Jersey, or *Nu Joisi*, not the flat near-midwestern neutrality more common here.

Luz nodded and gave a sympathetic smile as well as two of the half-dollar pieces.

"Yes, that's fine," she said, sliding back into California English with long-practiced reflex. "Is your husband in the Army, Mrs."—she glanced at the license displayed on the back of the driver's seat—"Cardola?"

"Navy, miss, and his destroyer's been transferred from the Pacific Fleet back ta Norfolk out east," the driver replied with a smile in return as she engaged the gear. "Wish dey'd pick one place! Foist it's Brooklyn, then we're here just long enough to settle in, like, then it's Norfolk—and there just *ain't* base housing in Norfolk now, so's me and the kids stayed here. An' da shipyard workers! I hear dey're hot-bunking 'em, got 'em hanging by da heels like dey was bats."

Another porter blocked the path for a moment, and the driver leaned out the window, shook her fist, and yelled:

"Get da hell outta da way, ya bum!"

Then in a pleasant conversational tone: "With three kids . . . well, the separation allowance is pretty good, I got da driver's-ed course free and dis job causa George, an' we get a special ration book with da Eugenic bonus, but every bit helps da way prices have gone. Couldn't drive dis heap a' junk at all if dose Scout girls didn't help out at the crèche."

The one-dollar charge with the meter off was a minor fiddle. She wouldn't have to pay her commission to the Metro Cabdriver's Cooperative, since it was automatically deducted from her meter's totals at the end of the day and the passengers would save about a dime out of it . . . assuming they'd intended to tip generously. The driver had probably chanced it since they were leaving the country, and made a snap judgment that they weren't the type to take her license number and report her anyway. Ciara turned and looked behind them, then said in Spanish:

"The next cab was a family with small children. Probably not a tail?"

"*Sí, tienes razón,*" Luz said. "*Mas—*"

"You Italian, miss? My George's folks met in Patterson, but dey were bot' boin in Palermo," the driver said. "Don't talk it myself. My maiden name was McAdoo."

"No, we're brushing up on Spanish for our work in the Protectorate, Mrs. Cardola," Luz said pleasantly.

Odd . . . it's harder to give a chatty female *cabbie a set-down, or at least it feels* that way.

The cabbie went on chatting, mostly with Ciara. Taking Spanish for Italian was a natural enough mistake for an East Coast city dweller like her to make, though not one you'd expect from an L.A. native. The languages sounded similar to an untutored ear, Luz could easily have been Sicilian as far as looks went, and the already massive pre-1914 immigration that had produced the cabbie's husband was getting plenty of reinforcement as prudent Italians looked north at the avalanche of disasters that was the Great War and scrambled to get out to the United States or Argentina or Brazil . . . or anywhere else, probably including Tibet . . . while they could.

Luz gave Ciara a glance out of the corner of her eye to say:

Don't just assume *someone doesn't speak a language,* and got a nod of acknowledgment.

They were out of the built-up area and its dense traffic quickly. The road went through a rather smelly oilfield, so new roustabouts were still capping a gusher that had left black sticky pools for hundreds of yards around and made the taxi skid dangerously, past busy-looking but ugly boxy factories with more under construction, and across pleasant leafy suburbs with brilliant gardens and palm-lined streets. Those quickly gave way to open farming country, heading northeast toward Pasadena. L.A. had still been a Mexican-flavored country town when Luz was born, but it seemed to grow inexorably by making a profit *off* that growth, as if it were grabbing its hair with both hands and pulling itself into the sky by main force.

"How pretty it is, and this November and all!" Ciara exclaimed in English, looking around at the countryside; her New England weather standards had been only slightly blunted by a short month's honeymoon in Santa Barbara. "And it smells lovely!"

The two-lane road had a smooth concrete surface, courtesy of the Rural Roads Program, and ran between rows of pepper trees through a flattish landscape of small densely planted farms; most were in bushy-green orange groves, surrounded by windbreaks of blue-trunked eucalyptus or palms. There was a green, slightly flowery scent in the air now that they were well past the oilfield, and the trees were thickly starred with yellow fruit. Here and there workers in overalls and broad-brimmed straw hats were bringing in the golden harvest, picking from the ground or stepladders and filling tray-like boxes, while others repaired the channels and pipes that carried water to the fields. Other fields were in different fruit trees—figs, pears, peaches, pomegranates, avocados—or grapevines, and open stretches showed rows of ground-hugging vegetables thriving through the wintertime in dirt as moist and rich and chocolate-brown as cake.

Even the roadside verges were green with the start of the winter rains. The distant San Gabriels had a dusting of snow on their tops, and it all had a feel of ripe, exuberant, well-tended fertility.

"Ah, you should see it in da spring when the citrus blooms, miss," the driver said over her shoulder. "It's like being inside a perfume bottle then! My George and me are going to get a place like dem dere over in the Valley . . . the San Fernando Valley . . . after the war, with da Veterans Settlement Program grants—we got it picked out an' registered already an' the water's ready to hook up."

Luz nodded politely; it had been policy to limit the size of irrigated farms for several years now. With strict enforcement, the bigger ranches were selling their surplus acres all over California and the rest of the dry West. The Veterans Settlement Program was a major beneficiary of that and the Bureau of Reclamation's giant projects.

The cabbie continued happily: "You don't need much to make a pretty decent living wit' oranges. A little house and a big garden and good schools."

"I sure hope that works out right for you, Mrs. Cardola," Ciara said, obviously sincere.

"Que Dios lo conceda," Luz said absently in agreement, which was just as sincere but less hopeful.

The cabbie's husband was on a destroyer, which meant convoy escort or sub-hunting work, and from what she'd heard the convoys were running fights all the way across, with advantage seesawing back and forth between the Entente navies and the Kaiserliche Marine with each change in tactics or gear. Just a few months ago Luz and Ciara had come back from Europe aboard U-150 . . . and had been depth-charged by American destroyers as they came west. And it had been . . .

Very unpleasant, Luz thought mordantly at the memory of fear and helplessness and waiting for the inrush of water as the blasts rang the fragile hull of the submarine like a bell.

For the escorts and merchantmen, *running fight* meant torpedoes slamming home out of nowhere, men flayed alive in seconds by superheated steam from ruptured lines, damage control parties working beyond all hope in total darkness as the water rose and rose, survivors clutching wreckage in the frigid North Atlantic and hoping for rescue before the chill penetrated to their hearts.

She carefully did not add aloud: *And I hope your George isn't blown into fishbait or drowned or burned alive.*

It was her job to stop that, after all; and now Ciara's as well.

We too are among the ones who put our mortal bodies between our folk and the desolation of war.

They saw the hangars first, immense rising skeletons of girder and truss still under construction and bare to the sky. Then the airship; it was an American development of the Zeppelin company's designs, but

Zeppelin wasn't a word much used since the declaration of war. You had to see it silhouetted against the bones of the immense buildings to realize the sheer *size* of the thing; it towered a hundred and fifty feet into the air and stretched nearly eight hundred feet long, like a great silvery whale ready to swim upward into the blue distance. It was in an outdoor cradle as they approached the haven, one that ran on circular rail tracks around the docking tower, with little electric locomotives to pull the whole assembly around to point its nose into the wind and ready it to be launched into the sky. Ciara's eyes opened wider as they approached the low-slung white neo-Spanish terminal building with its notice board reading:

American National Airways—flight southbound to: Mexico City, Caracas, Recife, Rio de Janerio, Buenos Aires w. connections to Dakar, Tunis via Recife.

Ciara's gaze grew more rapt and her lips parted in awe with a sigh as she took it all in and the airship loomed over them. The more so as the cab dropped them off and they waited for a moment for a redcap to move the luggage and she had time to admire this embodiment of *The Future.*

Luz leaned close and whispered in her ear: "Usually when you have that expression on your face it's because of something *I'm* doing with you, *mi corazón*. Should I be jealous?"

Ciara jumped as she was startled from her rapt contemplation of the airship, realized what Luz had said, and flushed crimson under her fair skin.

"Luz!" she said, laughing and scandalized and giving her a covert poke in the ribs. "Oh, you!"

Then she looked up at the great dirigible again and spoke in a dreamy tone:

"From Europe to America on a submarine . . . and now back on an airship! What an age we live in! The adventure magazines have nothing on this!"

"I've already flown once; I'm totally blasé," Luz said, grinning at the contagious enthusiasm, and read the name blazoned on the bows:

"Manila Bay. Uncle Teddy really is getting nostalgic for the lost days of his youth."

Though perhaps the nostalgia wasn't just for being the brash young rising star of the 1890s. Or even for that single magic hour when he shouted *Sound the charge!* to the bugler and went up the hill, and the roaring host rose as one man and followed him.

Perhaps it was for an era in which the United States could *choose* its wars, and not have them thrust upon it.

FIVE

Dining Room
American National Airways Airship *Manila Bay*
South-southeast of Mexico City
United States Protectorate of Mexico
NOVEMBER 19TH, 1916(B)

Luz put down her fork and laughed as she looked out at the huge crumpled landscape of central Mexico a thousand feet below, tawny-blue-umber-tinged at the edges with crimson in the last rays of evening and stretching to the edge of sight in every direction.

She and Ciara had an excellent view from their wicker-and-aluminum table with its snowy linen cloth, now that the lights had been dimmed; the middle deck of the *Manila Bay* was built into the lower curve of the airship's teardrop hull, and the dining room in its center had a view through the vast reach of inward-slanting windows along the galleries to either side now that the fabric partitions had been removed. Big airships could be lavish with space if not with weight, and the roof with its painted mural of constellations was eighteen feet above her.

"What is it, darling?" Ciara asked, patting her lips with the napkin and giving a pleased sigh; she had a healthy youngster's appetite.

"I was just thinking that . . . our employer . . ." Luz began.

She didn't say *Black Chamber*; those two words had gotten overly well-known lately. And down here in the Protectorate people often blanched, crossed themselves, and went elsewhere as quickly as they could without drawing attention when they heard *la Cámara Negra* mentioned. Key words like that often stuck out and struck the ear even when the rest didn't.

". . . has given us a very nice honeymoon cruise, regulations be damned and all expenses paid."

Ciara frowned. "Is . . . are *we* against regulations?"

"No, I don't think it *is* against regulations for operatives to be lovers," she said, mentally running through the—rather slim—volume of written rules the Chamber had accumulated in its brief, eventful career.

"Not technically," she went on. "Probably because the regulations assume but don't actually *say* that all operatives will be men, which isn't so . . . and that none of those will love other men, which I *also* know isn't so. Though that is *illegal* at common law for them, poor fellows."

"And we're not illegal?"

"No, we're not, in most places. Not *technically*, again. I looked that up . . . some time ago."

She trod a little delicately there; Ciara didn't much care to remember that Luz had been sleeping with the German agent Horst von Dückler when they first met, though that had been business . . . albeit rather enjoyably so. And Luz thought Ciara *really* wouldn't be too happy to hear of any past affairs with women, though she must know there had been. Lightly, she went on:

"But I suspect that's only because it never occurred to our august ancestral lawmakers that anyone without . . . the male organ of generation . . . was important enough to rate a mention in the law. *Tontos.* And now they'd have to throw Secretary of Education Addams in jail, too; everyone knows about her and Mary Smith. For that matter, I strongly suspect that's the reason Madison Grant—"

Who was a longstanding personal friend of the president, a co-founder of the Boone and Crockett Club, energetic savior of buffalo and redwoods, promoter of bird sanctuaries, and a major string-pulling, behind-the-scenes mover and shaker in the nature conservation and eugenics movements, both dear to the Party's collective heart.

"—has never married, for all that he's obsessed with getting people of *good blood* to have enormous litters of offspring."

Ciara grinned impishly and raised her wineglass in a toast.

"Well, long live laws and regulations based on false premises, then! Because this *is* a beautiful cruise even if we're going . . . somewhere bad."

Luz gave a slight nod of approval as she clinked her glass against her partner's and sipped the excellent California zinfandel. ANA was patriotic that way, and after starting out on sweet dessert wines Ciara was coming to appreciate the drier types.

She didn't say to Germany *either. Quick learner!*

The six brand-new vessels of the *Battle* class (Mk. II)—half of them were still under construction—were probably the last civil airships anyone was going to make for quite a while, but they made up for it in range and size and luxury, and even in a global war *some* people had to travel. Since an intercontinental airship ticket cost twice the average family's annual income, most of the passengers were either wealthy or working for a major corporation or traveling on some government's nickel, usually Uncle Sam's on this ship. Or all three.

Whoever the bill ended up with, the price of a ticket on ANA could buy you things nobody else could get, or even *could* have gotten until the last year or so. Things like this opportunity to dine while watching the lights of Mexico City twinkle on below and fade behind them. Ahead the sunset added a tinge of pale red to the crisp white snows on Popocatépetl, towering another ten thousand feet into the darkening star-spangled sky ahead as the airship droned southeastward at a steady sixty-five miles an hour.

The price you paid for it was also not entirely monetary; some of the passengers were probably a little short of breath. The city's mountain basin was around seventy-two hundred feet, and the airship was flying a thousand above that. The heat exchangers running off the engines were keeping the thin chill air of a high-altitude November comfortably mild inside the passenger sections, but they couldn't help with the *thin* part. The crew had discreetly hidden oxygen cylinders and masks ready if anyone started panting too badly.

"Let's take a look around at our fellow passengers, speaking of . . . business. Sizing people up quickly is necessary, because our business is people, *esencialmente*; but you can't get too wedded to first impressions," Luz said.

"Or you'd tailor evidence to suit it without even noticing," Ciara said, surprising Luz a little.

She went on: "That's what the textbooks say about lab work too, pretty much—you have to keep an open mind. It's very, very easy to see what you want to see. That's why you have to have independent confirmation of your experiments."

"Very good!" Luz said softly. "Don't whisper, it attracts attention. Just speak quietly. Now, starting with the people behind you, the three couples . . . that's right, drop your napkin and pick it up . . ."

"American? Rich? And all middle-aged. And they were talking about a cracking plant when we came in, I'm pretty sure I caught that and that means a Burton-Humphreys refining plant, so they're something to do with oil?"

"Excellent! The technical details are useful, and I wouldn't have known what that meant. And where does this airship stop?"

"San Francisco, Los Angeles, Mexico City—they got on in Mexico City—then Caracas . . . oh! Back two years ago they discovered oil in Venezuela, didn't they? Lots of it?"

"Yes, they did. And the concession was to a Dutch company."

"Uh-oh," Ciara said.

They'd both been reading the newspapers and magazines more carefully since they left Santa Barbara.

"And the Dutch just joined Germany. Well, were annexed, really," Ciara said.

Luz nodded. The official story from Berlin, and between gritted teeth from Amsterdam, was that the Kingdom of the Netherlands as a quote *kindred Germanic people* unquote had been invited to *come home to the* Reich on the same basis as the constituent kingdoms of Saxony and Bavaria and Prussia, and had joyfully embraced the opportunity to be protected against the brutal and perfidious Anglo-Saxons and depraved Latins.

She leaned forward and spoke a rhyming couplet, an old German folk saying:

"Und willst Du nicht mein Bruder sein,
So schlag' ich Dir den Schädel ein."

Which translated roughly as: *Be my brother, or I'll smash your skull.*

Ciara nearly snorted her wine out of her nose as she suppressed a laugh. Luz supposed it was all grim enough in Amsterdam, but if you couldn't laugh at *that* you'd probably had your Organ of Irony surgically removed. The Germans were throwing in the Flemish-Dutch parts of Belgium and French Flanders as a sweetener, while the rest of Belgium became the puppet Grand Duchy of Wallonia under Prince Bernhard of Lippe.

Horst had hinted that the Germans were thinking of something like that when he and Luz—under her cover as a pro-German Mexican revolutionary—had arrived in Amsterdam on the *San Juan Hill* not long ago.

A lot of German princely younger sons and Grand Ducal spare heirs are getting principalities of their own right now, Luz thought, and went on:

"Taking Holland off the board means a lot is up for grabs and everyone with a free hand is grabbing. We're impounding any Dutch merchant shipping we can get for the National Merchant Marine Authority and taking their Caribbean colonies—in trust, officially, but once our Marines are ashore . . . well. The Japanese are taking the Dutch East Indies, again *officially* to keep the Germans out of it, and French Indochina for the same reason, which is really a bit of a stretch and isn't going to please Uncle Teddy *at all*, but there's not much we can do about it except warn them off Australia and the British possessions—which might as well be ours, now."

Ciara frowned thoughtfully as she traced the implications of the bigger picture for the people in this room.

"So *we're* sending people to take over the Dutch oil interests in Venezuela?" she said. "Those people at the table are part of it?"

"Exactly. They're probably Standard Oil executives and their wives; they're too well dressed to be Department of Commerce or War Trade Board bureaucrats. It'll be more tactful if it's done through a private company and greased with bribes as well as threats—our troops and warships in Curaçao will speak for themselves. Standard Oil has learned it pays to cooperate with the Party, and they're big in the Protectorate these days, so they'd have appropriate people on hand."

"We're not wasting any time!" Ciara said admiringly.

"The president doesn't dither or hesitate, and neither does Elihu Root," Luz said, naming the secretary of state. "The War Trade Board will be putting the knuckle on in various ways all over South America since the declaration of war, snapping up Dutch and German investments and properties at a few cents on the dollar . . . and I wouldn't be surprised if a lot of the Belgian and French ones end up in American hands now too."

She indicated another table with her eyes. "Now, those soldiers. They got on in Mexico City as well, and so they're very probably from Southern Command GHQ."

There were five of them. Four looked as if they'd been stamped out by a press in a midwestern military factory; a Marine captain in dress blues with the globe-and-anchor tabs on his collar, a naval lieutenant, and two Army officers with the scarlet-and-white piping of combat engineers. The wiry Air Corps type with the new winged propeller badge was slighter and darker, and had a big nose and clever black eyes and black hair that was probably curly when it wasn't cut so short; he might be Italian or Greek or Jewish or Armenian by background, and he looked dangerous and quick. The Marine was a bit older than the rest, a weather-beaten thirty or so, and even tougher-looking than his comrades. She let her eyes flick on after a quick once-over; it was rarely wise for young women to stare openly at men.

"Recife . . ." Ciara said. "The new naval base we're building in Brazil? It's a short voyage over the Atlantic from there to Dakar in French West Africa. They'd be part of that? The engineers . . . and the pilots for the aeroplanes and airships that escort the convoys against U-boats?"

Then she added: "That was delicious!"

Sincerely, but apropos of nothing as two attendants arrived to clear the dishes. Luz sipped the last of her wine and enjoyed the vast panorama of field and mountain as the white-jacketed waiters took their plates, deftly scraped up crumbs with an ivory ruler-like tool, and put out coffee and brandy and *pastel de tres leches*, adding whipped cream and fresh strawberries to the top. The brandy was French, a very nice

Augier cognac. Therefore it would vanish soon, one more thing the Great War had destroyed.

So far you didn't need to use ration-book coupons in addition to money for meals on ANR or ANA either, though she supposed that would be coming quite soon. Herbert Hoover was a bit of a puritan. Also very, very thorough, and he didn't care whose toes he stepped on.

"So this is how Mexicans eat?" Ciara said, taking a first forkful of her cake.

They'd had *caldo tlalpeño*, a soup of avocado and shredded chicken in a spicy cilantro-flavored stock; mole poblano (the full twenty ingredients including ancho, mulato and pasilla peppers, cloves, cinnamon, plantain, garlic, and chocolate) over a cut of slow-cooked pork shoulder; red rice; and a number of other things. All very well done, if toned down just a bit for delicate gringo palates.

Luz smiled as she shook her head. Corrupting her lover's rather spartan Irish-American childhood eating habits with novel epicurean delights was great fun. Almost as much fun in a restaurant as it had been to cook for her with her own hands, and with the added pleasure of doing it on their field operatives' expense accounts, though she *could* have afforded airships as an occasional treat.

"No, most Mexicans eat tortillas and refried beans and chilies with a little chicken or pork or turkey in the vegetable stew when they're lucky," Luz said. "This is how the ones with enough money eat. If they're not too snobbish."

Their costumes were on Uncle Sam's account too, and they weren't using their Chilean identities yet, which would call for a more old-fashioned look and would be furnished by the Technical Section's experts; currently they were supposed to be upper-class Americans. Ciara was in an emerald drop-waist chemise dress that flattered her milky complexion, red-gold hair, and turquoise-and-sapphire eyes to perfection. Luz had no idea whether Coco Chanel had survived the wreck of France, but she certainly hoped so. Her own outfit was in a soft dark maroon knit by the same designer, and not only stylish but the most comfortable and least constraining semi-formal day dress she'd ever worn.

Which says something about the merits of finally *having a woman designing haute couture. Maybe with the war the New York fashion houses will have to hire more females too. Or the Chamber could send a mission to* rescue and/or acquire *Coco? She's been living in Biarritz, so she probably didn't get caught by the horror-gas . . . I wonder if I have enough pull to suggest* that? *She would be an economic asset for the country, after all.*

"The money I can see, but snobbery?" Ciara said. "It was exquisite! And . . . complex. You could tell cooking it must have been like a juggler keeping a dozen balls in the air at the same time."

"Rich, snobbish Mexicans . . . most of them would murder you if you offered them a tortilla. They like their menus in French and they'd rather eat haute cuisine . . . even second-rate attempts at it . . . than this, at least when anyone can see them."

Her family had moved in those circles while her father worked south of the border, back when the iron hand of cunning, ruthless old Don Porfirio kept the peace and kept foreigners respectful; Mima's exalted family background in Cuba had helped there, opening doors that a mere gringo engineer might have found closed or not even known existed.

One of el Necesario's favorite sayings had been: *Poor Mexico, so far from God, so close to the United States.* What happened after his exile gave spice to the jest; *el Necesario* meant *The Indispensable One*, and a great many people south of the border wished now that they hadn't decided in 1911 that thirty-two years of Don Porfirio were enough.

"They're like rich, snobbish Americans and their French chefs?" Ciara said with a chuckle. "And places that can't serve you a plate of beef stew with onions and mushrooms without calling it *boeuf bourguignon*, like putting a fancy Paris bonnet on a pig?"

Luz laughed. "Pretty much the same, but worse. And they avoid *indio* things because they like to pretend they're *de raza pura española* by blood, which mostly they're not, any more than the Arósteguis are. It would remind them of their many-times-great-grandmothers kneeling on the ground grinding corn on a *metate* when Hernán Cortés rode by on his horse eyeing their bottoms lasciviously. Now, back to work."

She inclined her head slightly to a nearby table.

"Those—no, don't look directly or meet their eyes! They'll take that for an invitation . . . those are men from Yucatán, and just the type

I meant. Let your gaze slide by and look out the windows past them, you don't need to focus directly to pick up details."

Ciara did, and shook her head. "Sorry, darling, all I can tell is that they're Mexican and very well-off . . . and there aren't any poor passengers here of any description, are there?"

Luz nodded. "Everything *they* ordered was French, or as French as upper-end Harvey House food gets; vichyssoise, *artichauts à la Provençale*, lobster Thermidor . . . all straight Escoffier."

"You noticed what they were *eating*?"

"It only takes a glance."

"And how can you tell where they're from, darling?"

"Well, their looks for starters; not any single thing, but the combinations."

She listed them. All three men were in their thirties or forties, with upswept waxed black mustaches and center-parted hair a bit longer than most Americans would wear it, and slicked back. They were slightly plump in a sleek sort of way, and extremely well-dressed in a very slightly out-of-date manner, lounge suits of light fabrics and high winged collars, with narrow four-in-hand ascot neckties and two-tone buttoned shoes that looked like spats but weren't. None of them wore the newfangled men's wristwatches, but all had elegant gold watch chains on their waistcoats with a few fobs, studded cuff links, and jeweled stickpins in their ties, and one wore a diamond ring on his pinkie. Their complexions were smoothly olive, not much different from her own, and their faces a bit broad across the cheekbones and full in the lips.

And all three looked enough alike to be brothers.

"What they're speaking is Mérida Spanish—the way they lengthen their vowels, and one of them said *SHincuenta* instead of *Cincuenta* for 'fifty' and called the one next to him *mi* h*ermano* instead of pronouncing it *mi 'ermano* the way most people do. And they're Casta Divina too, or I miss my guess."

"Divine . . . class?" Ciara said.

"Divine Caste is closer; it's sarcastic, even the Casta Divina aren't conceited enough to call themselves that. Henequen planters, the hacendados who own the State, a hundred families of *conquistadores* who've been marrying each other so many centuries that they're all first cousins. My papá did projects in Yucatán, during the *Porfiriato*—before the Intervention—and they were rich enough to pay well then. Now they're *very* rich, even if Plenipotentiary Lodge makes them toss their *peones* a few cents now and then instead of just flogging them. You'd have to spend seven or eight hundred dollars for what they're wearing. Each. Those are emeralds in the middle one's cuff links."

"Gosh!" Ciara said, her thrifty neighborhood shopkeeper soul slightly shocked and turning to stare at the *henequeñeros* for an unguarded moment until Luz tapped a foot on hers below the table. "Golly!"

Seven hundred dollars was a year's wage for a laborer in Boston, a dock-walloper or hod-carrier, and not the worst one either in a time of rising prices. It was about four-tenths of the respectable middle-class salary Ciara was now getting as a junior field operative (with the Order of the Black Eagle bonus), and which had struck her as amazing affluence when she learned about it. Though to be sure, part of the amazement had been because the Black Chamber's policy of paying women the same as men in the same grade wasn't common at all.

"Don't stare!" Luz said quietly but sharply.

"Sorry, love. I was just thinking of all the uses for henequen."

As they spoke the band had been setting up on the stand in the lounge area closer to the windows, where the light of the waning gibbous moon shone on the crumpled landscape of the Mexican highlands below. The musicians were all young Negroes in evening dress, and the bandstand had a sign reading *Morton's Red-Hot Ragtime Band* in jaunty curling script of a type she'd seen in New Orleans.

"Ah, I heard them on the *San Juan Hill*," Luz said. "They're very good—and very original, too!"

Ciara's ears perked up as the seven-piece band started their first number; presumably their leader Morton on the aluminum-framed piano, a cornet, a trombone, a clarinet, and a double bass and drum.

"You're right," she said, nodding along to the lively tune; she usually played the piano when they did duets, with Luz on the violin. "But that's not ragtime . . . not really . . . it's looser. Oh, my goodness, darling, just *listen* to the way the pianist is separating the rhythms of his hands!"

"Yes, one's doing a sort of tango thing and the other . . . that's five notes in the time of four. Which combination I wouldn't have thought was possible without your head exploding."

"Saints, yes! It makes my fingers ache thinking about it. And . . . and yes, he's doing the melody there with his right thumb and the harmony above it with the rest of his hand! Wouldn't that be lovely music to do a foxtrot to?" Ciara said wistfully.

"Four-four time except for that extra bit," Luz agreed.

The eighty or so passengers were about three-fifths male, but several of the couples had risen and were doing exactly that, their feet tapping on the spruce veneer that covered the aluminum deck. The foxtrot was all the rage these days, and had been since it burst on the scene in 1914.

"Yes, it's . . ."

Her head came around as she sensed motion out of the corner of her eye.

"*¡Ay, maldición!* I was afraid of that, if they realized we were talking about them."

"Sorry," Ciara said contritely. "I'll try to be less obvious from now on. Men are so very strange that way."

Luz sighed. "They'd probably all die as virgins if they didn't assume they were irresistible to every woman they see. *Some* of them are going to be right about *some* woman *eventually.*"

"Like a stopped clock," Ciara agreed.

One of the henequen planters made his way over to their table, with a broad white smile and a scent of very expensive French cologne . . . which was going to be even more expensive soon, with Paris gone and France wrecked, unless some refugee started making it in Algiers.

"Señoritas," he said, bowing slightly. "It is a tragedy that two such lovely young ladies should not dance . . . may my friends and I request the pleasure of your company on the floor? I am Don—"

Ciara glanced deliberately away, ostentatiously withholding her attention. Luz didn't think that pointed silence would work; neither would dancing. That would just encourage them. She gave the man a cool glance.

"Señor," she said glacially.

Putting on her best upper-class Mexico City accent, which would make the *henequeñero* feel like a provincial hick no matter how rich he was:

"My cousin and I could not possibly grieve our parents by speaking to or dancing with men to whom we have not been introduced by our families. Thank you, but no."

"Ah, but your parents are not here and would not know, so what harm?" he said.

Which made perfect sense and was just what you'd expect . . . if you knew the country. In her experience, the Latin lands—and Japan, for that matter—relied on the fear of being shamed before kin and neighbors to enforce custom; Yankees and Germans and Irish went more in terror of a scolding from the little schoolteacher-parent-priest who lived in their heads and tormented them with guilt. Both had their drawbacks.

And I, being what I am, can view both from the outside, she thought.

"I can keep nothing from my family, señor," she said, letting a slight edge into her voice. "Or from God. Thank you, but *no.*"

"Oh, come now—" he began.

Luz sighed and went through the same verbal circuit twice more with slight variations, with her side of it getting slightly less polite and the man's voice rising a little and a flush growing up from his collar. He was probably also very conscious of his friends' eyes and feared their scorn if he returned without the prize he'd doubtless boasted was his for the plucking.

Luz smiled sweetly and switched to English, pitching her voice very slightly higher so that it would carry:

"I am sorry, sir, but my cousin and I do not care to dance or speak with you and your friends. Please do me the courtesy of taking me at my word or I will have to ask for assistance."

Then, the smile growing a little cruel, she went on in Spanish again: "Señor, do you see those gringo soldiers two tables away?"

The man's head whipped around in alarm; whether or not he spoke English himself, he now recognized that she *did*, and fluently. It probably hadn't occurred to him that they were American once he'd heard her and Ciara speaking Spanish to each other, and unless he was even more stupid than she'd assumed, he was realizing just how far out on a limb he'd gone.

The officers had finished the steaks and pork chops, peas and creamed corn and baked potato and apple pie with ice cream that were their idea of a fancy meal. Now they were talking among themselves and drinking Carta Blanca or Siglo XX beer—which in her experience nine out of ten American military men preferred to the northern brews once they'd been stationed in the Protectorate for more than a month—and nodding and tapping their feet to the wild syncopations of the music.

In another time and place Luz thought they might have been a problem themselves, but give them a target they hated and despised, and a chance to show it by defending two fair flowers of American womanhood . . .

She didn't need to say anything more. Several of the soldiers had looked over at Luz's table as the voices rose and she nodded directly toward them, their gaze passing appreciatively but politely over the two young women, and then locking on the man standing by her chair. They'd been discussing a war they probably didn't expect to survive, and they were looking at someone who'd do nothing in it except add even more money to a fortune already many times larger than their combined lifetime earnings.

"You cannot speak to me like that!" the hacendado said, but kept his tone quiet; and the maître d'hôtel was also looking in their direction and frowning.

"Really, señor, it would be better if you left before others become involved."

The Marine rose and stood looking at them, cold killer's speculation in his pale eyes, a blank readiness to do anything at all. The hacendado flushed darkly, and Luz could actually hear his teeth grinding; she suppressed a happy giggle, for fear he would drop dead from a stroke or lose all sanity and attack her there and then.

"*¡Pelaná!*" he snapped, which was a regional insult and originally Mayan, and then over his shoulder as he stamped back toward his table something more broad-spectrum: "*¡Tortillera!*"

The hooked fish-shaped hilt of her *navaja sevillana* was in her hand, under the napkin in her lap; the one her mother's coachman-cum-bodyguard old Pedro El Andaluz had taught her to use.

He told me once I was the sort of girl who'd need it badly sooner or later . . . which I didn't understand at the time. Help may not always be at hand, but this *faithful little friend never leaves me.*

Ciara looked at Luz as she slipped the knife inconspicuously back into the special pocket of her skirt. Meanwhile the baffled man from Mérida tossed down his drink and then left the room equally abruptly.

"*Tortillera?*" she asked curiously. "Woman who makes tortillas? Why on earth would that nasty *abhlóir* call you that?"

"I'll show you later," Luz said, grasping the meaning of the Gaelic insult Ciara had used from context, and winked. "That's a promise. *Making tortillas* can be a lot of fun."

The Marine captain finished his beer and came over to their table, standing at a respectful distance with his blue-and-white peaked cap in his left hand, the one that bore a gold wedding band.

"Was that fat dago a problem, miss?" he asked. "You need him taught a lesson?"

His accent was a flat Cornhusker rasp straight off a Nebraska farm, and one big fist had closed into a knobby bone club, probably without his being aware of it. From the voice and the brawler's scars on his knuckles Luz decided he was probably a mustang, someone promoted from the ranks via a four-month Officer Candidate School course—there was a lot of that in an American military that had doubled or tripled in size every year since Uncle Teddy swept back into the White House and that now numbered in the millions.

"No, no problem after I took your name in vain and implied you'd thrash him if he didn't go away, Captain . . ."

"Moore, miss," the man said with a grin. "Yeah, that's what I thought you said; I know the lingo a little. Learned it from the missus."

He touched his ring finger with his left thumb, probably unconsciously. The grin said he'd have been delighted to do exactly that.

"Captain Vince Moore, USMC," he added.

"Our thanks, Captain Moore," Luz said, and gave him their aliases. "The music is fine, the choice of partner . . . no."

The Marine nodded. "It *is* pretty good, miss; that colored boy really knows how to tickle the ivories."

His eyes grew a little distant. "They say they've got a natural sense of rhythm . . . they say a lot of things, but don't believe anyone who tells you they can't *fight*. The Tenth Cavalry were right beside the Marine brigade at Veracruz back in '13—Black Jack Pershing's old regiment. Nobody had the fancy gear then we're getting now, but they could use Springfields and bayonets just *fine*, by God!"

"Veracruz, Puebla, *and* Mexico City," she said, reading the battle ribbons marked on his dress jacket; a fair number of civilians could, these days, but he still smiled.

She'd crossed the border overland with Pershing in 1913 herself, heading for Zacatecas via Juarez and Chihuahua while the Marines went ashore at Veracruz, but she'd been there for Puebla and Mexico City, doing things behind the other side's lines that never got into the public eye. Agents who could pass convincingly as Mexicans hadn't been common enough to let any sit idle.

He also had the Intervention Campaign Ribbon and the heart-shaped Military Merit badge, usually given for being wounded in action . . . with four circled lines around it to show how many times he'd beaten the odds.

"My, you have been busy, Captain Moore! The Tenth Cavalry were with . . ."

She stopped herself just before saying *Uncle Teddy*.

". . . the president in Cuba, as I recall. Thank you again, Captain, and your friends. I really don't think my cousin and I should accept *any* invitations to dance, though. We don't want to spoil anyone's evening with a set-to."

From the look of the Marine's fists and the rather battered-looking face below the cropped sandy hair, he'd probably spent a lot more time in dives with sawdust on the floor than in places like this, ones where a fight would just be the perfect ending to everyone's evening, and any females present would pick pockets during it, or screech and throw crockery or pull out straight razors tucked into their garters. But he'd obviously also picked up the etiquette expected of an officer and gentleman, and gave a slight bow to them both:

"Right, miss. And you, miss."

He smiled at Ciara. Luz was strikingly attractive in a slightly exotic fashion, but Ciara looked very much like most American men's subliminal conception of *younger sister* or *the girl next door*.

"And if there's any problem, we'll settle it—just give the word."

"That's what I told the gentleman," Luz said, and they shared a smile before he nodded to each of them with a murmur of:

"Miss . . . miss . . ." and returned to his friends.

Ciara looked after him and shivered a little. "He reminds me of Horst, even though he doesn't look like him," she said.

Luz mused for a moment. Both were big and fair-haired, but otherwise there wasn't much resemblance between the midwestern plowboy turned Marine and the Silesian soldier-intelligence-agent-aristocrat whom she'd deceived on the last mission. Except for one impalpable thing. It was good that Ciara was picking up on the subtleties.

"Both very dangerous men," she said. "There's something about someone who kills quickly and without a second thought. Most soldiers don't have it, but he and Horst both do."

And so do I, but I hide it better until it's time to let it out to play.

Ciara nodded thoughtfully. "And . . ." Luz continued, "*We* now have a perfect excuse to do that foxtrot together. Shall we?"

Ciara's face lit with a delighted grin. "And we'll just look too old-fashioned and prim and proper to dance with any man without an introduction!"

That sort of Victorian reserve was mostly dead at the social level of people who could afford an airship ticket . . . but mostly dead was not the same as altogether, *absolutely* dead. Luz suspected that it had always been used in ways other than the obvious. Even today, nobody expected women *not* to dance just because there wasn't a socially suitable male partner to hand.

As they made their way out to the floor with a nod and smile to the table full of officers, a pale and utterly unremarkable man stepped out from behind the shelter of a potted palm made of colored aluminum in the *moderne* style and looked after them speculatively through the thick wire-rimmed glasses that hid much of his moon-shaped face.

"*Ach, so,*" he murmured to himself.

SIX

Control Deck
Aboard ANA Airship *Manila Bay*
Approaching Recife
Province of Pernambuco
Republic of Brazil
NOVEMBER 21ST, 1916(B)

A hhh," Luz murmured.

She blinked against the brightness as they climbed the last stage of the stairway onto the bridge level. From the top you could see right out past the helms, and things got better as the group walked forward. The view from the passenger galleries was spectacular. That from the airship's bridge was . . .

Entrancing, she thought.

The horseshoe-shaped control room of the *Manila Bay* jutted out from the underside of the airship's blunt bow like a chin, and it was surrounded on three sides by tall windows slanting inward from the top at forty degrees and showing sweeping vistas of green sugarcane, bands of tropical forest, and endless palm-lined white beach fringed with white surf. They were about the same height as the tip-top of the Eiffel Tower—if it still stood in the blighted wasteland of central Paris—but they were *moving.* It was like the view from a cloud, or through the eyes of a falcon.

Ciara made her own unconscious sound of excitement, though Luz thought it was directed more at the airship, with the view proving how marvelous the great machine was.

They droned on across Brazil's Pernambuco province toward the regional capital of Recife, and the shallower water near the shore was jade-green, fading to a deep cerulean blue farther out and patches of white foam breaking on reefs. A windjammer was standing in below them, its four masts a white-and-black geometry against the ocean with the doll-tiny figures of the crew in the rigging plainly visible from a thousand feet up.

"Now, are there any questions?" the blue-uniformed third officer said brightly; his name was Alan McCredie and he was no more than a year or two older than Ciara.

He had already explained what the vertical and horizontal helms were for, and the banks of brass-rimmed dials and switches that let the bridge watch, monitor, and control the engines and gas pressure and dozens of other variables. He'd managed not to sound bored while he did it, but . . .

He probably is, Luz thought.

Dealing with the passengers on this tour was one of his duties, and it probably wasn't an accident that the junior deck officer got saddled with it. Another way an airship wasn't much like an ocean liner was that the crew was far smaller, sixty or seventy, and airships were vastly more fragile, new to everyone including their crews, and had to be *flown* every single moment.

Ciara was virtually dancing without moving her feet, and Luz was interested herself; how could you be so stodgy that you didn't pay attention to something so new in the world? Luz O'Malley was a young woman, but she could remember the day when Graf von Zeppelin launched the first of his monsters and touched off the airship race between the United States and his homeland.

Though we only started catching up when Uncle Teddy put his National Aeronautical Administration onto it, she thought. *Then we jumped ahead.*

Ciara raised her hand.

"Yes, Miss Duffy?" the officer said.

"I know you use gas for fuel on the latest airships because it has the same density as air and doesn't affect the buoyancy as it's used up, so you save on hydrogen lifting-gas and ballast," she said. "What I was wondering was how you deal with the way differences in ambient temperature affect buoyancy by making the lifting hydrogen expand or contract and altering its pressure and density."

The officer opened his mouth, then stopped as the question visibly made its way through his *ignorant-passenger* and *young-blond-woman-nice-figure* filters. Luz made a slight *tsk* sound; Ciara was attracting attention. It was probably, almost certainly, harmless, but she'd do some gentle reproof later.

Although that look on his face is priceless, she admitted.

"Ah . . ." He combed a hand through his cropped auburn hair.

The whole crew were rather young, since this was a new field, and McCredie had a blue-eyed, corn-fed, aw-shucks look to him like one of the covers for *Boys' Life* by their brilliant new artist, the one who was attracting so much attention now that the Scouts were part of compulsory school attendance.

Rockwell, that's his name.

When he smiled at Ciara his expression was genuine.

"Well, the control ballonets inside the gas cells can be expanded or deflated to maintain volumetric pressure control," he said.

He visibly aborted an explanation of what that meant when she nodded eagerly. It was an exceptional man who didn't appreciate that look of intense interest from someone like Ciara.

"And if we need to raise the temperature, we vent heated air from the engines around the gasbags," he said. "And if the sun and the outside temperature do that, we rise and it's cooler at higher altitudes so it's self-correcting to a degree. But we have to be careful not to rise or fall too fast, of course, or to porpoise, because then we would have to valve gas or drop ballast to maintain control."

"The same with rapid updrafts or downdrafts, I suppose," she said thoughtfully.

"Yes, that can be a problem, particularly in bad weather," he said, looking a bit desperate. "We use the horizontal rudders and dynamic thrust for active damping. Now, if you'll all step this way . . ."

At the rear of the control bridge where it was faired into the main body of the airship, a ladder ran upward. And up, and up, and *up*. There were murmurs from the passengers as their necks craned backward. The bridge had its own ceiling, but here they were out in the interior of the hull itself, vast and dim and shadowy and vibrating to the slip-stream and engines, lit by gleams from the windows along the galleries or bulbs spaced along the walkways.

The structure of the airship inside the smooth exterior teardrop of taut doped fabric was exposed, triangular truss-girders of riveted du-ralumin alloy, the bracing rings at intervals, and the long coaxial keel that ran through the center. Most of that space was filled with the cy-lindrical lifting-gas bags that limited the view; they were cut off at the bottom, and the remainder of their shape filled out by the smaller fuel-gas bags, all confined by henequen-rope nets that kept the huge con-tainers of canvas lined with goldbeater's skin from surging too much.

"The ladder here runs up a hundred feet to the observation dome on the top keel of the *Manila Bay*," the officer said. "That's where we take sightings of the sun and stars for navigation—not unlike sur-face ships. We also have other means . . ."

Ciara seemed about to say something; probably about the alarm-ingly new system of estimating location by triangulation from radio transmitters.

Luz gently nudged her ankle with one foot and got a muttered: *sorry!*

"The captain's day room is to your port . . . left . . . here, and the wireless communications room to the starboard . . . the right. And if you'll follow me, this is the side gallery where the engines are mounted; there's another just like it on the other side."

They were about one-third of the airship's diameter up from the ventral keel here. A long curving corridor ran along the ship's side, open to the hull on the inside and with occasional windows through the doped fabric of the outer skin on the other; they could see across to the other side because this was where the lift-gas cells were separated from the fuel-gas ones below. Once they were a hundred feet back from the bows, regularly spaced broad platforms marked the spots where each of the five engines on this side were mounted, with bracing beams and cables to transfer the thrust to the greater structure of the airship. A scent of oil and hot metal and solvents grew stronger as they approached the first one, though the way the engine pods were mounted outside swept the exhaust away in their wake; the platform had tables and work-benches, and there were racks and bins for tools and spare parts, all neatly labeled and fastened down—an airship of this size was usually extremely steady, but that could change if the weather was bad enough.

"It's not like aeroplanes that never stay up for more than an hour or two so that all the overhauls can be done on the ground; we're aloft for over a hundred hours on the longer passages. These bays can do anything up to a complete teardown when we dismount an engine and bring it inboard, and we carry several spares so that whole engines can be replaced while underway if necessary. Though that's a bit . . . bit of a big job and we only do it if we must."

Three men in mechanic's overalls of blue so dark it was nearly black had something complex and mechanical strapped to one end of the worktable and were doing things with brushes and screwdrivers amid a harsh chemical stink. They didn't look up after nodding to the officer, focused entirely on their task.

"Ah, working on a carburetor," Ciara said—very quietly.

Luz could recognize an automobile's carburetor easily enough, and even disassemble and clean one, because she'd had to help repair motor vehicles in the field in the Protectorate; however wedded some officers were to horses and mules, the American military and government did use more motor transport than anyone else. This one was rectangular, bigger than a man's head, and considerably more complex than the ones she was used to, but after her partner had given it a label she could see the resemblance.

The officer pointed outward. "As you can see, the engine nacelle is connected to the hull by a framework of girders covered in a wing-shape of hull fabric. It's big enough that mechanics can go out and work on the engine without being exposed to the wind while we're in flight, and since we have ten in all, we can stop up to four or five for maintenance if necessary—though it's rare for more than one to give real trouble at a time. The engines are the new Curtiss-Martin Mk. VII radials, nine-cylinder, three hundred fifty horsepower. The fuel is gas, and the pipes run under the walkway . . ."

Then he stopped and looked back over his shoulder; Luz followed his eyes. One of the passengers was bent over the walkway, holding the matting with one hand and his other underneath the metal planking at the side.

"Mr. Hansen . . . sir . . . what are you doing there?" he said.

"I ins . . . was inspecting it," the passenger named Hansen said, straightening up and pulling the section of tough woven henequen laid across the walkway's metal grid back into place.

Wait a minute, Luz thought. *He's an odd one. And . . .*

Her fine linguist's ear was twinging.

Something off there in the way he talks. It's slight, but . . .

"Why is there a covering?" Hansen asked. "My firm in Minneapolis makes industrial floor coverings. We're investigating new sources of supply in Brazil since henequen prices are so high."

That was as much as she'd heard from Hansen all voyage.

Interesting accent, she thought, keenly focused now.

Human speech in all its varieties was endlessly fascinating to her even aside from work.

Basically General American, Upper Midwestern, but there's definitely something underneath, whatever it was his parents spoke. Of course, that's true of every fifth American these days, more outside the South. Including me, if I weren't good at switching my voice.

She ran through the likely candidates for someone with that name from that part of the country.

Swedish? No, not hurby-gburby-yurgy enough. Not Norski *either, not* musical *enough. Harder and with more of a potato in the mouth and croaking . . . possibly Danish . . . but not German, not with the way he handles p- and f-sounds. Or not* standard *German at least, or any of the* Hochdeutsch *varieties. Low German? Frisian? Dutch?*

Most of the passengers had at least exchanged a few words in the usual social rituals of the polite world; Hansen had kept strictly to himself, more so than any of the other passengers . . . except the three hacendados. And they had an extra reason to avoid her and Ciara now, since the American military men were keeping an eye on them with malign intent.

Hansen had been *suspiciously* quiet, now that she thought about it . . . and doubly so in retrospect now that he was breaking the routine he'd established. Most human beings, particularly middle-aged ones, were nearly as attached to routine as cats.

"The floor covering makes it less slippery if lubricating oil gets on the metal treads, sir," the officer said. "And now if you'll all follow me . . ."

They did, but Luz was frowning. There was a jarring note in the pattern of the day. Seeing things that didn't fit, having them spring out of the picture and call for attention, was part of the set of skills that had kept her alive. It might be as simple as Hansen being the sort of person who somehow couldn't learn the basics of dealing with others and was awkward whenever he tried. Some people were just like that, though she'd noticed the same ones were often good at memory tricks or mathematics.

Ciara's a bit like that . . . a very small bit. Tesla considerably more so and just plain crazy to boot.

"Mr. Hansen, you're from Minneapolis?" she said, on impulse, dropping back to walk beside him; Ciara was sticking close to the third officer, the source of fascinating technical tidbits.

"Yes, Miss Robicheaux," he said.

He was a middling man—middling in height, an inch or two taller than her five-six, pale, with middling-brown hair that had a few flecks of gray and a rather ordinary snub-nosed generically northern European face, and blue eyes like paint on white china, so different from Ciara's turquoise, magnified by the large wire-rimmed glasses he wore.

If you'd looked up *moderately successful, slightly pudgy upper midwestern businessman* in an *Encyclopedia of Types*, he'd have been a good illustration.

He'd let himself go more than was fashionable these days, but there were still plenty who thought the *strenuous life* was folderol and useless sweat, especially if their families weren't long off the farm or from other manual-labor backgrounds. Some others shunned the *build your body to build yourself* maxim because it was a safe way to kick the Party in the shins, too.

In fact, he might have been designed to be inconspicuous . . . which would make him an ideal spy, far better than many in that line of work.

Men are far less likely to forget my face, for instance. But if you start thinking every inconspicuously average man is a German spy because they're so unremarkable, you'll go absolutamente loco. *Is there anything else? What is it that I'm noticing but can't put my finger on?*

That doughy bespectacled face was expressionless now . . .

. . . but he was sweating, sweating very heavily indeed. It was warm inside the airship's hull, with a stuffy feeling like a canvas tent in the sun, but they were also over a thousand feet up and flying, there was a steady draft designed to keep the air circulating and prevent buildups of leaking gas, and it wasn't *that* hot.

Sweating too much even with that duster-style coat he's wearing . . . which is stupid, because we are *on the equator, and that's the sort of thing you'd wear in the woods in Minnesota at Halloween. And it's not ordinary sweat. And a loose coat like that is perfect if you're concealing something . . .*

Working in the field in the Protectorate she'd seen, smelled, and shed most types of sweat herself; from the humid *selva* of Chiapas, where it lay on your skin and its folds like a coating of rancid bacon grease, to the sort that happened in the Sonoran deserts where the air shimmered over black rock like the beginning of a migraine and the sun sucked the moisture out of you so fast that the salt lay on your skin like fine white dust under the gritty alkaline stuff the wind carried.

This was a distinctive type and had an odor all its own—acrid but mealy. Usually *smelling trouble* was just a metaphor, but in this case . . .

Fear-sweat. That's a man who thinks death is coming soon. And fear like that makes you want to explode into action, lashing out or running. Fear makes you stupid. Add a little extra push, and . . .

Connections meshed in her mind, in a way she might have been able to describe afterward but that had nothing to do with the formal structures of logic. It was very much like hunting, where suddenly bird-sound and the movements of the tips of branches and things that couldn't be defined meant you were *sure* that there was a deer in that thicket, just about to come out, and the whole world told you exactly where to have your foresight resting.

Except that this time the game was another predator.

"Tell me something, Mr. Hansen," she said in a calm conversational tone that would press his *make a polite reply* button and put words on the tip of his tongue.

She was making a snap judgment. The downside didn't matter; if it worked she'd flush an enemy from cover.

Then she dropped into German—which she spoke like a native, if the native was a Bavarian *Uradel* noblewoman who'd gone to a girls' finishing school run by a certain impoverished but excruciatingly aristocratic countess near München, and hence trilled her *r*'s a little and softened the usually crisp sounds of *Hochdeutsch*.

"Are you working for Colonel Nikolai of Abteilung IIIb, or is it Lassen at the NIV, or has that dumb-head von Zimmerman at the Foreign Office stuck his spoon into the porridge again? They're even worse than Nikolai's people but they keep trying and we keep catching them. Still, as the saying goes . . ."

Then she threw in a proverb: *"Auch der kleinste Feind ist nicht zu verachten!"*

Which meant there were *no* enemies so insignificant they weren't worth attending to, which made it very, very Germanic.

The man actually started to answer. Then he stopped and *looked* at her, realizing he'd given away that he spoke German . . . which plenty of midwestern businessmen did. After all, German was the largest single element in the American ethnic stew, unless you threw the Irish, Scots, and English together, which she wasn't inclined to do. He hesitated on the edge of trying to brazen it out. Luz gave him her best carnivorous smile and leaned closer, whispering:

"You Germans are the worst spies in the whole wide *world*. We've been following you since you left for San Francisco. We're planning a little chat with you. I'm *Schwarze Kammer*, fool."

Which was a literal translation of *Black Chamber*; in Europe the term had usually referred to code-breaking operations, but if what she suspected was true, he would know exactly what she meant. In reality, as far as she knew nobody had suspected him at all, but a reputation for omniscience never hurt.

He'd also know that he was facing a trip to the Black Palace of Lecumberri, a grim-looking old pile of a prison outside Mexico City where the Chamber stashed—and interrogated—high-value prisoners under the Protectorate's martial law, far away from prying eyes and inquisitive lawyers in the United States proper. That still mattered a little, though less all the time and much less than it had before the declaration of war.

Going there was usually a one-way journey, capped by a death certificate reading *heart failure*, which translated into plain English as *shot in the back of the head*. That did generally make your heart stop, after all. Hansen's eyes narrowed a little and his right hand slid into a pocket...

And his left fist slashed out toward her face.

She'd hoped to spook him into revealing himself, and beyond that to paralyze him long enough to be subdued. Hansen, or whatever his name really was, reacted with rattlesnake speed instead, which meant he'd probably already suspected her at least a bit.

She barely managed to drop her chin onto her chest and avoid taking the fist in her face. A crackle of breaking bone was one or more of the man's fingers as they impacted off-center on her skull. The lance of pain in her head and neck was matched by a flash of satisfaction; skulls were fragile, but not *as* fragile as finger bones.

She went back in a controlled roll-fall that put her weight on her shoulder blades and brought her feet up; then she flipped back upright in a flexing motion that left her in a squatting crouch. The *navaja* snapped into her hand and clicked open in the same motion, the layered steel and honed edge glittering like the grin that split her face.

Unfortunately the German agent had been drawing his pistol with his right hand as he punched at her, and he fired in a panic as she catapulted back toward him with six inches of wasp-waisted Toledo blade flashing toward his neck in a lunge as precise as a surgeon's stroke.

CRACK.

And so quickly that it seemed simultaneous, the *ptank* of the bullet hitting the duralumin of a girder. There was a cry of horror from behind them, and then a banshee battle shriek of pure instinct. That was Ciara Whelan, without a shadow of a doubt.

That's my girl! some corner of Luz's mind thought.

The rest of her was a snarl and a blade moving in blurring arcs to *find flesh*.

Hansen was bleeding from a minor cut on the chin, which showed how well he'd ducked, or that she'd been thrown off a bit by the pistol firing next to her ear; if it had gone where it was intended it would have opened his throat in a slanting cut from just above the collarbone to the Adam's apple, crossing the jugular on the way.

"Tääv!" he panted, his eyes wild and showing the whites all around the rims.

That word was *bitch* in the Low German they spoke in Schleswig-Holstein, so his name really might be Hansen.

Crack-crack-crack!

Luz ducked and wove, lunged and cut at his right hand as he backed up, making him pull the arm back sharply and keeping him off-balance. All three bullets missed, though something tugged at the swing of her skirt and cut the knit fabric as neatly as a seamstress's shears.

The odds had been better than even on that as long as she kept him moving and off-balance. Many men carried guns but few were real snap-shooting *pistoleros*, not when fear and hate ran through them. Those few were as dangerous as they were rare—James Cheine was one, and Luz was nearly as good—but otherwise it took an amazing number of rounds to actually hit someone even at point-blank range. Lugers jammed a lot, too. The return spring was weak.

Of course, each time he shot at Luz made her odds a little worse, but one more step and she'd be closer than arm's length, *ojo a ojo*, close enough to *find flesh* with every attack. At that distance the odds were *all* on a knife, as she'd demonstrated for herself several times over the past few years. And he'd already used up half the eight rounds in a Luger's magazine. Knives didn't run out of ammunition.

Get inside, sweep the edge of her left hand into his gun arm . . .

Hansen knew that too. He turned and ran back along the way the tour group had come, back toward the control deck.

But he *leapt* over the spot where he'd been holding up the matting on the gangway and stooping to fiddle beneath it when the ship's officer called to him. That had started the whole business. Something was *there*. Something—

The knowledge of what it was flashed through Luz.

Bomb!

That stopped her lunge at Hansen's back. She halted herself with a desperate rearward jerk of her torso while her right foot was poised to land on the spot he'd jumped over, so violently that the leg shot out while she went down on her left knee, hard enough to hurt. The extended leg quivered as she withdrew it. If it had come down . . .

This airship is a flying bomb, metaphorically. Usually it takes hundreds of hits from machine guns firing incendiary bullets to bring down a zeppelin. But an actual *bomb will do the job nicely.*

Beyond Hansen the three mechanics who'd been working on the carburetor in the repair bay were gaping at the crazy passenger running toward them. One of them plucked a socket wrench from a rack beside the workbench; the other two spread out across the walkway with their hands extended. They were operating under a *running amok* assumption, trying to catch and subdue him, and it might get them killed.

"Gun! Gun! Gun!" Luz called, loud but not shrill; it was amazing what people didn't notice if they weren't expecting it. "Look out!"

Hansen whirled and shot at her, taking an edge-on range stance but rushed because he had only seconds before the crewmen reached him. This time the bullet went close enough to clip a tuft of hair above her left ear, with that distinctive *TACK* sound and wash of heat of a near miss. Then he whirled again and shot the man with the socket wrench with the muzzle nearly touching the target. Shot twice.

Two dots appeared on the stained dark-blue surface of the man's overall. He dropped the wrench and folded up with an *ufff!* she could hear, like a man punched in the gut. Unlike a punch, he wouldn't be getting up from that; he fell sideways, with his head hitting a support strut for the walkway's railing with a heavy *clung* sound, then landing facedown and exposing the much larger exit wounds glistening on his back, with fragments of bone visible before the blood covered them. The wrench spun down into the dimness of the hull's interior and clanged in the distance.

The other two mechanics were brave men. They didn't run, and froze only for a moment at their workmate's sudden death. That was enough for Hansen to twist between them, clouting one of them viciously on the side of the head with the pistol. Luz ignored him for an instant, because catching him was irrelevant if they all went up in a flaming torch. Instead she dropped flat, pivoted on her belly, grabbed the edge of the strip of woven henequen matting, and held it up with her left hand while she slashed with her right. It took three strokes with the keen working edge she kept on the weapon to cut across the yard width of the strip and throw it back.

The metal surface beneath was stamped grillework, and she couldn't see the details . . . but something was definitely under there, resting just above the six-inch pipe that brought the fuel-gas to the engine. Logic filled in what sight couldn't; it had to be some sort of bomb. When you threw in Hansen's jump over that spot it also meant a dual fuse, pressure and at a guess a timer too. Hydrogen would burn eventually if it was mixed with air, but the fuel for the engines was much more like the domestic gas used for stoves. It would *really* burn the moment flame touched it, and it would blow back into the fuel cells . . . which were below the hydrogen gasbags and would set it all off nicely.

Ciara was beside her. "Bomb!" Luz said, pointing.

The Boston girl's face had gone milk-white, but after she'd taken a long breath and let it out her lips were compressed and her eyes were steady. She was taking in everything that happened without a trace of shock or the glassy befuddlement a lot of people showed in situations like this as their minds rejected things they really, really, *really* didn't want to see or believe in. She threw herself down beside Luz and started to run her fingers—lightly, delicately, absolutely steady— around the section of perforated aluminum planking.

"I've got it. Go!" she said.

She *had* been raised in a Fenian family involved with the Irish Republican Brotherhood, after all. Bombs wouldn't be a total novelty, and given her technical skills . . . which would have included handling a lot of dangerous machines . . .

Luz came erect without using her hands. The young ship's officer was there, looking alarmed but bewildered too, with the passengers gabbling behind him—probably only a few of them had even realized that there had been shooting; people who weren't accustomed to it often did that, which was all to the good. The light was dim except where the overheads put a puddle of brightness on the worktable, and the acoustics inside the airship's hull were like nothing she'd ever encountered before.

"Your man's dead," Luz said to him.

She jerked her head to where one of the intact crewmen was bent over the one who'd been shot; the other was down groaning and holding his hand to the bleeding side of his head.

"Hansen's a German agent, and he planted a bomb. My friend's disarming it. No!"

He'd started to bend toward Ciara, probably intending to pull her away. Luz grabbed him by the throat with a pinching fingers-and-thumb hold that immobilized anyone, one her teacher had called the *tiger claw*—Uncle Teddy had been one of the first *gaijin* in America to study those arts and he'd gotten instructors for the Chamber. That stopped the officer long enough for Ciara to bark over her shoulder with the authority of total focus:

"Double-action pressure detonator—that and a timer. I can't let this go at all. Get me a pair of needle-nosed pliers and a Robertson-head screwdriver!"

"We're American secret agents," Luz said—which was usefully nonspecific, while holding the knife down by her thigh where hopefully nobody would notice.

"Understand? *Do you understand?*" she said, in a voice pitched to cut through the fog of shock.

If he didn't she was going to have to clamp on his carotids until he passed out, then stand here guarding Ciara while Hansen shot people and did *Dios sabe qué mas*.

"I under . . . *stand*!" he choked out. "It's a bomb, she's disarming it!"

She released him and saw that his fear was now tightly controlled, and he nodded; timid people weren't likely to become airship officers, and he was used to situations where everything had to be done right or people died.

Luz also hoped none of the passengers milling a dozen feet beyond had heard the word *bomb*. German saboteurs and bombs were even more in the public mind now than their *revolucionario* terrorist equivalents had been for the last few years of the Intervention, and that had already been true before the horror-gas attacks got people *really* on edge.

"Good man! I'm going after Hansen. Alert your bridge officer."

The young man wet his lips and called to the mechanics as he went to one knee and extended a hand:

"Jones! Robertson-head screwdriver and a pair of needle-nosed pliers, *now*! And then get the captain on the wire."

She dismissed him from her mind, leapt agilely over Ciara where she lay with the section of decking up, one hand blocking the plunger of the pressure trigger and the other beckoning impatiently for the pliers that presumably-named-Jones was stretching anxiously to hand over, and ran down the shadowed length of the walkway. Hansen was at the base of the ladder behind the control deck. He spotted her, leveled the pistol . . . and didn't fire, even though it was a straight no-deflection shot.

The one in the chamber was his last bullet, and he'd been counting. His unremarkable face wasn't mild at all as he looked at her onrush, then over his shoulder at where men would boil out of the bridge as soon as the intercom call went through. Evidently he didn't think he could hold either threat at bay with one shot *or* an empty pistol, which was a good bet.

Instead of firing he thrust the Luger inside his jacket, leapt onto the ladder, and climbed with the garment billowing around his calves. Luz gave a she-wolf grin; by the time she arrived below him he was high enough up that shooting downward at her was not likely to produce anything but a flash, a loud noise, and an empty gun.

"Let's not give him time to reload if he has a spare magazine," she muttered quietly to herself.

Then she put her knife between her teeth and began climbing the ladder after him. Luz had studied the schematics for the *Battle*-class airships before she made her first voyage on one a few months ago disguised as Elisa Carmody de Soto-Dominguez, agent of the Mexican Partido Nacional Revolucionario; and she'd also looked through a file of photographs. The hull was shaped like a symmetrical killer whale, or an elongated teardrop with the larger end forward, and it was just under eight hundred feet long and a hundred and fifty from keel to top at the broadest point. From bridge level to the circular domed observation chamber was about a hundred feet.

A hundred feet up a ladder wasn't much. She climbed economically, letting her feet do the work in a steady quick tap-tap-tap of pushing effort, keeping her hands on the uprights of the ladder and using them to guide her and breathing deeply through her nose. She was going to need limber quick-moving hands and arms when they got to the top, and for that you used your legs to do the donkey-work.

Hansen looked down to see her following like the shadow of incarnate Death, teeth showing around the *navaja* in an expression that would have been cruel on a shark; his face was a pale blur above, and she could hear him panting. She was probably even more of a blur to him, because a cone of sunlight came through the open hatchway from the greenhouse-like glass dome on top. It meant he was effectively standing in a lighted room looking into darkness, which destroyed your night vision.

She'd killed sentries standing beside blazing campfires and trying to peer out into the night, usually without much more difficulty than cutting a blind man's throat . . . less, because blind men at least *knew* they were blind.

Halfwits in training to be idiots, she thought.

Grinning around the taste of steel and brass in her mouth as she climbed.

Hansen drew his pistol again and pushed himself up into the observation chamber, leading with the weapon. There was a yell, and an instant later an echoing *crack*. Nobody up there would know that it was the last bullet, and there wouldn't be enough crewmen to be confident of mobbing him anyway.

Luz went into a full-out sprint up the remaining few feet, crouched on the third-to-last rung and *leapt* into the little room, slitting her eyes against the bright light. She landed with her feet astride the hatch, her skirt billowing up almost to her garter-belt for an instant because it already had a natural bell-flare. She spat the knife into her right hand as she landed.

The scene printed itself on her eyes like a photograph. There were two crewmen in the blue ANA uniforms there. One was down, clutching a shoulder with blood running out between his fingers. The other was backed up against the padded bench that ran around the circular room at sofa height, with his hands in the air.

Hansen was struggling into a big drab-colored cloth knapsack-like thing, one of the parachutes stored at duty stations throughout the airship like life rings on an ocean vessel. He was hindered by the complex straps and the need to keep his gun pointed at the ANA man, who was bigger and younger and glaring at him murderously, but had just about managed it by the time Luz came through the hatch. A rearward-facing door had been thrown open, and the thuttering whistle of the airship's passage filled the chamber with air that seemed cool by contrast with the stuffy interior of the hull.

The German agent was already backing out into it as Luz came up through the hatchway like a jack-in-the-box.

"Auf Wiedersehen, Schlampe!" he called, then threw the pistol hard at Luz's head and whirled to run.

That meant *Until we meet again, bitch!* but this time in High German.

Luz threw herself forward in a *pasada baja* the instant the balls of her feet touched the decking, a stepping lunge, falling forward, her left hand smacking down on the floor and the point of the knife in her right lancing out. The Luger whirled over her head.

The steel *should* have ended up in the back of Hansen's thigh, neatly hamstringing the man for capture, but the resistance she met felt entirely wrong for *finding flesh.* The parachute hung down below his buttocks. The long clipped point of Luz's *navaja* slammed home through the outer surface of the canvas container with a pop, then through the folded silk cloth and cords within . . . but it had the full weight of her body behind it, and she'd been moving very fast. The locking ring at the join of blade and hilt pinched the web of flesh between her thumb and forefinger as it kept her hand from running up on the blade.

Hansen lunged forward onto the top keel of the airship, leaping . . . and also pushed by the impact of a hundred and thirty-odd pounds of Black Chamber agent behind a very sharp knife. The walkway atop the *Manila Bay*'s hull was aluminum stampings too, with eyebolts every so often, to let crewmen fasten safety lines and rappel down to work on the hull. The German didn't try to stop himself when he staggered off the walkway; instead he laughed and went down on his belly, like a boy riding a toboggan down a hill. The hard, doped cotton was as slick as silk and smooth as a baby's cheek, and he gathered speed quickly until the curve launched him off into space.

"¡Joder!" Luz cursed softly, as the parachute blossomed below and behind the airship. "Now we'll have to try to find him, and do it through the Brazilians!"

Who couldn't find the ground *even if they tripped and fell on their* faces. *And who don't like us anyway, so they won't even really try.*

And if Hansen made it to someone who could communicate with Germany, he could probably scupper this operation; a description of a female American agent matching her . . . or of Ciara . . . would ring bells in Berlin, ring them very loudly. They'd be waiting at the border.

He probably will *get help.*

Brazil had plenty of German immigrants, and even more of their children and grandchildren. Someone would help, and the Brazilian authorities, such as they were, wouldn't really try to stop them.

In public Rio was very, very cautious and extremely polite around the ever-more-colossal Coloseo del Norte these days—hence the swift lease of extraterritorial basing rights at Recife when D.C. had made a polite *request.* But neither Brazil nor any of the other Latin countries were particularly happy about the way Washington had swallowed and consolidated everything from Panama to the North Pole into what amounted to a single homogenous political bloc over the course of Uncle Teddy's ever-increasing list of presidencies.

"*¡Qué coñazo!*" she snarled; this merited some *heavy-duty* cursing, and English profanity had never seemed very satisfying to her. "Maybe frightening him with the Chamber's name was a touch too much."

Then she stopped. The parachute had opened into a white dome shape with the doll-like figure of a man beneath it as he fell behind the speeding airship . . . but there was a rip in it, and one side sagged in with the cords flapping loose. As she watched the rip extended further and further . . . and the man fell faster and faster.

¡Toma! And it's a long way down, she thought much more happily; her lunge *had* killed the man, just a little more indirectly than ramming the blade into a kidney.

"*¡El que ríe último ríe major!*" she called, laughing, and almost went to the trouble of translating *who laughs last, laughs best* into German even though he was far beyond hearing.

Hansen was probably just realizing that he hadn't gotten away after all; though he'd avoided being questioned in Lecumberri, which would have been the *best* ending to their encounter from Luz's point of view. For starters, she would have liked to know if he was after the *Manila*

Bay in general or one Luz O'Malley Aróstegui in particular. Or, worse still, after Ciara.

She waited until the 'chute was a stream of rags plummeting through the sky above a figure with legs frantically pumping at nothingness before she turned, still chuckling. The expression on the crewman's face as she turned back into the observation chamber made her stop laughing. Although she was still smiling as she reached for the telephone with her left hand.

Her right wiped the blade of her knife on the sleeve of her jacket before she closed the weapon with a *clack*. Stabbing it into the parachute's silk would have cleaned any blood off, but you could never be too careful with your tools.

"Captain Woźniak, please," she asked as the airship's switchboard controller answered.

Now for the housekeeping.

SEVEN

Control Deck
Aboard ANA Airship *Manila Bay*
Approaching Recife
Province of Pernambuco
Republic of Brazil
NOVEMBER 21ST, 1916(B)

*N*a *zdrowie!*" the captain of the *Manila Bay* said, and raised his glass. "Cheers! Confusion to the Kaiser!"

"Amen!"

Luz knocked the small glass of vodka back, a shot of cold fire down her throat and into her stomach, where it exploded into a welcome warmth, pushing back that odd distanced feeling you got after violence, or at least which she did.

It was *good* vodka, if you could say that about unflavored alcohol, and the bottle she glimpsed as he poured the four of them a glass and put it away had the famous *Polmos Łańcut* blazon, which she'd seen in Europe. The toast, the drink, and his name didn't leave much doubt, but the man's neutral Pennsylvanian variety of General American also had a very slight musical accent, a tendency to lengthen *i*-sounds and turn the *r*'s crisp and stress the second syllable of words, which would have told her the same things; he'd been born to Polish immigrants and at a guess in a Pennsylvania coal town.

"Captain Woźniak," she said. "I appreciate your thanks—and this excellent White Lady vodka—but we must avoid all publicity."

Ciara had tried sipping at the glass she held in a slightly unsteady hand, and now she was wheezing and turning a bit red as the eighty-proof liquid struck. Luz leaned a little closer and said quietly: "No, sweetie, you toss it into your mouth, the whole thing, throw it at the back of your throat. Get it down, you'll feel much better."

The captain's ready room—it would have been his sea cabin in the Navy—on the *Manila Bay* was at the rear of the bridge, with the wireless room across from it. It was a windowless rectangle with room for a fold-down bunk and a desk and a few chairs, and reasonably private, but Luz wanted to get out of it and back into the anonymity of the passenger quarters as soon as possible—they'd be in Recife by evening. Ciara and Third Officer McCredie were there, by her request, but nobody else.

"Miss Robicheaux?" the captain asked, puzzled.

He was in his thirties and the eldest of the airship's officers, a stocky, muscular man with gray eyes in a broad face, but his close-cropped dark-yellow beard made him seem older; very few men his age wore beards at all these days, except in the Navy.

"It's a matter of State security, Captain," she said. "You have a Naval Reserve commission, I believe?"

The man's face was warily neutral; he hadn't been told precisely who she worked for, but not being a fool he could probably make a good guess. A woman as a field agent was unlikely in the Black Chamber but vanishingly so in the Federal Bureau of Security. That was one of the many reasons she wished it weren't necessary to have to have this talk.

"Yes, miss, I do; reserve commander. And I understand operational security. The reply we received to your wireless message was emphatic about your clearance."

"Excellent, sir!" she said sincerely. "Then here's what we're all going to say when questions are asked by anyone but the security services. Hansen was a German agent, which is true; a passenger saw that he planted a bomb on your airship, which is true, and informed your Mr. McCredie, which is true. Hansen attempted to escape, shooting several crew members, which is also true, and was killed after plunging to his death trying to avoid pursuit . . . pursuit by *passengers and crew*—which is more or less true too. Your third officer—"

She nodded to young McCredie, who blushed.

"Disarmed the bomb, assisted by several—unnamed—passengers. Which is more or less partially true."

"But . . . but all I did was hand Miss Duffy tools and keep everyone else back!" McCredie said. "I don't know if I *could* have done it myself. Not before it went off."

"You got the mechanics to pass the tools promptly," Luz said; they wouldn't have obeyed Ciara otherwise, or at least not in time. "You were operating on a tight margin there."

Ciara spoke, her voice neutral: "Hansen probably planted it earlier and then activated it while he was with the tour . . . you don't keep passengers strictly out of the hull, do you, sir?"

Captain Woźniak frowned. "Theoretically access is limited to authorized personnel, but that's not strictly enforced because we're shorthanded and never saw . . . well, I suppose we'll have to, now."

"Yes, sir, you will," Luz said.

"It had a dual trigger; a timer that armed the pressure switch," Ciara said.

The bomb, with all its connections severed and the blasting caps extracted, was resting on the captain's desk. The base of it was a bundle of half a dozen standard eight-inch tubes of dynamite, the type routinely used for demolition and construction projects, each half a troy pound. That would have been enough to rip the *Manila Bay* apart quite thoroughly, with explosions and fire in the fuel and lift bags to finish things off.

You forget this thing is fragile, because it's so big and feels so stable, Luz thought, with an inward shiver.

"Mr. McCredie was very helpful," Ciara added; she was still pale, and sat with her hands clasped together in her lap, but the drink was helping.

She's thinking the same burning-and-falling thoughts.

Luz put it out of her mind and nodded.

"He helped not least by keeping everyone else from seeing exactly what was going on by kneeling beside Miss Duffy. Probably Hansen was planning on getting one of the parachutes from the engineering stations farther down the hull and doing a header out of an engine nacelle."

"If you hadn't spotted him, Miss Robicheaux, he could have done that easy," McCredie said, appalled. "We even demonstrate the drill for grabbing a parachute and bailing out at the end of the tour, back near the stern docking station!"

That's what Hansen was counting on, Luz thought. *If he'd been willing to detonate it himself we'd have been overdone toast. Fortunately that's not very common, but it's the devil to stop when you* do *run across it.*

She turned her head to the airship's commander: "Captain Woźniak, people usually believe they saw what they're told they saw, especially by some person in authority," she said confidently.

That was true too.

"Especially when what they're *told* accords with what they expect better than what they really *saw*. Any lawyer—"

Or spy, she thought.

"—will tell you that. Their memories adjust to back up the story they believe; and they'll believe Mr. McCredie disarming the bomb with Miss Duffy handing him tools far, far more readily than the reverse. It's why untrained eyewitness testimony is often worthless, especially if you give the witnesses any time."

"It is?" McCredie said; he was young.

The captain nodded in unison with Luz.

She went on: "The mind's eye doesn't record facts in its memories like a cinema camera, it writes stories like a novelist. And if people talk, the strongest version drives out the others—and people come to sincerely believe it. We must strike while the iron's hot and get *our* story firmly in their minds."

The young man nodded slowly in turn, obviously a little queasy and disoriented at suddenly being introduced to the spy's-eye-view of reality.

"If you say it's necessary, Miss Robicheaux," Woźniak said. "Still, you and Miss Duffy did an astonishing thing. I wish you could get the credit for it."

Luz chuckled. "We're in this business to serve the State and the

American people, not for medals. And it *is* astonishing what you can accomplish . . . if you don't care who gets the credit," she said; which made the two airship officers laugh in return, and added to the admiration in their eyes.

"But the secret services—"

She was carefully nonspecific again.

"—of the U.S. government are on the job, believe me."

"Thank God for that, with this sort of deviltry creeping through the shadows!" Captain Woźniak said fervently, and his officer nodded emphatic agreement.

Which helps them get their *mental equilibrium back, which is all to the good,* she thought. *And makes them more cooperative. People like the idea that they're on the inside, privy to secrets others don't know.*

Woźniak frowned. "How can we tell if this was the only plot against ANA vessels?"

"It probably wasn't," Luz said, slitting her eyes in thought.

In fact, it certainly wasn't—the return message from Black Chamber HQ had said the attack hadn't been aimed at her specifically, which meant the mission could continue. But one disturbing incident was that a purported American citizen precisely matching Hansen's description and going by the name Karl Anderson had bought passage from Recife to Tunis on the *Gettysburg* doing the Dakar-Tunis run, through the same Minneapolis office that Hansen had used to buy *his* ticket . . . and on the same day and with a check drawn on the same bank.

An alert investigator making a quick dip into the accounts at the ANA office had spotted the oddity . . . because the hypothetical Anderson's ticket committed him to leave Recife too soon by far for him to reach Brazil any way *except* by air, which he couldn't have done unless he used the *Manila Bay* . . . and there was nobody of that name on this vessel.

Apparently a Karl Anderson of Minneapolis had expected to reach Recife by astral travel through the spirit realm and then fly ANA to Europe via French West Africa; and Karl Anderson and Poul Hansen had meticulous but eerily similar backgrounds as blandly anonymous and loyal midwestern businessmen of Danish descent from several generations back. The message to Luz had given the bones of it and included the code group for *investigation proceeding*, but she suspected down in her gut that both would turn out to be well-documented fakes . . . and the same man, now deceased after an unpleasant minute or two watching the ground coming up faster and faster under a non-functional parachute.

Had Hansen planned on parachuting from the *Manila Bay* just before it blew up, making his way to Recife, catching the *Gettysburg*, and repeating his sabotage? Or just using it to get to Tunis, now the only easy point of entry to Europe since the North Sea ports were closed except through distant Scandinavia?

Fragile either way, she thought. *Fiendish attention to detail, insolent over-confidence, and a plan that needs us to do what the Germans thought we would.*

Which fitted the way German intelligence agencies tended to act *perfectly*, when they went in for clandestine operations. It was a pattern that had led to some spectacular successes, and rather more abject failures.

They really are *the world's worst spies. But not for want of trying, and if you keep trying sometimes you get lucky.*

Captain Woźniak looked increasingly alarmed as she stayed lost in thought, and she continued:

"Measures to increase security on airships are in hand, Captain. You'll be hearing more about that soon."

She had little idea what the measures would be, but she *was* sure something was being done, and in jig time; even that monument to budding bureaucracy still wet from its eggshell called the Federal Bureau of Security would move fast when presented with something like this. At a guess there would be much more careful inspection of baggage and background checks on passengers, for starters, which would be annoying for travelers, and clandestine Bureau agents riding on every single airship flight to keep an eye on things. Which might help and would also probably be annoying for everyone except the Bureau agents who'd get prolonged holidays on a luxury vessel.

But not nearly as annoying as flaming death, and there will probably be competition in the FBS for that *duty.*

"And Captain . . . Mr. McCredie . . . please do your best to forget you ever saw us. This is extremely important and may be the difference between life and death for me and Miss Duffy. You'll be receiving official instructions . . . but I'm adding a personal appeal. Don't mention us to anyone; not your wives or fiancées, not your brothers, not the closest friend of your heart; and as far as possible don't think about us yourselves either. Do you understand?"

They both nodded solemnly and came to their feet to shake hands as she and Ciara rose.

"And call in say, six or seven pairs of passengers and ask them some routine questions to give us more cover, if you would. Here are some suggestions."

She handed them a page of notes. Luz judged that Woźniak probably would suppress his natural impulse to talk about the glamorous secret agents, and that McCredie might, as long as he was sober and avoided newspaper reporters. Fortunately, these days they could discretely use the War Emergency Powers or Subversion and Espionage Acts to quietly quash any press attempt to develop the story. It was amazing how resistant some people had been to the simple fact that your enemies could access massive amounts of crucial information simply by reading the press.

Or that it was a Bad Thing that they could. Bad! Very bad!

"Bless the Director," she said to Ciara as they went down the long staircase and landings to the passenger deck and into their cabin.

Then: "Shhhh, shhhh, *mi querida*. It's all right," as Ciara flung herself into Luz's arms and buried her face in the curve of the other's neck.

Luz was blinking a little in surprise as she stroked the red-gold hair.

She was terrified, but she held it down by sheer raw willpower. ¡Viva la magnificencia de mi querida!

"I was so frightened for you!" her partner said. "He had a gun . . ."

"It's all right," Luz said, sitting on the edge of the bed and rocking her gently. "It didn't do him much good. And you saved my life—saved us all. You're making a habit of that!"

When the quiet tears ended Luz found her a handkerchief.

"What did you mean about the Director?" Ciara asked.

After she'd blown her nose in a forthright manner; no finishing school had tried to make her do it in the ineffectually genteel style.

Luz smiled tenderly. "Well, Miss . . . Duffy . . . that the Chamber took the extra trouble to give us good cover for the first leg of this trip. If what happened on this airship *does* leak, the trail will head straight back north and it'll look as if we were on some sort of counter-sabotage mission."

She sighed. "I still don't like it, though. The best missions are utterly boring. We'll be getting off in Tunis and someone there will probably be expecting Hansen . . . Anderson . . . whoever . . . on the same flight."

EIGHT

¡Ay, Dios mío!" Luz said in astonishment, leaning on the airship's gallery railing and looking down at Tunis. "Now, *that's* all new!"

"What surprises you, my . . . Consuelo?" Ciara said, using the cover identity for this leg of the journey.

Her color was much better than it had been after disarming the bomb, or even when they'd left Recife on the *Gettysburg* eastbound across the Atlantic. Oddly, spending three days pitching and tossing into a Saharan sandstorm with half the passengers and some of the crew vomiting into every available receptacle had agreed with her. And she'd been mainly interested in the geology of the jagged fangs of rock passing nerve-rackingly close below while they sailed over mountains haunted by wild tribesmen who'd cheerfully rape and murder any infidel *giaour* who fell into their hands.

"Is it different from your last visit?" Ciara went on.

Luz shook her head. It was flattering that Ciara sometimes seemed to assume she'd been everywhere and knew everything about all those places, but she *was* only a well-traveled twenty-five years old.

"I've never been closer than Marseilles, but the guides give Tunis about two hundred thousand people."

Being well-read was almost as good. The books put out by Baedeker and Cook & Sons were as indispensable for spies as they were for tourists.

She went on: "Those shanty-camps around it must have a hundred thousand themselves now, and see how crowded the harbor is?"

Tunis had an excellent modern port at the end of a canal the French had dredged ten miles eastward across the sparkling salt lagoon to the sea, all of it laid out below like a map. Numbers didn't come naturally to Luz, but she'd learned to make good estimates quickly because it was a staple of the spy's trade—numbers of troops, weapons, supplies, rail cars, people. Ships were crawling in and out along the canal nearly nose-to-tail, and at the quays they were two deep, with more waiting their turns in dangerous proximity while harbor tugboats dashed about like hysterical yapping sheepdogs with toots from their steam whistles coming faint but clear.

"At least four times as many ships as it's designed for. And more people coming ashore all the time; they've got boats shuttling back and forth to the ones that can't get a berth."

Ciara nodded. "There are camps everywhere too, aren't there? All the open spaces in town, and like mushrooms in the fields."

"And look at the ships inbound along the canal. The decks and upper-works are absolutely *black* with people, like ants on a *pastelito de guayaba* left behind at a picnic. That's insane overcrowding, dangerous even if they were empty below-decks, and they're not. All since the horror-gas attack on Paris," Luz said. "Someone's moving very fast, full speed ahead and damn the torpedoes."

In the original sense of torpedo, *meaning hidden explosives*, she thought.

The old Maghrebi city of the Beys and the Barbary Corsairs spilled up a low hill in a pleasant mass of whitewashed cubical courtyard-centered buildings that reminded her of Mexico, spotted with occasional domes and minarets, and narrow alleys that opened out into small spaces too irregular to be called squares. The younger French colonial town along the reclaimed harborfront and on the low flat ground to the north was a vivid contrast with its broad tree-lined Haussmanesque boulevards and neat regular grid and scattering of parks and Beaux-Arts public buildings like some proud provincial center in the Midi showing off a nineteenth-century prosperity.

The gallery windows were tilted a little open, and she could faintly smell a frowsty compound of people and smoke and their wastes, even at eight hundred feet up, along with the salt tang of the lagoon.

Like essence of slum, Luz thought. *Or displaced-persons camp.*

"The rest of the country looked pretty," Ciara said.

"It reminds me of the southern part of California—both get better as you get closer to the sea," Luz agreed.

The desert had yielded slowly, first to scattered bushes and then to sparse steppe dotted even more sparsely with the goats and sheep and camels and black tents of nomads, with a herd of gazelle now and then, or an oasis dense with date palms. Closer to the sea was a landscape of olive groves and orchards, vineyards and fields plowed red-brown and smooth, planted with the winter wheat and barley and just starting to show sprouting blades. Field workers and carts were almost insect-tiny from the air, and then scattered adobe farming villages gave way to suburbs or villas. The overall color was tawny, with a first faint green tint from fall rains that had started early this year. The whole world's weather had been unusually cold and wet lately.

"But give it time," Luz added grimly. "The ripples of disaster are spreading out."

"Like the ones from a stone dropped in water," Ciara said, her voice troubled.

A few of the farming villages had been torched, recently enough that they'd still been sending squibs of black smut-smoke along the ground as the huge elongated shadow of the dirigible passed over them. Luz had seen that smoke before, during the Intervention—usually part of a procedure informally known as *showing them you're serious*. She didn't know if Ciara knew what the distinctive bent pillar of black meant, and there was no point in bringing it up.

As the *Gettysburg* sank lower over the outskirts of the city the aeroplanes that had met them twenty miles out buzzed near one last time, neat little modern single-seat biplanes with red-white-blue roundels on the wings; once they'd done a circuit of the airship they peeled off and climbed again, circling gradually upward to conserve fuel.

"SPAD Vs," Ciara said, craning her neck to keep them in view through the gallery windows. "The latest model, with the two Browning machine guns and interrupter gear . . . so clever . . . and that lovely two-fifty horsepower V-8 Hispano-Suiza. I wonder why they have a standing air patrol . . . oh."

"Zeppelins," Luz said grimly. "And a little after dawn . . . about now . . . is when they hit London and Paris and Bordeaux, to catch people on their way to work."

She tapped her foot on the *Gettysburg*'s deck. Ciara nodded, her face sober for a moment below her delight in the novelty of it all. When something could travel thousands of miles to drop ten tons of *Vernichtungsgas*, you wouldn't take chances . . . given that a single lethal dose was smaller than the period at the end of a printed sentence.

Then Luz looked down again; there was an endless fascination to seeing the maps come *alive* like this.

"It's a tribute to the human imagination that we came up with maps at all, before we could fly," she said, and Ciara chuckled.

"We've seen a whole geographical atlas's worth of them by now!" she said.

They were down to about five hundred feet, close enough to see how the streets were jammed tight with everything from hordes of pedestrians and bicyclists through donkeys hidden under enormous bundles to big French horse-drawn military wagons and a fair amount of motor transport . . . and even a few strings of camels. None of it was moving very fast, though she could see several trains pulling out of the central station with trails of black coal smoke behind them.

And faint but unmistakable, she heard the rasping stutter of an automatic weapon—a fairly long burst, too long to be good for the barrel, then a pause, then another, and then it fell silent.

Hotchkiss machine gun, she thought with a soundless whistle. *They feed from a thirty-round strip.*

She'd noticed the people weren't looking up as much at the great airship throbbing by overhead as she'd have expected, and that gave a hint of why.

Everyone's preoccupied, and someone *not very far away was* preoccupied *enough with what was in front of him that sending sixty quick rounds of eight-millimeter persuasion downrange seemed like a good idea.*

More French fighting scouts and light bombers were on the graveled dirt runways of the aeroplane base a little north of town, marked by its crisscross of dirt landing strips and ugly complex of hangars, fuel stores, workshops, warehouses, barracks, and administrative buildings of boards, canvas, and sheet metal. The airship docking tower looked as new as the flimsy squalor of the shantytowns, but it was a substantial section-built American National Airways design from the works in Patterson, with two circles of rail around it and a landing cradle mounted on them so it could be put directly beneath the big dirigible as it came in to the tower with its bow to the wind, and then shifted easily to keep it that way for storms, or for taking off again.

You could land without it, using hundreds of ground crew and lots of rope, but this was much safer; the installation had been flown out in pieces with the technicians to assemble it only a few weeks ago, though that meant plans and materials had been ready for some time. Pumps whined and there was a brief hissing roar as gas was released from the valves along the dorsal keel far above.

Most of the passengers were here in the lounge now, watching with interest as the ground came closer beneath the big slanting windows of the gallery. A few were sitting at the small tables, hands white-knuckled on the armrests of their chairs, and a few more would be lying on their beds in the cabins with their eyes closed. That was mostly just vertigo and funk, but while docking was as routine as anything so new could be, this actually *was* the most dangerous part of a voyage.

As a pilot in the Army Air Corps had said to her once—laughing, they'd been in bed at the time—taking off wasn't a problem and *flying* was dead easy . . .

But landing? he'd said. *Landing is* hard.

A cable with a cone-shaped weight on its end dropped free of the airship's bow. They could see it from here, unlike the similar one from the pointed stern behind the cruciform control fins. The airship bobbed slightly as both were caught by the ground crews and slotted into the matching winches in the tower and cradle. The cables pulled the great, fragile bulk gently forward, then down until it rested in the padded arcs that matched the traverse rings of the hull's structure and the restraints could be shot home in the recessed eyebolts. The engines went silent for the first time since they lifted from the stop in Dakar, and the quiet was greater for the fact that the droning had become a subliminal thing no longer consciously noticed at all; the living quiver of movement was gone likewise, replaced with the feel of a building on solid land as the craft went heavier than air.

Most of the passengers knew enough to stay where they were, but stewards politely headed off a few who headed for the exit ramp early. There were clunking and clanging noises, and then rumbles as the ballast tanks were pumped full, and subtly different ones as the process of pumping the lift cells empty began, so they could be opened and blown dry. Ciara leaned her head a little to the side, as if she were listening to a complex piece of music, and her lips moved silently as she listed the origins of the sounds.

Luz found her expression fascinating. They shared music; she tried to share this, as if the machines and their human tenders were an intricately structured piece by Bach, genius talking to God in mathematics. To see the clamor as her lover did, part of a thing that was whole and beautiful, a mighty expression of human intellect and will and purpose; and for a moment she grasped the edge of it.

The lights flickered as the dirigible switched to exterior supply. Luz affected a yawn.

"One gets bored with the procedure, after you've experienced it once . . . or twice . . ." she said, patting her lips with the back of one gloved hand, and grinned at Ciara's slight mocking *pffft!* sound.

A white-coated steward came through, rapping a little rubber hammer on a xylophone-like instrument held in the crook of his left arm in a pleasant chiming rhythm.

"Ladies and gentlemen!" he said, a spiel that would be repeated every ten paces. "*Mesdames et messieurs! ¡Damas y caballeros! Senhoras e senhores! Signore e signori!* Please prepare to disembark. Passports and identity documents must be ready at this time!"

"If I know the French, if they had their druthers we'd also have to do a short test on Racine's prose style and write an essay on Descartes or on the significance of the Realists versus the Impressionists," Luz observed. "To prove we're worthy of setting foot on their sacred soil . . . or I suppose on Tunisia's *quasi*-sacred soil."

"Did you spend much time in France?" Ciara asked curiously.

"About . . . eighteen months, counting long visits and the time I spent at school there in my teenage years. And one mission for our employers. It was all very educational."

"What was it like, compared to that school in Munich?"

"Let's put it this way; most Germans want to be liked and admired . . . or failing that, feared . . . but they're usually secretly afraid you're laughing or sneering at them, which is one reason they're always trying to bully people. The French are sublimely certain they're doing us savages an undeserved favor by letting us humbly approach the one true font of civilization, which if we work hard will let us become second-rate imitation French people, the highest state to which we could possibly aspire."

Ciara laughed, though Luz had been . . .

What's that expression? Kidding on the square?

They picked up their cabin bags and hatboxes; she preferred to keep those in hand. The hold baggage had been inspected and sealed in Dakar, their first stop inside the French Empire, and would come out directly since only the seals needed to be checked.

Though everyone anywhere near the European war had gotten much more persnickety about documents and searches lately, compared to the carefree years before Princip shot the archduke and blew up the world. They all walked forward and past the ship's second officer, who stood at the head of the departure ramp nodding and wishing them a pleasant stay in Tunis in a downeaster *r*-swallowing Maine accent. The ramp was built into a hinged section of the forward hull, and as it went down, stairs folded up and a railing rose on either side. She could see figures moving behind the glass walls of the bridge high above as they disembarked.

"Before the war usually only Russia asked for passports and visas. And they might call you a spy even in peacetime, and threaten to call the Okhrana unless you bribed them," Luz said, and then added: "Also fairly often they'd be drunk."

American military and government personnel, of whom there were about a score, were whisked away immediately in a minor convoy of staff cars. The French *did* need the *Gettysburg*, and the goodwill of its passengers, and above all that of the American government, so they'd also given ANA's on-site personnel the use of a Fordson tractor pulling an open cart rigged with benches to take the U.S. civilians and Latin American neutrals bumping and jolting through the mild sunny day to the big frame structure where they were processing the newcomers. That only took a few minutes to cross the aerodrome and its noises of engines and harsh military shouts.

One universal constant of Army life everywhere was that people in uniform yelled a lot. The French added a good deal of arm-waving, which Luz found comforting. She could mimic Anglo-Saxon body language easily without sitting on her hands and did so automatically in some contexts—ones that would get you classified, and dismissed, as a gibbering gesticulating dago monkey on a stick if you didn't—but she'd never *liked* that unnatural stiffness.

The wood-frame building with the high truss roof was a hangar in ordinary life, judging from the huge open doors, the nameless chemical stains on its concrete pad floor, and the smell of exhaust and burnt castor-oil, which French designers used as a lubricant on the Gnome-Rhone rotaries they preferred as power plants for many of their aircraft.

"Things feel . . . bad," Ciara said, looking around doubtfully as they stepped down and walked toward the sign that had been hung from the roof truss.

It read *Douane*, which meant *customs*.

"You're right," Luz said. "Very quick of you, *querida*!"

Nearly everyone she saw was French military, and they were going about their jobs well enough. But there *was* a sour grating feeling to it, like clenching tinfoil between your back teeth. These were men doing what people usually did while a disaster unfolded, keeping going until it actually landed on their heads.

"Those aren't a good sign, either," she said, nodding.

Those were a large squad or short platoon's worth of infantry standing by in two ranks at the former hangar's doors, in neat but worn and slightly threadbare khaki uniforms and red fez-like caps with red sashes around their waists under their equipment belts, rather than the blue-gray outfit that French regulars wore and called *blu horizon*. They were Negroes except for their lieutenant, many with ritual tribal scars on their faces like chevrons of raised tissue and all of them looking tough enough . . .

To chew iron and shit rivets, as the old Army saying goes.

They stood at parade rest, not rigidly but precise, and the long, worn, and rather old-fashioned Lebel rifles they carried glinted with loving care. So did the *coupe-coupe* machetes at their waists and slim cruciform bayonets fixed to the rifles, stabbing weapons that French soldiers nicknamed "Rosalie."

They called a bayonet charge *taking Rosalie to breakfast.*

"Senegalese *tirailleurs*," Luz said. "French West Africans . . . mercenaries, basically, or men their village chiefs decided should *volunteer* to keep the French *commandant de cercle* happy with them."

Ciara looked at them with interest. "How very black they are!" she said; the skins of some of the soldiers almost absorbed light like velvet. "Not much like most American Negroes I've seen."

She'd learned that *Negro* was the polite, modern, Party-approved Progressive word to use for black people, and there were a fair scattering in Boston, which had been an important node on the Underground Railroad in their grandparents' time.

"Which is odd," she went on, "because our Negroes' ancestors came from West Africa, didn't they?"

"Their *African* ancestors mostly did, but there are a lot of white men in that woodpile; American Negroes are the *mestizos* of gringoland."

"And why are the Senegalese a bad sign?" Ciara asked. "They look like good soldiers, not that I'm a judge."

"On average they're better than French regulars, I'm told by people whose judgment I respect; the Germans certainly don't like fighting them, and tell each other horror stories about their eating the dead. But the French use the *tirailleurs* the way they do the Foreign Legion: for nasty dirty jobs in dirty nasty places, or where ordinary conscripts from mainland France aren't reliable, or because the conscripts could write to their deputies or to the newspapers and cause a scandal. I suspect they're here because the French high command is worried about discipline in their regular army. The government in Paris is . . . gone, France is wrecked, so who's got a right to obedience?"

"That'll be settled by the bayonet, then?"

"*Absolutamente*; but bayonets are carried by people who can have opinions of their own. Smart generals worry about that. Especially French ones, given their history."

Right now the hangar had a set of tables with clerks behind them in the quasi-military uniform of the *Régie des douanes nationales*, which in France included battalions of paramilitary border police. The hangar *also* had several dozen slightly frazzled but wealthy-looking civilians with their children and baggage off to one side waiting to get *on* the *Gettysburg*. Since turning the big airship around was going to take all day at least considering the storm damage to the outer fabric, that said something about how anxious they were to make sure they were aboard when it began its return passage across the Atlantic to safety in Brazil or Argentina or wherever they'd transferred their Swiss accounts.

"Or wherever they're planning on selling the diamonds sewn into their clothes," Luz murmured to Ciara. "Some of them won't stop running until they reach Santiago de Chile, I'd guess!"

Which was about as far away from the Hell's Cauldron of modern Europe as you could get, barring an Asia that was having its own agonies.

"Why would they sew . . . oh, much more concentrated and easier to hide than gold," Ciara replied.

Everyone from the *Gettysburg* queued to have their documents examined and baggage searched, and with the meticulous care taken the lines moved slowly even though there were four of them. That didn't bother Luz. Ordinary physical impatience had never been a problem for her, not since about age eight; you had to get over that when you learned to hunt, and she'd have done far more than learn not to fidget to see her father's smile and nod of approval.

Some of her finishing schools had mistaken the result for placid lady-like decorum.

Two keen-eyed men waiting behind the bored customs officials *did* give her a prickle like the sight of a jaguar's spotted coat glimpsed in the jungle.

The older one was in a blue frogged officer's walking-out jacket and kepi and the younger in a civilian suit that might as well have had rank epaulettes, with a trench coat over his shoulders and a thin mustache in the modern fashion, as black as his senior's was white and as close-clipped as his senior's was bushy with turned-up tips held in place with musk-scented wax. She spotted a shoulder holster through the fabric, probably carrying the same 7.65-millimeter Star automatic as the one his uniformed comrade had on his belt, and then carefully avoided looking at them more than a civilian would.

Deuxième Bureau de l'État-major General, Luz thought.

Which meant the military secret service, who besides ordinary intelligence work did some of what the Black Chamber and FBS did in America.

Colonel Dupont's little helpers, if he made it out of Paris alive, or whoever his successor is if he didn't.

Not long ago she'd helped Horst von Dückler massacre an entire Deuxième Bureau snatch team in the Netherlands, in her Elisa Carmody de Soto-Dominguez persona, a process that had included leaving stacked bodies in a bath on the seventh floor of the Hotel Victoria in Amsterdam with their throats slit as well as using rifles and grenades around a train the French agents had wrecked near the Dutch-German border.

The French secret service wouldn't be very interested in how she had been playing the Abteilung IIIb man then, or how convincing that joint action had made her, or that she'd done her probably . . . unfortunately . . . not *quite* successful best to kill Horst herself in Boston a little later.

And she strongly suspected that if they knew or suspected the truth of it all they'd quietly disappear the Black Chamber operatives to various fates worse than death, followed by death, American alliance or not. Their mission had saved America's coastal cities on the Atlantic, though it hadn't saved London. What would be much more important to these men than either was that it hadn't saved Paris, or stopped the breaking of the Western Front and the ongoing ruin of mainland France.

Though single-handedly preventing everything *would be a bit much to ask . . . even of me!* she thought whimsically, with an undertone of seriousness.

Vanity is a sin; also, in this business it leads to premature death and burial, not necessarily in that order.

Another prickle went over her skin as she moved willingly toward the danger, not entirely disagreeable, and she looked away with an appearance of bored insouciance over a tingling sense of *aliveness*. Between losing her parents and meeting Ciara, nothing had made her feel that way except an operation like this.

And revenge on Villa and his men, but that was . . . hotter.

And she felt a new and unpleasant shiver and gut-clench of actual common-or-garden-variety fear, but that wasn't for herself.

I'll just have to get used to that.

She valued her own life, now more than ever, but the knowledge that the mission was more important had long ago sunk down to the level of the heart. With Ciara, she only knew it with the head. But Luz had studied Aristotle in her philosophy class at Bryn Mawr: the difference between animals and human beings was that if you were truly human, the *dianoētikon*, the intellectual part of the soul that knew reason and duty, was meant to rule the rest of you as an Oriental king did his subjects, tolerating no other power.

It was natural for two young women traveling alone to be a bit nervous around foreign officials, anyway. Just letting a little of an unrelated fear show was easier and more authentic than outright acting. You used everything that came to hand.

There were posters on the inside of the hangar, presumably there to keep up the troops' morale. One was rather old and a bit ragged and ripped; it showed a muddy French *poilu* in horizon-blue and ridged steel helmet brandishing his rifle and backlit by shell bursts in a landscape of flooded craters and tumbled wreckage, with the slogan below:

On ne passe pas!

That had been about Verdun, but the Germans *had* passed, back in the spring, albeit at hideous cost. That had been an unrecognized tipping point leading to a downhill slope. If she'd been in charge here she'd have had the thing torn down long ago, but they might simply have been too busy to get around to it. Or just reluctant to be seen doing it because of the admission involved. Still . . .

Nothing is more demoralizing than a reminder of a boast you couldn't make good.

A more recent one showed the citadel of Angers, a medieval castle in Anjou, with:

La Loire tient!

That meant: *The Loire will hold!*

That would have been *much* better propaganda without the previous one about Verdun on the wall mocking it. The current Western Front ran mostly along the Loire River, and then through the difficult hilly terrain eastward to the Swiss border. If you didn't count the shrinking perimeter the British held around Calais and Dunkirk as the Germans hammered them back and back and back toward the waiting sea and the frantic shuttle of boats large and small.

"Will it?" Ciara said softly, tracking the direction of her eyes to the poster. "With . . . the help they're getting."

Luz used a blunt proverb current all over the Spanish-speaking world:

"Cuando las ranas crian pelo."

And that meant it would happen *when frogs grew hair.* Which was even appropriate, since amphibians with fur *were* more likely than pigs with wings, but not much more so than the Loire holding. As far as she knew the Germans had just stopped and dug in when they outran their supplies, with the smoldering wreck of Paris and the poisoned horror-gas wasteland of the old trenches behind them, and were marking time against the French until they kicked the last British troops into the sea and repaired enough railways and bridges to bring up the heavy gear for the next push.

"We have enough troops and equipment to tip the balance thanks to . . . you-know-who . . . but we can't *send* enough to Europe fast enough, not now that we can't stage through England, or supply them if we could. Probably not enough shipping, certainly not enough ports to put the ships in if there were. Everything has to come all the way across, into the Mediterranean, and then to the harbors in southern France . . . and there are only two of any size."

"You can only put a certain volume of water through a given diameter of pipe no matter how hard you pump," Ciara said sadly, which Luz thought expressed it very neatly . . . if you thought like an engineer.

There wasn't much chance of being overheard, but they were both being careful. Fortunately, it was entirely natural for them to speak softly with their heads close together; half the other passengers were doing that too, the ones who didn't bray self-importantly at the world in general. People who had the money, pull, or both to get passage on a transatlantic airship were *very important* people, and if you didn't know it already many of them were quite willing to tell you about it, in detail and at length.

"We *can* delay things long enough for more of the French to get here," she replied equally quietly. "The new leaders in charge here are ... playing a long game. Though I'll bet anything you care to wager that ... you-know-who ... have told ... the other two ..."

Uncle Teddy and *General Wood* would have stood out from the flow of the Spanish conversation. So would *Foch* and *Lyautey*, the men currently running France and its possessions. As much as anyone was.

". . . has told them the last rearguards outside Marseilles holding the Germans out of artillery range of the docks will be French, not Americans. The delay will keep France ... or at least France-*outre-mere*, overseas France ... in the fight. Though the Germans aren't stopping the civilians from running south even where they're in effective occupation. They're letting them through their lines—the fewer French people in France, the easier to control."

And she knew the Germans were squeezing every last loaf from the occupied zone for their troops and not even *trying* to feed the civilians anymore now that Hoover's Belgian Relief Commission had closed up, also for the same reason; they wanted the territory but not the population, and there was nothing like the prospect of dying of starvation to set masses of people in motion. There was a poster here about that, too. It didn't say or even outright imply anything so pessimistic, but it was big and new and it was right behind the customs officers.

It showed two generals in embroidered kepis, Foch and Lyautey, both trim figures in their early sixties with old-fashioned bushy mustaches upturned at the tips like the horns of a Cape buffalo and that grim predatory I-am-going-to-kill-you-right-now stare that some men had and a good photograph could convey.

Foch currently commanded what was left of the French army in Europe as it fell back inch by slaughterhouse inch, scorching the earth as it retreated. Lyautey—a long-time colonial bigwig, the conqueror of

Morocco in the last prewar years, and very briefly minister of war in Paris—was heading up the new Committee of National Salvation in Algiers. They were effectively military dictators now, along the lines of Hindenburg and Ludendorff in Germany.

Between the generals was a drawing of burning ruins with machine-gun tracers snapping over them and a gaunt-looking woman with a child in her arms crouching behind a snag of broken wall. A French soldier stood beside her and fired the odd-looking Ribeyrolles machine carbine his army used back over it, while a Frenchman and a German lay dead inches from each other in the background, each with a bayonet buried in the other's body.

The caption on that one was blunt, too:

To the Last Man and the Last Bullet.

It was considerably more honest than the others, which said something about the two generals.

They came to the head of the line. The blue-uniformed clerk was methodical; also middle-aged, balding, with olive skin about the same shade as Luz's. He went through their cabin baggage carefully but neatly—without noticing any of the expertly concealed secret compartments—and then his bushy black-and-gray eyebrows went up as he examined the documents.

Their cover identities were from Chile, which was a prosperous country and quite advanced, not an impoverished, *caudillo*-ridden backwater like Bolivia or Paraguay where even the police couldn't afford shoes or count to twenty-one without dropping their trousers. But it was very remote and hadn't gotten around to putting photographs in travel documents yet.

The beautifully forged entry visas purporting to be from the French and Italian embassies in Buenos Aires—the forged German ones were inside the secret compartments—did have them, stapled to the documents. The likelihood of the orphaned French authorities here checking with their embassy in Argentina anytime soon . . . now that central France was a wasteland and the Quai d'Orsay was a tomb . . . was probably in the frogs-grow-hair range.

That wouldn't be true in Germany.

"*Aïa!* Chileans! We don't see that very often!" the customs official

said, speaking singsong Algerian-French that was melodic and guttural
at once; the dialect of the *colons* here in North Africa bore strong traces
of both Spanish and Arabic.

He made a sign that brought the hard-looking young man in civilian clothes over. The intelligence officer went over the passports and
visas again, and used a jeweler's loupe he pulled from a jacket pocket to
examine the details, glancing up at them in turn. Ciara met his eyes
and then glanced away, which was perfectly normal; Luz raised a brow.
Their ladies' day dresses were in the best French style and suitable for
travel . . . but the style was that of 1914, just before the Great War,
with ankle-length skirts pleated a little in front, and with plumes on
the brow of the low-crowned hats.

"You two ladies are Mlle. Consuelo de la Barrera y Meza and Mlle.
Maria O'Doul?" he asked, pronouncing the Hispanic names as if he
spoke Spanish well and speaking French like a graduate of one of
the Grandes Écoles, as precise and as uncolored by anything regional
as water in a mountain spring.

"Oui, monsieur," Luz said.

French was certainly the foreign language an educated Chilean
lady would be most likely to speak well, but the problem was that Luz
would be *too* fluent if she used her perfect upper-middle-class collo-
quial Parisian. She reminded herself to speak slowly and hesitate now
and then, rolling her *r*'s and hissing a little on the sibilants to put an
under-layer of the archaic Chilean version of Spanish into her pronun-
ciation. And to think in that language and then translate mentally,
composing her French sentences as if she were reading them from a
book, formal diction like using the full *ne . . . pas* for the negative rather
than the *pas* alone after the verb that was more common in younger
people's ordinary speech these days in Paris.

Or that had been until October sixth, when there still was a Paris.

"We are representatives of the Circulo de Lectura de Señoras de
Chile," she added, producing a—forged—letter from that worthy
women's rights organization.

While he read it she went on: "We are here to study developments
in the education of women and of girls in Europe and to make a report.
Our founder and leader, the very distinguished Señora Amanda

Labarca, studied at the Sorbonne before the war and is a great admirer of French culture."

She smiled as she took the name of Chile's foremost feminist in vain and touched her bobbed shoulder-length raven hair, modeled—except for the absence of curls—on that of the famous and scandalous French actress Polaire.

Who's probably dead, whether she was in Paris or doing one of her fund-raisers in London, Luz thought suddenly. *That's a pity; it really is. She made thousands of people smile and laugh and be happy, and she never hurt anybody.*

The bob was a fairly daring style even in Europe or the United States, and would have been *extremely* daring for someone who actually was from South America, but the man's half-conscious glance said he knew its origins. He was much more likely to know Polaire's name than to be closely familiar with the social customs of Santiago de Chile.

From a secret agent's point of view it was very convenient sometimes that there was no universal reference book that could be accessed on the spot and used to look up obscure facts about faraway places.

"And . . . our trip was planned before the . . . the so-terrible events," she said, letting her face fall.

It is *terrible to think of Paris. I wouldn't want to live there, but it was a splendid place to visit, an ornament to the whole human race, all politics and nations aside. So many generations to build it, and all destroyed so quickly . . . Who knows if the Germans even managed to secure the Louvre before fire or flood got to it?*

"You have chosen a very bad time to travel in Europe, mesdemoiselles," he said severely.

Luz nodded anxiously and made her eyes go wide, since it would be entirely out of character for Consuelo de la Barrera y Meza to simply tell a functionary to mind his own business, though completely *in* character for Luz O'Malley Aróstegui. Of course, Consuelo wouldn't know what the man was, apart from some French bureaucrat, either.

Ciara silently frowned and clutched her hands together in quite genuine grief and horror at the fate of Paris.

"But surely Italy and Switzerland are neutral?" Luz said with appropriately naïve hopefulness.

"Belgium was neutral until 1914, mademoiselle. The Netherlands were neutral, until last month," the Frenchman said dryly. "Now they're both under Germany's boot."

"But we are going to Italy and Switzerland, not the Netherlands also as we originally planned."

"I do not think that the Boche or their Austrian hangers-on have forgiven Italy for their . . . one supposes they will call it treachery. They are merely biding their time until more powerful enemies have been destroyed."

Italy had formally been one of the triple alliance of the Central Powers in 1914. Rome had stayed out of the war on the technicality that it was a defensive alliance and Austria-Hungary had attacked Serbia rather than vice versa. Which was even true if you didn't count the head of Serbian military intelligence engineering the assassination of the heir to the Austro-Hungarian throne.

Not even the Black Chamber was sure if his government had known about the plot, or whether they approved if they did, but they were *quite* sure Colonel Dragutin Dimitrijević, code-named *Apis*, had been behind it. He'd paid for that with his life, along with, by now, well over half of Serbia's total population . . . and still counting.

The Chamber was also sure that Rome—and nearly everyone in that pit of cannibalistic vipers collectively known as "the Balkans"— had been planning on jumping in and biting off chunks of the Austro-Hungarian dual monarchy or German-aligned Turkey if things went against the Central Powers. Except Bulgaria, which in 1914 had decided to bite a really juicy chunk off Serbia instead, by way of revenge for the Second Balkan War of 1913 in which Serbia had done exactly the same thing to them. Italy was now thanking God they'd—just barely—managed to resist *that* sort of temptation at least. Unlike, for example, the dim and luckless Rumanians, who were now paying a very high price for their optimistic greed.

Luz thought the Deuxième Bureau agent was probably right in the long term, though; Germany wouldn't forget Italy either. And there was that old Hungarian joke that Zsófia from Budapest had told her at the *Reichsgräfin*'s school, asking why God had created Italians.

The answer: so that even Austrians would have someone *they could defeat.*

Just as he'd said, it really was a very, very bad time to visit Europe.

"The Circulo de Lectura de Señoras and our own families have spent a great deal of money to send us here," Luz said, firming her lips like someone taking their courage in both hands. "We cannot simply turn around and go back, as if we were . . . were nothing but *tourists* concerned with being safe and comfortable."

The man shrugged in a resigned Gallic fashion, apparently accepting that they were interesting international flotsam but not professionally significant. Getting themselves gruesomely killed would be their problem and none of his, since Chile wasn't a player in this game.

"Be very careful here in Tunis, then, mesdemoiselles," he said.

He probably wouldn't have bothered to warn their male equivalents.

"And make your passage to Naples as quickly as possible. Food is already growing very scarce throughout the National Redoubt, despite what the Americans have sent us, though they promise more soon, which the Good God grant. Many of the refugees are hungry; *les indigènes* even more so. And people who have been through much fear, much horror . . . sometimes it makes them very strange, very dangerous."

He tapped a finger on his temple to show what he meant:

"We keep order vigorously in general—"

Well, vigorous *is one way to describe firing multiple thirty-round bursts down a crowded city street*, Luz thought dryly, behind her anxiously intent expression.

"—but unfortunate things still happen in particular, to individuals, if you take my meaning."

He gave them an ironic salute as he waved them on; a portly Argentine exporter who'd been chattering to his secretary in Italian-flavored *Rioplatense* Spanish was next in line, no doubt with mountains of grain and tinned corned beef waiting for a market if he could find ships that the U-boats hadn't sent to the bottom. And if the esoteric problems of industrial-scale credit and payment could be solved, now that the Bank of England and the currencies it had anchored were one with Nineveh and Tyre. Shock waves from the hammer blows that had fallen on Paris and London were rippling and stuttering back and forth through the world's networks of commerce and finance as surely as they were through war and politics, leaving deathly famine from France to China while farmers went bankrupt for want of customers and food rotted in warehouses on the other side of the ocean.

The two Black Chamber operatives walked through the back of the ex-hangar, not the first of the passengers to clear the officials but far from the last, with a soldier trundling their trunk from the baggage compartment behind them and dumping it unceremoniously by the roadside in a puff of dry dust. Luz took a long slow breath, fighting down the dizziness of relief with one hand braced against the trunk.

"Darling?" Ciara said, her voice worried.

"That was . . . more dangerous than it looked, *mi corazón*. Just give me a second."

In an actual fight action purged your blood and left exhilaration, at least for her, but right now it surged in her veins for a moment with a feeling almost like nausea. Something deep in her knew she *had* been fighting for her life . . . and Ciara's . . . and had primed her for *anything* but standing quietly and waiting, which was precisely what she had to do. She fought the feeling back and down with a practiced effort of will and returned to the moment. Suddenly bending over and depositing her breakfast on the roadway might attract attention.

Then she blew out a breath and felt her lips twist wryly. "You know, life is too short and too full of risk and pain to take seriously all the time."

Ciara smiled, but with a little puzzlement in her eyes.

"Let's see about getting to the hotel. I suspect that's not going to be as simple as I'd like, judging from what we saw."

A sign by the rear entrance promised with pompous assurance that transportation would arrive . . . but didn't specify exactly when, or how, or in what form.

Whoever came up with that maxim about French being such a clear, precise language never ran into a Frenchman trying to be vague, Luz thought as she read it again. *It's actually the perfect language for sounding so absolutely definite that you don't realize until fifteen minutes later that nothing was said at all.*

"You should have gone on the stage, Consuelo," Ciara said admiringly, rolling her eyes a little back toward the French officials. "You had *me* half-fooled!"

"We both have done exactly that, Maria," Luz replied, feeling what she thought was pardonable pride.

I did save both our lives, after all. My imitation of an earnest, naïve, brave, but slightly dim Chilean do-gooder completely out of her depth and swimming with sharks was enough to convince a professional. ¡Viva la magnificencia suprema de mí! It's just that it wasn't as much fun as it used to be. I don't think I've ever done it better, though. I had double the reason! Lying for two, you might say.

Then she chuckled, and at Ciara's look said: "Plato once said something about an army of lovers being invincible. I see now there's something to that, as far as motivation is concerned, and it seems to hold for . . . teachers . . . too."

The word for *spy* was another of those conversational standouts, and very similar in all the Romance languages . . . and for that matter in German and most of the Slavic ones too.

Ciara nodded solemnly and quoted a free translation of Plato's *Phaedrus*:

"For love will guide a human being to strive for imperishable honor in the eyes of the beloved, more strongly and beautifully than public acclaim, or wealth, or even blood ties. That makes more sense to me now."

Luz nodded back with equal gravity, thinking for a moment of the Lion of Chaeronea sitting its long watch over the bones of the Sacred Band of Thebes, where they had stood to meet the charge of Alexander the Great and won the hero's privilege of a common grave. Stood, and died in their tracks to the last man—to the last pair of *erastês* and *erômenos*, lover and beloved, their locked shields facing the Macedonian lances side by side.

The roadway was graded dirt with gravel, and fairly busy. Dust settled on them, and Luz was glad of her broad-brimmed hat, though not as much as Ciara would be with her tender milky skin; even in late November the sun here had a California-like authority, and it was rising toward midmorning. The passengers standing near their piles of baggage were getting more and more restive as they realized they'd be waiting for some time for transport, since they were mostly people accustomed to the world catering to their whims or at least their convenience. Luz thought that discontent would get worse soon; she also thought that ANA's civilian passengers weren't all that high a priority for the French army right now when it came to allocating road vehicles. This was a bigger pond than the ones they came from, boiling hot and full of piranhas.

There are times when fast beats subtle, and when it comes to people not talking afterward, there's nothing like complicity and self-interest. We already lost days in that sandstorm. The closer we get to Germany, the more likely someone is to trip over us. The clock is ticking.

She decided to solve the problem while she could and before it occurred to the other travelers to take direct action, and put her cabin bag on top of their trunk and opened it to rummage for a moment, stripping off her gloves as she did. The Technical Section had made the secret compartments in this version much more accessible without being any more conspicuous.

"What an age of progress we live in!" she murmured; the best flavor of irony came with a piquant sauce of literal truth. "Cover, please, *querida*."

Ciara stepped between her and the other passengers, pulling out her compact to examine her nose and apply a little dab of powder with the puff . . . while examining everything behind her as well. Compacts were still a new and slightly racy fashion in the United States, and possibly out of character for respectable Chileans, even members of a feminist organization. For a spy they were *so* handy . . . not least for giving you an excuse to have a mirror in your hand. Luz bent over the open case as if rooting for something, slipping her automatic into the holster sewn into her jacket's lining and two rolls of coins into her purse in the process. Nobody was in position to see, and wouldn't have even if they were closer because she palmed the objects neatly.

Official French wartime regulations banned civilian firearms; she knew exactly how much attention she was going to pay to that, with Tunis so unpleasantly reminiscent of Mexico City at the beginning of the Intervention and before the new proprietors got things well in hand. She'd drawn her automatic *there* half a dozen times in the first month. That wasn't counting Chamber business, just times she deterred or shot dead locals who thought she was Mexican too and could be robbed, raped, murdered, or various combinations of the three amid the initial chaos.

Nowadays Mexico City was safer than New York, which meant by no coincidence at all that she was unlikely to be sent there very often.

The French rules also required travelers to exchange bullion and foreign currency for a paper franc that had been heading downhill rapidly even before the Bank of France and its gold reserves became a poisoned ruin with the rotting corpses of its directors and accountants slumped across their desks and ledgers. Fortunately, they said nothing about people on French territory *spending* pre-1914 currency, probably because even in good times French citizens trusted the glint of precious metals far more than government promises.

A boxy snub-nosed Berliet CBA motor truck was coming toward them, with two French soldiers in the cab and three more riding behind. It wasn't going very fast, because the roadway behind the hangars was narrow and crowded, and besides that the only way to get that model above fifteen miles an hour was to drive it off a cliff. Luz fished in her purse as she stepped into the roadway, slit open one of the paper rolls of coins with her thumbnail, and raised her hand, swinging it out with the palm toward the vehicle's steering wheel.

Five twenty-franc gold coins showed in it, one slotted between each finger, one more held by her thumb and the last resting in her cupped palm.

To anyone more than a few paces away it would look as if she were just hopefully waving at them, but the man behind the wheel got a much better view, especially since the truck had no windscreen. He showed alertness and quick wits then. Berliets didn't have very good brakes either, but the driver managed to stop it with a spurt of red dust from under the smooth-worn solid rubber of the forward tires. Someone riding a motorcycle-sidecar combination behind him just barely managed to halt in time too, with a *hoog-hoog-hoog* from a squeeze-bulb horn and a heartfelt scream of:

"*Nig'doulle!*"

Which was *imbecile* in *chtimi*, the patois spoken in Picardy, up near the Belgian border. The shout sputtered on in the thick peasant dialect with variations on *con* and *merde* and comments about the truck driver's mother and sisters and his relationships to and with them and livestock and God and Satan, and as the motorcycle swung past, the beefy blond-mustached driver with the leather helmet and aviator's goggles made a gesture which meant *everything OK* in America and either *you are a zero* or *you are the lower end of the digestive tract* in much of Europe.

The corporal driving the Berliet ignored him—while the trio in the rear of the truck replied in kind—and leaned out of the doorless cab toward Luz as she stepped closer, a delighted yellow-toothed smile on his stubbly rat-like face beneath the blue fore-and-aft Bonnet de Police cap. A rice-paper Gitane sent up a trail of harsh-smelling smoke from one corner of his mouth.

The smile grew even broader and yellower as she made the coins disappear with a stage magician's gesture—the Chamber had retained a couple of those, too—stepped closer, and showed them in the palm of her hand in a neat overlapping row for an instant before returning them to her pocket.

"Oh, the roosters, such a great big flock of pretty little roosters!" he crooned.

In slurred argot right out of the gutters of the 20th arrondissement; the gold pieces had a Gallic cock on one side and the head of Marianne, France's incarnation, on the other.

She'd been fairly certain *someone* would stop, and not much surprised it was the first one by. Not many French soldiers ever saw a twenty-franc piece even in peacetime, since their daily wage was a miserable twenty-five centimes, less than a tenth of what a farm laborer made and worth about an American nickel. The attitude of the Third Republic was that a citizen privileged to bear arms for France should be glad to suffer for *la patrie* without being shocked and insulted by the offer of gross, demeaning material incentives like decent pay, edible food, regular leave, or adequate medical services. And late in this year of grace 1916 they'd get that nickel's worth in collapsing paper money.

Whereas twenty *gold* francs would buy, for example, a hectoliter—nearly thirty American gallons—of quite drinkable *vin de table*. She judged it was just the right weight of bribe, lavish enough to be irresistible but not quite so outlandish that it was frightening.

A quick glance at close range made Luz sure that the driver wasn't an Apache himself, the sort of tattooed street-gang horror who ended up doing his military service in the Saharan penal units of the Bat d'Af.

He was definitely the smarter first cousin of the type, though, which was promising. The other soldier beside him in the front of the truck was still blinking in slow yokel bewilderment and visibly trying to decide what he'd seen and whether it could possibly be what he *thought* he'd seen, like a mental equivalent of a cow chewing its cud.

"*Bonjour*, mademoiselle!" the noncom said, pulling off his cap with one hand and putting on fine manners like a duck trying to tap dance. "What can I do for you ladies on this fine day?"

Who do you want killed? ran beneath the statement, though that would probably require a little more cash if she took it literally.

"My friend and I need to get to the Grand Hôtel de France, 8 Rue Leon Roches," she said briskly.

This time speaking like someone born and raised in the household of a banker or senior civil servant in the 8th arrondissement and who'd gone to the sort of schools Luz had, in fact, attended long enough to absorb the dialect.

"One beautiful rooster for each of your comrades and two for you if you take us there now. It's worth that much to me. It isn't worth any more . . . so decide quickly now, *Monsieur le caporal de Ménil'muche. Vite!*"

He blinked and his eyes went wide, along with an involuntary grin that meant she'd picked his neighborhood correctly.

The soldiers would know she was well-to-do—stinking rich, in their terms—from her excellent if slightly old-fashioned clothes and Ciara's similar outfit, and the mere fact that they'd come in on the airship whose spine loomed over the hangar behind them. That she'd guessed the noncom's specific stamping ground and knew that *Ménil'muche* was the nickname in Apache argot for that extremely louche part of the rather louche 20th arrondissement would make him more respectful in an entirely different way, rather than thinking she was *un pigeon*, an easy-mark rich girl with more money than sense.

The corporal met her eyes, nodded in instant decision, and snapped over his shoulder without disturbing the cigarette:

"Erwan! Jean! Henri! Help the beautiful, generous ladies with their bags! We're taking a detour, and telling Lieutenant Le Haricot—"

Which translated as *Lieutenant Dimwit*.

"—we had another block in that *salope de merde* of a fuel line."

When the three soldiers in the back of the truck looked at him, he added:

"A rooster for it. For each of us."

At that they jumped down and slung their stubby Ribeyrolles machine carbines—they had curved box magazines jutting out below, rather than the Thompson's drum—and grabbed the brass-bound brown leather trunk and the two cabin bags and heaved them enthusiastically onto the bed of the truck.

Luz gave a half skip and sprang lithely after them, extending a hand down and pulling Ciara after her, just as one or two heads started to turn toward them among the other stranded travelers. There were wooden bench seats along the sides, but the women folded their skirts around their knees and sat on the floor cross-legged with the plain brown trunk between them and the tailgate of the motor truck . . . which kept their heads below the level of the sides as well. That left them nearly invisible unless someone leaned in the rear where two of the men stood, each with a hand on the overhead hoop that carried the canvas cover when it was up and the other on the grip of his weapon.

The soldiers gave them brief happy grins of complicity over their shoulders; the corporal looked back at them, nodded approval at how they were making things easy for him, and the truck lurched into its slow racketing motion once more.

"Is this safe?" Ciara said quietly, in Spanish and leaning close. "That man driving looks like a nasty thief to me."

"*¿Quizás un pícaro?*" Luz said, giving her own quick estimate of the man; perhaps a rogue rather than simply a thief, though certainly anything lying about unguarded would find its way into his knapsack. "So it's . . . reasonably safe."

She touched the side of her jacket where the little FN 1910 automatic rested in the molded silk-and-chamois pocket.

Needs must, three head shots for the ones in the back with us, catch one of the machine carbines as it falls . . .

"The corporal knows I'm probably French and certainly rich and that I recognized where he came from and its name in street argot, so he probably *thinks* I'm a very successful criminal or more likely the daughter or mistress of one," she told her partner softly.

She was watching what she said, since *French* North Africa also had plenty of Spaniards and Italians in it; so did the slums of Paris, for that matter, or had before the city was gutted by the horror-gas and then abandoned in panic, riot, and fire.

"Just dropping us where we asked is much, much safer than trying to rob us. Besides . . . professional courtesy."

They came to the perimeter of the air station quickly; there was a trench all around it, coils of barbed wire, a swinging gate . . . and two bunkers of sandbags and concrete on either side of that, with overhead protection and a pair of Hotchkiss machine guns pointing their finned barrels outward through the firing slits, which said something. The bunkers were very new, which was also a comment on the situation.

A sergeant came out and spoke to Corporal Willing-for-the-Golden-Roosters, then waved them through as he got a glib two sentences about checking the docks for the arrival of the families of the garrison; the defenses were to keep things out, not in. The trio in the rear hadn't made any attempt to talk to or even leer at the two attractive women, either, and as soon as the truck was beyond the perimeter they all looked alertly outward, their automatic weapons ready.

That was *also* a comment on conditions . . . which were already very unlike the orderly and mildly prosperous colonial city described in *Cook's Practical Guide to Algeria and Tunisia with Maps, Plans and Illustrations (Thos. Cook & Sons, 1914).*

She touched Ciara's elbow and they both rose and sat on the trunk; that put their heads above the sideboards of the truck without making them too conspicuous. Spies had a duty to be curious when they could, and the U.S. security services hadn't been looking this way much until very recently.

At the first major intersection that crossed the southbound road they stopped for a column of people on foot, several thousand in all, moving out westward toward the open country and carrying bundles and bags wrapped in bedding. They didn't look much different from anyone else around the Middle Sea, dark hair and olive faces that would have been only a little more swarthy than average in Palermo or Cadiz or Athens. It was their clothing that marked them as locals; striped hooded robes, *jebbas* and burnooses in various combinations with Western dress, huge *sefsari* shawls wrapped around the women and drawn over the head and across the face.

Squads of Senegalese with fixed bayonets kept the column moving in the cloud of dust it raised, sometimes with air-jabs or threats from the steel-shod butts of their rifles. After a while the West African troops made a pathway through the crowd for the truck, at the corporal's obscene urging and frantic arm waving, deliberately delaying a little, pretending to misunderstand him and then grinning whitely at the regular's fury.

"Oh, les joyeux," one of the French soldiers she'd bribed muttered in a sour tone; it meant *the happy ones*, and it could be a compliment . . . or, as now, very much not.

The column included women of all ages, old men, and plenty of children, but no healthy young men fit to bear arms that Luz could see, interpreting those conditions liberally. A few faces turned blankly toward the truck; others wept or prayed; most just stolidly trudged with their eyes down. Luz winced slightly as one toddler with big dark eyes riding on his grandfather's shoulders where he could look over the edge of the truck waved a hand holding a piece of flatbread at them and called out to Ciara in shrill pidgin:

"B'jour, joli mam'zelle blonde!"

Ciara blinked and looked away quickly.

"Que se passe-t-il ici, soldat?" Luz asked; what was going on?

One of the soldiers—he was the big one named Erwan, and had a reddish mustache and a musical Welsh-sounding Breton accent when he spoke in his very basic French—shrugged and said:

"Pas de logement, pas de pain."

Which meant *no room, no food*.

The next east-west road had traffic in the other direction, inbound toward the city center, and it made them wait longer: flocks of sheep and goats giving off an earthy barnyard smell, and wagons drawn by mules and oxen piled with farm gear amid sacks of grain, green fodder, clay crocks of pickled olives or olive oil, baskets of fresh or dried fruit and vegetables or wicker cages full of chickens . . . and it was all much more heavily guarded, this time by white French soldiers whose knapsacks looked suspiciously full.

Since most of the troops were peasants themselves they weren't having much difficulty keeping the livestock moving, but they were getting a lot of fixed stares from the crowds to either side and hanging out of the windows above. Occasionally someone would make a move toward the passing bounty, and stop at a harsh warning . . . or when they ended up looking at the points of half a dozen bayonets, or once when a round was fired into the air.

They've certainly got flexible rules of engagement for a supposedly friendly urban area, Luz thought—what went up always came down somewhere. *That's* another *sign of the situation.*

Overwhelming firepower and an obvious willingness to shoot to kill at the slightest resistance were keeping the lid on.

For now.

The French refugees they saw crowding the streets more and more densely as they got closer to the docks didn't look much happier than *les indigènes* as they milled around with *their* miserable bundles and crying children, or lined up for meager bowls of slumgullion at soup kitchens mostly run by harried-looking nuns or soldiers, or argued with harassed bureaucrats and policemen and soldiers trying to move them somewhere else, or just slumped on the ground and dully watched with exhausted indifference. A good many of them had countrymen's tools as well: sickles and scythes, shovels and pitchforks and hoes and the like, or bundles of the gear rural artisans like carpenters and cobblers and harness makers used.

The refugees obviously hadn't been eating very well lately either. And even when you mentally subtracted the heavy military vehicle traffic crowding the streets there were a *lot* of them, from everywhere in metropolitan France.

And I swear ante Dios *that I heard someone shout:* How long must we stay here in this awful Corsica place? *In Burgundian patois, to boot.*

"Why are they dropping so many of their people here?" Ciara asked in a subdued tone.

She was awed by the sheer *scale* of it all, and so was Luz. Not to mention by the smell; it was very fortunate that Tunis had an excellent drinking water system based on repaired Roman aqueducts from sources in springs a long way out of town where they couldn't be con-taminated by the insane chaotic crush.

"This isn't even the closest port to France; Algiers is much closer. Wouldn't it be better to spread them out instead of sending everyone here?" she asked Luz.

Luz translated, though she suspected the answer. The corporal laughed, a harsh humorless nasal honking that made a newly lit Gitane dance at the corner of his mouth, and spoke over his shoulder with a very French disregard for looking where he was going.

"*Merde alors*, madam! She thinks *this* is bad? Tell your *petite amie esp-agnole blonde*—"

Which was possibly disconcertingly sharp of him. The phrase *petite amie* literally meant "little (female gender) friend" but usually implied a more intimate relationship. "Little blond Spanish girlfriend" *definitely* did, in context.

"—that it's like this at every port in the National Redoubt! From here to Casablanca! Or to Agadir, for all I know. I *do* know Sfax and Bizerte are just like this because I've been there; Bône and Algiers and Oran farther west are ten times worse, they say."

"*¡Dios mío!*" Ciara blurted, crossing herself as the implications sank in.

Luz whistled very softly herself, as they looked at each other. She'd known refugees were pouring across the Mediterranean, but the *scale* . . .

Her mind drew maps and calculated numbers. It wasn't that far from France to Tunisia or even to half-pacified Morocco, and as Ciara had said the Algerian ports were closer still, two days' sailing or less. On that short a voyage you could use anything from liners down to little fishing smacks and cram people in as tight as convict ships and slavers had in the old days. On today's ships that would mean multiple thousands even on a single ordinary-sized freighter. And probably the convoys of American transports landing in Marseilles and Toulon were doing a dogleg to the nearest part of the National Redoubt on the way back west as a favor to their new allies.

There had been forty million people in France when the war

started, though she mentally subtracted a couple of million dead since. The French colonies of the Maghreb stretching between Italian-ruled Libya and the Atlantic had around twelve million, including a million or so long-established European settlers, the *colons*. So . . .

How much of A *can you pump into* B *before something goes* boom? *Or* splat? she thought.

Luz's expert guess from the air had put at least a hundred thousand refugees in the camps here. The view from the ground perhaps doubled that, if you counted everyone who'd been stuffed into an attic or was dossing in a warehouse or—with appropriate bribes or influential friends and relations—was inheriting some luckless local's house and was happy to get a place in what had been a native-quarter slum before the war. Multiply that by every port along the shores of the Maghreb . . . or what *had* been the Maghreb . . .

At least *a million already, maybe two, since Paris was destroyed. And something like . . . ¡Recórcholis! Ten thousand . . . twenty thousand a day? No, even more than that! Just* one *big passenger liner like the* SS France *could take that many tight-packed and they've still got a fair number of those. The mind boggles. The biggest mass movement in history!*

"Most of France will be over here by spring," the corporal said over his shoulder. "And nobody's going back north for a long, long time."

He spat into the roadway—again without shedding his cigarette, but with magnificent disdain.

"La Loire tient, les ânes disent-ils? C'est des conneries absolument!"

He was quite right; saying the Loire would hold *was* absolute bullshit told by donkeys who obviously didn't believe it themselves. Ordinary people weren't necessarily stupid, and they didn't necessarily swallow propaganda whole all the time either, not unless it told them things they at least half believed already.

All the major intersections they passed had sandbagged machine-gun nests, or once a pair of back-to-back seventy-five-millimeter field pieces with their muzzles depressed to point straight down the roadways, no doubt loaded with zero-fused shrapnel to dispense the proverbial whiff of grapeshot.

Sometimes the *oooga-oooga-oooga* of the truck's squeeze-bulb horn would clear a path, sometimes the horn and curses, sometimes the waving muzzles of the machine carbines. Once the soldiers in the truck had to fire a burst into the air to get past a mob besieging a feeding station that was handing out big round loaves of coarse dense Army ration-issue bread; even then most members of the mob just moved slowly aside as they tore the loaves apart and stuffed them into their mouths with ferocious concentration or scurried off to find their families, hiding the bread beneath their clothes or glaring around murderously.

Also an indication.

French tricolor flags were everywhere, but Luz noticed that many of them had a highly unusual addition sewn onto the resolutely secular banner of the very secularist Third Republic, a stylized red heart shape and cross: the Sacred Heart of Jesus.

Aha, she thought, as things she knew clicked together. *Foch is extremely Catholic, in the French political sense of the word, and I seem to remember reading or hearing somewhere that Lyautey said in public that at least the war might make the Députés and party politicians shut up. The Third Republic is gone with Paris, and the things it kept its foot on are springing up again. Countries dying, countries being born.*

Ciara jumped slightly at the ratcheting clamor of rounds going up and the shower of hot brass that rained down on the front of her dress— the soldier obviously wasn't worried about where the *bullets* would come down either—and then craned her neck as the truck pulled over to the side of the road and slowly crept by a long, long convoy of big wagons pulled by hitches of eight horses each.

That transport meant a high priority. The wagons were moving at barely walking pace themselves, and loaded perilously high with rough slatted crates holding mysterious metallic shapes; there were armed French troops in filthy ragged uniforms riding—or sleeping—on the loads too. Several of them were bandaged, walking wounded, and they all had the haggard hollow-cheeked look of men pushed to their limits.

Another train of lighter four-horse wagons right behind was full of people—a few of the soldiers but mainly family groups, with the adult men all wearing cloth caps or berets and what the French called *bleu de travail*, tough blue overalls that were a virtual uniform for factory workers. They were just as physically miserable as the other refugees but unlike most of them looked relieved and happy as well, except for the uncomprehending children.

They came here with the equipment and knew where they were going, Luz thought. *Or escaped with it by the looks, rode with it on the roads, on the railway, on the ship, and now they're all keeping company to the final destination because it's so ground into them it's automatic by now and they've all turned into a nomad clan who don't trust anyone else. There's a story there, and it's an epic by the look of it.*

"Machine tools on the big wagons," Ciara said quietly to Luz. "Turret lathes, drill presses, milling and boring machines, and the power shafts and belting for it all and a knocked-down Corliss-valve engine . . . there's the boiler shell under that sheeting. Gauges and jigs in the smaller boxes, I think, and maybe a disassembled steam forging hammer, too, under the tarpaulins. Very capable equipment, you could make a lot with it."

"Make what?" Luz asked.

Ciara gave her a baffled look that Luz had come to recognize; it meant she'd just asked a question that revealed she didn't even know enough to ask the right questions.

"Well . . . anything, darling. Lots of . . . anything. That's everything you'd need for a fair-sized jobbing engineering shop, one big enough to make . . . oh, a locomotive or whatever. And to duplicate all its own equipment. That's if you had a foundry too for castings, but a foundry's mostly a cupola furnace and some masonry and sand-molding work. The complicated stuff there is—"

She tapped her forehead and made a gesture with her hands, indicating that it was in the memories stored in the minds and muscles of the workers. Luz remembered that Ciara had mentioned *visiting* her brother when he was working on repairs to machinery in a foundry in Milford near Boston and that she'd *looked at* what they did there.

Those words from Ciara Whelan meant *memorized everything she saw* and *put hands on anything she could wheedle them into letting her touch.*

"And you could use that gear to build specialized machines for mass-production lines," she finished. "It's tools to make tools."

Luz nodded grimly. "Our friend the corporal was right to be

skeptical. I don't think those . . . two generals whose faces we saw on the poster . . . expect frogs to grow hair either. This load's probably from someplace like Schneider-Creusot."

One of the soldiers looked at her for an instant in surprise, and Luz quietly cursed herself for naming the famous armaments and heavy-industry firm. It wasn't as odd for a woman to mention it as it would have been before the war, but the French names interrupted the flow of a Spanish sentence. She made a note to be more careful and continued:

"And the people are the workers and their families. Probably they're running all the factories they still hold until the last moment, then stripping everything they can and shipping the labor and machines here to the National Redoubt as soon as the German shells start landing within a kilometer or two."

"*Could* they do that?" Ciara asked, numbers flickering behind her eyes.

"Some of it, obviously. A lot of the other refugees we've seen are peasants. Some with the basics of their farming gear. Next season's wheat and barley has already been planted by the local farmers here, but who's going to be around to bring in the harvest come next May is a different matter. The French are relocating their whole country across the Mediterranean, or as much of it as they can. It's . . . impressive, especially for a quick-and-dirty improvisation. Probably the leaders just told their local commanders and the departmental prefects what they wanted done and left them to get on with it—messy compared to detailed planning, but it can work if you care more about speed than wastage."

And they're kicking the previous inhabitants out of the way to make room and killing anyone who resists. That's an old, old story in every time and clime, over and over again; older than America, older than the Old Testament.

"*Salus populi suprema lex esto,*" she murmured, then translated: "The good of the people is above all law."

They turned off the broad Avenue de France—a French colonial civil engineer planning a city could be absolutely relied upon to put one of *those* anywhere he worked—and right again onto a relatively quiet side street lined with newish buildings in a densely packed southern European style reminiscent of the recent quarters of Barcelona or

Nice. People there had enough room to get out of the way of a truck full of soldiers with automatic weapons, at the sound of the horn and vigorous verbal encouragement and waving gun muzzles. They looked to be mostly local French settlers or at least Frenchified Italian and Spanish ones anyway, from their dress and demeanor.

"Voilà!" the corporal said as he halted the truck, as proudly as if he'd built the place himself. "Le Grand Hôtel de France!"

They hadn't made much better time than an ordinary walking pace over the same distance, but Luz was profoundly glad they'd done it in a motor truck, and with armed . . . heavily armed . . . guards.

Cheap at the price, she thought. *Very cheap, even if it wasn't Uncle Sam's cash. It's dangerous here, and getting worse fast.*

The hotel's five stories loomed over them in a bulk of cream-colored stucco decorated in a vaguely Art Nouveau–Moorish style; the main train station was a block farther north, and the harbor only a little farther east, with the old Arab town about the same distance westward. They wouldn't be here more than a day or two unless things went badly wrong, but it was time and more than time to be careful about possible bolt-holes. They had several sets of French identity papers for several different identities, and given how . . .

"Masivamente jodido" *about sums it up*, Luz thought.

. . . things were here it wouldn't be hard to walk two blocks and blend in to the ongoing chaos if they had to run for it. Luz could fit in perfectly, and Ciara could be of Breton or Norman or Alsatian stock without much of a stretch.

"Erwan, Jean, Henri—give the fine ladies a hand, you ignorant peasant *salauds!*"

The hotel had its own security. Two soldiers in khaki with white covers on their kepis that had flaps to cover the neck and broad blue sashes underneath their equipment belts stood on either side of the entrance. One was dark, one fair, both tanned to the consistency of old leather apart from the white marks of scars and both wore full beards. They had the latest Meunier semi-auto rifles, and they ignored the regulars with lofty disdain as Erwan, Henri, and Jean dropped the luggage before the door. The Legionnaires were probably the reason there wasn't anyone lingering around the building with *Grand Hôtel de*

France on the sign above it in the hope of begging or stealing something, and their eyes moved ceaselessly down the street and along the rooflines.

Picking up a little drinking money by working while they're off-duty, Luz thought.

Which was an old tradition with their corps; before the war the French Foreign Legion's daily pay had been a princely *five* centimes, which made one whole sou … and *not worth a sou* had been a French proverb for *worthless* for a long time, like *one red cent* in English. You didn't actually have to be suicidal or on the run from the law to join the Legion, but you did have to be very thoroughly out of better choices.

These two looked as if they'd been chasing Tuareg through the Sahara and fighting Berbers in the High Atlas or wading through the jungles of Indochina looking for Can Vuong guerillas for years before Archduke Ferdinand ignored one last piece of good advice and took his trip to Sarajevo. The Legion had turned out to not be such a bad choice of career for them after all, since they were alive when tens of millions of cautious stay-at-homes weren't.

She shook hands with the driver as he sat behind the wheel; he transferred the coins in her palm to his pocket gracefully and without exposing the glint of gold to the inquisitive, but his eyes went a little wider as his nimble fingers counted the extra one.

"In case you must make a little gift to someone to smooth things over about your blocked fuel line," she said quietly. "And because none of us will see *Ménil'muche* again, not as it was, and I learned some very interesting things there. May luck ride on your dice, Corporal, and drink a toast to the *gars* of the 20th arrondissement for me; also to *les minettes.*"

"A pleasure, miss," he said soberly, a faraway look in his eyes for a moment, something different from the feral wariness they usually showed.

He and his squad bundled back into the truck and left without further ado, anxious not to have more time than they must to blame on the conveniently troublesome fuel line. Luz looked at the tall arched door and its intimidating guardians and whistled a snatch of a slow rhythmic tune, then spoke casually with her eyes on nothing in particular, while rolling a silver one-franc coin across her knuckles:

"Ils sont les dégourdis, et peut-être les lascars aussi! Mais jamais des types ordinaires."

The faces of the Legionnaires remained impassive, but she thought she saw the hint of a smile in their eyes, and the fair one turned his head to shout in rough Slavic-accented French that substituted *a* for *o*, mangled *r*-sounds, and was laden with a deadly contempt besides:

"Sartez ici, petites andouilles, mes mignans, petites tireurs au cul! C'est sur, nous sammes ici."

Two men in badly fitting hotel livery scurried out to take the baggage at the assurance that it was safe because the Legionnaires were there . . . which it was, except that it wasn't safe from the Legionnaires themselves. Who'd just called them thick, dim, cute little shirkers fit only to shoot themselves in the ass. Luz stepped closer, and the coin slipped into the hand of the black-bearded soldier.

Gold would have been suspiciously excessive here. She'd bribed the corporal with the truck heavily, to take five men off-base with a valuable vehicle during a high-alert emergency. This was just a *pourboire* to smooth things a little . . . though at two days' pay for each, a generous one.

Both the bellhops were middle-aged European French, and from their looks they'd been provincial bourgeois town dwellers until recently, solid respectable fathers of families, and still couldn't quite grasp that they were abjectly thankful to have servants' work in a colonial hotel. And thankful enough for the two ten-centime bronze coins she bestowed, a regular tip this time.

They glanced sidelong at the Legionnaires out of the corners of their eyes as they picked up the trunk and the bags and hatboxes, rather the way cats would at a pair of large, unfamiliar dogs on the other side of a screen door.

Luz and Ciara stepped through the hotel's busy lobby, all cool white-and-blue tile and horseshoe arches on columns with gilt tops, while a doorman in a uniform with more gold braid than a field marshal bowed them forward toward the desk . . . though usually he'd have been outside himself.

Ciara leaned closer as they waited in line again. "Darling, what did you call the soldiers at the door?"

"*Dégourdis, et peut-être les lascars,*" Luz said, smiling. "Clever rascals, or possibly cunning thieves. *Mais jamais des types ordinaires*; but never ordinary respectable folk."

"I thought so, but . . . you insulted them? Why did that make them so helpful?"

Luz laughed, and whistled the tune again.

"That's 'The Blood Sausage,' the Legion's marching song. And those words are in the lyrics, which they made up themselves. I was showing I knew their history, sweetie, which is a compliment to a Legionnaire's way of looking at things. Donating a franc to their inebriation fund helped too, but showing respect for their true homeland—"

"Homeland?" Ciara said, puzzled.

"*Legio Patria Nostra*; the Legion is our Fatherland. That did just as much to put them in a friendlier frame of mind as the money. Not that they'd be safe company if you were alone with them. Not at all. They have the only honest recruiting slogan in the history of armies, after all."

At Ciara's look, she quoted a Legion commander's well-known words, ones inscribed later above the depot in Marseilles: "*You legionnaires are soldiers in order to die, and I am sending you where you can die.* It doesn't attract . . . *des types ordinaires.*"

She looked past the desk to the courtyard, which was full of an affluent but frazzled and rumpled crowd milling about, too many of them for the seats and tables.

"Let's hope our reservation holds. I have a feeling that Tunis isn't a safe place for us . . . Chilean feminists . . . to linger."

L uz sat on the edge of the bed and dried her hair contentedly on a large, fluffy towel. One of the many advantages of the Polaire bob was that it dried out much faster than the style—long enough to sit on—she'd had to wear for most of her life after she turned twelve.

And *it doesn't get caught in things as much*, she thought. *Mima would never let me just braid it once I was in my teens, either, she said that was common.*

The Grand Hôtel de France was rather recent, and while not quite as luxe as the very best European or American establishments, it had several water closets on every floor and bathrooms with big enameled tubs and hot water. The shower-baths with hand nozzles on ANA's airships were as progressive and modern as next week and quite satisfactory when it came to keeping you clean, but just not the same as a soak.

Though speaking of satisfying . . . she thought. *I doubt the engineers who designed the hand nozzles were thinking of the uses my darling found for them. There are unforeseen advantages to having a lover with engineering expertise!*

Their room was pale and high-ceilinged, with a marble fireplace, an overhead fan not working right now, and an interior balcony behind folding doors that looked down on the leafy plantings and umbrella-studded tables of the hotel's courtyard. That it was on the fifth floor and the elevators weren't working was acceptable if you were young and fit . . . and she suspected that no amount of inconspicuous bribery would have made "M. Ferrier (propriétaire)" honor the quite genuine reservations made falsely by wire in the name of the Chilean feminists if they insisted on a room lower down.

Ferrier was elderly, shrewd, and looking to his family's future if her guess was right. That meant that the hotel was stuffed with influential people or the metropolitan relatives of people who he thought *would* be influential soon in the still embryonic structure of the National Redoubt of Overseas France, after things settled down a bit. Even hard currency couldn't always buy you that sort of insurance.

"What is it, *mi corazón?*" she said gently.

Ciara was also in a robe, and her hair was dampened to a darker red than the usual fiery half-golden blaze, spread over her shoulders and back to dry. Her mood seemed to be likewise subdued, and she wasn't really reading the book on wireless transmissions she held in her lap.

"Luz . . ." she began. Then: "Luz, I keep remembering those poor people the Negro soldiers were driving out of the city. They're going to starve, aren't they? Like . . . like what the English did to our ancestors in Cromwell's time, driving them out to *hell or Connaught.* I know the Germans are doing more and worse, but . . . these are our allies. It makes me feel . . . sort of bad. Guilty."

Luz put aside the comb and went to sit in the chair across from hers, taking the younger woman's hands.

"*Mi corazón*," she said, meeting the troubled turquoise eyes. "No, it isn't like Cromwell or the famine, though it was ugly enough."

Even the actual famine hadn't been as simple as the Fenian mythology of English wickedness tormenting Irish helplessness either, but Ciara didn't need a lecture culled from the Bryn Mawr history faculty's demonstrations of the way incompetence and ignorance were more common than malice and conspiracy. Best keep to the simple truth, which worked even from a perspective formed by Irish Nationalist visions.

"The English were the strongest, richest nation on Earth then, and at peace; it was their responsibility to help when the potatoes failed. The French are losing a war now, and are beaten and desperate and starving themselves. They've died by the *millions* this year, civilians and soldiers both; they're dying by the thousands every *day*; and God knows how many millions more have been plundered bare and driven from their homes in winter and are a week's food or another bit of bad luck away from death by cold and hunger and the plagues that come with it and with sleeping in ditches and haymows."

"Well . . . that's so," Ciara said. "But do they have to do this?"

"It's this or submit to the Germans . . . but I suspect the Germans want them dead anyway, or most of them, to make an end of any threat of vengeance by their children or grandchildren."

"The way the Turks have with the Armenians?"

"Close enough. And they've got a way, if famine and plague aren't enough, that doesn't involve doing it face-to-face."

"The Germans haven't been using the horror-gas since . . . since Paris and London, though."

"They haven't been bombing cities with it or using it on the battlefield in France, because we captured two hundred tons of it from the U-boats in Boston and New York and the other harbors the same day they bombed London and Paris—which was our doing, you and I. And we've told them through secret channels that if they use it that way we'll send it right back at them."

"Oh. And we'll be making our own soon, too. It's a . . . what do they call it . . ."

"Mexican standoff. But," Luz said with a prompt in her voice.

"But—" Ciara's brows knotted in thought. "But that's *us*. We can retaliate in kind, and if both sides have a weapon there's no defense against, it's a lot less likely to be used."

Luz nodded; Ciara was rarely slow on the uptake. She went on:

"Right. But behind their own lines . . . you could spray that *cosa horrible* on whole countries from the air, town by town, village by village, and farm by farm, and then when it washed away you'd have an empty wilderness to settle, but with the roads built and the fields cleared and the houses ready."

Once you'd sent in cleanup teams to bury the bones, she didn't say.

Though you'd have to be careful about decontaminating cellars and such.

You could use prisoners for that, and then shoot them *too*.

"Couldn't *we* take them in, like those English we saw in Los Angeles?"

Luz sighed regretfully. "No, not this many . . . not nearly this many; the ships would have to travel so much farther, exposed to the U-boats. There's no *time*. France isn't going to hold that long, not unless those frogs get hairy."

Ciara nodded unwillingly, obviously doing the numbers in her head; there was a huge difference between one trip in two weeks and three trips in one week that couldn't be wished away, any more than two-plus-two could; and the shorter trips could carry four times as many people per voyage tight-packed, many in vessels that couldn't cross the Atlantic in any case. She was naturally much better at math than Luz anyway, and numbers were instinctively real to her soul in a way that Luz had had to learn by hard effort. Luz went on:

"The generals and politicians could get to America, maybe, and some of the very rich . . . but they're getting out as many ordinary people as they can instead."

"Well, *that's* to their credit," Ciara said, a little unwillingly; she had radical reflexes.

"It is," Luz said, and thought:

And to be sure, it also means the generals get to stay big . . . frogs, shall we say . . . in their new pond here in the National Redoubt; but still, it is brave of them. Because it means staying nearer to the Germans. Who's to say they won't find some means of getting the horror-gas here *sooner or later? And here they can govern themselves and stay French . . . not in the old way, but in one way or another.*

"And there's not enough room here for all?" Ciara said with a sigh.

"No, there isn't," Luz said flatly.

Which was true; simply not enough farmland between the sea and the Sahara to feed the influx and the locals both, even with the most careful rationing, and not enough surplus anywhere else or enough shipping to carry it here past the U-boat packs if there had been. If the movement was anything as big and rapid as she thought, there still wouldn't be enough when the local harvest came in . . . and it wasn't as if you could wait six months to eat anyway. The Germans would be reaping whatever crops there were in mainland France next year.

"Some problems don't have solutions. Or no good ones, at least."

"The Great War . . . it's a Moloch, devouring the world," Ciara said sadly.

Luz nodded. "Truer words were never said, *querida*," she said. "And they worshipped Moloch here when it was Carthage."

And sacrificed their children to him in the red-hot brazen belly of the idol . . . and Rome slaughtered the Carthaginians and sowed Carthage with salt. So have things changed all that much?

"And if someone's going to starve no matter what you do, you keep what there is for your own folk and your own kin and your own children, don't you?"

"I suppose so," Ciara said. "It would be a strange breed who didn't put their own children and their own folk first, and I wouldn't want to meet them."

She frowned in thought. "All those French people looked . . . well, like they'd lost everything."

"They have." Luz nodded. "Everyone has a right . . . and a duty . . . to be on their own side."

"Well . . . yes," Ciara said, after a moment's thought.

It was refreshing to be with someone who not only had native wit but actually *used* it even when her feelings were involved. Too many smart people simply treated their abilities as a way to think up better reasons to *not* change an opinion once they'd grabbed on to it.

"It's happened before," Luz said.

"It has?"

"Something very like it. Back a long time ago, in Roman times, the Huns beat the East Goths in what's now Russia. The survivors fled the Huns and fell on their neighbors to the west, the people they hit moved, and then the people *they* hit moved . . ."

"Sounds like billiards!" Ciara said, startled.

"It was, and it finished with Vandals from Poland trekking all the way across Europe and crossing from Spain to Morocco and then cutting and burning their way east again until they ended up right here in Tunisia! Folk died, by the sword and by hunger and by plague all across Europe and North Africa, and farms and villages and cities burned at the hands of desperate famished warriors storming out of nowhere, all because of a battle on the banks of the Dniester between two tribes nobody else had ever heard of before."

She tapped her bare foot on the tile floor. "This is the same . . . and once again it's all the Huns' fault. Nobody made them invade France because a Serb killed an Austrian, or drop horror-gas on Paris and London and Bordeaux, or try to destroy New York and Boston and the others."

"Yes . . . yes, you're right, my love. Still . . . I feel sorry for the people here."

"So do I, *querida*," Luz said, and added to herself: *truthfully enough.*

Though she wouldn't lose any sleep over things she couldn't affect happening to strangers outside the bounds of kin and country and oath—whether they were French or Tunisian or for that matter Siamese or from the mountains of Peru. Her loyalties were she-wolf fierce, but just as tightly held. The important thing about your own pack or tribe or barrio was that it *was* your own, as your comrades and your loves were.

Uncle Teddy is my clan chief and war chief, the lord I've given my oath to as they said in the old days; America is the land of my folk, where I was born; and the Chamber is the pack I run with. And Ciara is the darling of my heart and the mate I'll share a life and home and make a family with, if we're spared by mala fortuna.

Aloud: "They didn't ask to be caught in the gears; but neither did that corporal who drove us here who'll never see his home in Paris again, or those factory workers we saw on the wagons, or those French peasants on the streets outside who've lost their little farms forever and the churchyards where their ancestors were buried for a thousand years. What we do, you and I, is make sure that it isn't *Americans* who lie starving on some roadside somewhere with their children dead beside them."

Ciara sighed and nodded and sank down beside Luz, who put an arm around her shoulders.

"And if we're going to fight the Germans, we need every ally we can get, I suppose." Ciara sighed again. "It's a hard bit of history we're caught up in, though, my darling, and that's a fact, and I'm glad I have you to hold me while I sleep."

"No dispute, *querida*. Let's get some of that sleep; we'll be dealing with the Società Nazionale Servizi Marittimi tomorrow to get passage to Naples, and that will take all our strength!"

She rose and extended a hand. "Come. You need to be held so you *can* sleep . . . and so do I."

NINE

G ood day, Fräuleins," the customs inspector said.
The interior of the customs station at the border crossing between Switzerland and Baden-Württemberg looked bigger than it was
because there were so few people in it, and it was perishing *cold* anyway, with that dank, dark penetrating North European winter evening
chill that Luz had always detested with a cat's loathing. Evidently the
Germans still weren't wasting coal on heating, however great their recent victories. The chill had a sad, tired scent to it too, though that
might be her imagination.

"Papers, please. Baggage over there."

Luz hid a reminiscent smile hearing him speak in a Bavarian dialect. It always reminded her of her girlhood, and he'd just said *do drüm*
for *over there.*

She tipped the porters a few pfennigs for putting the trunk up on
the table. Neither of them was actually a German at all; she'd have said
Polish, or even Russians from the way they mutilated *danke, gnädige
Frau* by rote and doffed their shapeless caps and bowed, and also from
the fact that they were young men and not crippled and yet not in uniform, if you didn't count some bundled-up rags that might be Russian
khaki. Besides their ragged clothes and grime both looked hungry and
underweight, too, but then most people in Germany did two and a half
years into the Great War, unless they were in the military, were

black-marketeers, were very rich, or were among the considerable minority who grew nearly all their own food.

"Open the trunk and the hand luggage and hatboxes for examination, if you please."

When a German bureaucrat said "please" like that, the temperature always seemed to drop several degrees all on its own and you felt
an unspoken barked-out *sofort*, a word that meant *immediately* with over-
tones of *or else* if used by a functionary or superior.

A little before the war a seedy down-and-out grifter named Voigt
who'd dressed up in a second-hand Army officer's uniform from a
pawnshop had commandeered an entire town in Prussia, thrown the
mayor in jail, and absconded with the municipal funds, and had gotten
away with it until he switched to civilian gear because it simply hadn't
occurred to anyone to disobey or question him . . .

"Your destination within the empire and the purpose of your visit,
please," the inspector said, going over their passports and visas and
making a note of everything on a form.

"Yes, Mr. Officially, traveling Berlin-like we will be," Ciara said in
her rather eccentric German, and smiled at the customs officer as his
face went blank, his eyes narrowed in thought, and his lips moved, trying to parse what she'd just said after he worked his way through the
accent to the syntax.

*She may have been exaggerating it a bit or saying the first thing in her head,
like that Irish writer who wrote* The Dubliners *has his characters do. Her German isn't quite* that bad anymore. *Though Customs men hear every way of
butchering their native tongue imaginable.*

The German official was middle-aged, was built like a fireplug, had
a face like a suspicious squint-eyed boot, wore an odd uniform that
included a leather shako with a bill, and looked as if he'd rarely smiled
since puberty himself.

*Except possibly at things like watching a cripple fall under a train. But even
so he's a bit staggered by my* querida's *turquoise eyes and innocent charm.*

Luz's own lips turned up a little in rueful approval; her partner
wasn't acting, exactly, but she was learning to use her natural affect
under conscious direction.

She's going to be formidable if she stays in this line of work, she thought. *Not in my style, but in her own. And* scientific *espionage is certainly a promising field!*

"Education in Germany has the famous for its great advancement is in years and years been," Ciara went on.

Which remained quite true even with the extra misplaced past-tense verbs; before the war people had come from all over the world to study any number of subjects here, including thousands of Americans. Every second Progressive thinker back home had fond memories of first supping on economic historicism or Hegel at Tübingen or Jena, not to mention the technical schools, which made the present falling-out all the more bitter.

"Your methods we will study for making of our own country's great advantages and advancements to childrens and of into special girls and that is to coming across the sea to Germany from *República de Chile* we why are."

And in this case, her German is naturally *odd, which is perfect for a foreigner.*

Letting Ciara take the lead and pretending not to understand the conversation let Luz keep an eye out all around. That really wasn't necessary this time, since the only other people with them were four Italians here to buy electrical generators and a pair of nondescript types from a Swiss ball-bearing firm muttering to each other in *Schwi-izertüütsch* so thick that even someone who knew the related Bavarian form couldn't follow. But good habits kept you alive.

Ciara sounds as if she picked up German from someone whose parents were Bavarian or Upper Austrian peasants but who spoke something else most of the time, and then refined it by reading a lot of books in Hochdeutsch *... and that's the exact truth, and perfectly plausible for a third-generation member of an emi-grant colony in southern Chile, though it actually happened in South Boston. Someday I'll have to talk to her auntie Colleen and Auntie Colleen's special friend Auntie Treinel and find out how they happened to meet.*

Ciara's innocent looks and his occasional twitch of the lips at some strange construction didn't stop the customs man from examining ev-ery document carefully and opening all their baggage, but at least he didn't throw things out on the table for them to put back themselves. When he'd finished he even touched his cap and addressed them as *gnädige Fräuleins*, gracious misses, and hoped they'd enjoy their stay in Germany, while plying his rubber stamp with a will.

There was little enough for sale on the platform as the porters manhandled their baggage back, though in peacetime the boarded-up kiosk had probably dispensed coffee and the lavish pastries the locals— with good reason, as she remembered—adored. A thin insistent drizzle mixed with slush was blowing in under the overhang, but Luz managed to pick up a set of newspapers before they re-boarded their sleeper car on the overnight Lucerne-Berlin express. Newspapers were something Germany had in profusion, even in wartime; unlike most European countries but rather like the United States, the press wasn't totally dominated by the national capital.

The *Norddeutsche Allgemeine Zeitung*, the *Berliner Tageblatt*, the *Münchner Neueste Nachrichten*, and the semiofficial *Kreuzzeitung* between them would give you a fair glimpse of how the world looked through German eyes . . . or at least as much of it as Colonel Nikolai wanted German eyes to see, since Abteilung IIIb had picked up press censorship in its jackdaw's-nest of powers back in 1915. Aside from keeping up for its own sake, fairly soon they'd be impersonating Germans and you had to be able to carry on a general conversation without appearing suspiciously ignorant of what the papers were saying.

"Good work with playing that customs man, *querida*," Luz said.

They settled back into their compartment and the train gave that shrill European whistle before chuffing back into motion for the nonstop journey to Berlin, winding at modest speed through a hilly landscape of forest and narrow ribbons of pasture and scattered villages and farms. A few lights came on, dim flickers seen through the water-streaked window; it wasn't quite sundown yet, but darkness came early this time of year. Not even the most northerly parts of the continental United States . . . or the continental United States as it had been until it included Canada . . . had nights as long as this.

The weather wasn't affecting Ciara's mood as much as it was her tropically reared companion, and Ciara was smiling as she spoke:

"He was acting very gruff, but he was just an old grandpa-bear underneath, I could see that, fond of his pipe and a mug of beer and children and dogs underfoot before the fire of an evening. Maybe a canary fancier, like Auntie Treinel! There was a magazine about them on the shelf behind him. Auntie Treinel reads those."

Luz blinked as she remembered the inspector's mean piggy little eyes, but said nothing. It was certainly possible she'd gotten a bit too jaundiced about people in general; but then, secret agents working for the Black Chamber usually didn't see folk at their best. It had been very perceptive to notice the magazine, too.

The cars of the overnight train from Switzerland to Berlin still bore the Compagnie Internationale des Wagons-Lits blue-and-gold livery with the two lions on either side of an ornate letter *W*, the firm that nearly monopolized high-quality sleepers and restaurant cars on the Continent. She'd recognized that from before the war, but the ticket agent in Lucerne had said that its assets had been acquired—

For which read stolen, *more or less*, Luz thought with ironic amusement. *To the victors, the spoils.*

—by a new joint German-Austrian concern, Middle Europe Rail and Dining Cars, or Mitropa for short. They'd also been, behind a stiff reserve, very pleased to sell the two tickets. Most of Germany's railways were very crowded and very slow these days; this express was slightly less slow and not crowded at all, with the way international trade and travel had slowed with the war and then suddenly fallen off a cliff after the horror-gas bombings. They'd pick up again, but it was lucky that nobody had gotten around to cutting back trains like this yet.

Switzerland in general had reminded her of a wolverine trapped in a cave with a bear—not exactly terrified, but taking things seriously and keeping its backside to a corner while showing its teeth. Under a shell of bravado, the Italians had been in a pitiful funk, cursing their decision to desert the Central Powers in 1914 and hoping against hope that God, fate, or the United States would rescue them, or that Germany's rulers would forgive and forget . . . which was about as likely as brotherly love from a crocodile.

The Swiss hotel had done up a traveling basket for them that included a big thermos of hot chocolate, creamy and sweet. Luz unscrewed the top and poured them both a cup, a skill that took some practice on a moving train. They sat side-by-side on the fold-down bed they'd be sharing—they'd stripped the blankets off the other on the opposite side of the compartment and added them to this—and sipped gratefully. The electric light was working, but Mitropa wasn't wasting much fuel on heating their trains, and the hot liquid steamed even more than their breath. They'd both kept on their fur hats and overcoats for the same reason, hers of sealskin with a mink collar, Ciara's of lamb's-fur, both French but authentically several years old, and both well-lined. The way the metal cups heated up made them pleasant to hold and allowed them to shed their gloves.

"Let's see . . ." Luz said.

She unfolded the *Kreuzzeitung* with its Iron Cross in the center of the top line—that had given the paper its name, since it was technically the New Prussian Newspaper, the *new* referring to 1848.

"*¡Quién lo diría!* Germany has been officially renamed—it's not just the Deutsches Kaiserreich, the German Empire, anymore!"

Ciara's brows went up, and Luz read on: "It's the Großdeutsches Kaiserreich now. The Empire of Greater Germany. In celebration of the Dutch and Flemings *coming home* to their Germanic kin, not to mention a few other things picked up in the process of breaking the Iron Ring of Encirclement fastened around the blameless nation by the wicked Entente, on whom God's just punishment has fallen."

"God uses Zeppelins full of poison gas?" Ciara said; the dry tone had a little of Luz in it.

"Apparently. The *coming home* was done with a pistol stuck up the nose to ensure the new members' enthusiasm, but . . . *así son las cosas*, eh? Perhaps the Empire of Greater Germany should replace 'Hail to Thee in Victor's Crown' with a new Greater German anthem, one with a chorus that goes: 'Our Boot Is on Your Throat Today! *Hoch! Hoch!*'"

Ciara giggled and then frowned: "Isn't *Reich* the word for *empire*? *Kaiserreich* . . . Emperor's Empire? Empire of the Emperor? Emperor-ish Empire?"

"*Reich* is . . . sort of realm, empire, domain; it's got a broader meaning than *empire* does in English. *Kaiserreich* is specific, *realm ruled by an emperor*. That ought to give the All-Highest something to think about besides the loss of his British relatives, not that he actually rules much now beyond what uniform to wear on any given day and whether to have white wine or red."

Oddly enough, I believe the stories about his fainting when he heard about the British royals being killed, Luz thought as Ciara nodded the way she did when committing a new fact to memory.

He always loved and hated them at the same time and wanted them to take him seriously, starting with his grandmamma Victoria . . . no, probably with his English mother and the way she rejected him because of his damaged arm . . . the fleets of battleships and the uniforms covered in medals and the silver helmets with big golden eagles on top and those worthless colonies he spent so much blood and money on were all for that . . . but I don't think he ever really wanted them dead. A silly little man. But now he's the prisoner and puppet of the generals, and they aren't silly at all.

"And there's to be a new king of Georgia—the one in the Caucasus, not our Georgia," Luz noted dryly, reading on to the next article. "The younger son of the king of Saxony's getting the throne—Friedrich Christian of the House of Wettin. Albert Leopold *Friedrich Christian* Sylvester Anno Macarius in full."

"To be fair, sure and they're probably thankful to get him," Ciara noted. "Since the Turks are the other choice, and with what's happened . . . is happening . . . to the Armenians . . ."

Ciara shuddered with a queasy expression, and Luz nodded with a grimace, remembering photos of tumbled, naked skeletal bodies in huge windrows a mile long. She was less tender-hearted about strangers than her lover, but even by the ever-lower standards of the Great War the aftermath in the wake of the triumphant Turkish onrush across Armenia proper and toward the Caspian was grisly. Though she suspected it was just the first case of many to come.

As a matter of fact . . .

She scanned down in the *Kreuzzeitung.* A certain Birinci Ferik—which meant General—Halil had ridden his horse into the Caspian and proclaimed it all to be part of the Türk Yurdu, the exclusive national home of the Turks, and he was the uncle of Enver Pasha, Turkey's younger, better-looking version of Ludendorff.

Which probably meant nothing good for *anyone* ethnically or religiously inconvenient who was thoughtless enough to clutter up the National Home.

Pointless to dwell on that now, Luz thought, and went on a little more lightly:

"That's the ... let's see, Georgia, Finland, Courland ... the third new throne just lately. Things are moving quickly! The fourth, if you count Bernhard of Lippe—Bernhard Kasimir Wilhelm Friedrich Gustav Heinrich Eduard, *¡Dios mío!* how these *Hochadel* collect names— getting to be the new Grand Duke of Wallonia. All of them completely independent, if you don't count the treaties giving Germany permanent control of their central banks, foreign policy, tariffs, trade, railways, postal systems, telegraphs, telephones, law courts, armies, and police. Plus German military bases, and unlimited rights of transit and handing all their important mines and industries over to German cartels and nice stiff annual *contributions* to pay for the privilege of it all."

"Well, if you're going to get upset at trifles and quibble over every little thing ..." Ciara said, and they both laughed.

The only reason Germany wasn't annexing all those areas directly was because they didn't want to give them seats in the Reichstag and Bundesrat, or their residents the rights of actual *German* Germans.

Then Ciara went on, looking at her own paper: "It says here that the bread, potato, and coal rations are to be increased by one-fifth. And oh ... the headline's *Land Won by German Swords to Be Tilled by German Plows* ... it also says that after the war, all honorably discharged veterans will be able to claim a farm of one hundred hectares if they settle on it and live there ... they have to be married, too ... a hundred hectares is two hundred fifty acres, or a tiny bit less. That's for privates, more according to higher rank. They're calling it *Häuser für Helden.*"

Which meant *homes for heroes.*

"Rather like the Homestead Act after the Civil War, or our Veterans Settlement Grants in the irrigation districts now," Luz said. "They're letting ordinary people know winning doesn't just mean new thrones for the *Hochadel.*"

"Two hundred fifty acres ... that would be quite a good-sized farm in America! Bigger than most, in fact. It's very big here, isn't it?" Ciara said.

"That's . . . *huge*, by German standards," Luz said, her brows going up as she thought.

She checked and found the same announcement in the *Kreuzzeitung*. It was right after one offering German coal miners well-paid positions, free four-bedroom houses on half-acre lots, and lavish benefits as supervisors in something called the Donets Basin Coal Cartel, to be managed by the emissaries of the Oberschlesisches Kohlenkartell in the new General Government of the Ukraine. Which was a new term too, apparently now a subdivision of OberOst, the military government of the eastern territories.

She nodded and explained: "In Germany *ten* hectares is substantial and five is adequate."

"That's about the same as the grounds around your house back in Santa Barbara."

"*Our* house, but yes," Luz said, and Ciara chuckled and laid her head on her shoulder.

Luz went on: "And there are millions of German peasants scratching out a living on one or two hectares each and whatever work they can scrounge up on the side. Not to mention plenty of villagers here who've no land at all and live by day labor on others' farms, or rent a plot."

"So a hundred is wealth, then?"

"A gentleman farmer's property," she agreed.

"Someone who has hands to help in the fields and a maid in the house, putting meat on the table there every day?" Ciara asked.

"Exactly. There are Junker estates with only a little more," Luz said. "Probably a lot of peasants and their sons are feeling very happy about this, so it means . . . oh, at least tens of millions of hectares total."

She read further. "And millions of votes for the brand-new German Fatherland Party, because that's who is sponsoring the necessary legislation in the Reichstag, not that anyone would dare vote against it— even the Social Democrats aren't objecting much, what's left of them. And the Fatherland Party is the generals' creation. Well, well, well!"

"But where would they get enough land to give out to so many . . .

oh," Ciara said, biting her lip. "Didn't mean to be silly. Like Cromwell and King Billy handing out Ireland to their soldiers in truth, then."

"*¡Verdaderamente!* Very like, but on a much, much bigger scale," Luz said. "Europe is *crowded*; that's why we think a couple of acres is a big backyard for the dog and kids to run around in, and these Europeans think it's a small *farm* for a family to *live* off."

"I just hope they're counting their chickens before they're hatched . . . or before they've cut the heads off and set the stewpot boiling," Ciara said.

"Brr! I'm freezing!"

"Let's get under the covers, then," Luz said.

They hung up their day dresses and chemises and hurriedly switched into flannel pajamas and then ankle-length flannel nightshirts over those and bathrobes over all, and put on knit caps and two pair of thick wool socks each; the car might be Wagons-Lits, but it certainly wasn't being heated to prewar standards by the new owners, though doubling the blankets and cuddling close would make them comfortable enough.

"But that gruff old uncle who looked over our papers is going to follow procedure," Luz said, getting back to the immediate future as they shivered at the initial chill of the sheets and she poured more cocoa and continued: "Which means the clock is ticking now, because the German embassy in Argentina will forward a list of visa approvals we're *not* on. It won't have arrived yet and it's Wednesday by the time we arrive. The Foreign Office keeps banker's hours which means it takes them more days to process their lists. Even though we did lose three days with that storm; sometime in the next week to two weeks they'll know there's been an entry under forged papers."

Ciara frowned: "We'll be switching identities again, won't we?"

Luz nodded as the train gave that shrill European whistle once more. She was used to Continental trains, and they weren't as toylike as their British equivalents, but rail travel west of Russia always seemed a bit like kids playing with scale models to an American.

Ciara hadn't really asked a question, but Luz answered anyway: "At least once, starting as soon as we get to the safe house in Berlin, *querida*.

Well, in Spandau, Siemensstadt in particular. But Abteilung IIIb are going to realize there are ringers loose and that it's two women of roughly our descriptions, unless they're careless. And if there's one thing Germans aren't, it's careless about details. Bells will go off."

Ciara smiled gamely. "You always say they're the worst spies in the world."

"They are—when they're dealing with foreigners on foreign ground. At home, not so much . . . and they'll be looking for our faces. Are you hungry?"

"Starved! The boiler needs fuel in this cold!"

Fortunately the same wartime decline in standards that made the compartment so chilly gave them a perfect excuse for avoiding the watery soup and potato-starch bread of the dining car and keeping out of view at the same time; every passenger who could had bought food in Switzerland, where they weren't rationing it . . . much . . . yet . . . and if you could afford high prices you could get something edible without being plugged into the black market.

In the way of business Luz had lived on varieties of loathsome swill from time to time—she'd crossed the Atlantic on a German U-boat, for example, which had been rather like being locked in a Chamber softening-up cell in the Black Palace at Lecumberri, only colder and wetter—and had endured plain boring fodder like Army rations and stale tortillas with dubious *refritos* for rather longer ones, but she saw no reason to do so when she didn't have to.

"We won't have to go out much, will we?" Ciara said. "Until we've gotten the information we need and then leave."

"Until *you've* gotten the information, probably, *mi corazón*! Yes, if we're lucky and everything goes exactly according to plan," Luz said. "Which in my experience it never does. Let's eat."

Ciara grinned as she opened the basket the Grand Hôtel National had packed for them and they shook out the napkins, tucking them into the collars of their nightgowns with the blankets rucked up around them.

"This is like a picnic!" she said. "Da and Colm and I and the aunties used to picnic on the Common in Boston sometimes—the Fourth, and sometimes St. Patrick's Day if the weather was good that spring. And even a bright March day in Boston can be near as chilly as this, so we'd bring blankets."

Well, apart from the risk of torture and death, verdaderamente, *it is like a picnic,* Luz thought, and grinned back. ¡Dios mío! *But this* is *better than doing it alone . . . is that selfish of me?*

"Reminds me a bit of Bryn Mawr," Luz said.

The weather did too, but traveling through it was harder than just scurrying from building to building or an occasional excursion to skate on ponds or toboggan down hills.

"Sometimes friends would get together in each other's dormitory rooms in Denbigh Hall and sit up with biscuits and cocoa and talk the hours away and solve all the world's problems."

"That must have been nice," Ciara said wistfully.

Ciara's self-education had been better academically than what she'd have gotten at school—for one thing, nobody had been around to shame or mock her out of pursuing her technical interests, and Aunties Colleen and Treinel had helped her quite intensively, being an off-book accountant and certified high school teacher respectively—but she had missed the social side.

"I used to read stories about girls in schools and places like that, with friends and fun and adventures."

"And you'll have just as much fun at Stanford after the war," Luz said. "With better weather. You *should* have classroom friends, and go to musical evenings and parties and dances, and cheer yourself hoarse at the Stanford-Berkeley football games—"

"Waving one of those silly little triangle flags?"

"Exactly! And play tennis *y todo ese tipo de cosas.* I'll do a few courses too, to keep you company. My spoken Japanese is fair if very rustic and I know the kanji script, and there are some courses on Japanese literature I've always wished I had time for. I can understand just enough of the *Heike Monogatari* to tantalize."

"That'll be wonderful! But this . . . this is like our own little moving cocoon, too."

They leaned their heads together quietly for a moment, and then began unpacking the basket. There was a loaf of *Zopf,* braided wheat bread with a golden crust brushed with egg yolk before it was baked, cut and buttered for them and in a neatly folded waxed paper bundle sealed with a ribbon. Luz took a bite and smiled.

"We used to have this every Sunday morning at the *Reichsgräfin*'s school," she said reminiscently. "With cocoa like this, too, and jam, like a finishing-school sacrament after Mass in church."

You went to Mass fasting, of course, something they'd both been brought up to do.

"It looks like that Jewish bread . . . what's it called . . ."

"Challah," Luz said.

"That's it! I've had that a few times. Mmmm! The crust is so crisp, and it's so buttery and smooth!"

The supplies inside the basket included *Bierschinken*, a cold sausage of pickled pork, bacon, and spices with small chunks of smoked ham embedded in it, two cheeses—hard tart mouth-puckering Berner Alp-käse and soothing, creamy Vacherin Mont d'Or—and a variety of pick-les and hard-boiled eggs and the like and some Italian olives. And *Kartoffelsalat*. American ideas of potato salad were to this as a paint-by-numbers kit was to the *Mona Lisa*, because these Central Europeans really knew how to handle the humble spud; for starters, the potatoes were cooked in broth rather than water, and it went on from there.

They had a bottle of a very nice red Salgesch to go with it, and then they finished by feeding each other pieces of *Bündner Birnbrot*, a pastry bread filled with chopped dried pears, raisins, nuts, plums, and figs all marinated in pear schnapps, spiced with coriander, cinnamon, star anise, anise seed, and cloves. Fairly soon the bites were inter-spersed with kisses, which went on after the dessert was gone.

"Oh! That makes me feel all lovely and swoony," Ciara said dream-ily, as Luz nibbled an earlobe. "Like a wonderful tingly tickle *all over.*"

"It's nice to be appreciated," Luz murmured. "Now, some toe-nibbling . . ."

Then there was a giggle and Luz felt a soft touch on the soles of her feet through the thick wool:

"But you can't *find* my toes, all bundled up this way."

"Oh, I think I can, *querida*," Luz said with a promise in her voice, slowly sinking down beneath the blankets.

"But in the dark I'll have to do a lot of exploring," she added.

And did.

Much later they lay curled together in darkness in the warm nest of blankets, listening to the *clack-clack . . . clack-clack . . .* as the train swayed through the cold night.

"It's like you're purring again, Luz!" Ciara whispered.

"You have that effect on me," Luz said. "Especially when you do certain things. *I* feel like a floating wisp of cloud now. *¡Dios mío!*"

After a pleasant silence Ciara shifted and said: "Luz . . ."

"Mmmmmh?" Luz said against the back of her neck; the tone had been serious.

"Luz, do you ever wonder what happened to Horst? After he hit me with the pistol and you shot him. I don't remember much of that at all."

"Mmmmh," Luz said, shivering slightly.

Ciara had been the one who turned the IRB men and Germans against each other, but she'd been mostly half-conscious at best during the shoot-out in the warehouse and the pursuit through the streets of Boston with Horst and the sailors from the U-150 firing machine guns at them. Though she'd been awake enough to throw up in the backseat of the Ford Guvvie Luz had been driving.

Concussions did that to you, and getting pistol-whipped across the side of the head by a man as strong as Horst von Dückler was no joke even if she'd been dodging at the time. Though it was probably for the best that her memories were mercifully blurred; a lot of people had ended up dead in the warehouse, some Germans, more just South Boston types misguided enough to get involved with the Irish Republican Brotherhood.

Though to be fair, not even Sean McDuffy realized until the last minute that their German friends intended to destroy Boston and their homes and kill their families, not just attack the Navy Yard, Luz thought. *And he'd have fought, if Horst hadn't shot him the moment he started to hesitate.*

Luz had done much of the killing before the Germans realized how they'd been played and chased her out into the night, firing Lewis guns from their trucks . . . one of which had been on fire. Horst had been limp at the end as his men dragged him to their surviving truck and fled, too, and though it had been dark and some distance away she thought . . .

Certainly he was badly wounded, I got him twice and one of those was in the face; possibly he was dying, but I won't count on it. He's a man with his life nailed tight to his backbone, as Uncle Teddy's beloved frontiersmen used to say.

Despite the best efforts of the Black Chamber, the FBS, the military, various local police forces up and down the East Coast, and everyone else down to and including the Scouts, they'd never found a trace of them *besides* that Ford motor-truck, abandoned in southern Pennsylvania. Which actually *had* been found by a patrol of Boy Scouts. They might still be hiding out somewhere, but Luz's working assumption was that they'd made a pickup appointment with a U-boat and had been back in Europe by the time she and Ciara arrived in Santa Barbara.

It just wasn't possible to keep a close watch on that much coastline. She said—honestly—after a long moment of thought:

"I hope Horst is dead, *querida*. I hope that very, very much. I doubt he is, but *con optimismo* . . . there's that word again . . . that's just pessimism."

"Do you hate him so?" she asked. "He always frightened me. Like . . . like a bomb. You didn't know when he was going to go off."

And you were jealous, though at the time you didn't realize it yourself, Luz thought; sensing that had been one thing that convinced her Ciara wanted her, even if she didn't know it yet.

"No . . . no, I don't hate him, precisely," Luz said. "I'm not *happy* that he hit you. Or that he told me . . . well, told Elisa Carmody, really . . . to shoot you because you'd become inconvenient to him. I was very angry at the time, killing angry. But that was really just . . . work."

Horst and I are both as ruthless as we must be, when we must be, for our countries, she thought. *Ciara knows that, but she doesn't like to dwell on it, I think. You don't have to dislike someone to want them dead, though that makes it more fun. It just has to be necessary for . . . work.*

"I'm pretty sure he hates *me* now; I was playing him, after all, and that's always very annoying on the receiving end, *si solo un poco*. And men . . . the way they get when you've wounded their pride . . . well . . ."

She shrugged. "But I respect him, respect his *abilities*, a great deal, and *that's* why I hope he died. He's far too able an enemy. If he's still alive, he's doing *something*, I'm sure of that, and he'll move heaven and earth to get on our trail again. I very much hope we never see him again . . . but I wouldn't bet on it."

TEN

Warsaw
Kaiserliches Deutsches Generalgouvernement Polen (Imperial German Government-
General of Poland)
Großdeutsches Kaiserreich (Empire of Greater Germany)
DECEMBER 1ST, 1916(B)

Even the world's weather seemed to be conspiring to afflict the world, first with drenching rain at harvest time and then redoubled record cold just when fuel was in dire short supply everywhere. It was drier inside Warsaw's Royal Castle than it was outside, but not much warmer, and it smelled cold and of damp walls.

Hochwohlgeboren Hauptmann Horst Julius Albrecht Freiherr von Dückler—High and Well-Born Captain Horst Julius Albrecht, Baron von Dückler—wasn't happy as he looked at the Russian automatic rifle on its stand in the center of the table and listened to everyone else at the meeting argue, despite thinking highly of the weapon. He felt every one of his twenty-nine years, and about twice as many more besides.

At least we've got the electricity working reliably, he thought. *I doubt the Russians ever did.*

The chandelier overhead cast a puddle of brightness on the steel, leaving the eyes of the humans glinting through shadow and highlighting their faces like the brutal South Sea masks in some museum. It had been only two months or so since the murderous fiasco in Boston, but he was off the morphine now, and thanks be to Almighty Lord God and the mercy of His Mother there hadn't been any serious infection in

the ruined socket of his left eye even in a return journey in the filthy
stinking crowded prison that a U-boat inevitably was.

But there was still a deep ache, and worse ones of the spirit. Having
to chair a committee on whether a new weapon got production priority
wasn't helping at all.

"We must have it!" Hauptmann Röhm said from across the expanse
of mahogany, not for the first time.

I suppose even rear echelon work keeps me from thinking too much, Horst
mused.

Röhm pointed to the gunmetal gleam of the Fedorov Avtomat rifle
with his left forefinger and slammed his right fist into the solid wood of
the table.

"I have sixteen experienced *Stoßtruppen* here with me for the tests,
and we all concur. We must *have* it!"

"It's not as simple as that, Hauptmann Röhm," said von Dorn, the
pale thin man with the carmine collar tabs and stripe down his breeches
that marked the General Staff.

The staff captain spoke impeccable aristocratic *Hochdeutsch* with a
Holsteiner accent and he didn't *quite* add: *you ranting Bavarian peasant
clown*, though his face and tone made it clear.

Horst sighed and lit a cigarette as he listened to the stormtrooper
and the General Staff officer argue, enjoying the mellow bite. At least
reasonable Turkish and Bulgarian tobacco was finally getting through
in quantity, which was almost as important for morale as food.

Particularly my *morale. Perhaps I could take up one of these land grants
they're talking about after the war. Somewhere far away from everything . . . the
Crimea, say.*

All his father's sons had the title of *Freiherr,* baron, but the rich Silesian lands not far from here would go to Horst's eldest brother, Karl,
and his children—he and Elke already had three healthy boys.

I've changed too much to be comfortable at home in the Schloss. *There's too
much I can't say. A thousand hectares for a captain . . . a very nice little chunk of
the world, off somewhere quiet and warm, with a view of the ocean and plenty of
sunshine. After that* Vermasseln *in Boston . . .*

He wasn't sure if he wanted to get leave to go home for the

holidays, either, despite the palpable and universal air of gloom as cold and hunger and disease stalked the occupied city. Though the Jews were still glad to be under civilized German control after the unspeakable Russians and their pogroms and death-march deportations.

"And we must have it now!" Röhm barked. "No more delays for further study! No more whining about logistical difficulties! We *Frontschweine* are sick of that pack of excuses!"

The ugly facial scars the man had picked up leading a company at Verdun in the spring went with his squat muscular build and dark coloring to make Ernst Röhm look exactly what he was: a murderous killer with the personality of a cannibal troll from the old sagas. The fact that he was also a fairy, a *Schwuchtel*, didn't matter much to Horst, apart from a personal revulsion; Röhm was one of the hard mean type of arse-bandit, not a poof. You used what was at hand to work for the Fatherland.

The General Staff man sniffed disdainfully at the Bavarian officer's coarse bluster.

Röhm was right about the weapon, but he was in danger of sabotaging his own argument by sheer bloody-mindedness. Nobody here was an *Etappenschweine*, a rear-echelon pig, and even the lone civilian in the room had seen action earlier in the war. There was probably some resentment of the *Adelborn* on the ugly scarfaced man's part too.

Not that I'm so handsome anymore, Horst thought with detachment.

Before the loss of his eye he'd looked much like his distant relative Manfred von Richthofen, the newly famous fighting-scout pilot they had started to call the Red Baron.

But plenty of women like scars, and I can still get the job done. I'd rather command a company or battalion at the front; you don't need looks for that, or both eyes either.

The civilian among the officers was a sleek sallow dark-eyed young man of Horst's own age, in a natty dark suit and wing collar and a pair of beautifully made shoes that didn't help with a bad limp. He was named Grunstein, and wore his astrakhan-collared overcoat buttoned up against the cold and his gloved hands thrust into his pockets.

"Herr Hauptmann?" he said, which was almost his first comment, and one made looking at Horst. "I would be interested in your opinion."

Grunstein was a troubleshooter for the Abteilung für Kriegsrohstoffe und Industrielle Gleichschaltung, the War Raw Materials and Industrial Coordination Department, a huge new bureaucratic fiefdom of its own under that other clever Jew, Walther Rathenau.

"It's a formidable weapon, that's not in dispute," Horst said, and everyone fell silent immediately, for a wonder, perhaps because he didn't gabble as much as the others. "And reasonably serviceable. Not perfect in the way a time-tested model might be, since it is designed to fill an entirely new tactical *concept*. It will have weaknesses only combat service can reveal. But unlike some *perfect* weapons it is available now rather than an eternally receding date two years in the future."

Röhm laughed aloud at that, and the General Staff man winced slightly.

The Fedorov Avtomat machine carbine before them was Russian, a chunky, ugly-looking piece of machinery, functional though without the high finish you expected from German industry, with a curved detachable twenty-five-round magazine and a wooden hand grip on the forestock just ahead of it. It could use single shots like a semi-auto rifle, and for close-range work fire on full automatic.

"My men all agree it's absolutely ideal for *Stoßtruppen*," Röhm insisted. "More firepower than a bolt-action carbine, but more range and punch than a machine pistol and much lighter and handier than a light machine gun, even the Lewis."

Which the Emperor insisted we adopt back in 1913 because he saw that cinema clip of President Roosevelt firing one from the hip and grinning like an enraged bull moose. The All-Highest was right that time . . . more or less by accident and motivated by his childish envy, but still.

The General Staff officer ticked off the negatives on his fingers: "This Russian thing overheats if you put several magazines through it one after another. That was why we developed the quick-change barrel for the Lewis."

"This isn't a machine gun and doesn't need that sort of sustained-fire capacity!" Röhm snapped.

Von Dorn continued: "It's mechanically complicated and requires careful maintenance in the field, and encourages waste of ammunition."

Horst snorted slightly and intervened: "Hauptmann von Dorn, that's what they said when we introduced magazine rifles to replace the single-shot models in my father's time . . . and when we replaced muzzle-loaders with needle guns in my *grandfather's* time. And before that the armorers for the *Landsknechte* probably complained that harquebus balls weren't reusable like crossbow bolts."

Even the General Staff man smiled at that, though he concealed it quickly.

"But the light Japanese cartridge doesn't have the range or stopping power of the standard 7.92 Mauser," von Dorn put in; he was probably really more worried about the logistical complications.

"If it were chambered in 7.92, Hauptmann *von* Dorn, you couldn't *control* it on automatic fire," Röhm said. "It's not a rifle for hunting antelope in Africa or exterminating paper targets a thousand meters away. Those ranges are for machine guns and *Minenwerfer* anyway. This is . . . it's . . . it's . . ."

Horst smiled as a thought came to him: "An . . . *assault rifle* . . . perhaps, Hauptmann Röhm?" he suggested.

Röhm grinned like a happy hyena about to rip off a face and slapped the table.

"*Sturmgewehr!*" he repeated. "Assault rifle! A perfect name. *Sturmgewehr* for *Sturmtruppen*."

Sturmtruppen was the alternative designation for *Stoßtruppen*, elite assault troops the German army had developed to deploy new tactics and gear. They were everywhere on propaganda posters this year too, the modern face of war, like fighting-scout pilots. Ludendorff doted on them, being a self-proclaimed military modernist, and a hard-charging assault-troop officer like Röhm could often get his ear.

"The question, *meine Herren*," Grunstein said smoothly, "is whether the benefits of deploying this weapon are worth the additional costs of yet another model of small arms and yet another caliber of ammunition."

"*Cost!*" Röhm said with a sneer of contempt; he might as well have said *you cheap kike* aloud.

Grunstein let it roll off him; he must have been used to it, but Horst wouldn't have cared to be on the receiving end of the cold glance he shot Röhm for an instant. It was the sort of look that *remembered*.

"The war may be over in any case before we could tool up to produce the weapon and its ammunition in quantity," the Jew added.

Horst von Dückler didn't care much about Jews one way or another; for a generation now the man of business in Breslau who marketed the crops and livestock from the von Dückler family's Silesian estate had been a smart Jew. There was no more point in despising a Jew for being a Jew than there was in despising a dog for being a dog, and like dogs they often had their uses. Röhm was evidently one of those who didn't think that way.

"There my . . . superior . . . may be able to offer some help," Horst said in turn . . . also smoothly.

That got everyone's attention. Rathenau's organization was a power in the land now, but Abteilung IIIb was a growing power too, and so was its chief *Oberst* Walter Nicolai. These days Nicolai was a *political* power as well, one of the hidden guiding hands behind the new *völkisch-*nationalist German Fatherland Party the High Command favored.

"We have been sending agents throughout Russia since the collapse to secure valuable assets, and one of them exercised initiative—"

Which whatever foreigners believed was a quality very highly thought of in the German military.

"—and secured the manufacturing plant for the . . . *Sturmgewehr* . . . in Kovrov."

He waited a beat and raised his eyes slightly before adding in a flat tone:

"As authorized by the reparations provisions of the peace treaty."

That got a set of predatory smiles from everyone present; the treaty pretty much *authorized* Germans to go wherever they wanted in Russia and take whatever they pleased, down to the monogrammed nightshirt of the puppet Regent Grand Duke Nicholas, and nobody objected. Nobody except the plentiful bandits and rebels, which was why Germans wandering in search of booty did it in heavily armed groups.

It will be best to drop the Fedorov designation if I want anyone to take it seriously. The reputation of Russian engineering . . . Though it doesn't do to count on them being totally beschissen, *and the exceptions can kill you.*

For example, the Fedorov.

The assault rifle, he reminded himself.

And shuddered to think of what might have happened if they'd been around in quantity in 1914. Despite the official propaganda painting the Russians as pale-skinned equivalents of the Hottentots and Hereros who'd been butchered en masse in African colonial campaigns.

Well, might-have-been doesn't count, he thought. *They're beaten now and we just have to keep our boot on their throats so they can't get up again.*

"It was only necessary to kick in the door before the whole rotten Russian house came crashing down," Röhm said. "Even the yellow monkeys of Japan could defeat them! They're just meat to be carved."

Horst coughed, reflecting that the stormtrooper was a good example of his thoughts about believing one's own propaganda. Then he went on briskly:

"The equipment is packed, under guard, and ready for transport. My thought is, *meine Herren*, that we could establish the plant here in Warsaw, where it would be under the authority of OberOst, who would supply the factory space and workers."

The Oberbefehlshaber der gesamten Deutschen Streitkräfte im Osten—OberOst for short, the supreme command in the East—was currently under Prince Leopold of Bavaria. But Generals Hindenburg and Ludendorff had been its first masters, and they still backed it against its many bureaucratic rivals.

And Americans think that Germany is a single smoothly organized machine! How Bismarck would have laughed! Now they try to imitate a Germany that exists only in our *propaganda and their* dreams, Horst thought dryly as he continued:

"That would require the General Staff to organize the transport, of course." He nodded to von Dorn. "But if anyone can cut through the chaos in Russia, it is the Great General Staff Railway Department."

A little flattery never hurt, and they did do very good work. Whether anything or anyone at all short of *der Herrgott* descending in glory on a storm cloud could make the Russian railways in their current state give results superior to a train of oxcarts was another matter, but not his responsibility.

I would bet on the oxen, assuming plenty of peasants to push the oxcarts out of mudholes and someone to hit the moujiks *with a whip.*

Just converting the Russian rail system to the European standard gauge . . . He shuddered at the thought. But if someone had to starve, it was going to be the defeated, not the victors. That was the natural order of things.

"And the Ordnance Department would cooperate on the technical side, as consultants," he went on and inclined his head to the General Staff officer.

"Meanwhile," he went on, "Abteilung IIIb has secured all the . . . *Sturmgewehre* . . . that the Russians had in their supply pipeline, and concentrated them and their ammunition here in Warsaw, more than enough to reequip an entire battalion of *Sturmtruppen* immediately. We gain operational testing in the field, and the factory would be turning out a thousand or more a week within . . . three to six months, perhaps?"

He looked at the Jew. Grunstein gave him a long look and a slow nod, his dark eyes conveying:

Clever, my good baron.

"That is agreeable to the Abteilung für Kriegsrohstoffe und Industrielle Gleichschaltung," Grunstein said aloud. "A most efficient disposition of resources, Herr Hauptmann. We have gotten good use from other foreign weapons in this war: the Lewis light machine gun, the Thompson machine pistol, both of which we manufacture in Belgium . . . the former Belgium, that is."

"In our loyal and independent ally the Grand Duchy of Wallonia," von Dorn said pedantically, with a serious expression on his face until everyone joined him in mocking laughter, or in Grunstein's case a thin smile.

"Excellent, Hauptmann von Dückler!" Röhm said. "I know just the battalion to get the assault rifles first; namely, my own. We'll be ready when we break the Loire front and drive south to chase the insolent Yankees and their squealing little French bitches into the Mediterranean. And then after that . . . who knows?"

The General Staff officer shrugged, and added his own less enthusiastic acceptance. Grunstein was quite right: it always made things more harmonious when you could hand out slices of someone else's cake.

And as the saying goes, stolen goods are rarely sold at a loss, Horst thought with a sigh. *Am I to be a military bureaucrat from now on? I never wanted a pink stripe on my trousers; I'd rather shovel out stables.*

"And we shall call it the von Dückler Assault Rifle Project," Grunstein said.

That brought another general laugh and nods. Horst shrugged, though he'd thought himself that some new designation was a good idea.

"All I did was come up with the name," he said, waving a hand in dismissal.

"And plunder the weapons and machinery in good soldierly fashion," Röhm pointed out, grinning and jovial now that he'd gotten his way.

"And names have power, Herr Hauptmann," Grunstein said, and quoted from a Scripture not his own: "*En archē ēn ho Lógos.* In the beginning was the Word."

"Carried by acclamation, *meine Herren,*" von Dorn said dryly.

The meeting broke up with promises to exchange memoranda of agreement and detailed plans and Grunstein volunteering to find an experienced project manager within the next week. Who would almost certainly be highly competent and would *most* certainly be indebted to Grunstein and hence to Grunstein's patrons.

The corridor outside the meeting room was just as cold but slightly less gloomy, since it had tall windows looking out on the (triangular) Castle Square, though the light was a gray suitable to his mood, and cold rain mixed with sleet streaked the glass. It would turn to snow overnight and then freeze to ice that would turn the streets to skating rinks like the rivers that threaded Breslau, hindering the death carts that went around every morning to collect the bodies of those who'd died of cold or typhus.

His new orderly stuffed the book he'd been reading back into the pocket of his greatcoat and sprang to attention.

The tome was *Die Grundlagen des neunzehnten Jahrhunderts* by the renegade Englishman Chamberlain: *The Foundations of the Nineteenth Century.* Horst had read it himself despite the thickly turgid style, and it was very fashionable since it basically boiled down to a claim that everything good and noble in the entire history of the human race came from the blood of Germandom.

Horst von Dückler was a patriot fiercely proud of his people's world-shaking deeds and their vast and growing power, but he took the book's popularity as proof that Germans were . . .

Alas, no more immune to flattery than any other folk.

The orderly saluted smartly, and Horst returned it punctiliously. Routine helped you get through the days without drinking yourself insensible . . . and the man had earned the gesture of respect. A limp, two missing fingers on his left hand and three thick scars running down the left side of his face beneath the brimless red-banded field cap to the edge of his small black mustache showed how. As did the Iron Cross First Class on the left breast of his tunic. Horst had one too, but enlisted men almost never received that award, not unless they'd done something unsurvivable *and* done it while an officer was watching.

"Sir!" the man said in his Austrian-Bohemian yokel accent. "Did you get what you needed from the dirty Yid shirker, sir?"

"Yes, Corporal, I did," Horst said quellingly.

The noncom had even less use for Jews than Röhm, if that was possible, but he was a first-class scrounger and pathetically grateful for being taken off boring border-guard duty with a third-line *Landsturm* formation of pimply myopic boys, doddering old men, and recovering cripples.

Experienced combat veteran and *slightly insane* were often much the same thing anyway.

"There is a message, sir," he said, and produced it.

"Almighty Lord God in Heaven!" Horst said when he'd read it, and turned on his heel; he'd have walked out of the meeting if he'd known, and been glad of the excuse.

The beat of the heel plates on his polished pair of officer's *Marschstiefel* was steady, but by the time he'd reached the third-floor office billet he kept his hand off his side by an effort of will. In the X-rays the bone looked a bit frayed where the bullet had glanced across it, and there was the earlier damage near there from the French shrapnel he'd taken on the Marne when the war was young.

Two guards he didn't recognize were standing outside the office door, in gray-painted *Stahlhelms* and field uniforms without rank or unit insignia, their drum-fed machine pistols—copies of the American

Thompson in nine-millimeter parabellum—across their waists in assault slings, another invention of the modern age.

"Sir," one of them said to Horst, and opened the door. "The colonel will see you now."

Then through the door: "Herr Oberst, Hauptmann von Dückler."

"Enter."

Colonel Walter Nicolai was sitting at Horst's own desk reading through a report; a man in his early fifties with a neat mustache and graying brown hair cropped close at the sides and a little longer on top, an unremarkable German officer's face except for the eyes. He laid a cheroot in a short ivory holder down in an ashtray made from the base of a French seventy-five-millimeter round and nodded in return to Horst's salute.

"Be seated, Captain von Dückler," he said calmly, with a slight Braunschweiger accent that stretched out the *a*-sounds in a Lower Saxon fashion.

Horst hoped he looked calm enough himself. He'd recognized the report; it was his own, on the debacle that had encompassed the attempted Projekt Loki strikes on the United States. It was unsparing, too. There had been an element of self-punishment in it, and of course the pain of the wounds and the effects of the drugs had been stronger then.

"Sir, I take full responsibility—"

"No, you don't, Captain von Dückler," Nicolai said with a slight wintry smile. "First, the Carmody woman—the woman we *thought* was Elisa Carmody, the Mexican revolutionary—had her identity confirmed in *my* office by a source *I* thought credible; we were both there, and we both know I am at least equally culpable. And all else in this *Schweinerei*—"

He tapped the report with a forefinger.

"—followed from that. Second, the Black Chamber operative impersonating Carmody secured the details of Projekt Loki's American strikes from *my* heavily guarded and inaccessible office in Castle Rauenstein. How she did it, the Almighty Lord God alone knows; that is still under investigation. I am inclined to credit satanic witchcraft, invisibility, and a talent for walking through walls."

He gave another of those cold smiles. "If I thought she had . . . charmed . . . any of that information from *you*, Herr Hauptmann, believe me, you would have convalesced in a far less pleasant place than the Royal Palace in Warsaw."

In an unmarked grave, Horst thought, nodding. *Without any excessive time-wasting formalities.*

"But you did not even *know* the complete details of the attacks yourself, only those for Boston. The others were available only from my files and at 70 Königgrätzer Strasse."

He shrugged; that was the Imperial Navy's headquarters in Berlin, and Naval Intelligence cooperated with Abteilung IIIb only grudgingly.

"We played a game with the Americans, and we lost that roll of the iron dice," Colonel Nicolai said.

Then he sat silent, taking a draw on his cheroot and contemplating something with hooded eyes, before continuing in a meditative tone amid the curls of smoke:

"As the old saying goes, *All marksmanship is in vain when a little angel pisses in the touchhole of your musket.* But two-thirds of Operation Loki . . . which we in Abteilung IIIb were heavily involved in planning and which the *Luftstreitkräfte*, which is part of the Army, carried out . . . succeeded brilliantly. The American portion was always a high-risk gamble . . . and carried out by naval personnel, for the most part. I am not in the habit of shifting blame to subordinates. The Fatherland will not win the empire of the Earth at a single stroke, or in a single war, or without failures and setbacks along the way. We learn from our mistakes, close ranks after losses, and continue."

"Thank you, Herr Oberst," Horst said, ducking his head in gratitude; something thawed a little inside him.

He is not a likeable man, or even a gentleman—

Nicolai's family had been minor civil servants and clergymen. He'd never aped Junker manners either as so many bourgeois officers did, which was to his credit.

—but he is a man, *by God. And a chief worth following. There are plenty who would have used me as the sacrificial goat rather than sheltering me.*

Speaking of old sayings, failure runs downhill and credit flows up; and victory has a thousand fathers while defeat is an orphan.

"Are you now fit for more active duty than this?" Nicolai said. "Not field service, but counterintelligence work in Berlin?"

"*Jawohl*, Herr Oberst!" Horst said enthusiastically. "The medics say I will make a full recovery. Except for the eye, of course. I have been practicing diligently at the assigned exercises."

Also as self-punishment, but no more!

"Good," Nicolai said. "Now, here are the relevant developments. We attempted sabotage of the American commercial airship *Manila Bay* some little time ago; those craft are an asset that it would be most convenient to deny to the Yankees. The attempt was foiled, as far as we can tell by misfortune or incompetence on the part of the saboteur, who paid for it with his life. The official releases are bland and uninformative—the Americans are finally learning not to publish quite so many important secrets in their newspapers, which makes our work harder."

Horst waited in silence when Nicolai paused, recognizing that he was debating with himself how much to tell. Briefing subordinates was a tricky business in intelligence work. You had to give *enough* in the way of facts but not one iota more, while remembering that the occupational disease of the field was obsessive hoarding of information instead of using it in a timely fashion.

"But we have an agent in Tunis who managed to secure confidences from unwary members of the crew of the airship *Gettysburg*. Here."

Horst took the paper and scanned through the brief report; it was redacted, with passages that would let him identify the agent or containing irrelevant material blacked out.

"Elisa Carmody," he breathed, reading the description of a woman dashing up a hundred-foot ladder in pursuit of a man with a Luger and then knifing him . . . or fatally knifing his parachute, at least. "No, the bitch who impersonated her, in fact."

"Possibly. Carmody herself, the real Mexican revolutionary, was almost certainly interrogated and then executed at the Black Chamber's headquarters at Lecumberri in Mexico City," Nicolai said with a shrug. "That is their standard and very sensible procedure in such cases. The agent impersonating her traveled north under her name to provide a back-trail."

He shook his head in grudging respect. "A very skillful operation and it hurt us badly."

"Definitely the pseudo-Carmody," Horst said.

The blood was pounding in his temples and his mouth was dry. He controlled the beginning of a tremor in his hands, but his simple *Frühstück* of terrible ersatz coffee and rolls with some soft quark cheese that his mother had sent from home suddenly sat sour and leaden in his stomach.

Nicolai raised an admonishing finger. "Very probably, not certainly. Also, the official news release and interviews with passengers indicated that an unnamed but female civilian *assisted* the *Manila Bay*'s third officer in defusing the bomb . . . and one of the passengers mentions striking titian blond hair. Significantly, that part of the story was suppressed after a single appearance in a minor provincial newspaper . . . the *Kansas City Star*."

"Whelan!" Horst said, making the name a curse.

"Yes. I have my own score to settle with the so-scientific young miss, but she has undeniable technical talents."

Nicolai stubbed out his cheroot and lit another. "Now, the *Manila Bay* completed its trip to Buenos Aires, and returned."

He unrolled a map of the Americas. Horst leaned forward as the intelligence chief's finger traced the routes of American National Airways' long-distance routes, one from New York to Manila, one from Recife in Brazil to Dakar and then Tunis, and a north-south route connecting the two running from San Francisco to Buenos Aires.

"They no longer use the North Atlantic route from New York to Europe; that is too risky now," the spymaster said. "But there is this—"

Nicolai's finger moved from San Francisco through Los Angeles, on to Mexico City, then down through South America to Recife, Rio, and the Argentine capital. Then he ran it back up to Recife and eastward across the Atlantic.

"Two female passengers—traveling as Madeleine Robicheaux and Mary Duffy . . . disembarked from the *Manila Bay* in Recife. The next vessel on the transatlantic route was the *Gettysburg*, and no persons of those names boarded it. Mary Duffy and Madeleine Robicheaux stayed on in Recife . . . apparently . . . and reembarked on the *Shiloh*, the next flight northbound, checked into an expensive tourist hotel in Mexico City for several days of sightseeing, and were last seen traveling north on the *Aztec Chief*, a luxury express of American National Railways that operates between Mexico City and Chicago."

"Why would anyone traveling for pleasure stop in Recife and return to the United States?" Horst said, suppressing a twinge of nationalist envy at what America had been able to do with a technology Germans had developed. "Rio de Janeiro is a major tourist destination and Buenos Aires is an important business one, but Recife . . ."

Nicolai smiled, the satisfied smile of a mentor at a promising student.

"I am glad to see that you are still capable of seeing the discordant element in a pattern, Captain. Recife is a backwater only important because of its location close to West Africa, which is why the Americans are developing it as an air and naval base. There is nothing to see in Recife but the sea, scruffy half-breed Negroes doing lascivious dances, jungle, sugarcane, and decaying Portuguese buildings. All infested with many very large blood-sucking and disease-carrying insects."

He went on. "But the next eastbound flight across the Atlantic, the *Gettysburg*, did embark two Chilean nationals named Consuelo de la Barrera y Meza and Maria O'Doul. Whose documents and itinerary show them crossing from Santiago to Argentina by rail, securing visas to enter French territory, Italy, Switzerland, and Germany from the appropriate embassies in Buenos Aires, and then taking the airship to Recife with a transfer to the transatlantic flight. Purportedly on some sort of educational tour."

Horst could feel his mind make a leap as he considered the overlapping dates.

"The Robicheaux and the Duffy who went north again were doubles," he said. "They started as the Chileans in Buenos Aires and switched identities in Recife, delaying there so that they would be on a northbound airship where nobody had seen the faces of the *first* Robicheaux and Duffy. Easy enough to find two operatives with roughly similar appearances to confuse matters . . . though we are lucky they did not attempt to secure genuine visas from our embassy. Would there be any reason to deny them?"

"No, Hauptmann von Dückler, *they* are lucky they were not quite so insolent as to try that—their descriptions were circulated to all our embassies some time ago, with instructions to issue visas and quietly alert us . . ."

Horst ducked his head to acknowledge he should have thought of that.

"And our agent records that the day after the *Gettysburg* docked in Tunis, the two women traveling as Chileans—one dark of complexion who spoke comprehensible Italian with a strong Spanish accent—booked tickets from Tunis to Naples. The official of the Italian Società Nazionale Servizi Marittimi he spoke with remembered it because young women doing so by themselves are so unusual—even more so in that part of the world—and because they paid in gold francs. Perfectly legal, but gold has disappeared into socks buried under hearthstones in what remains of the French Empire as their paper currency loses value."

Nicolai spread out another folder. "Now here is a report from the customs and border service. Two persons—young women—with *apparently* valid passports and entry visas as Chilean nationals entered from Switzerland on the overnight Lucerne-Berlin express on the twenty-eighth of November and were recorded as arriving at the Anhalter Bahnhof the next morning. But the latest records from Buenos Aires routed through Stockholm show no such persons receiving visas; this was spotted by our routine correlation check. How I wish we had photographs of them, or that the *Bildtelegrafie* facsimile transmission between here and the New World had not been interrupted by the war! Or that the Foreign Office did not work by prewar habits of aristocratic languor . . . But pay careful attention to the attached descriptions."

Horst did, and felt his hands begin to tremble in earnest, and his mouth go papery with a terrible longing, as if he were a wolf thirsting to feel blood dripping from his fangs. He'd known what he would read, but having it in front of him hit at a level below the intellect.

"That is . . . the one impersonating Carmody . . . and the Irish girl from Boston, Whelan. Beyond any doubt."

"Control yourself, Captain!" Nicolai said sharply.

Horst became aware that the bestial snarling had been coming from *him* and cleared his throat in embarrassment; the fantasies running through his mind shocked him a little too. He knew he was a ruthless man and killing had never bothered him when it was necessary, but he'd never considered himself a bloody-minded one before. Nicolai took another draw on his cheroot and gave him a long, considering glance.

"I require that you be honest with me and yourself, Captain. Have you sufficient self-control to conduct this operation? Hatred is like fire, a fine servant but a bad master. Fire in the belly is good. Between the ears, no. There you must be cold as ice."

Horst took a deep breath and forced an iron control. "Yes, sir. *Jawohl*, Herr Oberst."

"Good enough. You will personally interview the customs inspector, who has been brought north—and who seems to be an honest dullard—and then pursue the matter in Berlin."

Nicolai raised a hand. "I am aware that letting us think Berlin is their goal may have been deception on their part. We have no real notion of their true intentions . . . but Berlin has our greatest concentration of valuable intelligence targets, and we know that these are capable agents, cunning, ruthless, and resourceful."

"Or they may have been using the prospect of Berlin being a deception as a way to hide that it is in fact the true object," Horst said; intelligence work was like a hall of mirrors in a circus sideshow, image within image within image, all unpredictably distorted.

"A *double bluff*," he added, using the English phrase.

He'd learned to play poker while working in the United States. It was an oddly difficult game, requiring mental gymnastics and psychological insight rather than just the ability to calculate odds, and excellent training for intelligence work.

"Just so," the intelligence chief said.

Then another thought struck Horst. "Project Heimdall is being run out of Berlin—from the Siemens works, as far as research and production are concerned, under the supervision of the Kaiser Wilhelm Gesellschaft's War Projects division. And Whelan, despite her youth, knows the technologies."

A memory prompted him to pound his fist down on the arm of the chair, once.

"And she saw the preparatory work on the battleships and battle cruisers at Wilhelmshaven! And *asked* me about them!"

Nicolai made a *tcha* sound of annoyance. "That code name is absurdly overinformative, as well. Our naval colleagues have been to Bayreuth too often and imbibed overmuch at the spring of Wagner. But yes, and that is our single most important secret project now that Loki has been implemented. Its success is the difference between partial victory and immediate, complete triumph in Europe and Africa and western Asia."

"And it's at the riskiest possible stage, just when the equipment is being widely distributed."

"Just so, and with Naval Intelligence in charge," Nicolai repeated. "Other agents will pursue the alternatives . . . which may or may not be a diversion of resources from the *Schwerpunkt*, the decisive point, but which is unavoidable."

Horst shrugged. "Numbers are less important in this type of operation. Too many agents can be a handicap if they trip over each other."

Which was true; but he didn't lie to himself. *I want her blood myself.*

Nicolai nodded. "You will keep me updated at reasonable intervals and will in turn be informed of any relevant developments, and you will receive documentation that secures the full cooperation of the Berlin police and the *Preußische Geheimpolizei*. And any other resources you need, within reason and at your discretion. Understood?"

"Fully understood, Herr Oberst!"

"Then you are dismissed. I will be leaving within the hour."

Horst stood, saluted and clicked his heels, and left the office. Four paces outside it, he halted almost in midstep, so abruptly that only catlike reflexes kept his orderly from stepping on his heels.

"Corporal," he said, writing quickly on an order pad he kept in a tunic pocket.

"Herr Hauptmann?"

"You are to take this to Captain Röhm in the transient officer's quarters, and inform him that I will have need of a special force for an important mission . . . about half a *Zug*'s worth. They've already been seconded for special duty."

A *Zug* was a unit of forty or fifty men, what they called in English a platoon, though by this stage of the war few were at full strength. By no coincidence whatsoever, Röhm had sixteen men with him, there to participate in the testing of the new rifle. As long as he didn't keep them too long and arouse the wrath of their battalion commander at the front, getting suitable movement orders cut wouldn't be a problem.

Not when Colonel Nicolai has just given me the power to bind and loose, he thought. *And as far as I know we have no serious offensives planned on the Loire for the next few months at least.*

Then he went on aloud: "Picked men, with an experienced officer . . . and equipped with the new *Sturmgewehr*."

The orderly's eyes lit with martial curiosity at the mention of that unfamiliar name.

"If this Hauptmann Röhm questions me further, sir?"

The orderly's eyes slid backward for a moment toward Horst's office and its illustrious current occupant.

"No names, Corporal. My . . . superior prefers to operate from the shadows. But you may let the good captain assume whatever he pleases."

The other man grinned like a wolf, and Horst went on:

"Oh, and an extra pair of the new rifles for you and me, Corporal, and a few hundred rounds and some magazines for each."

"*Jawohl, Herr Hauptmann! Zu Befehl, Herr Hauptmann!*" the corporal barked.

They were words that might have been sarcastic in another tone, one of the few ways a subordinate had of letting a superior know his feelings while being formally blameless, but now simply indicated wholehearted enthusiasm.

Röhm owed Horst von Dückler a nice fresh new favor, and it was time to collect before it went stale. It was probably dropping an anvil on a cockroach . . . but that worked. Giving the nasty pests a little tap often didn't. At worst he'd have wasted some of Röhm's time, which would be Röhm's problem, not his.

And the problem with relying on the police for backup was that they had police reflexes. German police reflexes, at that; the *Reich* wasn't the Yankee Wild West where their cowboy president had blazed away with six-shooters and chased bandits down frozen rivers, like something Old Shatterhand would do in a Karl May novel. German police were trained to be careful not to endanger bystanders on the rare occasions they had to use the weapons they carried as symbols of authority.

A half platoon of veteran *Stoßtruppen* with automatic weapons could be expected to show an entirely different set of responses.

Especially under the command of Hauptmann Ernst Röhm, if I have read him correctly.

ELEVEN

Berlin, Anhalter Bahnhof
Königreich Preußen (Kingdom of Prussia)
Großdeutsches Kaiserreich (Empire of Greater Germany)
NOVEMBER 29TH, 1916(B)

Luz and Ciara arrived in Berlin's largest train station at quarter to eight Wednesday morning, nearly an hour before sunrise and amid a steady soft snowfall. It left them feeling as if the great city were muffled and they traveled through a tunnel, noise fading away in the black-and-white stillness even as the train chugged through mile after mile of Berlin's mushroom sprawl. More and more lights blinked on in the darkness, as the lord-city of an empire woke to another day of strain and dreadful toil in the titanic struggle it directed.

The Anhalter Bahnhof's train shed was big even by American standards and brilliantly lit, an arched enclosure nearly three hundred feet across and half that high over the arrival and departure platforms. It was a thronging mass of light and color as their express pulled in with a *shuff-shuff-shuff* of steel wheels on steel rails, crowds and wisps of steam and smoke and the harsh smell of low-grade coal burning. There was another—brief, this time—document check as they detrained, to make sure that people who'd crossed the border on an international express actually went where they said they'd be going; that was the reason they were keeping the Chilean identities this long.

It *might* delay the alarm a few days until the border crossing documents were checked, which *might* be crucial. If they'd disappeared en route the rocket would go up immediately.

Once they were past that, Luz looked around the huge, bustling rectangular concourse plastered on the front of the train shed. Forty or fifty thousand people a day went through here in peacetime, and it was probably more now. The style was pure Wilhelmine 1880s via Byzantium, the chest-beating of the newly founded Empire, all tessellated tile floors and tall red-marble columns to the arched and domed ceiling far above and symbolic terra-cotta bas-reliefs, with huge round-topped windows giving onto the street outside . . . and no heating even in peacetime.

Though it was very well lit; Germans had taken to electric light nearly as soon as Americans and just as enthusiastically, and Berlin itself was known as the *electric city* because of both how much it used and the gigantic factories here that produced everything from turbogenerator sets to exotic novelties like electric toasters. Germany and the United States were neck-and-neck in technology, with the Germans ahead in some areas and America in others, and both vastly superior to any of the other Great Powers . . .

If there are *any other Great Powers now,* she thought grimly.

Austria-Hungary was Germany's poodle, or doddering ill-tempered poor-relation spinster aunt; Russia was gone into the monster's maw and could at most give it indigestion; France was broken and ruined; Britain was maimed. Italy was even more of a joke now than it had been before the war.

Well, there's Japan, I suppose. Not greatly great just yet, but working hard and coming up fast. Give them twenty years to build up the chunks of territory they're grabbing off now . . . ¡Y Basta! A cada día su propio mal; let's survive the next couple of days.

The traffic had a heavy higher-ranking-military bias, which meant a lot of greatcoats and shiny boots and a fair number of old-fashioned spiked helmets as well as modern officers' billed caps, but there were plenty of civilians on their occasions as well, and the sound of voices and footsteps was a growling surf-roar of echoes.

"I haven't been through here since . . . 1909," Luz said. "It's where you come into Berlin from Munich, and I was playing hooky from the *Reichsgräfin*'s school. Oh, the trouble I got into! Mima was convinced I'd run away because I'd gotten pregnant."

"It must have been such a relief for her when she found out you weren't, darling!"

"Yes," Luz said. "To put it mildly. Especially after I'd telegraphed . . . five times . . . and convinced her not to go rushing to Europe herself."

Especially since pregnancy was a distinct possibility at the time, which made the monthly news a profound relief to me, too. Someday, perhaps, but at the time and circumstances of my choosing.

Ciara snorted. "Sure, not something *we* need to be concerned about!" she chuckled.

Luz nodded. *"A falta de pan, buenas son tortas,"* she sighed with mock resignation. "My sweet cake."

Ciara frowned. Her Spanish was enough for the literal meaning, but it took a moment before she realized what *Lacking bread, cake is good* conveyed as a metaphor, and she chuckled.

Luz went on: "She was so relieved that she *almost* forgave me right away when her fears didn't materialize. Papá didn't, though; it took a bit of time and persuasion before they shipped me off to Bryn Mawr. Though that was a bit illogical."

Bryn Mawr had had its own risks, or opportunities in her case, but getting knocked up there hadn't been a significant danger; about as likely as being devoured by crocodiles in the middle of the Mojave Desert—technically possible, but requiring a combination of intense effort and very bad luck.

"And weren't you the wild one as a girl!" Ciara added, halfway between admiring and shocked, having been a dutiful homebody who traveled and adventured only in her imagination and in books.

"Oh, that's not the half of it, *querida,*" Luz said, with an inward-looking smile. "But then I fell into an old-fashioned novel."

"How?" Ciara said.

"I was a wicked Byronic hero . . . ine . . . saved from my wild and wandering ways by the redeeming love of a Good Woman."

Ciara took a step that halted halfway, swallowed a laugh so hard that she nearly choked, and gave Luz a poke in the ribs.

"Oh, *you!*"

I think most of the people mi corazón *grew up with didn't have a very subtle sense of humor, but she's coming along nicely.*

Then Luz went on briskly: "Let's keep them confused!"

A porter—German, this time, and on the upper end of middle-aged, with a white mustache—took their trunk and cabin bags and hatboxes.

"To be checked in at the Hotel Excelsior," Luz said, providing a further false trail, along with a fifty-pfennig tip, very generous before the war but only moderate now with rising prices. "In the names of *Fräuleine* Consuelo de la Barrera y Meza and Maria O'Doul."

Then she had to write it down for the porter to show the concierge over at the hotel, since he could no more have pronounced the foreign names reliably than he could have sung Brünnhilde in the *Ring*. The Excelsior was right across the street: 112/113 Königgrätzer Strasse, if you wanted to be technical.

Luz had never seen it before, since it had opened in its present form only a year before the war, while she was off in Mexico deceiving, suborning, and/or killing people and blowing things up; according to the 1914 Baedeker *Berlin and Its Environs* it was now the largest hotel in Germany, and it would be the first place the police or Abteilung IIIb looked for them once they had the detraining document check in hand . . . which was exactly why she'd made the reservation there from Switzerland.

We want them to keep *looking in hotels as long as possible. If we're not in* one *hotel, they'll look in the* others. *Where else would foreigners stay? Berlin has hundreds of hotels . . . but it has hundreds of* thousands *of houses. Hopefully they'll concentrate on searching every hotel, boarding house, and place with rooms to let who've had a recent change of tenants with true Prussian attention to detail. Give them a choice and Germans will do tactics over strategy every time. They're absolute wonders at* doing *things and absolutely hopeless at figuring out* what to do. *If you're careful you can lead them by the nose.*

"Now for the fun part where we make them scream with rage and frustration until their heads explode," she said. "Let's put on a little show with your crowning glory, *querida*."

Ciara pulled out a few long pins, as if to adjust her hat. Luz grabbed her by the arm and hurried her off to the ticketing booths; they were in side halls to either side of the main concourse. Ciara squawked artfully and clutched at a tumbling fall of red-gold hair. The sight attracted glances; blondes were a large minority here, but mostly ash or golden in shade. That exact combination of yellow and molten copper wasn't really *common* anywhere except possibly the Aran Isles or the Hebrides, though it was obviously natural.

"Linz, on the thirtieth of November," Luz said to the first agent, a tired-looking mousy woman in mourning black with a *Reichsbahn* armband.

It would have been men's work here before 1914, but the Great War had its own demands. Her weary eyes flicked up to Ciara, then back to the documents that consumed her days.

"Two, first-class overnight shared sleeper car, please, if possible."

Then Luz and Ciara crossed the concourse to the ticket counters on the other side, working their way through the crowds as the younger woman fumbled with her hair under an apparent impatient tugging that produced a few smiles and laughs.

"München, second of December, first-class sleeper, please," she said.

This time the clerk was a man, in his sixties from his looks and coughing wetly into a handkerchief. She completed *that* transaction as fast as she could, didn't touch anything he had except the tickets themselves, and found herself trying to hold her breath as she signaled Ciara to stand back. Consumption usually spread with crowding and poor food and prolonged contact with the infected, but you *could* catch it from one touch, and people in all countries dreaded the inexorable "white death." It was a major source of mortality at all ages, and everywhere.

Luz discarded her gloves as soon as they were away from the booth and she'd dropped the tickets where she'd planned. Then she switched to a spare pair of gloves from her pockets. Luckily, ladies were expected to keep several such.

"Where are those tickets?" Ciara said, as they headed for the concourse again.

Luz grinned. "I left them on the benches," she said. "Which is asking to have them stolen. Even in Germany there are thieves in railway stations . . . and if they're stolen and used, which is highly likely, all the better! Though the people who did will get a very rude shock. And we're going to buy ones for Breslau and Vienna and Dresden, too! And to Hamburg, and we'll inquire about a connection from there to Wilhelmshaven. *And* we'll have the trunk shipped out from the hotel to one of those destinations; let them chase it. Now, tuck up again."

Ciara ducked into an inconspicuous corner to actually put her hat back on when they'd finished, and Luz made sure that every bright lock was covered; fortunately, manners meant women didn't need to take their hats off indoors in most of the circumstances where men did. They went out and crossed to the Excelsior, ducking their heads as the wet snow flicked into their faces and holding their hats on with one hand.

It was technically around sunrise, though you could barely tell, but street traffic was already heavy. It included fewer motor vehicles and more horse-drawn ones than you'd expect in New York or San Francisco, but plenty of both and a fair number of bicycles despite the weather. The startling thing was that nearly all the motors and many of the bicycles were riding on steel wheels; Germany was *very* short of rubber, and it gave the traffic a distinctive grinding, squealing sound . . . and made it much more dangerous because the grip of the tires on icy pavement was so feeble and stopping likely to mean skidding and slipping.

Darkness and swirling flakes hid the no-longer-illuminated sign across the façade of the vaguely Renaissance hotel building, though the streetlights were mostly on, but once through the revolving door there was plenty of light and at least a welcome semblance of warmth.

The lobby was vast, but even more crowded as people checked out to catch the morning trains or arrived with the overnight sleepers. And winter crowds always looked bulkier with the overcoats that gave the air a strong scent of damp wool, amid the marble-and-gilt splendors that were now slightly shabby with reduced wartime maintenance. Even the potted palms were looking a bit tattered. This wasn't a cheap hotel, though, and Luz kept her ears cocked with a spy's reflex as they made their way through the line toward the registry desk, inconspicuously sweeping up bits and pieces of speech like one of the newfangled vacuum cleaners.

You never knew when something you overheard would be useful, hence the universal and usually futile wartime warnings against "loose lips." Of course, if you looked at it from the talker's point of view, the likelihood of a spy being within hearing distance was very low. Which didn't mean zero, as she was demonstrating right now.

Snatches of conversation were abundant. She caught one:

". . . English . . . Calais . . . surrender . . . announce . . . today! Fifty thousand prisoners . . . crown prince's army group . . ."

That was a heavy-set military man with graying blond hair cut an inch long to make a flat tablelike surface on top, a wide waxed mustache, and the gold knotwork of a *Generalmajor* of infantry on his shoulder boards. He shouldn't have been talking about it in public, but it was understandable he was so volubly happy; that left only the shrinking zone around Dunkirk in British hands, and not for long.

Unlike his father Kaiser Wilhelm, the crown prince was actually commanding forces in the field, and from what she'd heard, not entirely as a figurehead, though his chief of staff would be doing most of the technical side. The prince's grandfather and great-grandfather had both been competent working soldiers, so it wasn't as surprising as you'd think from his father's comical pretensions in that direction. The general's aide leaned closer and said something and the conversation moved on.

There were plenty of civilians chatting as the two women made their slow progress toward the desk; they tended to have even worse conversational discipline than soldiers, and mostly they were talking about booty rather than battles; holdups with barges of plundered Rumanian grain on the Danube, how to get your hands on Serbian bauxite or Ukrainian manganese. A plump man who hadn't missed any meals since 1914 was planning a trip to Baku now that the Trans-Caspian Railway was up and running again under the control of the Central Powers. Luz's sabotage-and-assassination ears pricked up at that. Baku was chock-full of oil wells and refineries, both rather flammable . . .

From what the man was saying . . . gloating over and practically drooling over, in fact . . . the Russians had also shipped a mountain of cotton from Central Asia across the Caspian and piled it up at Baku on the west coast . . . and then just left it standing on the docks when their government collapsed and their army dissolved in defeat, mutiny, mass desertion, abdication, and revolt over the last six months.

Perfect for someone like James Cheine with a suitcase of incendiaries. I'm collecting a lot of valuable information already, she thought mordantly. *Unfortunately, it's all* bad *news for my side so far. Germany's whaled the stuffing out of everyone they've come up against except us . . . and they came close to breaking us with the Breath of Loki. I'd hate to be in Secretary of Public Information Croly's shoes right now, tasked with making this* catástrofe en progreso *look good to the public.*

Ciara was looking around with happy interest; she'd been to Germany once before, but that had been mostly a matter of riding under guard on trains as Abteilung IIIb's agents hustled their Irish Republican Brotherhood asset through the country to Castle Rauenstein in Saxony at maximum speed. This was more like what she'd hoped for from foreign travel.

Granted, with a risk of death added to the tourism, but she's just naturally brave, I think.

They finally came to the head of the line and Luz unobtrusively nudged Ciara to check in with her distinctive German; that took some time, since foreigners had to sign a special registry, and even the Germans behind them were muttering and stirring by the time the last careful entry was made. The clerk—this time a younger man, but with a steel hook in place of his left hand—shook his head at their request for an en suite, though a hotel as modern as this would have a fair number of them.

"My apologies, gracious misses," he said. "But all our rooms with an attached washroom are engaged. The war . . ." He made an ironic gesture with his hook. "It makes many things difficult!"

Ciara gave him a sad smile, which made him stagger a bit; her pleading-puppy-eyes were formidable weapons.

"You are sure?" she said plaintively. "So nice, for ladies especial, one's own plumbing!"

And so necessary for what we have planned, Luz thought; you didn't want to attract attention, but . . .

She reached around and slid a palm onto the marble desktop; she'd taken the glove off that hand, and used it held in the other to pat at a yawn. For some reason, yawns riveted the attention, and then the people looking at you were preoccupied for a few seconds with yawning themselves. It was a useful trick, using the same principles as a stage magician's prestidigitation.

The young man with the hook glanced down and blinked . . . as he yawned . . . his eyes widening slightly as he saw the denomination of the bill peeping out between her fingers; a week's salary for him, even at wartime prices. If there was a place in the world where rich people didn't buy their way past inconvenient rules at least sometimes, she'd yet to visit it, or even hear its name. The Party was trying hard to turn America into such a place, so far with mixed results.

He blinked again, twice, and then smiled broadly. "A thousand apologies, gracious misses! There *is* one left, on the seventh floor; I see Generalleutnant von Beseler didn't request an en suite, they are an innovation and he is a conservative man . . . But I'm afraid it's a single-bed room?"

"That is to be not a problem," Ciara said cheerfully; you had to get well up into the middle class in any country before sharing beds with someone of the same gender was unusual if you were crowded. "War is bad and badly making problems and problems is opportunities one must with energy grip."

He deftly flipped the register around, and Luz equally deftly slipped the fifty-mark note under it. They signed, and then again and again as he noted their visa and passport details on the requisite forms.

"Enjoy the Hotel Excelsior's hospitality!" he said, when the time-consuming business was past and the money had inconspicuously vanished. "Boy! The luggage of these gracious misses to room 737!"

They pushed back through the fortunately orderly crowd to the elevators, with more patient waiting involved. When they stepped out of the ornate brass cage, the skinny teenager closed the accordion-pleat door behind them and sent the machine upward with a twist of the controller and a whine of motors.

That gave them privacy. "Do you know the great thing about bribery?" Luz said.

The bellhop was waiting well down the corridor with the baggage, presumably whisked up via a freight lift.

"Ummm . . . it gets people to do what you want?" Ciara said; she was still a little uneasy about things like that.

"*Solo un poco,*" Luz said. "The other part is that it makes them your accomplice. They have a vested interest in saying nothing and denying everything if anyone asks them, because anything they say has to start with: 'And then this beautiful enigmatic lady smiled disarmingly and handed me money to do something I knew perfectly well I *shouldn't* do and I took it because I'm greedy and broke the rules.'"

"That would be . . . embarrassing."

"Lethally in some cases—if Abteilung IIIb or the Prussian *Geheim-polizei* were asking, for example. So the temptation to say: *Not me! I would* never *do such a thing!* is overwhelming. And once they've denied things when someone official asks questions, they're practically guilty of espionage themselves. Bribery is a recruiting tool in more senses of the word than one! Only blackmail is better, and it's not as easy to apply . . . but bribery leads to blackmail too."

"Consuelo . . ." Ciara said just before they came too close to the waiting bellhop; she'd gotten good at using the name in public. "Darling, has anyone ever tried to blackmail *you?*"

"Ah," Luz said. "Well, yes, a few times."

"What happened?"

Luz thought for a moment and pursed her lips; she wasn't above a little bit of gentle *suppressio veri* to let Ciara get gradually accustomed to how things worked in the world of espionage and black operations . . . or just in the world of people who worked in that world . . . but she didn't lie to her with outright *suggestio falsi.* Sometimes that self-imposed rule was slightly awkward, but sticking to it was worthwhile.

"Well, you did specify *try,* as in *attempt,* sweetie. And . . . *por decirlo así* . . . nobody who's tried it with me once has ever tried again," she said.

Which had the virtue of being strictly true without saying why or how. *Some* of the would-be blackmailers *had* survived being warned off, after all, if they just went away in a hurry. There was no need to be specific about the other one; he'd gone someplace where it would require dynamiting a dam supplying water to a large Californian city to get at the skeleton, that being an unexpected side benefit of the Party's love affair with rearranging hydrography. And even then, there wouldn't be any clues; soft tissue damage, for example a slit throat, didn't show on the bones.

Ciara blinked. "Oh," she said thoughtfully.

Then with a sardonic edge she showed sometimes, to Luz's pleasure:

"I'll never try to blackmail you, then, darling . . . despite all the wonderful secrets I know!"

And it's one of the benefits of being in love with a woman—we pick up on hints better.

The bellhop wheeled their trunk in and set it and their cabin bags on little folding stools, glancing down with a quick smile as Luz extended a fifty-pfennig piece between forefinger and index and dropped it into his palm. That was generous, but not notably so. Rich people weren't *necessarily* stingy, but many were surprisingly mean about small things. Luz had always tipped well when she was playing affluent traveler—in life or for work. If you shorted the staff it was like *asking* to have people spit in your drink when you weren't looking.

Hitting just above the median was the best way to be unremarkable. Though the bellhop would remember two attractive women more than most of his middle-aged and male clientele regardless.

"Woof!" Ciara said.

She slotted the chain into the door's holder and looked around their room—which *did* have an attached bath and WC, and steam radiators that were keeping the temperature acceptable if a little lower than an American hotel would have chosen.

The décor was plush and heavy, rich in a way, somber and fussy at the same time, with a lot of carved varnished wood and plump upholstery on the chairs and settee and a rather high bed with four posts and a canopy; the windows had dark green velvet curtains. A competent oil painting showed peasants in dirndls and lederhosen raising steins around a table at a harvest festival, all of them rather shiny and tidy compared to the dusty, sweaty exhaustion of the real thing, with a dog and a kitten and a plump flaxen-haired moppet rolling about in the foreground.

There was also a portrait of the current Kaiser in one of the comic-opera white-and-gold uniforms with polished breastplate and eagle-topped helmet he favored, and a reproduction of a famous set piece by Anton von Werner of his grandfather being hailed as the first Emperor of Germany with flourished swords and loyal shouts in the Hall of Mirrors in Versailles in 1871. Bismarck and von Moltke the Elder looked on from the middle of the crowd as their masterwork was accomplished.

You couldn't live in Germany for more than a week without seeing *that* one. The *Reichsgräfin*'s school had had a round dozen copies.

Possibly it's my imagination, but I always get the impression that they're look-ing at each other and the Father of the Great General Staff is muttering: We did it, Otto! We did it! *And the Iron Chancellor is whispering back:* You can bet your sweet buttocks we did, Helmuth!

"It's all a bit old-fashioned," Ciara said. "I would have expected something more . . . more up-to-date. Didn't you say this hotel was built only a few years ago?"

"Eight years and then it was closed for renovations, but those are German years."

"Like dog years?" Ciara said. "Only running backward? That would make it 1902, and this would be about right."

Modern American taste in interior decoration—at least, the Party-sponsored version you saw in the magazines and model homes and public buildings and housing developments—ran to something consid-erably more spare and stylized than this, with light, bright colors and things like decorative murals in Tiffany favrile glass at the uppermost end. Possibly because so many of the movement's thinkers were react-ing against their Victorian parents and *their* tastes.

"Germany's a very modern country otherwise!" Ciara added. "Though mostly I know about the scientific and engineering side. But Castle Rauenstein wasn't very modern at all; it made you think of vam-pires and werewolves and those old fairy tales about ogres."

They shared a glance, knowing that they shared a thought: Colonel Nicolai was enough of an ogre for *any* age or land.

"Germany *is* modern if you're designing dynamos or poison gas or artillery," Luz agreed.

She skimmed her hat onto the bed and stretched with her hands finger-linked over her head; something popped slightly in her lower back. Luz loved travel, except for the continuous *sitting*.

"Or modern if you're keeping company with the *Berliner Secession* type of artistic radical, from what I've seen and heard of them. This is more the Kaiser's taste—he has 'gentleman's evenings' for his cronies at this hotel sometimes, the Baedeker says, or at least did before the war."

"Wild parties?" Ciara said.

"Well, if you think *wild* means middle-aged German men with *von* in their names singing and spilling their wine and telling mildly smutty stories," Luz said, and sighed. "Let's be about it."

"Yes, darling . . . though I'm *almost* tempted to take a nap. That was a bit of a struggle, and we only crossed a street!"

"Big city, big war, big hotel on a street right across from a big railway station, *querida*," Luz said. "It's one reason I like visiting cities but live in Santa Barbara. After a while taking so long to *get* anywhere starts to be wearing."

Ciara wrinkled her city-girl nose. "But in a city like Boston there are places *worth* spending some time getting to, like the Brattle Book Shop or the Museum of Fine Arts, or the Boston Public Library, or a lecture at Faneuil Hall."

Luz snorted—it was unanswerably true, since Santa Barbara just hadn't been there long enough to acquire many public sights beyond the Mission—and went to the trunk. She carefully checked the lock-plate for any scratches she didn't recognize. That along with several other indications said it was clean, as far as she could see, and she twisted the key and heaved it open. Then she pulled out several plain paper containers.

"We'll dispose of these hair-dye containers somewhere they won't be found," she added. "Then let them circulate your description! And a pale-skinned woman with green-blue eyes and brown hair is about as inconspicuous as you can get, hereabouts. Freckles aren't as common as they are at home or in Ireland, but they're not rare either."

Ciara looked at the hair dye a little dubiously. "Wouldn't we be just as well off if *you* were a blonde instead of me dyeing my hair brown?"

she said. "Blondes are common as dirt here, more than Boston; it seemed like every second woman we saw. You'd be very striking that way."

Luz smiled. "Attracting the eye more than our inherent magnetic beauty makes inevitable is the last thing we want," she pointed out. "Besides . . . to be any *less* convincing as a flaxen-haired Nordic type I'd have to be a Zulu, or Japanese. Whereas that milky skin of yours—*¡Dios mío!* how beautiful you are when you turn pink!—looks just as natural with darker hair. My father was nearly as pale as you are, though he didn't burn in the sun, but his hair was black like mine and Mima's."

"Black Irish—I'll venture his eyes were blue?"

"Almost as blue as yours, though not with that lovely turquoise tint. Mima's were very dark, but she said one of her uncles was blue-eyed; the Arósteguis were Basques, a long time ago."

"And didn't the Milesians come to Ireland from Spain?"

"So the chronicles say. And so no dye for me, but I'll be washing my hair in strong lye soap."

"But that will dull the lovely sheen it has!" Ciara said.

"That's the point, *querida*; and it'll make me look older, or at least more tired and run-down. Don't worry, that's temporary. And later I may have to shave it and wear one of the wigs we brought—I can claim it was because I had a fever."

"Oh, no, your beautiful hair!" Ciara said, genuinely distressed.

Luz grinned at her. "It'll grow back. Besides, wouldn't it make an interesting change for some things, with me bald?"

Ciara looked puzzled for a moment, then flushed deep pink. This time her poke in the ribs had real force.

"*Luuuuz!*"

"Now, let's turn you into a brunette. I'm afraid we'll have to renew it every so often, too, or the roots will show."

"Oh, all right, but I've never dyed my hair. Or anyone else's!"

"I have, and with a bathtub it's not even too messy," Luz said briskly. "Disrobe, miss!"

Ciara chuckled. "You just like getting me to take my clothes off. In daytime, or with the light on, too—scandalous!"

"Business before pleasure, but I'm going to give you a very thorough dye job, I warn you."

"Oh, *you!*"

L uz, why did those two rude biddies call us *Katzenfresser?*" Ciara said some time later, as the streetcar swayed through the murk and bustle of Berlin.

She directed a glare at the two elderly and rather dumpy German women who'd made the accusation; they were down by the driver and the exit of the streetcar now, ready to get off.

"I love cats!" Ciara went on. "It's not really a home without a cat or two padding about lordly-wise demanding better of the servants. What a horrid thing to . . . golly, that was just *mean!*"

Luz grinned at the indignant tone. With the two who'd aroused Ciara's ire gone they had the rear of the streetcar to themselves, since it was nearing the end of the line. Together with speaking Spanish that gave them a fair degree of privacy.

"They probably said it because they thought we were Italian, *querida*," she said. "Like that cabbie's husband in . . . the city amid the orange groves. And local folklore in Germany is that Italians eat cats."

Now Ciara looked disgusted as well as indignant. "They do not! I've had some wonderful meals at little places in the North End back in . . . back home, so tasty and so economical too, only a dime for that lovely bread they make and a nice big plate of noodles and meat sauce—"

Then she stopped, appalled as the realization of *why* the marinara sauce might be so cheap struck.

"They *don't* eat cats, do they?"

Luz patted her hand reassuringly; the thought of involuntary ailuropophagy was making her visibly ill. Luz liked cats herself, but wouldn't have hesitated to eat one if there wasn't anything else but rutabagas.

Though not a cat who was a personal friend. And in any case I'd try quite hard to convince myself it was really rabbit in the Hasenpfeffer. Close your eyes and think of bunnies . . . bunnies . . . bunnies . . .

Aloud she continued: "Italians are no more likely to eat cats than other people are; which is to say, not unless they're very hungry, *mi amor.* And anyone would if they were hungry enough. There are probably German tabby-nappers in Berlin right now. But Italy's a poor country and the Italians that a German sees are probably migrant workers from the poorest parts like Calabria, so . . ."

Their long tram-ride had trended north and west, nearing the outskirts of Berlin proper, through a sprawl of dingy working-class tenement buildings of four or five stories built around grim-looking paved courtyards, what the Germans called *Mietskaserne*—rental barracks—together with shops and churches and schools and all the paraphernalia of a modern city, complete with a maze of overhead lines.

Half the people she overheard along the way were exclaiming or complaining about how bad the weather had been this year, and the rain-sleet-snow combination certainly wasn't letting up, though she thought the temperature was somewhere in the low forties. Looking out at the chill soot-and-wet ambience of it all was enough to make you think . . .

Let's go conquer the world, it can't be worse than this and we might end up owning somewhere warm *the way the English did*, she thought whimsically. *Or that may just be the Californian in me speaking.*

The other main topics among the shabby, bundled-up, and hungry-looking passengers she'd overheard earlier . . . besides the inevitable and universally popular personal items, like the way that tomcat Hans-or-whatever was carrying on with that slut Margarete-or-whatever . . . were the price of food and coal, and where to get food and coal, and who had gotten food and coal and how, spiced now and then with complaints about clothing and shoes and the amount of time spent waiting in lines at shops. The war news got tucked in at the end, despite the storm-and-thunder level it had been hitting lately; today's headlines had announced the fall of Calais in heavy Fraktur type.

Ordinary people go on with their own lives as long as they can, Luz thought, not for the first time. *Until the anvil falls on their heads. It's irritating sometimes, but . . . in a way, it's sort of endearing, a sign of strength.*

Everyone who mentioned it seemed happy enough about the way the great struggle was going, naturally enough, albeit occasionally wistful on the *when will it all end and Hans comes home?* side, but whenever someone mentioned *Vernichtungsgas*, Annihilation Gas, their voice unconsciously dropped to a half whisper.

And she heard one *outright* whisper of: *but what if they use it on us?* That was hastily shushed by the person sitting beside the whisperer, who got off at the next stop looking flustered. Evidently even the Germans were a little disturbed by what they'd unleashed, the common people at least.

"It all . . . doesn't look as old as I expected," Ciara said, rubbing at the fog on a window beside their seats with a cuff of her plain dark cloth coat. "Italy did, what little we saw of it—"

"Someday, after the war . . ." Luz said with a sigh; half the world must be saying that. "I'd like to see more of Italy myself; I never got farther than Venice while I was in Europe, and that was with the *Reichsgräfin* shepherding us around in a gaggle making appropriate *oooh* and *ahhhh* sounds at St. Mark's and taking gondola rides . . . and the gondoliers sang—badly—and you couldn't get away or even pitch them into the canal and beat them to death with their poles, however tempting it was."

"Were they *that* bad?"

"Like miserable cats on a roof complaining about cold wet weather and a lack of love. There's nobody a Venetian despises more than a tourist, and they've been perfecting the art of fleecing and tormenting them at the same time for four hundred years. To be fair, Venice really is worth seeing; they plundered widely and spent their loot splendidly, in their great days."

Ciara sighed. "I remember reading Edith Wharton's *Italian Villas and Their Gardens* over and over again when I was a girl—I left my favorite copy with Auntie Colleen back in the spring because I couldn't bear to part with it when we sold the store. Those Maxfield Parrish illustrations . . . And then we had to rush through without seeing much."

Luz nodded. "After the war . . . that phrase again! After the war *we* could rent a *pension* in Florence, say, in the spring when the orchards are in bloom, and rent an auto too, and tour from there; move up to Lake Como for the hot months, then back . . . Though the Italians are inveterate bottom-pinchers, worse than the French, even French from *le Midi*."

Ciara nodded and smiled admiringly. "Well, you've a blunt way with that, my darling one! And just what he deserved, the masher. Which saved me the trouble of—"

She touched one of her six-inch heirloom hatpins. Luz smiled too; she didn't think the man in question had quite realized exactly how his thumb came to be dislocated since it happened so quickly. But it had certainly concentrated his mind on his own affairs as he staggered off clutching the wounded member as it started to swell and uttering incredulous agonized shrieks of:

"T'hanna magna' i cani i canciello!"

Which meant *something* about dogs eating people in the doorway, but in such thick Neapolitan that the rest eluded Luz, since her command even of standard Italian was no better than competent and what they spoke in Naples was nearly as distinct from that as either was from Spanish. Meanwhile the two of them had walked calmly but briskly away from the Naples docks and toward the railway station.

And the chances of a man in Naples going to the police alleging that a woman successfully *assaulted him are somewhere between zero and* absolutamente nada, *considering how hard they'd laugh at him. Odd how a terrible fear of being humiliated by women sometimes makes it* easier *for a woman to humiliate a man and get away with it, if she knows what she's doing and doesn't have any inhibitions about* la violencia. *And . . . I don't think I ever did have those. Tactical caution, yes; inhibitions, no.*

Most people did have some sort of mental stoppage, needing to push themselves for a while before their blood was hot enough to strike and then doing it wildly; it was an odd handicap and had saved her life several times.

Human beings are strange creatures.

Ciara went on, while peering out the patch of cleared glass: "But sure, and most of what we've seen of Berlin isn't any older than most of . . . the place I grew up, from the looks of it!"

"It isn't," Luz said. "A hundred years ago Berlin was a sleepy little fourth-rate garrison town and never had been anything more, not in all the centuries since the Wendish Crusade."

"How it's grown!"

"Like a weed, darling, and most of all since the Empire was founded in 1870."

"It's a major manufacturing city and center of the sciences, I know about that, but I hadn't realized it was all so *recent*," Ciara said thoughtfully.

Luz nodded: "Berlin is Germany's version of . . . that city on the lake with the giant stockyards."

Ciara nodded to show she knew Luz meant Chicago. Few Germans would understand Spanish, but millions would recognize the name, not least because so many of their relatives lived there.

Luz went on: "It's big and new and powerful and sort of ugly . . . though not as ugly as Essen, say. And even the parts right in the center that *were* older have mostly been rebuilt in the last generation; these Prussians are like thrifty old farmers who suddenly came into a great big inheritance and went berserk with money and bad taste."

Finally they went past Berlin's legal boundaries, into ground that had all been green fields only ten or twenty years ago. Ciara whistled silently at the size of the huge brick and glass and iron structures they saw, set amid crowded railway sidings with long trains of flatcars and freight cars, and as they clattered over a canal crowded with barges, mostly of coal. Even if you'd been through Chicago and Gary and Pittsburgh or seen Ford's monumental new plant at Highland Park, all of which Luz had, it was impressive; dirty and grimy and the essence of unpicturesque, absolutely nowhere she could conceive of dwelling or working for long herself, but pulsing with life and power all the same.

"I've seen pictures and prints of this, but gee, it's not the same," Ciara murmured. "Golly!"

Smoke poured up into the lowering sky from tall chimneys, and electric light glowed harshly through the dull north German winter's gloom from endless rows of tall factory windows. Even through the clatter and clang of the trolley came a whining and grinding of great powers at work, and a smell of ozone beneath the coal smoke. Hordes of men and women poured in and out of the entrances as shifts changed.

"Siemensstadt," Luz said.

Ciara nodded vigorously and spoke with the rapt intentness of someone discussing an interest close to her heart:

"It's a company town like Pullman, named after the founder of

Siemens und Halske. The equivalent of Westinghouse or General Electric."

In fact its only real rival in Germany was the Rathenau family's equally huge Allgemeine Elektricitäts-Gesellschaft AG, which meant . . . General Electric Company. America wasn't the only country where someone with drive and genius could rise to be a titan and found a dynasty.

"Say what you like about them, the smokestack barons, but they dream grandly," Luz said quietly.

Ciara nodded eagerly again; she loved efficient industrial giganticism in an oddly aesthetic way, as something pleasing or even beautiful in itself, and this was one of her first opportunities to see it in person, rather than photographs and books. Her New England home was a thriving manufacturing region, but most of its plants were smaller and very specialized.

"Siemens employs more than twenty thousand people in the factories here, all built from nothing! Well, a lot more now—that was before the war, I read it in *The Electrician* a couple of years ago. And their lovely, lovely central labs are here . . . they're huge too, hundreds of research people who can just . . . just *discover* things . . . and make things *work* . . . and so beautifully equipped, everything you could want in the electrical line, and electromechanical and electrochemical! The Chemisch Physikalisches Laboratorium. I've read lots and lots of articles on them," Ciara said.

She clasped her hands together below her chin in a gesture that was almost reverential. Luz didn't chide her; talking about the neighborhood they were riding through wouldn't seem odd in foreigners . . . a fair number of whom worked here. Some even voluntarily.

"Werner von Siemens made the first really practical dynamo in 1866! Siemens installed the first heavy reversible electric drive in a steel rolling mill near Osnabrück in 1906! And their new tantalum-filament lamp, oh, it's so clever and elegant! So . . . so *efficient.*"

"And now they also make engines for fighting scouts and a good deal else as well," Luz said.

My beloved is a better Progressive than I am! she thought ruefully; *efficiency* had become more or less a synonym for *virtue* lately. *Mind you,*

Papá would have loved it all too. He'd have thought the same things, just expressed it with less girlish glee.

Aloud she went on: "I can see why Horst said you ought to be boxed up and shipped to Siemens and Halske just before we got on the U-boat in Wilhelmshaven . . . but I think that was a revealing slip of his, because you were asking about the rangefinders at the same time he said that. Mental association does that if you're just speaking on impulse, which is why I'm betting whatever-it-is they're doing with the . . ."

"Telem—"

Ciara started to say *Telemobiloscope* and Luz gently laid a finger on her lips for an instant.

"That would stand out and we're far too close to the factories to use it, *querida*!" she said. "It's natural to talk about the Siemens works while we're riding past them, but not that. Even if we've got most of this trolley to ourselves now."

"Sorry, darling," Ciara said, abashed. "I got carried away."

"*De nada*. But that's why I think Siemens is the best bet for the location, and more importantly the Director thinks so. Though I'd be surprised if someone's not assigned to sniffing around AEG too."

Luz and Ciara rose as the stop on Dihlmanstrasse was announced, picking up the small plain brown suitcases they'd been carrying as their immediate baggage . . . and for the various surprises built into them, transferred from the trunk at the hotel before it was shipped out to Munich to waste the time of the German intelligence services both before and after they tracked it down. The items left in it included coded nonsense calculated to drive cryptographers mad, and others that could be broken with enough skilled, concentrated effort, to reveal disinformation aimed at diverting them to nonexistent networks and sabotage plots.

They descended into the wet cold murk and hopped up on the sidewalk; the other side of the street was one of the lumpy fields of open ground in the process of becoming a park, though there were fairly well-grown trees, mostly oaks or beeches, along the street itself, probably left over from its days as a country lane.

"Rapsstrasse should be in this direction," Luz said, setting her hat more firmly; they were both wearing plain dark cloth coats, and hers was losing its fight against the rain.

"I'd be glad of an umbrella in this weather," Ciara said with a sigh, pulling down the brim of her own hat; the rain was still half sleet, and it was getting harder.

"Sometimes I forget the disgusting northeastern climate you grew up with, sweetie," Luz grumbled.

"And you've been weakened by the lotus-eater ways of . . . that place," Ciara replied cheerfully. "It's just *bracing*, that's what it is! And this *is* the northeast here. Northeastern Germany!"

Luz made a small rude noise as the street sign loomed out of the wet and they turned. Rapsstrasse was a curving laneway to their left— heading northward—just wide enough to let two vehicles pass, lined with recently built row houses and low blocks of flats set back slightly from the sidewalk. Young trees along it showed bare, wet black twigs like arthritic hands and there were still a few fallen leaves in places; in late afternoon only a few windows were lit, because many of the women living here were working in the factories now too while their children were in schools or nurseries.

It was always best to be inconspicuous, which was not always . . . usually not . . . the same thing as hiding and skulking. They strode briskly up the lane.

There wasn't all that much time before alarm bells rang and the enemy started moving in.

TWELVE

Warsaw to Berlin
Schlesischer Bahnhof (Silesian Station)
Königreich Preußen (Kingdom of Prussia)
Großdeutsches Kaiserreich (Empire of Greater Germany)
DECEMBER 2ND-4TH, 1916(B)

Amazing how one wartime rail transport is exactly like another, Horst von Dückler thought. *At least when you're not in a boxcar lying on straw with a bucket for a chamberpot.*

They were all in a single hard-seat car, with no marks of rank except that he and Röhm and Fuchs and their orderlies had some space to themselves at one end. Their transport priority was very good, but not exalted, which meant that they didn't spend *too* much time on sidings waiting to be slotted into a new mix of cars.

The inevitable game of skat had started, in the intervals between competitive stripping and reassembling of the new assault rifles, as they rocked westward through the night. Men were handing around loaves of black bread and pungent Polish sausages or sharing a quick slug of schnapps, adding their smells to those of gun oil and coal smoke and a fug of smoke from terrible tobacco and the smell of male bodies. Albeit they were cleaner than soldiers usually were, since they were starting out from a billet with baths and laundries. Some talented soul opened a can of liver paste he'd liberated from somewhere and shared that too, spread on the rye bread with a bayonet. It was obvious that Röhm's *Stoßtruppen* were experts at living off the land and instantly plugging into the local economy wherever they were.

At least nobody has started singing yet.

The first to do that was always someone who thought they could carry a tune, and couldn't. Horst, who'd had formal training in music and actually did sing well and could play the piano quite passably, found it almost unendurable.

It was mildly surprising that this pack of wolves Röhm had brought to test the new . . .

Assault rifle, Horst reminded himself. *Or possibly the von Dückler StG-16 assault rifle after the man who discovered . . . or stole . . . it.*

. . . included such an array of odd skills in their ranks, besides their obvious competence at their main work of slaughter. Most of them were noncoms, except for Oberleutnant Fuchs, who despite his name had white-blond hair and came from Hamburg. Röhm had obviously combed his company, and probably his battalion, for the smartest troopers and the best tacticians. He didn't like the man, but the Bavarian knew his business.

Interesting that more than half of them are city-born, too. Before the war we called up the peasant lads by preference, but perhaps that was just nostalgia on the part of the high command. Twentieth-century war is more . . . more industrial. True, not many farm boys were Social Democrats, but . . . does anyone still believe in the international solidarity of the working class at the end of 1916? The war has proved *it's blood that matters: blood shared in your veins, blood shed together.*

Dice had also come out, and the odd book, and some were reading or writing letters.

Horst's own—short, slight, black-haired, and rather sallow-faced—orderly was deep in an issue of *Ostara: Journal of the Manly Blonds*, a truly weird rag run by a Viennese occultist named Lanz von Liebenfels who was given to works with titles like: *Theo-zoology, or the Science of the Sodomite-Ape People and the God's Electron.*

There were times when the little man's preoccupations were very tiresome.

Still, he's less troublesome to a superior than an ordinary soldier always prowling for drink and whores. He doesn't even gamble or smoke, and he'd be death in a fight.

One of Röhm's *Gefreite* had been an art student in Dresden in civil life; unlike most German units, this half-experimental elite outfit drew recruits from all over the *Reich* rather than from a single military district. After Horst had given them a first briefing on the mission— waiting until they were underway was good security—the Dresdener had an almost visible stroke of inspiration. If he'd been in an American newspaper cartoon, a little electric lightbulb would have gone on over his handsome youthful face.

"Herr Hauptmann, we will need to know the faces of these two for whom we search," the ex-budding-artist said, pulling a rolled-up sketching pad and artist's charcoal out of his knapsack.

Horst looked at him in surprise. "You could work from my description," he said. "But would that be good enough? Better not to mislead by an approximation, I think. And I have no photographs for you to work from, Corporal."

"That is not necessary, sir. I have developed a method which works much better than trying to do a portrait of someone I have not seen in one attempt. It is . . . scientific and methodical, in the spirit of Germanism. See, Herr Hauptmann, I will do a sketch of a young woman."

He did, the stick making scritching sounds on the paper as he filled the upper left corner with a small portrait. It could have been any generic pretty young face.

"Now, sir, you must tell me specifically what is wrong . . . Nose too short? Too long? Ears? Shape of the eyes? Chin? And I will correct a bit at a time, over and over until we reach a version that accords with your memories. I have done this before, to make pictures of their families for my comrades."

Röhm opened one eye for a moment and grinned, looking even more like something from a folktale that lived under a bridge and devoured passersby, but depraved and mutilated in addition. Horst wasn't sure if the one eye was a joke about his own mutilation.

"It's a good idea, Horst. I've seen Wulf do it before; it's like a magic trick. *Du wirst erstaunt sein*—you'll be amazed."

Horst pushed down a stab of annoyance at the familiarity as the man pulled his greatcoat closer and his peaked cap down over his scarred face and apparently went back to sleep. He hadn't invited Röhm to use the familiar *du* form rather than the more formal *Sie*, or address him by his first name either for that matter. Still, they wouldn't be working together that long, one way or another, and he *was* doing Horst a favor . . .

Best not to be too stiff and to allow him a little baron-taunting.

"I could do that too, sir!" Horst's orderly said, putting away his magazine. "I made my living doing drawings and watercolors in Vienna and Munich, before the war."

"I'm sure you could, *Gefreiter*, but this man has experience with this technique. We will start with him."

Horst turned to Corporal Wulf's drawing and used his finger as a pointer, conscious of the orderly watching closely:

"First, the hair is too long—she wears it bobbed, just above the shoulders and it is quite straight, not curling at all. The nose is a bit too short and wide—hers is narrower. Lips quite full and bowed, face more oval, with high cheekbones and cheeks themselves not quite so plump . . ."

Horst became fascinated by the process as they went on. By the time they were down to the lower right-hand corner of the sheet of paper . . .

Elisa, he thought, as the image struck him like a rifle-butt in the gut. *Or whatever her real name is.*

His emotions were a complex roil that his mind refused to accept or even analyze, except that none of them felt good and most of them made him want to kill. In fact, most of them felt like the way you did when you woke up from a nightmare about combat, sweating and fighting with the blanket and yelling incoherent orders to men long dead, with the *crack-hiss* of shrapnel shells echoing through your mind as the *fauchage* swept whole battalions into carpets of chopped meat and gray-green cloth.

He'd had a couple of women bolt from his bed in terror after episodes like that and never look back.

But Röhm was right; it is like a magic trick. Someone who has never seen her has drawn an accurate line portrait taken from my mind . . . and the only thing I can draw are tactical maps.

"Now I will do a full-sized drawing," Wulf said, and turned the sheet over.

"That is a striking likeness," Horst said ungrudgingly when he'd finished. "An excellent thought, Corporal Wulf." *And so much better than the written description I telegraphed before we left Warsaw.*

"I could copy that, Herr Hauptmann," his orderly said.

The stormtrooper offered a piece of paper and a stick of charcoal; the orderly's hideously scarred face knotted, but his good hand produced a competent copy in a series of quick assured movements despite the swaying of the train. He never complained of his missing fingers, and managed soldierly tasks well enough despite the hand and the limp, by sheer willpower. It was another reason to tolerate his oddities; Horst suspected that if he'd been better-born . . . or even just not born in Austria . . . he'd have reached much higher rank by now.

Horst looked at the drawing and nodded; it was very competent. In fact, *competent* was the word that came to mind. It was just as good a likeness, but . . . lifeless. Odd to think so of a series of black marks on paper, but it had none of the feeling of animation the first man's work had produced. Wulf's work was a sketch of a living woman; this might have been drawn from carved stone stored in some airless mausoleum on the dark side of the moon.

"Excellent, Corporal," Horst said, and thought:

You probably did not make much of a living with the pencil and brush.

Aloud he went on: "Make eight copies, so that there will be one for every second man. And *Gefreiter* Wulf, you may now start on a second one, for the other enemy spy."

"I could do a color wash, too, Herr Hauptmann," the orderly said. "If you give me directions. I have a small kit in my bag."

He did, with Horst giving instructions, and one set of the drawings acquired Luz's smooth dark comeliness and Whelan's fresh-faced blond-and-pink looks.

The train clanked on over the nearly six hundred kilometers between Warsaw and Berlin; rarely at much more than forty kilometers an hour, sometimes stopping for fuel and water or a new locomotive, sometimes stranded on sidings while freight cars of coal or timber or unidentifiable goods went by, once while a huge set of stinking slatted boxcars stuffed with miserable-looking Ukrainian cattle went westward toward the packing plants and tanning pits and renderers to be turned into meat paste and boots and belts and the stuff that held aero-plane frames together.

One of the *Stoßtruppen* pointed that out, and his comrades put up a chorus of plaintive mooing sounds uncannily like those from the cattle cars before dissolving in laughter. Then a couple of troop trains passed them and then they were back on the main line—it was standard gauge all the way now, a process that was currently grinding its way eastward beyond Brest-Litovsk and heading for Moscow. Those rails would carry Berlin's power in the future.

They arrived later than scheduled on a Monday afternoon, pulled over the last stretch by a worn and wheezing French locomotive ac-quired as war booty after the Western Front broke a little while ago and obviously fed bad coal. Rail movements weren't his specialty, but Horst spared a moment to hope that things were going well enough for the Central Powers to stop gambling by skimping on upkeep of the transport network. If everything seized up the way it had in Russia before the Czar's ramshackle realm collapsed . . .

That would be very bad. We had to put everything into one strong set of at-tacks and they worked . . . but surely we have a little more effort to spare now that we are winning?

By then they had copies of the drawing that Horst had looked over and approved for all sixteen enlisted men, Fuchs, Röhm, and himself plus the colored set. He'd even managed to doze, though not deeply. Anyway, going without sleep was another feature of military life you just had to get used to, and learn to operate well with your brain feel-ing as if it had sand in the gears. You could sleep as long as you wanted *after* you were blown into dogmeat, as the saying went.

"Well, this is like old times," Horst murmured to himself as they pulled into the Schlesischer Bahnhof, the Silesian station.

He stepped down, stretched after the long cramped ride, and swung his greatcoat around his shoulders, lighting a cigarette as he looked up. The von Dücklers had visited Berlin two or three times a year when he was younger . . . when sugar beet and schnapps and pork and cattle prices were good, which they were more often than not. They took the express from Breslau, where the family had a town house for extended visits during the social season when they weren't living in the *Schloss* on the estate. Those trips ended in the Silesian station, naturally enough; nearly everything for the east ran out of here, and returned.

Horst smiled slightly, as he remembered his father, stern and fork-bearded with his walking stick and cape, stepping down from the carriage and pulling out his watch and snapping it open and nodding in Jove-like majestic approval if it was no more than a minute either way of the scheduled time. The baron would hand down Mutti. Horst and his brothers would do the same for their four sisters, all of them eager for the great stores and the theater and museums and dinner parties. And for the teenage boys there would be some slightly less reputable outings to beer cellars and the like. Behind would come a gaggle of servants and baggage . . .

In his earliest memories, his eldest brother Karl would be preening a bit in his infinitely envied cadet school uniform, loftily ignoring the younger boys.

The building itself wasn't much changed, with its odd side entrances and false front and twin neo-Gothic towers flanking the train shed as they pulled in. Inside was a huge metal-and-glass arch, two hundred meters by fifty-four; a thin mist of smoke and fog clung to the numberless slender tie rods of iron above, turning it into a phantasm that might have been the web of a giant spider in the halls of the dwarf-kings below the mountains.

He'd thought of that in those days, and after the family's first time at a performance of the *Ring* cycle he'd seen himself as Siegfried Fafnir's-bane, with an enchanted sword to slay the monsters.

Even that ceiling looks a little different, now that I'm a Cyclops myself. I'm getting better at estimating distances with only one eye; something compensates more and more, but it's not the same.

The crowding might not be much worse, but even Berlin hadn't shown nearly as many uniforms in peacetime as he saw here now, and there was a good deal more plain field gray and much less peacocking of regimental finery than in those innocent far-off days back when the century was young and braid and bright cloth, plumes and polished metal were still the fashion.

Back when they thought war still meant men sitting on the backs of animals poking at each other with pointed sticks! Of course, that was also before we realized it was more important for soldiers to be inconspicuous to the enemy than to look dashing and attractive to the girls. At least we did *realize it before the war started—the French looked like Napoleon III's men even then.*

Röhm looked at him when he glanced around and chuckled. Horst decided to explain: they did have to work together, and that meant they were comrades of a sort.

"I was thinking, Hauptmann Röhm, of how uniforms have changed since I was a small boy—and how the French looked at the beginning of the war, with their big blue coats and kepis and cherry-red trousers and shining buttons and packs with polished mess tins strapped on top so you could see them blinking in the sun kilometers away, and their officers in their white gloves, flourishing their swords out in front. And colors waving and their regimental bands playing as if they were going to a dance. But it turned out to be a *Feuerwalze* by our artillery, instead."

The *Stoßtruppen* commander barked a laugh, and several of his men within hearing smiled as well, the ones who'd survived since the halcyon days of the frontier battles, when the German armies had swept forward like a scythe of death and Paris beckoned temptingly like a vision of victory just out of reach.

And now we have *reached it. Admittedly it's a poisoned wasteland where even the rats died, full of a million bloated rotting corpses writhing with maggots and those pretty buildings we dreamed of devastated by unchecked fires, but it's* our *devastated corpse-stinking smoldering poisoned wasteland, by the Almighty Lord God!*

"Yes," Röhm said. "I remember that too. Jesu-Maria, what targets they made in the summer sun! Wheat fields, forests, villages, it was all the same, they were like a circus poster in glowing colors! I was in Lorraine then, with the Tenth König; we were part of Kronprinz Rupprecht's Sixth Army. That's where the French made a start on prettying up my face. I swear before God that I saw one little baby lieutenant straight out of Saint-Cyr with white kid gloves *and* red and white plumes in his kepi!"

"And you shot him, I suppose," Horst said.

He'd heard rumors about getups like that, extreme even by French standards, but hadn't seen it himself.

"No, he was already dead and swollen and black and stinking."

Horst nodded, sharing a memory that nobody who hadn't been there could know.

"It was a hot August. The dead horses stank even worse. And their cavalry . . . polished breastplates and brass helmets with plumes!" he said, remembering them charging into the stutter of the Maxims.

Dying horses scream even louder than men, and they don't know why.

Röhm nodded too, and went on: "Their infantry was a joke back then, but those seventy-fives were a menace on the defensive the way they could sweep open ground, and our own formations were too dense. Much too dense, and we paid for it in bone and blood. You'd have been with von Kluck in Belgium, I suppose?"

"Yes, that's right. I went back to Intelligence after I collected some shrapnel from the Black Butchers on the Marne. Which put me in hospital just before that idiot . . . or traitor . . . or traitorous idiot . . . Hentsch decided we should follow up a victory by turning around and running away. I wanted to get out of bed and strangle him myself when I heard."

"*Jawohl!*" Röhm said. "But I'd have used a bayonet. Wouldn't want to touch him."

At Horst's raised eyebrow—Röhm hadn't struck him as in the least fastidious—the stormtroop officer went on:

"In case traitorous idiocy was infectious, like scrofula," he explained, at which it was Horst's turn to laugh unwillingly.

The *Sturmtruppen* attracted more than a few glances—and the curious-looking assault rifles slung over their shoulders even more. He thought some of the passing officers needed all the resources of military discipline not to stop and ask eager questions. Nobody thought you could overwhelm firepower with numbers and superior morale anymore, and the *Sturmgewehr* breathed firepower's very essence even at first glance.

The men gathered around at his gesture after they'd filed off, holding their drawings of both women. He'd noticed that discipline in the *Stoßtruppen* unit was much less stiff than among the regular infantry of the German army, but it seemed to be just as functional if they respected the officer in question. They certainly looked and, to a subliminal sense that Horst relied on, *felt* deadly enough. One of them held up the pictures of Elisa . . . or whatever her real name was . . . and Ciara Whelan . . . which he was fairly confident really *was* her name.

"Can I kiss them before I shoot them, sir?" he said, and there was a collective goatish male chuckle, except from Röhm and a few others.

Horst smiled thinly; the false Elisa might have been a lying, treacherous, murderous bitch, but there had never been a dull moment in bed, and she'd shocked *him* a couple of times. He'd always thought that fornication was something a man did *to* a woman, but she'd disabused him of that notion fast enough. It had been rather disturbing, in fact. Very pleasurable, but . . . disorienting.

I hate her guts, but the memory makes most women seem a bit bland.

"Private Haas, do you think I am a weakling, an *Etappenschwein* who shrieks and faints at the sight of blood?" Horst said.

I need to get them concentrating on the mission. Distraction means death. And much worse, failure.

The man came to attention. "No, sir! Of course not, Herr Hauptmann!"

Horst von Dückler didn't feel he was being vain when he believed nobody who knew fighting men would think that about *him*. He looked around, meeting each man's eyes with his single gray one and speaking with slow emphasis:

"Then listen carefully. This woman—"

He held up Luz's color-washed picture and pointed to it.

"—I met while she was pretending to be a Mexican revolutionary friendly to Germany. Not long after, I saw her take down a big . . . tall as I am, muscled like a bear . . . *indischer* mercenary in British pay, a killer going for her with a garrote, while I dealt with the *Engländer* and his pistol. She dislocated his arm with a kick and knocked him unconscious with her elbow, and it took less time than it does for me to describe it."

There were a few thoughtful whistles.

"And she did it naked," Horst added: "We both were then, when the *Engländer* and his helper broke in."

That drew some laughs . . . but they were thoughtful too. It probably got him a little extra respect as well, for being able to bed such a she-devil, with good-natured envy thrown in.

"Then in Amsterdam, which then was not yet a city of the *Reich*..."

There was a grimmer chuckle at *that*, and Röhm shared it. Whatever the legal technicalities declaring the enlarged Netherlands exactly equivalent to Bavaria or Saxony, Amsterdam would have some hard work to do before its inhabitants or any of the Dutch and Flemings were regarded in the same way as the folk of Dresden or München.

"I saw her kill several Frenchmen, all Deuxième Bureau field agents and all soldiers. One she kicked in the crotch hard enough to ruin him for life—"

A collective wince. They knew what that meant when it was done in earnest to crush and rupture the testicles, not the painful but passing barroom brawler's tactic. There were certain wounds even the hardest feared.

"—but that didn't matter because in the next instant she hit him over the head with a lead-filled sap and crushed in his skull."

Horst tapped the back of his head. "She took him by surprise. The next she killed knife-to-knife; that one was ready for her... he thought, and she stabbed him through here—"

He put his index finger to his throat a little back from the chin.

"—and into his brain, so he was dead before he hit the ground. The next day the train we were on was derailed in forested country by more French agents, all heavily armed, and I think all soldiers with combat experience. The ones I killed certainly gave every sign of it. I saw her shoot..."

He paused for thought. "Four of them, with a Meunier semi-auto rifle, at ranges from snap shots at about ten meters, to aimed fire at better than two hundred while under fire herself. She walked away from that exchange; the other shooter didn't. He got close, very close... but close only matters with artillery and grenades, not rifles. Twelve, perhaps fifteen rounds including suppressing fire, four kills."

Another long whistle. That was *good* practice. Usually even at close range it took hundreds of bullets fired for a hit in actual combat. There were genuine gunmen who routinely hit more often than they missed even in the hot jittery stress of lethal violence, but there weren't many of them and they moved through average combatants like snarling wolves amid bleating sheep; if most men fought at that level, mass infantry combat would be impossible.

Because it would end in mutual annihilation at the first engagement, he thought.

"And she killed several more with grenades. This was in two linked episodes in a twenty-minute space of time . . . you know how it is in a skirmish, flurries of action between spells of crawling and hiding."

A universal chorus of nods or grunts of agreement or both.

"Then we stole one of the French motorcars and fled at high speed, and she knocked over one of them, he was on a motorcycle, with a grenade and kept the others at a distance by suppressing rifle fire so their pistol shots missed and they couldn't get close and throw grenades into our motorcar. *Gefreiter?*"

His orderly nodded vigorously. "I was guarding a frontier post between the *Reich* and the Netherlands—there was a border, then, of course—when the Herr Hauptmann's car came through the barrier. Smashed through; the brakes had been disabled by enemy fire. I'd been assigned there after this healed as much as it was going to."

He held up his mutilated hand and went on: "I saw the last of that pursuit, and I saw the woman. An unnatural creature, but deadly."

"The Herr Hauptmann has led an eventful life!" someone murmured in the background, amused and impressed.

Beautiful naked seductive killer spies and high-speed chases in autos sounded much better than the lice and mud and stench and rats and being jarred out of inadequate snatches of sleep by frantic poison-gas alarms and burial alive by endless *Trommelfeuer* barrages and the general anonymous omnipresent misery and random death of the trenches.

"How do you go about getting posted to the Intelligence service, sir?" the man said impudently.

Horst ignored it, since it was more or less the reaction he'd wanted, and went on: "Then in . . . America, you don't need to know just where . . . when she revealed her true colors, she killed German sailors and a number of Irishmen working for us with a machine pistol and a Lewis gun, and then gave me this with a pistol—"

He tapped his eyepatch.

"—*from a moving auto* and another wound in the side and escaped to warn the Yankee authorities. She is clever, and quick as a viper, very skilled with the knife and a fine shot with pistol and rifle both. A combat shot, not a target shooter, and she strikes to kill, instantly, without mercy or hesitation."

By this time they were all looking sober; they knew how important that unflinching willingness to kill at close range was. It was one important reason that a minority of soldiers did a majority of the damage in close combat and were crucially important in leading the rest on by example in the heat of battle. That was especially true when the action was face-to-face, close enough to see sweat on the other's face and smell the onions on his breath, where your groin and gut knew you were ripping and smashing another human being. Not like pulling a cannon's lanyard, or even firing a Maxim from a sledge mount at faceless doll-sized targets hundreds of meters away.

Not at all.

Horst had heard fighting-scout pilots say the same was true of the *Überkanonen*, the top guns—what the other side called fighter aces—in that form of combat too. One with the Blue Max on his tunic had told him with a laugh over beer that if bits and pieces of the enemy aircraft didn't hit yours when you opened fire, you weren't nearly close enough. Getting to bayonet range with a pair of machine guns, he'd called it.

"She speaks perfect German like a gentlewoman—with a slight Bavarian accent—and several other languages, and is cunning and deceptive in the extreme, and as constantly alert as a ferret. Once you have made a positive identification, shoot without hesitation and shoot to kill. Make no mistake, comrades, your lives will be just as much in danger as if you were part of a team stalking a French machine gun dug into a bunker. I do not expect us all to survive this mission, if we find the target."

Oberleutnant Fuchs nodded soberly and ran a hand over his white-blond hair. "Any other identifying marks, sir?"

Horst looked at the drawing, patiently corrected and recorrected to his description and color-washed by his orderly.

"Please, everyone take note of the splendid job my orderly has done in adding color to the line drawing. Her hair as you see is very black and her coloring is rather dark, dusky olive skin; you would take her for a southern Italian or a Greek. And her eyes appear black, but if you see them closely there are blue streaks around the iris. Though if you get that close you will probably be paying too much attention to the knife ripping open your gut to appreciate the finer points."

Another chuckle; in their line of work, that grisly sort of humor was usually the only one available. Horst went on:

"Whelan is a bright blond with red tints in her hair, blue-green-eyed, and with very fair skin and freckles. A little younger and less hard, less . . . vivid . . . but with a high technical aptitude—she recently disarmed a bomb one of our agents had planted on an enemy airship only minutes before its timer expired, which would take nerve and concentration. Both are to be shot on sight."

A man in a civilian suit with a long belted black leather coat over it and a black hat had come up during the brief conference, flanked by a stout middle-aged blond man dressed in the spiked helmet and brass-buttoned blue uniform of the Berlin city police, saber and pistol at his belt; their subordinates stood well back.

They exchanged a combination of salutes and handshakes with Horst and Röhm—the civilian was named Gustav Diehl and was actually a captain in the *Preußische Geheimpolizei*, the Prussian Secret Police, an organization that had been tasked with counter subversion work for a long time and had branched out into counter-espionage lately. These days there wasn't much of a difference, and they worked closely with Abteilung IIIb and the *Geheime Feldpolizei*, the Secret Police branch of the Army's *Feldgendarmerie* that filled a similar role in the occupied territories and ran their puppet native police forces.

The regular police captain was named Kurschat, and very taciturn with expressionless pale gray eyes; Horst thought he probably realized why the stormtroopers were there, and resented the implication that the regular police couldn't handle the matter. He probably also resented the way the civil police were more and more subordinated to both Abteilung IIIb and the *Preußische Geheimpolizei*. Horst reflected sourly that sometimes dealing with Germany's enemies involved combat less desperate than the bureaucratic infighting he had to wade through to get *at* the enemy.

"We received the briefing papers, also," Diehl said; he had a thin, almost French-style dark mustache.

And he's a native Berliner, Horst thought; he'd said *ooch* rather than *auch* for *also*.

"Your little talk just now was also impressive, Herr Hauptmann."

Röhm helpfully handed him one of the sketches and explained the process his man had used.

"This is an accurate drawing?" Diehl asked.

"Very accurate, as good as a photograph—better, perhaps, because it has color and depth," Horst said. "Hauptmann Röhm's man is extremely talented, as is my orderly."

"This is an interesting technique," the uniformed policeman Kurschat said, with respect in his tones now. "We have been trying out a similar one using an assembly of precut features, but it is not as effective; the final results look stiff and not nearly as lifelike. If your man could come with me for a few hours, we could have him do ink originals for our hectograph printer and run off many copies that can then be distributed to the police and public."

Horst cast an eye at Röhm.

"See to it, Lieutenant," Röhm said to Fuchs.

"Now, I have arranged quarters for you all at the Siemens plant," Diehl began.

Horst felt a grim satisfaction. The hunt had truly begun, and when you were hunting a fellow predator, your best bet was to prepare a hide near the bait and sit up waiting. He'd spoken to men who'd hunted lion and leopard in the German colonies in Africa that way, with a goat staked out for the big cats.

The spies would have to come to him, if he'd guessed right about the target. Perhaps even calling the electro-ranging device *Heimdall* wasn't as much of a blunder as he'd thought.

You *wanted* the lioness to smell the goat, after all.

THIRTEEN

Siemensstadt (Northwest Berlin metropolitan area)
Königreich Preußen (Kingdom of Prussia)
Großdeutsches Kaiserreich (Empire of Greater Germany)
NOVEMBER 29TH, 1916(B)

No. 27 Rapsstrasse was one of the semi-detached cottages that packed both sides of the street, modest single-story structures topped with steep-pitched red pantile and each with one dormer window in the street-facing roof and another to the rear. That still made them quite fancy by the standards of a big German city, even this far from the center. Usually the working class lived in apartments, often of only one or two rooms. Middle-class people mostly lived in flats too, though nicer ones; usually you had to go well up the social scale to find families with houses of their own. Europe's crowding showed in more ways than the size of farms.

Luz gave a quick look to either side. Nobody was on the street and the house across was darkened, so . . .

"Keep a lookout for me, *querida*," she said.

Then she turned, leapt, got her fingers on the ledge above the door, and pulled herself up like a chin-up on the bar in a gymnasium. What she was looking for was near-as-no-matter invisible from the ground, and the sill was too high for even a tall man to reach without standing on something.

"*¡Ajá!*" she said.

She dropped lithely back to the brick pathway with a small tinned box painted a dull matte black in her hand, the type people used to keep oddments like buttons and needles. Inside was a set of brass keys, a piece of green glass, and a little slip of paper with *1-Steinbrech-2* written on it. All three were coded confirmations that the preparation teams had gotten in and out without trouble.

Steinbrech was a flower name in German: *stone-breaker.*

She suspected someone was having a bit of a joke at her expense in the Codes section, and thought it was a certain "Specs" McGuire, since he spoke good enough German to joke in it, and this had his leaden misogynistic touch. She made a mental note to inflict some stinging petty humiliation on him at the next opportunity.

"Did I ever tell you about McGuire in the New York station, *querida?*" Luz asked.

"Just that you didn't like him and he's a woman hater," Ciara said. "And that you have to keep giving him set-downs."

Luz smiled as she tore the piece of rice paper in four and lifted it to her lips. "My sympathy for him is underwhelming; he can't grasp that he's trying to fight out of his weight."

She ate it as she opened the door with one of the keys and they both stepped inside. It was very dark, since the shutters and curtains were all shut, and it wasn't significantly warmer than the outdoors. But as you'd expect from housing built by Siemens und Halske for its skilled workers, there was a switch for electrical light by the doorway and Luz threw it, blinking against the sudden sharp brilliance. The air had a damp, still, musty scent, that of a house that hadn't been heated or lived in for at least a few weeks at this miserable time of year and in Berlin's miserable climate.

"Not bad at all, darling!" Ciara said cheerfully, looking around. "It'll be cozy!"

It was; there were still plenty of far worse things in the immigrant slums of any big American town despite all the Party's work on rehousing programs, and compared to the way a *pelado* lived in Mexico City it was paradisiacal. There was a sitting room or living room to their left, then a bedroom, and the corridor ran back to the kitchen; there was an indoor bathroom, or at least a water closet, under the stairway to the attic, which was normally more bedrooms for children; the whole was bigger than the apartment over the shop Ciara had grown up in. The furniture was well-used but sound, and the rooms even had that characteristic almost painful cleanness that modest German homes with pretensions to respectability usually showed, with a scattering of patriotic prints and religious ones of a Catholic variety in frames on the walls. Besides the inevitable Madonna and Child, there was one of St. Benno, patron of Munich (and fishermen) with the familiar odd depiction of him holding a fish with a key in its mouth.

"Let's get settled in," Luz said.

The bed was made up with a plain *Daunendecke* on top, a thick quilt stuffed with eiderdown and encased in a linen bag; Luz was glad to see it, since they were a lot warmer than any practical number of blankets. Suitable lived-in lower-middle-class clothes and shoes in their sizes were in the cupboards and drawers. It all had the stamp of a family that would fit right in to this neighborhood, one whose income permitted a steady comfort, decent if modest . . . *if* it was combined with strict thrift and unremitting self-discipline and *if* nothing really bad like a serious workplace accident happened.

The kitchen had the usual coal-fired iron range stove, ready with kindling piled and briquettes of compressed lignite around it when she opened the little metal door. Luz lit a match on the sole of her shoe and touched it gratefully to the splints and paper, and then did the same for the plain brick-enclosed black metal rectangle of the *Dauerbrandofen* in the parlor, the continuous-fire heating oven common in these parts that you could keep going indefinitely with an occasional scoop of fuel. They weren't as comfortable as central steam or hot-air systems, but they were a lot cheaper and did the job, more or less, especially in a small dwelling like this of only six or seven hundred square feet in total.

The kitchen range and the *Dauerbrandofen* sandwiched the interior walls of the bedroom between them, which would at least take the curse off it by the time they turned in; she found a little water heater in the bathroom, which did have a small semi-upright tub, and lit that too. A quick check in the cellar showed plenty of coal for a week's stay—which would make them the envy of the neighbors, if only they let the neighbors know, which they wouldn't—and a small sack of potatoes, which would do likewise.

Ciara opened the door of the pantry, which was also a cold store this time of year, given the thick door and the wire-screen openings to the outside up under the ceiling that kept it at temperatures that would be hovering around freezing most of the time in a bad winter like this.

"Well, and this would last us a month!" Ciara said, looking at the sacks, boxes, and shelves of canned goods. "Or two weeks, at least, with healthy appetites."

Luz smiled. "Better to have and not need—"

"—than need and not have," Ciara finished. "And isn't there something comforting about a well-filled pantry on a wet, cold wintry day like this, to be sure?"

"Not much comfort in this city right now, then. Though it wouldn't help anyone if *we* didn't eat."

Ciara made a gesture with palms up. "Whatever we leave, *someone* will have the benefit of it, too."

"And food is good as gold here and now; better, in some respects," Luz said, which wasn't quite agreement.

There was a stack of large envelopes in one of the kitchen cupboards; Luz put them on the table and carefully inspected the seals and numbers, showing Ciara what to look for to reveal tampering if a courier had been caught by the opposition. You could make anyone talk; the problem was that, particularly if the subject was a trained agent, it was extremely difficult to detect the little nugget of falsehood they might insert that would render all the rest worthless.

Though the downside is you have to hold out long enough to make being broken convincing, which would be extremely *unpleasant.*

Luz was good at interrogation but didn't enjoy it and avoided that sort of duty as much as she could . . . which was one reason she was good at it; the last person you wanted dealing with hostile subjects was a sadist. The proper approach was clinical, objective, and based on evidence and detached reason . . . *progressive,* in other words.

So far everything looked good . . . though there was always a nagging kernel of doubt, of course. But on the whole the work of the team—teams—who'd come in to set things up for the actual spying mission was first-rate. Everyone worshipped efficiency these days in theory . . .

They wouldn't have to waste any time on finding food or a roof, neither of which were very easy in Germany right now, and both of which meant unnecessary contacts with people who might notice something wrong.

"Who are we this time?" Ciara said.

She braced an elbow on the table and leaned her chin on her palm, waiting with an air of interest as Luz opened the envelopes, arranged the contents on the table, and fed the brown paper containers into the stove along with their previous cover documents. The Chilean feminists went crackling up the chimney, and she stirred the flames with a poker to make sure everything caught firmly.

"Let's see . . ." Luz said, seating herself and wiggling her fingers like a pianist limbering up for a performance.

She looked through the mass of identity documents, residency permits, letters of recommendation, and other artful forgeries. Those included laundry tickets for Munich, for the small town in Bavaria that was supposed to be their starting point and local ones here, canceled train tickets and food and clothing ration coupons of many different types, with the appropriate stamps and solemn warning that they were *nicht übertragbar*, not negotiable or transferable. Germany would be an easier target than most for this sort of thing because there were so many German immigrants in the United States and so many long-standing family ties, which made it easier to find the necessary talent. The same would have been true in reverse, if it weren't for the insularity of the German ruling class; the British did much better running propaganda or other semi-clandestine work in America, and not just because they spoke more or less the same language.

"German bureaucracy is like the proverbial little girl," Luz said, and at Ciara's raised brows she went on: "When it's good it's very very good, and when it's bad it's horrid."

"Why do we imitate it, then?" she asked.

"The Party tries to imitate the good parts, or an idealized version thereof people remember from their student days."

There was also a rental agreement for this house. In fact the rental was a sublease, since the original agreement was between a certain Herr Kaulwit and the Siemens subsidiary that managed company housing; it was complete with a string-bound bundle of rent payment stubs. Ciara took each piece of paper in turn; they were both fast accurate readers. She also understood German much better than she spoke it, and had still less trouble with the written form.

"My goodness; for all the progress we've made in America, the Germans are still ahead of us in the documentation of everyday life!" Luz said sardonically. "I'm Bavarian again—good, I can do other German accents but that's the one I'm most natural in. I'm a childless war widow, Frau Huber, that's imaginative . . ."

At Ciara's raised brow she explained:

"Huber's the commonest name in *Oberbayern*, like Murphy in Ireland or Smith in most places in America or González in Mexico."

She slipped the helpfully provided plain gold band on the ring finger of her right hand: it had *Myn Genyst* for *My Heart* engraved on the inside, in authentic dialect. Ciara looked another question.

"Germans wear gold bands on the *left* ring finger when they're engaged, then shift them to the *right* ring finger when they're married. Usually the same ring."

Luz smiled and kissed Ciara's left ring finger, where the Claddagh rings they'd exchanged would rest when they were back home, and Ciara followed suit with hers. Then she went on:

"I'm from Munich . . . no, I moved there as a child from a small village . . . and used to be a schoolteacher; my husband was a watchmaker by trade and was killed at Verdun this spring serving in a machine-gun company . . . nice touch, that's just the sort of military job a watchmaker would end up in."

"Because he'd be good at repairing mechanisms with many small parts," Ciara said, nodding as she filed it away in her relentless process of self-education.

"*Freilich, Süsse.* You're also Bavarian, a simple country maiden from the village of Uffing am Staffelsee . . . which is clever, Lermoos is just over the border and it's where your honorary Auntie Treinel's parents came from, isn't it?"

"Indeed it is! So I'll sound right?"

"Except that you sound a bit as if you came from there sixty years ago and spent the time in between on Mars, *querida*. Incidentally—"

She switched languages.

"... from now on, we speak German."

Ciara groaned and rolled her eyes. "Do I have to?" she said ... in English.

"Auf Deutsch!" Luz said, with mock severity, and went on:

"And you're named Fräulein Bauer, which means ... farmer. That's so unimaginative it's imaginative!"

Ciara fluttered her eyes, a gesture Luz found a little distracting even now, and laid two fingers on her cheek as she tilted her head.

"A simple, innocent village maid, I am! Oh, you wouldn't want to *corrupt* me, would you, now, you wicked woman from the big city with your sophisticated Sapphic vices?"

Luz grinned and kissed her. "Every chance I get, my beloved, though I've never heard Santa Barbara called *the big city* before, not by a Bostonian girl."

"It's bigger than Uffing!"

"A point. And your cover is that you're *literally* simple; it's common up there in the Alpine valleys. Lately the doctors say it's because of not enough iodine in the soil, like a goiter. You're feeble-witted and have a speech impediment; just stammer and look tongue-tied and a bit baffled."

Ciara nodded, and looked thoughtful. "And then everyone will ignore me. Try not to look at me because it'll make them feel odd."

"Very perceptive, *Schnucki*," Luz said. "There are whole categories of people ... servants, the mad ... who are invisible because people decide ... without noticing it, usually ... not to see them. Sort of a focusing problem. Very useful for espionage."

Ciara rolled her eyes. "Servants, the mad, and girls?"

"Sometimes. Annoying, but it can be extremely useful when you're *trying* not to be noticed. Now ... we're here because I took you in as a household help ... and an act of charity ... and we're getting ready to look after a wounded brother of my deceased husband, as soon as he's released from hospital—he's a petty officer in the Navy, which accounts for a man from a farm outside München being in hospital in Berlin, at the Charité. He was badly steam-burned when a line in the engine room ruptured under fire at Jutland and is named ... more stunning originality there . . . Bruno Huber, and he's going to need full-time care . . . that's gruesomely credible from what I know of steam-burn cases. It's like being a lobster dropped into the pot, but much faster. Are you following me?"

"Well enough, but strains puts upon me through attention-compelling. Is there a real Bruno being?"

Luz absently corrected her, and then remembered to smile; it didn't do to assume that what was easy for you was for someone else. In fact that could be profoundly irritating, and she knew that languages were much easier for her than for most people, even very intelligent ones like Ciara Whelan. If you wanted to stay in love forever, you worked at it every day; she'd learned that from her parents, by osmosis.

"Yes, there is. But he's not going to complain we're imposters if some officious twit asks at the hospital, since he's blind and can't talk, poor fellow, and they're pumping enough morphine into him to make an elephant see elephants. And he's not going to be released for at least a couple of months, either, if ever."

She thumbed quickly through the last of the pile. "And here's a nailing certificate!"

"What's that?"

"There's a huge—hundred-and-twenty-foot—wooden statue of General Hindenburg next to the *Siegessäule*, the Victory Column in the Königsplatz park right across from the Reichstag building; they've got other things in other towns, medieval knights and heraldic shields and I think I heard one place has a bear in a cage, which is unpleasantly accurate symbolism if you think of what's happened to Russia. If you make a donation that's used for the war effort you get a nail to drive into the statue and a printed form like this. They call it the Iron Titan now, which it is with all the nails."

"I know the nail location pick would I," Ciara said. "And drive it in very hard I would, Lord General Hindenburg saying ouch ouch *ouch*!"

"That's *I know where I'd like to put the nail*," Luz corrected. "And Germans say *aua!* Not *ouch!* But the sentiment's perfect. Still, the Documents Section and support people seem to have done us proud. We should still check the documents against the clothes and such."

"Check the clothes?" Ciara said.

"That things like the initials sewn in collars and hatbands match the paperwork, that sort of thing. You can never be too careful."

A methodical search revealed no discrepancies.

Ciara looked around. "Golly . . . no, *Donnerwetter*! It's amazing, all the detail!" she said, or at least that turned out to be what she meant, after some backing and filling. "It must have taken a lot of work, and all done so quickly. I wonder . . . no, I *shouldn't* wonder, should I?"

Luz held up a finger in a *that's it!* gesture. "Right you are . . . *mein Bärchen*!"

She'd added the endearment in German at the last moment and chided herself mentally to keep thinking in that language. One of the problems with being thoroughly multilingual was that you could lose track of which one your interior voice was using. She could also speculate in an informed way about how it had all been set up. The house lease might well have been acquired well before the declaration of war, when America was still formally neutral, because Siemens was a natural target in a modern war where science and technology were crucial.

Everyone in the Chamber had known America would join the fight sooner or later from the moment the Germans lunged across the Belgian border in 1914 in the teeth of Uncle Teddy's strong protest at the violation of neutral territory, and especially when they lost their gamble on a quick victory after the Battle of the Marne in September of that year. Presumably the General Staff had known the same thing; the word was that the only reason the United States hadn't come in earlier was that General Wood had convinced Teddy that the military needed to get Mexico nailed down tight first and build up its own numbers and weaponry. She'd put money on a pool the people at Lecumberri had running back eighteen months ago, in fact, and lost ten dollars because she'd picked June of this year for the American declaration of war.

Establishing safe houses in the enemy's capital was just as much a part of getting ready as training millions of conscripts and stockpiling trench and field guns and building shell factories. Copenhagen would be the most likely base for this operation; that was probably where most of the fresh food in the pantry had come from, and it would be a lot less likely to cause a stir than trying to source things locally.

And of course . . .

"This is for you," she said, handing Ciara a smaller sealed envelope. "Memorize it and then burn the location and directions; keep the identity documents and money somewhere you can get at them quickly but don't tell me where. It's your escape route if we're separated."

"Luz . . ."

Their eyes met; they both knew that *separated* was a euphemism for *taken* or *killed*.

"It's part of the game, darling," Luz said gently.

Ciara nodded, and Luz turned her back until she heard the grate of the stove go *clink* followed by the quick crackle of burning paper.

Then she smiled and looked back over her shoulder. "Shall we go up?" she said. "And see what presents Santa left?"

They went up the stairs, holding their skirts up a little, gripped in front of the thighs in that immemorial gesture with thumb and first three fingers you learned as a girl, though if hemlines continued to rise it might not be necessary much longer. Luz carefully noted which treads squeaked and where. The space had been for a brace of small children's bedrooms, stripped and vacant now . . . except for a dozen crates that were revealed when Luz switched on a bare bulb hanging from the roof of the windowless room at the south end.

Ciara blinked. "Bicycles?" she said. "I had one once, but . . ."

There were two pre-war Adler touring models with authentic post-1914 grooved tires of resilient steel, probably a trial to the back and kidneys but usable.

"Somebody was being thorough," Luz said. "You can move a lot faster and farther in a city on one of these. Europeans use them a lot more than we do—they never went out of fashion for grown-ups here."

A prybar had been helpfully left on top of one of the crates, weighing down another sheaf of documents in envelopes and neatly organized blueprints in pasteboard tubes. Luz took the tool up and drove the wedge end under the lid of one of the pine boxes, levering it up with a brief screech of nails and a scattering of straw packing.

"Electrical equipment," she said.

Ciara looked in. "Capacitors and cables," she said. "Oh, and a set of three-electrode thermionic regulator valves! How I've wanted to examine those since I read about them, they're the very latest thing! The possibilities for modulating and amplifying currents are fascinating! I can't wait to get to the notes on how to use them! And this is an oscilloscope, they're so expensive . . ."

As far as Luz was concerned, the already-low comprehensibility ratio went down from there; as she'd noted on their last mission Ciara's German got a lot more precise and regular when she was talking in technical terms . . . but that might as well have been Greek to her lover, language aside. Ciara went on:

"The problem is determining range. Hülsmeyer got consistent results on *direction* with his Telemobiloscope ten years before the war, but direction isn't very useful without being able to tell *distance*. He did some work along those lines by using triangulation from two transmitters, but that's awkward and slow, just proof of concept. He showed that it could be done, not how to do it in practice. I'm pretty sure and . . . N . . . agrees—"

She'd remembered just in time that the guiding light of the Technical Section went by that initial.

"—that from what we saw at Wilhelmshaven, they're using multiple transmission antennae with pulsed bursts and a receiver . . . they hadn't installed that then, what a pity . . ."

"*Süsse*, if they'd installed that . . . stuff . . . then we'd be too late now, wouldn't we?"

"Right!"

"They probably wish they could have; if they could have sortied and beaten the British fleet at the same time as the horror-gas attacks the war would have been theirs before we were in it."

Ciara nodded. "But there are always last-minute delays with a new technique. And then . . . then they're somehow using the measurement of time from the reflected object . . ."

Her voice trailed off into a mutter, then:

"Oh, Luz, *look!*"

She did; what was revealed was a case of tools, from the familiar to the exotic, topped by a rectangular box with a little typewritten note in German: *by my order and with my compliments, N.* Ciara opened it; there were tears in her eyes.

"It's . . . a slide rule, isn't it?" Luz said.

"It's a double-sided Faber-Castell from their Geroldsgrün works," she replied.

Ciara looked up, blinking and holding it to her heart. "Oh, darling, I wanted one of these for *years*. They're the best in the world! I saved and saved and bought one by mail order secondhand, and then I had to fix it myself because it had been damaged, and I did . . . and then I left it behind in Boston. This is new . . ."

Luz hugged her. "Well, you'll be getting good use out of it!"

The last box revealed something a bit different.

"¡Ay!" Luz said. "This is my area!"

There was a pump-action shotgun, a modified Winchester model with a twenty-inch barrel and a cut-down stock; it was much easier to conceal than a Thompson gun. She'd used the like before, mostly in towns and other cramped places hunting *revolucionario* agents and terrorists—there was nothing like going into a room behind seven loads of double-ought buck to make sure someone or someones stopped being a threat to American interests and an impediment to the Progressive Project once and for all, one way or another. It was especially useful when undercover, in that moment when the horrified realization that she was a Black Chamber agent hit the target who'd been convinced she was someone else.

Then there were a dozen of the latest lemon-shaped fragmentation grenades, the new ones with notched coils of wire inside the sheet-metal casing. Those were even easier to conceal, and they gave much more predictable results than the older type with a cast-iron shell.

And a shallow rectangular case about forty-five inches long that she set on top of the crate and clicked open; this was a Black Chamber model, made to look like a light suitcase on the outside. Inside was a padded hollow shaped to hold a Sharpshooter Springfield '03 Mk. V, the sniper's model made by Remington to incorporate the lessons of the Intervention and reports from the not-so-small legion of observers that General Wood and Uncle Teddy had sent to the Western Front. It had a cut-down forestock, free-floating heavy barrel, pistol-style grip, adjustable cheekpiece, and glass-polished selected action beneath an eight-power telescopic sight with a two-inch forward lens for low-light work and dual drums for adjustment. Beside it were several boxes of .30-06 cartridges with *SBI* for *Special Batch Inspected* on the plain gray pasteboard covers, and one with *ITAP* for *Incendiary Tracer Armor Piercing*.

Luz sighed; she certainly hoped she wasn't going to use any of this, and she'd probably have to ditch it all when they got out, destroying it if there was time . . .

. . . *but better to have and not need than need and not have*.

And Luz had used a Sharpshooter of an earlier model on a certain memorable bright but chilly dawn day late in 1914. A patrol of the 2nd Mechanized Cavalry she'd briefed had chased some fugitives past a hide in the Sierra Madre Occidental. She'd been lying up for forty hours, on the advice of a network of local informants she'd developed through a judicious combination of generous bribery, viciously believable and entirely sincere threats, fast-talking charm, and an earnest desire on the part of the locals that the fighting just *stop*, or at least move far away from their villages, their children, and their cornfields and goats.

And through the scope she'd seen and recognized one José Doroteo Arango Arámbula—better known as General Pancho Villa, professional bandit turned revolutionary chief turned bandit-cum-underground guerilla leader once his "army" was smashed in open fighting the year before—just as the informants had said she would.

Luz had put the first round through the head of his horse at five hundred yards, as close as he was going to get, in that one perfect moment when you *knew* that it was time to squeeze gently with your fingertip. Which had dropped the beast from a gallop into a limp collapse like a rag doll falling into a big puff of dust, and pinned Villa's leg to the ground under a thousand pounds of dead equine. There had been some luck as well as good shooting in that, but it *had* been very good shooting and she was proud of the memory.

The Black Chamber had wanted to interview so-called General Villa badly . . . badly in every sense of the word . . . and at length. Nobody would have been very happy with her if she'd just killed him. Dead men, as the saying went, told no tales, and it would have been put down to womanish spite. She wouldn't have been all that happy herself, for the same professional reason and for personal ones. As far as she knew, being suddenly and unexpectedly struck dead didn't hurt in this life, and she'd lost any confidence in any other some time ago.

And she wanted him to *suffer*. Suffer as much as she had from the grisly murder of her parents by his followers and the trials of her escape, with her mother and father's own pain and fear thrown on top. Along with the worth of everything all three of them had missed because of the lives cut short, and then with the whole bundle of debts recalculated at high compound interest applied every day for four years, to be paid in full and to the ounce. Emotional pain by preference, but physical would do and a combination of both would be just dandy. Followed by death done while he could see her smiling at him, after he realized everything in the world he loved and valued had been destroyed.

She'd emptied the rest of the magazine at four-second intervals, and killed three of the men with him as they tried to rescue him by dragging the dead horse away, dropping their sprattling, bleeding bodies across his, which had the additional bonus of sparing their innocent horses; she had nothing against *them*. The fourth and last had spotted the muzzle flashes and rode at her screaming in frustration and firing his carbine with about as much effect as the curses; she'd waited until he was two hundred yards away and then punched him neatly out of the saddle with a round through the breastbone.

Then she'd displaced to her secondary position, reloaded, meticulously checked the surroundings by unaided eye and binoculars, walked down, popped a red-smoke grenade, and settled in to await the 2nd's armored war-autos and trucks full of motor dragoons . . . and to explain matters to a sputtering and disarmed General Villa after she poured his canteen over his head to wake him.

Not least how shortsighted he'd been to allow his men to do things like butchering her parents. Her first words had been:

Mi nombre es Luz O'Malley Aróstegui y estoy muy contenta de encontrarle así al fin, mi general.

"My name is Luz O'Malley Aróstegui and I am so very glad to meet you like this at last, my general," she murmured now, laying a finger on the gray Parkerized steel.

"Luz?" Ciara asked.

In Santa Barbara that rifle still hung on the wall in the study, not far from her parents' wedding portrait. Whenever the vision of their deaths wouldn't go away, remembering that day among the mesquite helped quite a bit.

"Nothing, *querida* . . . just a bittersweet memory from long ago," Luz replied. "Perhaps one I need to let go . . . to let the dead go free."

FOURTEEN

Siemensstadt (Northwest Berlin metropolitan area)
Königreich Preußen (Kingdom of Prussia)
Großdeutsches Kaiserreich (Empire of Greater Germany)
NOVEMBER 29TH, 1916(B)

Luz blinked back to the present and continued the examination of the gear. There were various burglar and climbing tools; handy miniaturized cameras with a miniature mechanical dark-room to develop film; a complete invisible-ink kit, not used very often but very useful when you did, and . . .

"You might be interested in this, *Süsse*," Luz said, holding up an object like a rectangular cake of hand soap wrapped and sealed in waxed paper. "It's the very latest thing, only just being issued for special purposes this year."

"It smells like almonds . . . oh! It's an explosive, isn't it? Some form of malleable gelignite? And those are detonator timing pencils?"

Luz smiled widely. "That's my girl! You know, your brains were *actually* the first thing I noticed about you?"

"And here I thought it was my toes!"

"You had your shoes on at first, though I *did* think they were the most kissable toes in creation when they finally came to light; but it was the way you seized the opportunity to keep Nicolai in the dark and came up with details to convince him . . . Yes, it is an explosive, and you can shape it like putty. Marvelously handy, and it's more stable than dynamite—you can hit it with hammers and it's safe as beating clay. Even if you put a match to it all it does is burn . . . though it burns very fast and hot. You just have to remember that handling it with your bare hands and breathing the fumes isn't a good idea."

"No, it wouldn't be!" Ciara said. "Mononitrotoluene or something of that order!"

Luz knew one thing she was going to do with them right away; she took four of the bricks, pushed detonators into each, and distributed them inconspicuously by shoving their soft bulk into convenient nooks and crannies, rubbed the pale brown surfaces with dirt, linked them with flash cord around the baseboard—the cord was conveniently a dirty dark-brown color and inconspicuous, not much different from the wires for the lighting system—and then pushed a timer pencil into the one she'd left nearest the head of the stairs.

"See this, sweetie?"

"That's the timing device?"

"Right. It's set for five minutes, but you can increase the time or decrease it by turning it like a screw, see? Then twist this loop at the top and pull straight up, hard. Then leave, quickly."

Ciara looked bright-eyed at the locations, then around at the little house, and then paused for an instant:

"And if it went off, it would drop the ceiling right into the ground floor. And probably set the place on fire, too, and I'd guess the walls would collapse inward."

"Smart girl! Needless to say, don't do it unless you're sure it's necessary!"

Ciara swallowed a little, looking from the explosives to the box full of weapons.

"I thought . . . I was supposed to quietly get the frequencies they use, and then we'd go?"

"Ideally, yes. But better to have and not need than need and not have when it comes to unexpected opportunities or problems." She nodded to the documents. "And those are the plans for . . . whatever it is you're building?"

Ciara opened the pile of documents and gave a squeak of excitement. "Luz, these are by . . . N! Oh, this is the suggestion for the receiving antenna, since we can't use a moving . . . that's so . . . so *clever*! I would have . . . but yes, he says this is better because . . ."

"Ummm . . . will we have to put wires or anything outside, sweetie? Like a wireless transmitting station?"

"Oh, nnnn . . . *nein*," Ciara said absently. "There isn't enough metal in the roof to interfere—not if the transmissions are as powerful as I think . . ."

Another sound of girlish glee. "And he agrees on the most probable range of frequencies! Te . . . I mean, N agrees with me!"

Luz took her by the hand. "Well, bring the documentation and come along. It's going to take a while for *this* part of the house to warm up!"

Ciara did come along, but abstractedly; she sat at the kitchen table in her overcoat under the bright light, spread out the plans and descriptions, and began reading again. After a while she pulled out a pad of paper and began to make notes with a pencil; a few times she used the slide rule, with the pencil clenched in her teeth. Occasionally she paused to blow on her fingers, but the concession to the chill was obviously not penetrating to wherever her mind had gone.

Luz shook her head with fond affection.

Well, she's gone for a while. ¡Dios mío! You don't see focus like that very often; not outside a fight to the death, and only by the best even then. I can see that one of my tasks in life is going to be keeping her from walking into walls and off cliffs. My wife, the absentminded professor!

Instead she examined the chilly pantry again, selected ingredients, and made a *tsk!* sound.

Not that I don't appreciate it, but someone in Copenhagen should have checked a little more carefully on what's available to ordinary people in Berlin nowadays.

It was probably because, in the nature of things, their people had a lot of contact with corrupt officials, smugglers, and rich black-marketeers, and *they* wouldn't be going short of the better things in life. That kind never did, whatever ordinary people suffered and went without.

No question of what I'm going to use up first! Easier to eat it than to throw it away.

She removed her coat—it had gotten warm enough for that, if you didn't plan on sitting still—and tied on an apron as well. Then she tested the heat on the elements of the stove, putting her fingers close and counting the seconds until she had to jerk them away and shake them.

"That'll do," she murmured to herself. "And better to use this up before it's noticed. Really, *mi compadres*, that was a bit extravagant!"

She selected a saucepan—sound but showing signs of use again, which was a nice touch—and poured in a three-to-one mixture of whole milk and heavy cream, heating it gradually while she added cocoa powder, some sugar, and a pinch of salt, whisking it now and then to keep it from developing a skin. In between she chopped a small piece of the milk chocolate that shouldn't have been there at all and beat some of the cream; when the mixture was steaming she added the chocolate and whisked it until all was smooth, adding a touch of vanilla just as she removed it from the heat.

It was just the thing on a cold raw day . . . and there were probably people in this city, running into six figures, who'd quite literally kill to get it. Germans loved chocolate about as much as they loved coffee, and they hadn't seen much of either lately.

"Here, *Süsse*," she said, putting down a mug and adding a dollop of whipped cream on the top.

Ciara gave an abstracted murmur. A moment later her hand went out with a movement obviously not under conscious control and she sipped.

Then she stopped, looking up with a white whipped-cream mustache on her upper lip and cradling the cup in both hands to warm them.

"This is very good, *Süsse*!" she said. "Even better than the thermos from the hotel we had on the train, and that was lovely. And it feels so nice on the fingers!"

"*Na Freilich*, it's fresher than the hotel's," Luz said with a fond smile, and held out a napkin. "The pot's on the stove when that one's done. I'm going to take a quick turn around the neighborhood before I make us dinner. It's never too soon to make sure of the lay of the land in a new place. People will talk, but they'll talk less if they see me and get a story handed to them rather than making up their own. And the one I give them will be much less interesting and less likely to spread along the gossip telegraph."

"Mmmmmphh," Ciara said in absent agreement as she wiped her lips and her eyes went back to her plans and notes.

Luz looked over her shoulder: Ciara had just written: *But if three in series then KVL where Q =*

Luz smiled again; it faded off into mathematical symbols after that. *And I'd have gotten the same if I'd said . . .*

"Let's strip naked and dance down the street with our hair on fire, doing cartwheels," she said quietly.

"Mmmmmphh."

Luz chuckled, washed four quite small and rather misshapen potatoes from this year's miserable European harvest, and put three of them in the oven to roast, then put her coat and hat back on and slipped a couple of small packages of biscuits into her pockets in case she needed to generate some goodwill.

It was full dark outside, and the cold slushy rain had turned to a light fall of something still wet but definitely snow; the pavements glistened, but it was starting to stick on strips of garden. There weren't any streetlights on this recently built lane yet, only a pair down at the junction with Dihlmanstrasse, but enough windows were showing light to keep it from being pitch-dark.

The smell of coal smoke and cooking was in the air, though mostly the scent of cabbage and root vegetables being boiled rather than meat; the housewives were back from their day jobs, or from the endless queuing for food and fuel that stole so many precious hours from their lives, and now they were making dinner for themselves and their children and kin, and for such husbands as weren't in uniform or dead.

Holding down two jobs, or three, in other words. And anyone who thinks keeping house for a family isn't work just because it doesn't get you paid in cash has never done any of it. No wonder they all look tired!

Her mother had grown up with servants, but she'd been taught and had taught Luz all the tasks herself, on the theory you couldn't supervise what you didn't understand, and you needed to understand it through your hands and fingertips. Household servants did honest work for honest pay, but one thing she'd learned along with the techniques was that it was most certainly *work* and not an easy type either.

She wasn't surprised when women greeted her from their doorways, even though nobody was lingering with the door *open* the way they might on a long summer's evening, and she responded politely with a few words each time, using the *Grüß Gott* formula of southern Germany and saying she was the new tenant at No. 27. At one house the greeting was accompanied by a wave of invitation, and she stepped in to join four women in the hall of a building almost identical to the one she was using, and two more managed to "just drop by" immediately, panting slightly in their haste. Several school-age children wearing overcoats looked up from their books in the parlor and then bent back obediently to work at their mother's imperious gesture, though they were probably listening keenly.

Everyone here was naturally curious that someone had finally moved into the vacant house and eager to know who and what and why, and what the people with the wagon had brought in earlier.

"Guten Abend, sehr geehrte Damen," she said, careful to be friendly but a little deferential.

Luz could feel their eyes appraising her person—face irritatingly comely and even more irritatingly well fed, very dark indeed for a German but just about believable in a Bavarian or Rhinelander—and her clothes, muted in dark blue and black, good-quality in a severe way but not new, never particularly fashionable, and respectably plain down to the black crepe mourning armband, which every third or fourth person in Berlin wore in November 1916. That made her outfit suitable for a skilled workman's widow in these days of shortages when elaborate formal mourning clothes were far beyond the ordinary budget.

Here the lack of a corset was very much a minority habit even among women her age and especially among the working class, but from what she'd seen it wasn't all that *small* a minority either among those her age. The expense and difficulty of getting the materials in the grinding hardship of wartime put a patriotic sheen on the change of fashion.

"Thank you for greeting a stranger so courteously."

She introduced herself in the rather formal German manner, with handshakes all around and a bit more distance than Americans would employ, particularly Americans of this class, at least outside New England or its offshoots. The positive side was that they'd mostly refrain from the bluntly direct questions Americans were given to. Frau Blücher, whose house this was and who was apparently the neighborhood's unofficial chieftainess, was fairly quivering with curiosity but managed to suppress it.

"Please accept this token of my thanks," Luz added, and presented the horse-faced woman with one of the little packages of Leibniz butter biscuits. "They're not what they used to be before the war and the packages are so small, but they're available, which is something."

That produced genuine smiles; the little cookie-like things were a German staple but hard to get now, and sorely missed.

Mrs. Blücher opened it, in accordance with local custom, and handed them around as envy fought with delight, and the children gave theirs concentrated attention. Luz reminded herself to make her München accent less upper-crust than it was naturally. A schoolteacher would be expected to use the correct *Hochdeutsch* forms and speak bookishly, but not like a personal friend of the House of Wittelsbach . . . or like the *Reichsgräfin*, who *had* been at court in her youth.

Real invitations will come later, she thought. *I can't turn them all down, either, alas, and I should return them if we're here more than a week or people will assume I'm hiding something.*

Her story—schoolteacher and war widow preparing to care for her badly burned brother-in-law—got her sympathetic clucks and smiles. Explaining things would arouse interest and gossip, but much *less* interest and gossip than trying to play hermit or being evasive. And it enabled her to explain the special baths and apparatus a burn patient needed, which accounted for the wagon and boxes and accounted too for any assembly noises people heard over the next few days and let her explain how Bruno's commanding officer and comrades had contributed to the expense.

"The girl's simple, I'm afraid," she warned of Ciara's cover identity as the unfortunate Fräulein Bauer.

"How simple?" someone said warily, afraid of a lunatic lurking in their neighborhood.

"She can dress and clean herself and even speak after a fashion and say her prayers, but she's like a little child in her mind and sometimes she'll just wander off, or babble nonsense or talk to people who aren't there—like a child talking to her dolls. And she still plays with dolls, and at children's games when she can . . . *Katz' und Maus* and the like."

"A little girl in a woman's body," Frau Blücher said sympathetically. "How unfortunate!"

"Exactly," Luz said. "A strange place among strange faces, that frightens her; she's a timid thing. They often are like that, the ones from the villages in the mountains."

North Germans would certainly believe *that*. Berliners tended to view Bavarians in general as thick, dim hicks anyway, and Bavarian mountain villagers as pig-ignorant yokels from the Middle Ages given to inbreeding and overly affectionate relationships with the livestock. It wasn't too different from the attitude of Massachusetts or Manhattan toward Arkansas and its hillbillies.

"How did you come across her?" one asked.

"The priest of the parish asked for someone to take her in when her mother couldn't cope anymore. My husband's family were farmers, though he moved to town to apprentice with a watchmaker; I've been living with them until recently and helping about the place . . . I was a villager as a young girl too, and I remember the work . . . and the girl could do some things, enough to be worth feeding. She's good with animals and at simple chores."

A return to the farm would account for Luz's callused hands and fitness, too, otherwise a bit odd in a female city dweller with a sedentary job. Many German men were sports and outdoor enthusiasts, even this far down the social scale—the trade unions and Social Democratic Party had had their own network of hiking and gymnastics and soccer clubs—but it was much rarer for women. And it would explain why Luz and Ciara weren't ten pounds underweight, and for their access to foods city wage earners hadn't seen in some time. She could delicately imply that her dead husband's family were sending her (and their wounded son Bruno) parcels, which was both technically illegal and extremely common for those with rural connections.

The German food-rationing system was a spatchcock mess that just didn't work very well for town dwellers, and a reminder that Teutonic efficiency wasn't a universal rule. In a reversal of the pre-war situation, peasants who grew their own food were now deeply envied by city workers, and although supplies had gotten a little better recently because of wholesale plunder abroad, things were still bad. The new-comers' food supplies would be resented, but without astonishment, and a few gifts would win a lot of goodwill.

"She's sweet-natured and there's no harm in her, and she's useful around the house for scrubbing and such if I watch her, which will be a godsend when Bruno's released from the hospital. And it's a good deed to protect her—she's a pretty girl, and so trusting and innocent and not used to the wickedness of the world, well, you know . . ."

Luz let her voice trail off discreetly. Others were quick to fill in the implications.

"Wickedness of men, you mean, they'll take advantage of anything in a skirt like the shameless he-goats—"

"Shameless sniffing *dogs*," another put in.

"—that they are, simpleton or not," the first woman finished. "Honestly, some of them wouldn't care whether she was *breathing*."

Luz rolled her eyes to nods of resigned, disgusted agreement from all around; you rarely met women anywhere who didn't share that general opinion, mainly because it was true so depressingly often across all barriers of nation and class.

"It's very Christian of you to take care of her, Frau Huber."

"I try, for the Lord's sake and the Virgin's," Luz said, and crossed herself.

Frau Blücher, the householder, did likewise. The presumable Protestants among the neighbors didn't look too disapproving. A new neighborhood in a big city was more likely to be religiously mixed and tolerant, too. And this working-class area was probably full of Social Democrats, even if they were keeping their heads down and mouths shut now, which would mean a sprinkling of outright unbelievers among their menfolk and many more who were indifferent and stayed away from any church except for weddings and funerals. With socialists in central Europe anticlericalism was part of the package.

"Thank you again, ladies. I must be on my way; the girl can't be left alone too long."

Then when she opened the door again she asked: "What's that?"

That was a column of women heading down the road toward one of

the low-rise apartment blocks a little farther north. It was led by a soldier elderly even by the standards of the third-line *Landsturm*, in an
obsolete blue uniform under his greatcoat and with an equally obsolete
Gewehr 88 rifle and bayonet over his shoulder and a lantern hanging
from the point of the long blade, smoking a big clay pipe and showing a
bristly white mustache that almost glowed in the snowy dimness. His
military appearance wasn't improved by a long scarf wound around his
head to cover his ears and then under his chin and over his round brimless field cap, with the ends tucked into his coat.

One of the housewives made a disgusted sound as she buttoned her
coat and stepped out after Luz.

"It's those French harlots. They're working at the Siemens plant. I
suppose we must use what we have. But why do they have to kennel
them in our neighborhood? Put them in a warehouse! Let them sleep
less and walk farther!"

Another went *hrummp*. "Working at what, I ask you? Making eyes
and shaking their backsides at our men—when they're not doing more
than that."

The other German women kept silent, though Luz thought that
several would have said something rather different if they weren't being discreet, either from fear of the authorities or reluctance to fall out
with neighbors or both. Frau Blücher silently kissed her crucifix and
looked aside.

"Well, it's the war, and the war is the mother and father of all mis-
eries," Luz said, which brought more resigned sighs and nods all
around. "I must be going back—the girl will be getting restless and I
can't let her wander off or get into a state."

She made polite good-byes, shook hands again, and headed up the
street. That led her parallel to the column; there were about two hundred of them, walking by twos in the street itself, which was safe
enough given the sparse traffic.

Wooden-soled shoes clattered at the wet pavement, and most of
them had shawls, or sometimes outright blankets, around their shoulders or over their heads. Their clothes weren't nearly heavy enough for
this weather and had the sort of ragged appearance that would go with
having only one set and months of hard use and not much in the way of

thread, needles, or cloth to make repairs; Luz thought some of the patches she did see were from burlap sacks of the type heavy goods were shipped in. All the dresses had a large blue letter *F* in coarse cloth sewn on the front and back.

But those aren't all working-class clothes, she thought, catching sight of the ruins of a hat once fairly chic, and tailored shirtwaist day dresses.

There was a murmur of voices, though most of the women were trudging on silently, too tired or too hungry to chatter. The conversations were in French that mostly wasn't quite the *chtimi* patois that peasants in Picardy spoke, but heavily in debt to it. Many of them were sniffling or coughing as well.

So they talk like city dwellers from northern France, the areas the Germans overran in their first offensive right at the beginning. And they've been here for a while, six months or more, since spring or summer. Probably from Lille, Luz thought.

That was a big industrial town near the border with Belgium, or what had been the border, full of textile mills like a French equivalent of Manchester or Lowell and which she hadn't dreamed of visiting herself while she was in the country; otherwise if she remembered correctly it was mainly famous for the rumor that it had one bar or cabaret for every four houses.

There was that big scandal early in the spring when the Germans started deporting women and girls from Lille as laborers and the neutrals all got in an uproar . . . which didn't stop them from doing it, of course. Part of Ludendorff's new Total War policy. And some of them ended up here, working in the very same set of factories and labs I'm tasked with penetrating if I can . . . Now, is this an excessive risk, or is it a golpe de buena suerte *to be seized?*

A few of the women glanced up at her. Their faces were gaunt with hunger, not merely looking underfed like ninety percent of Berlin's population. At a guess, the managers were trying to feed the workers just enough to keep them going but also too hungry and exhausted to think about making trouble, or anything but food and sleep.

With irony intentional or otherwise, one of the propaganda posters at the trolley stop on Dihlmanstrasse had shown a stalwart Imperial Navy sailor against a mélange of U-boats and battleships and zeppelins, protecting a skinny German woman with an even skinnier child clutching at her skirts, and *Break the Hunger Blockade!* as the slogan.

Whether ordinary Germans themselves were actually dying of hunger because of the Entente blockade of food and fertilizer was a game of definitions; undoubtedly the death rates for the most vulnerable, children and the old and the sick and the inmates of asylums and such, had gone up sharply, and even bread and potatoes were still very short, not least because fertilizer and explosives used the same basic ingredients and shells had priority.

But these forced laborers certainly *were* starving, just in very slow motion. Things were almost certainly every bit as bad or even worse back in their homes. Hoover's Belgian Relief Commission had fed millions of civilians in Belgium and most of the occupied zone in France, making the difference between hunger and killing famine, but it had closed up shop with the declaration of war. Reports were that the Germans were seizing every scrap of food in France for their troops, and while they weren't stopping refugees, they weren't helping them either. God alone knew what the millions Hoover had fed in Belgium and in the occupied zone in France were going to do.

Run south if they can, I suppose, like those ones we saw in Tunis.

Which meant getting past the shattered, shell-churned, poisoned wilderness of the old Western Front. There the horror-gas lingered, invisible and impalpable and infinitely patient amid the legions of the unburied dead, where three great armies had bled each other for month after mortal month since the front froze into deadlock in 1914.

To die when they touch the gas, or by the roadsides of starvation and dysentery and cold and leave their bones in ditches if they can't make it to the French lines. No wonder everyone in unoccupied France who can is heading for the National Redoubt while they've still got a chance!

The body smell wasn't too bad even considering the cold— presumably the Germans had taken the recent findings about the role of lice in spreading typhus to heart, and feared the killer disease as no respecter of nationality. All the women had their heads covered, mostly by kerchiefs, but the way some looked as if they'd been close-shorn argued for inspections and delousing. Luz crossed herself again as she passed them, and some of them repeated the gesture before they filed into a modest set of flats that had been built just before the war and then modified recently; there were bars of cast-iron pipe on the windows on the first two floors, an exterior bolt on the door, and a sign reading:

Unterkunftsstätten für Ausländische Arbeiter.

Which meant *Quarters for Foreign Workers,* rather blander and more anodyne than the unpleasant reality. Luz did a quick count of the windows in comparison to their numbers, and her brows went up at the degree of tight-packing it implied. The crowding would be bad, though at least the body heat would help a bit with the cold. There didn't seem to be much internal lighting, just quivers as from tapers or candles, and there was no smell of cooking. They probably got their rations at some sort of factory canteen, which would make it easier to precisely control amounts and prevent the slightest waste.

The male equivalents are undoubtedly behind barbed wire and working in mines and forests and on farms and roads and the like as well as factories, she thought. *The Germans took two million Russian prisoners last year in central Poland alone and more since, not to mention plenty of every other nationality fighting them, and I doubt they're letting them sit idle.*

Luz walked past the militiaman standing outside the door, who looked only a little less miserable than his charges, then turned and stopped and nodded to him. It was a sign of how thinly Germany was stretched that the *Landsturm* man was alone there, or was in uniform at all; he might well be sixty or even older from his looks, though with wartime privations it was harder to tell.

"Good evening, Mr. Sergeant," she said as he perked up at something to break the discomfort and monotony. "I am the new tenant at number twenty-seven. This is cold duty! Surely your superiors don't expect you to stay out here all night? You should be at home with some good hot soup on a day like this!"

The coals in the bowl of his pipe glowed in the darkness as he took a pull; by the smell it was terrible tobacco, mixed with some pungent weed, and the overall effect was like burning horse dung. Though Luz admitted she was prejudiced, and agreed with Uncle Teddy's distaste for tobacco in general.

"Good evening, Fräulein! Yes, it is cold, by God! But no, I have only to stay until midnight. By then all the Frenchwomen are long asleep, the unfortunate creatures. Ah, it's a hard world for us poor common working folk!"

Unlike most of the housewives, the militiaman did sound like a Berlin native, or at least someone who'd spent all his adult years here.

"But then it's back at five for their reveille and to take them to the Siemens works. I can sleep a bit on a cot there and get a crust and something hot to drink, even if it's brewed from roots and leaves. At least it's warm inside."

Luz exchanged a few more pleasantries and expended another package of Leibniz biscuits. The old soldier—who turned out to be named Schultz—looked as if he'd been built like a chubby bear once but had rather fallen in on himself lately, and he mumbled eager embarrassed thanks for the gift and corrected himself and called her Frau when she said she was a widow.

"The soldiers at the front—"

He didn't use the blunt and rather coarse *Frontschwein*, frontline pigs, the term they used for themselves, probably guarding his tongue when talking in front of a woman.

"—like my sons suffer much worse than this, in their trenches. None of that trench business when I fought the French at Sedan as a youngster in 1870, thank God, or these terrible gases and all these awful new weapons. Then it was rifle against rifle in the open fields, a shot for a shot and a blow for a blow, and all over quickly. Still, with God's help it looks as if the war will be won soon—another great victory over the stubborn English in the papers today! Our boys will march past the Victory Column before His Majesty as I and my good comrades did in our day before His Majesty's grandfather, and all will be well."

"Yes, God grant it! May the Virgin throw her mantle over your sons, Mr. Sergeant."

"Amen to that, *gnädige Frau*. Then when the Fatherland has its rightful place in the sun, we ordinary folk will have some of the good things too. Plenty of food and land of our own, they say, better houses, better work, and chances for my grandchildren to rise in the world."

"God grant it," Luz said piously. "Good night, Sergeant Schultz."

I actually rather like a lot of ordinary Germans, Luz thought as she walked briskly back home through the snow, hands in her pockets and thinking hard. *There's no particular harm in them, it's just circumstances . . . my empire and theirs, and you have to admire the way they keep their shoulders to the wheel. Generals and emperors can accomplish nothing*, save the temper and disposition of the common people be stout, *as the old saying goes. I hope his sons* do *come home safe and give him more grandchildren to spoil. Without the victory parade, of course.*

"Sweetie! I'm home!" she said softly as she opened the door.

Ciara looked up from the table and smiled when she came into the kitchen, gave her a swift kiss, and then returned to her papers. Luz shed her coat again, hanging it near the heater in the parlor to dry better, and resumed her apron. Cooking had always been a hobby of hers, and she found it soothing and something that made thinking easier. Since she didn't want to go shopping if she could avoid it, she dealt with the most perishable goods first.

Veamos, she thought. *These pork chops look good, if not very large; some Danish pig ate well and died happy. In fact, they're thick enough to split and they'll go further that way. Aha! And I can trim this bone out and use that for the soup.*

Sometime later Ciara blinked and looked up. "That lovely smellingness is to be having! No, *that smells lovely!* What are you making?" she said.

"Well, this is going to be *Schweinschnitzel*," Luz replied. "You managed to ignore my pounding it flat, so here we go. Dredge in the flour . . . dip in the beaten egg mixture . . . dredge in the crumbs . . . and into the pan!"

There was a dragon's hiss as she dropped the two cutlets into the hot oil. Ciara clapped her hands.

"Oh, I love that! Auntie Treinel used to make it for us! Colm and Da loved it too when we visited her and Auntie Colleen together of a Sunday. She said it was even better with veal and we had that on special occasions, but I liked it fine either way."

"Did she? Well, I hope I'm up to her standards. The secret is to get the oil quite hot, but not too hot, not smoking—just enough you can cook it quickly and the coating is crisp and almost dry. I judge it by flicking in a drop of water and listening to the sound."

"How did you learn to cook German-style?" Ciara asked.

"By mildly scandalizing the *Reichsgräfin* and hanging about the kitchens," Luz said. "But she expected an American to be eccentric. Or mad. Or déclassé. Or all three together; she thought I must have fought Indians and bears as a girl. Seriously, she asked me once if my house had a stockade around it. There! Now I'll put it on this dish on the back burner, and the boxty to the fore."

That was a mash of potatoes roasted soft, with grated raw potato, a little onion, milk, a touch of flour, salt and pepper, and a bit of butter. She formed the little cakes with her hands and popped two for each of them into the oil, flipping with a long fork as they turned golden-brown.

"Boxty!" Ciara said, laughing, and sang an old Irish tune in an exaggerated brogue:

Boxty on the griddle,
And boxty on the pan;
The wee one in the middle
Is for Mary Ann!"

Luz laughed too, and began to whistle along to the jaunty lilt; it was safe enough, as long as they weren't loud—the walls were reasonably thick and you had to shout at the top of your lungs to be heard through them:

"Boxty on the griddle,
boxty on the pan,
If you can't bake boxty
sure you'll never get a . . . woman."

"You changed that last bit!" Luz said.

"Well, sure, I'd marry you for your cooking any time, my darling dear," Ciara said in answer, putting still more of an Irish lilt into her voice. "But no man, be his boxty never so good. I love it when you cook for me, though."

"My pleasure, *Süsse*. Remember when we had those *coquitos* in Castle Rauenstein?"

"I'll never forget it . . . and they crossed the Atlantic by air! The first coconut cookies baked in New York ever to fly to Holland and be eaten in Saxony!"

She looked down and smiled a little shyly: "I remember thinking at the time . . . you *were* a little frightening, you know . . . and then . . . *she makes cookies*. I knew that it didn't . . . well, it sort of reassured me anyway. And I was sort of . . . fascinated even then, though I didn't know why. It was . . . was . . . like being hit by a *soft* thunderbolt."

Luz gave her a smile, and she went on: "What's the rest of it here, the fine feast of the world?"

"Mostly as German as schnitzel, and potato pancakes aren't exactly foreign here, either," Luz said. "These are *Möhrengemüse*—a couple of carrots in a little butter. And a handful or two of Brussels sprouts done in beer, which sounds odd but tastes nice. All very German. The beer's *Berliner Weisse*, and here's a bottle each to go with it all. The quality isn't what it was before the war, but even so it's better than most of ours—I usually don't bother to drink beer in America, though the Mexicans do it well."

"And fine Irish soda bread!" Ciara said as they sat and she dug in with thoughtless youthful voracity, pausing to break and butter one of the irregularly shaped rolls of drop bread with raisins and dried apple in its steaming interior. "Now, *that* Auntie Colleen used to make."

More of it was left on the sideboard wrapped in a dishcloth.

"You made a fair bit of it, I see!"

"That's in pursuit of an idea I had," Luz said, and told the story of her walk amid sips of the pleasantly bitter pale ale.

Germans took beer seriously, even amid the Great War.

"You'd give some of it to those poor hungry French ladies, then? That's a good thought!"

"Yes, but I'm not being altogether altruistic," Luz said. "I remembered something from Seneca, you see."

Ciara frowned for an instant, then smiled as she remembered. "Not the town in New York, surely? Ah, no, you mean the Roman man."

Her self-education had included a little Latin for its technical uses, but not much of the literature. Luz found that Latin prose was often fun, and she loved the poetry. Catullus was one of history's great humorists, if you approached him in the right way; when Catullus insulted someone, they were *insulted*. Seneca was a sententious hypocritical preaching bore by contrast, but now and then . . .

"That's him. And he said once that the Romans had a proverb . . . *totidem hostēs esse quot servos.* Which means . . . pretty much . . . that: *If you want to know how many enemies you have, start by counting your slaves.*"

After a moment she added: "And since the enemy of my enemy is my friend . . ."

Her smile grew wolfish. After taking a moment's thought in turn, Ciara echoed it.

FIFTEEN

Siemensstadt (Northwest Berlin metropolitan area)
Königreich Preußen (Kingdom of Prussia)
Großdeutsches Kaiserreich (Empire of Greater Germany)
NOVEMBER 30TH, 1916(B)

Ciara murmured sleepily as Luz slipped out from under her arm and then out from under the duvet; then Ciara turned over, grappled a pillow in a grip like a drowsy, warm-blooded, and very affectionate octopus, and went back to sleep as Luz pulled the covers over her and eased the bedroom door closed behind. Thankfully, Luz had always been able to set an internal timer to tell her when to wake up, and she rarely needed an alarm clock. The house was chilly, and Luz shivered a little as she padded into the parlor and stood in front of the *Dauerbrandofen*, wishing that Germany were located seven or eight hundred miles farther south.

And ideally, was a nation interested only in art, music, food, wine, and carnivals and too civilized or too selfish or both to make war seriously. Of course, then it would be Italy . . . but between worrying about bottom-pinchers and worrying about Abteilung IIIb . . .

She added a little fuel to the stove and the *Dauerbrandofen*, and used the lukewarm water in the bathroom heater for a quick wipe-down. She'd hung her clothes before the heater, so they weren't too painful as she dressed. After that she went into the kitchen to pour a cup of— lukewarm—chocolate, still drinkable despite being left on the stove. She didn't dare offer any of that, which was a pity and too bad for poor old Sergeant Schultz.

Then she set several handfuls of raisins and chunks of dried apple rings to soak in a little *Śliwowica łącka*, a Polish plum brandy of which the setup team had thoughtfully left a couple of bottles. It was accessible to Germany and had been since the Russians were run out of Poland and Galicia last year, and hence a plausible possession to anyone who had soldier relatives sending things home, and would make excellent bribes if necessary.

There are people who'll take food or drink who wouldn't take money. Odd, but human beings are *odd. Also it's good stuff.*

The house stayed cold, just less so. There might be plenty of coal in the cellar, but they couldn't be too lavish in using it; people would notice the amount and duration of the smoke, and the results could range from eager, embarrassing questions as to where they were getting it— she could scarcely cite the American secret services putting it there— to resentful denunciations to the authorities for black-marketeering, which would be potentially disastrous.

Then she wrapped up the soda bread in two packets and put them in a wicker shopping basket, and tucked her hair up and pinned it so that it wouldn't show under her hat . . . and most importantly, wouldn't draw attention to the French-inspired bob-cut, which was uncommon in the States and much more so here. Her kit included hair extenders and some very good wigs in several different shades of brown, but she didn't want to use those yet.

Outside was very chilly indeed at the dead time of five on a winter's morning with her breath showing in white puffs. Thankfully it wasn't snowing or raining, though everything remained icy and slippery from the night before. Luz walked carefully, looking down at her feet occasionally and smiling a little; that ice couldn't have been arranged better if she'd ordered it from the Technical Section. It was blacker than midnight, though lights showed in a few windows.

And here's Sergeant Schultz with his lantern and pipe, Luz thought. *I wonder if anyone's fired that rifle in the last twenty years even on a range? And the last thing* Schultz *shot in anger would have been a Dreyse needle gun in the Franco-Prussian War, paper cartridges and all.*

Not everything *everybody knew* about Germans was true, but they really did tend to be punctual to a fault, particularly these Prussians. She'd lived in countries where precise times for anything were polite fictions or at best more in the nature of guidelines, but hereabouts being late was regarded in roughly the same way as publicly picking your nose and eating the results.

They make Yankees look like Mexicans that way.

"Good morning, Mr. Sergeant!" Luz said. "I remembered you said how early you must rise, and here is a little something for you from the dinner I made last night—biscuits with raisins—an old family recipe."

She pulled the smaller bundle out of the basket, unwrapped the two lumps of soda bread, and held them out. Many families in Bavaria did have a particular recipe for some sort of baked goods, though this one was actually from her father's mother, who'd been born an O'Sullivan. Grandma O'Sullivan had died not long after Luz was born but had fortunately left a collection of recipes among her effects, and Mima had studied them so that Papá could have some of his childhood favorites like soda bread or Dublin Coddle.

Schultz was flustered, but she could tell his nose twitched at the scent; when you were hungry, your sense of smell got better, for some reason.

"No, no, Frau Huber, I could not, you are too kind. Times are still very hard, I cannot take the food from your mouth."

"Please. If my own father or grandfather were serving the Fatherland so, I would wish that people be kind to him. And my husband's family are farmers and still very kind to *me*, and I'm going to be looking after their other son, but he's not out of the hospital yet so it's no hardship. We have plenty; it's a sin to let anything go to waste with things as they are."

"Since you put it that way, Frau Huber. Many, many thanks!"

The column of Frenchwomen behind Schultz was silent but restive, anxious to get out of the cold and to whatever vile potato-peel-soup excuse for a breakfast they were given. He led the way again, happily eating one of the pieces of soda bread as he went, and they pressed toward his heels.

Wait a minute, she thought, glancing back.

Schultz ate the first lump of soda bread the way a man would an apple; but at the same time he held the other behind his back, almost ostentatiously not looking as one of the women darted forward and grabbed it, took a bite, and then with a truly impressive display of will-power passed it on to the one walking next to her. It disappeared rather more quickly than the first one had, and the fourth laborer in line got a bit of crust and licked crumbs off her hand.

Nice to know my people-sense is still working, Luz thought. *Schultz is a good patriot, and probably he was a good soldier in his long-distant day, but a bit of a softie.*

She'd chosen a spot where light from the windows fell on the women's faces, and she watched carefully but inconspicuously. One was approaching—scalp-cropped hair under a ragged kerchief, but the remnants of a good shirtwaist outfit, and bony in a way that emphasized that she was about five or six months pregnant. And something about the way her eyes flicked, dark and hot, not lowered in blank misery like many . . .

Luz waited for an instant, picked her moment, and then let her foot skid out from beneath her and toppled, windmilling her free arm and crying out:

"Huif! Huif ma!"

Which was an appeal for help, in broad Bavarian as if she'd been startled out of a schoolteacher's educated speech and back into the patois of her childhood by feeling herself topple. Her target did help her, though involuntarily; when someone fell into you there wasn't much else you could do, especially if you didn't have the room or good footing or time needed to dodge. If you just let them fall they'd be very likely to pull you down with them.

That might have happened anyway if it had been a genuine slip; the Frenchwoman felt like a bundle of sticks thinly encased in gristle and rags. Luz braked the fall expertly, digging a heel into the slick surface of the road and propping them both up without appearing to do so. The Frenchwoman's face had shown only annoyance and surprise; the surprise increased as she felt the strength of Luz's grip and realized that it hadn't been an accident after all. The Black Chamber operative whipped the second bundle of soda bread out of the basket and into a fold of the blanket the other woman wore wrapped around her shoulders.

"Courage, ma soeur," she said quietly.

While their faces were close she went on in the French of an educated woman with a very slight Provençal accent, based on that of a girl from Arles she'd gone to school with and who'd looked a good deal like her:

"Take this. Tonight, a candle across your window three times at half past seven. Then wait for three pebbles hitting the window, much later!"

The Frenchwoman gave a quick nod. Luz straightened herself with a louder:

"Danke," to the woman and a cheerful:

"Just slipped a little! Nothing hurt!" to Sergeant Schultz.

And the beauty of it is that even if Schultz noticed anything, he'll most likely just think I was doing them a kindness but that I don't want it seen, Luz thought. *He's a nice old* abuelo *who pities them himself, and he'd just look the other way.*

Luz waved again, which Schultz answered with the bowl of his pipe in his hand, and then he trudged off, contentedly brushing crumbs off the front of his greatcoat, doubtless not wanting to have to explain them to anyone at the factory canteen.

Luz went back up to No. 27 and let herself in, grinning slightly. Spying usually involved manipulating people's fear, hate, ignorance, greed, and the more unpleasant types of lust. Occasionally you could take advantage of the better angels of their natures instead, which was a refreshing change.

Ciara emerged from the bedroom while Luz was busy in the kitchen. She was encased in pajamas, nightgown, robe, socks, and knit slippers and went over to stand as close as she could without being in the way. They exchanged a quick kiss.

"Brrr! That quilt thing is lovely, but the stove's welcome once I'm up! And how did things go?"

She explained, and Ciara asked: "Well, good! It's nice that the sergeant's got a human heart, but why did you pick a lady who's in a family way?"

Luz sighed and paused in beating the egg whites and looked at her wordlessly. Ciara thought for a moment, flushed, and said with angry indignation:

"The poor woman!"

"Exactly. We'll see how things develop. I have full confidence in your abilities, *Süsse*, but . . ."

Ciara nodded. "I'm trying to *build* something to *detect* something we don't know much about! I think . . . I hope . . . it'll work, but it won't work the first try. Better to have belt and suspenders both, darling."

Luz nodded and went back to work. She'd separated the yolks and mixed them with the flour, sugar, salt, and a touch of vanilla—more precious than rubies in wartime Germany, but still available at a high price in neutral Scandinavia or places that smuggled therefrom—into a thin dough. Then she folded the stiff egg whites into it, and mixed them until the dough was fluffier.

"It's pancakes, then?"

"*Kaiserschmarrn*," Luz replied, as she turned the dough into a hot pan with some melted butter popping in it, then added the raisins and dried apple chunks that had absorbed the plum brandy and folded it over them.

"Imperial or Emperor's . . ." Ciara said. "What's *schmarrn*?"

"*Messed-up stuff*, or near as no matter," Luz said, and when Ciara chuckled through her yawn: "Or *chaos*. Really. The story is that it's the Emperor of Austria's favorite breakfast—no, I lie, that would be the last Emperor, poor old Franz Joseph, his grandnephew Charles has the title now, and the sublime privilege of doing exactly what Hindenburg and Ludendorff tell him to do, though he probably still gets to set his own menus. The *Reichsgräfin* was very fond of it too, though she insisted on Preiselbeeren jam on the side."

She used a knife and fork to rip the griddlecake into shreds and then scooped it out onto two plates and set them on the table with a jar of apple-butter jam, convincingly an unlabeled homemade variety.

The tea she made was some nameless herbal concoction.

"We couldn't get coffee?" Ciara asked wistfully, who liked her morning cup, though she preferred tea—strong and milky—in the afternoon.

"We probably could have, but I'd have thrown it down the plumbing if the setup team had been stupid enough to leave any," Luz said. "Coffee has such a wonderful smell, much stronger than chocolate . . .

and even leaving us chocolate was really more risky than wise. I'm going to note that in my report."

"Yes, coffee does smell . . . oh," Ciara said, and plied her fork. "We'd have curious, drooling Germans about the place if we brewed coffee? Standing outside the door making piteous faces and whimpering like mournful puppies?"

"They do love their coffee here, almost as much as Scandinavians do," Luz agreed. "And most of them haven't smelled the real bean for going on two years now; I could scarcely claim my Bavarian in-laws grew it on their farm outside München! Pigs and grain and potatoes and apples, yes. Even grapes and homemade raisins, if it was in Franconia; and real ones come in from Italy via Switzerland and Austria. Coffee no, not for ordinary folks of the type we're supposed to be."

"They can't import coffee *through* Italy?"

"A little, but the Entente restricts what the Italians can import, so the domestic price is set very high indeed and it's diluted with various vile substitutes. The smell would draw the people in this neighborhood the way blood in the water does sharks."

"This Emperor's Mess tastes wonderful, though!"

"Emperor's Mess for the queen of my heart, sweetie. What's on *your* menu?" Luz said, after her first forkful. "I'm basically here as your support, after all."

Kaiserschmarrn was just the thing on a cold day in a badly heated house, when your body needed more fuel simply to exist. She could see Ciara thinking the same thing, then thinking of all the people in Berlin who *weren't* getting what they needed on a cold day in cold houses, and sighing before she put it out of mind and got back to business:

"Well, the first thing I need to do is get the receiving antennae set up in the loft," she said seriously, then took another mouthful and chewed and swallowed before she went on:

"You see, I'm going to have to make and remake the circuitry—it's called breadboarding by experimentalists, because it's like pegging things to a breadboard—but that's where the input will come from to test each iteration, and then I rewire . . . the length of the receiver is crucial . . . I have the general outline from Mr. . . . N's notes, but I'll have to adapt as I go along."

THEATER OF SPIES —

She gave an impish smile. "That's assuming . . . N . . . and I are right about the Telemobiloscope and what's been done with it. They'll absolutely have to have included a tuning circuit, and different antennae for providing a ranging bracket . . ."

"I *think* I understand that," Luz said. "Meanwhile I'll fall back on traditional espionage; sneaking around, stealing, lying, cheating, deceiving, conspiring, and suborning. And that will start with . . . cooking!"

I can begin testing tomorrow," Ciara said over dinner; it was well after dark outside, sunset being around four in the afternoon this time of year and this far north. "Thank you for all the help!"

Luz chuckled. "Move this here, put that there, hold this while I do that?" she said. "Really, sweetie, all I did was what you told me. It's fascinating, too, watching you work. You're so *precise.*"

"Well . . ." Ciara ladled more soup from the crock into her bowl, her eyes downcast. "I've always dreamed of doing experimental work like this. And . . . nobody ever did that before."

Luz cut and buttered a slice of the bread. She'd made a simple dinner: something that would make the neighbors green with envy of her farm connections if they knew about it, but not bewildered or disbelieving or suspicious. On the contrary, it would confirm her story . . . and the smell had probably done exactly that. Thick lentil soup with onions and carrots and just enough ham for an occasional small taste; fresh-baked farmer's bread of rye mixed half-and-half with wholemeal wheat flour and none of the various Ersatz extenders ordinary people had to put up with when they bought from bakeries; and some nondescript hard cheese. Not to mention real butter, when even the oleomargarine available locally was like something from an auto's grease sump and very expensive to boot.

Perfectly satisfactory in itself, and they were both eating with gusto after a hard day's work in the chilly upper story, in her case including the relief of being able to do a full set of stretching and limbering exercises and spend an hour or so running up and down the stairs in her stocking feet swinging a half sack of flour over her head, which had also kept her blessedly warm. The forced inactivity of travel had been wearing on her; she'd been aggressively physical even as a tot, which had been the despair of various deportment teachers, and her life to date had confirmed the habit.

And the meal would provide her with some essential props for the next step.

Ciara cleared her throat and spoke, looking down at her bowl.

"Nobody . . . nobody ever helped me like that before. Oh, Colm and I used to do things together, but he was my older brother—he taught me things, hands-on things he could do more of in his work. I was the clever little sister who helped him, and he'd show me off and they'd laugh and tousle my hair and call me the Girl Engineer—and that let me see and do more things, but . . . nobody ever . . . just helped *me* like that, just trusted that I knew what I was doing."

Luz looked at her, with a piece of bread halfway to her mouth. "But sweetie . . . you *do* know what you're doing, and I know you do. Those first days we met you saved my life when you told me about that electrical alarm trap in Nicolai's office. And you figured out how to disarm it and I hadn't even noticed it was there at all! I *love* your mind and what you've learned all by yourself and what you can do with it. It's . . . it's very impressive and it's *beautiful*."

Ciara started to say something, then jumped up and rushed out of the kitchen. Luz put the bread down and stared after her.

"*El alma humana es un cuarto oscuro,*" Luz murmured to herself. "And in that darkened room of the soul we're always bumping into something we don't expect. Well, she and I will get to know our way around each other eventually."

She went into the bedroom and found Ciara weeping quietly into a pillow; Luz sat by her and took a hand, one that closed on hers with almost painful intensity.

"I haven't made you sad somehow, have I, my darling?" she said. "Tell me if I did."

"No. Just . . . very happy, and it makes me feel . . . confused."

"Do you need to be by yourself for a bit?" Luz asked, and Ciara nodded into her pillow. Luz gave her a kiss on the top of the head.

"Well, I'll put the crock on the back burner if you want more soup, *querida*. And now I've work to do."

She finished her own soup first, rinsed out the bowl and filled it again, put a plate on top of it to keep it from spilling and wrapped it in a towel, then cut several thick pieces of the bread from the loaf she and Ciara had been sharing and buttered them. Those she put in a cloth as well, before stowing it all carefully in a basket, throwing a scarf around her neck, buttoning up her coat, and going out the front door.

Someone had scattered a little sand on the sidewalks, which was welcome, and Sergeant Schultz's lantern provided a beacon. What was a little less expected was the presence of Frau Blücher, the horse-faced lady who'd invited her in to run the gauntlet of the neighborhood's informal *Hausfrau* Review Committee that morning.

"Frau Huber!" the woman said, politely extending a hand in a patched-and-darned glove. "This is a surprise!"

"Frau Blücher!" Luz said, shaking it equally politely and with the slight but definite degree of deference due from a younger newcomer to a neighborhood matriarch. "So good to see you again!"

Sergeant Schultz was eating a small ill-looking boiled potato, the fruit of 1916's disastrously scant and soggy harvest; that root—singular—had apparently been brought to him by Blücher, as she was folding up a cloth she'd used to carry it and keep it warm. As things were, even a questionable potato ungarnished except for a little salt was nothing to turn down. He finished the last bite with every sign of enjoyment and swallowed, saying thickly:

"Frau Blücher and the other good ladies of the neighborhood bring me a little something sometimes," he said. "It's very welcome, for an old man living alone, as things are."

It's probably very welcome and the difference between real suffering and not, Luz thought.

"Your daughter should take you in," Blücher said tartly. "*Or* your daughter-in-law."

"Both of them offered, *gnädige Frau*," Schultz said. "But I refused. Times are very hard with their husbands away at the front, and a useless old man shouldn't take food from the mouths of his grandchildren.

Ulrike and Katrina stint themselves for the little ones as it is. And you kind ladies help me so well!"

Luz laughed and inclined her head to the other woman. "I had the same thought, Frau Blücher. It is good to know that I and my brother-in-law will be living among people who have a good German Christian spirit and are ready to care for our soldiers."

She put the basket down and opened it, taking out the bowl and uncovering it in a puff of fragrant steam.

"I made some soup for our supper today, nothing much, just an *Eintopf*—"

Which meant *cooked in one pot*, what you did when you didn't have much time, or many ingredients, or just needed to use up odds and ends before they went bad.

"—with lentils, and I thought you might like something hot, Sergeant Schultz, since the weather is so cold and you must stand still outside."

"That is very thoughtful, Frau Huber! A thousand thanks!" he said.

His mustache twitched at the smell, and he set the lantern on a ledge to take the spoon and the steaming bowl.

Blücher deftly twitched the spoon out of his hand and took a small taste, just enough to get the flavor, and likewise tore off a small corner of the first piece of bread. Schultz submitted meekly, then dug in blissfully himself, smacking his lips and making wordless appreciative noises.

"That is good lentil soup," Frau Blücher said; her long look showed she thought Luz had gone short to bring Schultz this much. "Some carrot and onion . . . and with actual *ham*, isn't there?"

"Well, I had a ham bone left," Luz explained mendaciously. "My mother-in-law sent it with us when we left the village. If you bake the bone first it makes good stock, so I had it in the oven with the bread for a while and then into the crock; I think the marrow makes it so good for the taste, don't you? *Ach*, with some chicken feet too, though those you must simmer a long time to get any good from them. Then the pigs can eat what's left, back in the village. I brought a small jar of the broth with me, though the merciful Lord God knows what I'll do when it's used up. Do without, I suppose."

"The chicken feet work well when you can get them," Blücher said, with regret and an element of surprised respect, and popped the little tag of bread into her mouth.

"Hmmmm. I thought I smelled someone baking—that wasn't very common here even before the war. Most people buy from the shops; it's so much less trouble, and cheaper since the bakers can buy their flour and fuel in bulk."

"Nor in Minga . . . in München either, Frau Blücher," Luz agreed. "But my father was a harness maker in a very small village when I was young before he moved to the city for factory work, and my mother a farmer's daughter who always baked her own. It wasn't until I was twelve she let me make my first loaf all by myself. I find the kneading so soothing, you understand."

Which happens to be partly true, with the names and a few details changed. Mind you, in Cuba when Mima was a girl ordinary people lived on rice and beans and plantains and cassava, with risen wheat bread a luxury for the rich merchants and hacendados like the Arósteguis.

"She taught you well," Blücher said. "Very good *Bauernbrot*, and nobody can get *Weißbrot* anymore. Very nice crust!"

"*Ach, so*, that is the water. Brush the loaf with a little water, or milk when there is any, after it has risen—after you score it—and put a little cup of water in the oven, and the crust will never fail, so my mother taught me and so it is. And good crust makes the strike when you put the loaf in better, the bread rises higher and is lighter, I think."

"So it isn't all books with you, then, Frau Huber!"

"No indeed, Frau Blücher," Luz said. "Though with all the skill in the world, these days it's so hard to get what you need; there are no spices, chocolate is a memory, and even the official flour, well . . ."

Both the women grimaced and Schultz snorted agreement with their opinion of the awful adulterated Ersatz stuff, though he didn't stop his busy spoon to talk. Luz went on:

"Now, I grant you, I've been very lucky with my husband's family's generosity, even though God didn't bless us with children though we prayed so often He would—our time together was so short. It's only right that I come and help to look after Bruno here; that would be so difficult back in the village, more of a burden than they could bear with all the strong young men away and half the horses gone too."

She paused and went on, casting down her eyes: "And . . . it would be very hard, if his mother had to see her son so every day, so soon after losing my Karl . . . so hard anyway, for a mother to lose her son, and then this . . . The burns, you understand, they heal so slowly and badly. In the long run . . . there isn't that much hope, but it may be a long time."

"I heard hammering today," Frau Blücher said. "That will be those special things you mentioned the men with the wagon brought? The baths and so forth?"

"Yes, there is the special bath, and a bed with adjustable frames where he can sleep without pressing on the terrible wounds with slings to lift his limbs, and medicines and bandages and other things. We will be taking lessons in how to care for him . . . well, me really, the girl can't follow such things . . . at the hospital, the Charité."

Schultz hadn't wasted any breath on words while there was anything to eat, and then used the last of the bread to wipe the bowl gleamingly clean and the spoon too.

"A thousand thanks, *gnädige Frauen!*" he said, handing Luz the bowl and utensil, but not forgetting to thank Blücher as well; that one potato was a real sacrifice for a family like hers with young children.

He chuckled with satisfaction: "When I write to my Franz and Alfons and Ulrich . . . Alfons is in the east, at some place called Rostov on the edge of the world, Frau Huber, and Franz and Ulrich are in France . . . south of Paris now, not fighting the English, thank Almighty Lord God . . . I will write to tell them how beautiful kindhearted ladies bring me good hot food and fine bread and real farm butter while I am on sentry-go. How they will envy me, and curse, and swear to their fighting comrades that the damned old fool lies, lies, lies!"

"Nichts zu danken, Herr Sergeant," Luz said, waving it aside and stowing things away in her basket.

It had been a big bowl of filling soup, and probably much more than he was accustomed to at one sitting these days, with a potato for foundation and several thick slices of bread and butter on top. With any luck he'd be drowsy and very ready for his bed by the time he went off duty, especially since he had to get up as early as his charges.

One of the basic skills of a spy was watching without looking, and not showing it when you saw something you were waiting for. As she spoke a candle passed behind a window at the corner of the building once ... twice ... three times. It was a little late, but only a few minutes, and she doubted the laborers had many watches left. After cash, timepieces were the first thing prisoners had stolen from them.

Frau Blücher bid her good night with a smile; Luz had passed several tests and was, though probably provisionally, in her good graces as a capable housewife and cook devoted to caring for the members of her family, pious, kind, and patriotic—and suitably deferential to an established, respectable pillar of the community. Someone well worth cultivating for her rural, food-producing connections, too. If the hypothetical injured brother-in-law had actually shown up, Luz would have been absolutely unsurprised to be deluged with offers to help, given with an unspoken hope of getting part of the parcels from the countryside in return.

The fact that Luz's cover identity and Blücher were both Catholics in an area long dominated by Lutherans and in a notably irreligious city probably didn't hurt. Unless Luz's social antennae were much less sensitive than the electronic ones Ciara was running around installing in the rooms of the loft.

Sergeant Schultz beamed at her with grandfatherly affection.

"That soup was nearly as good as my Luise used to make, Frau Huber!" he said, and gave a little bow as she headed back to No. 27.

Luz nodded to herself as she stopped by the pathway to their temporary home and bent to select three pieces of gravel that she slipped into her pocket. Then she opened the door, darted through, and closed it as quickly as possible, which everyone hereabouts would be doing to lose as little heat as they could.

I hope there aren't any repercussions for the folk of Rapsstrasse from all this, she thought with affectionate amusement. *I like them. Not that I'll alter anything I do one bit because of it, but I do hope.*

Luz hung up her coat; the kitchen was comfortable, if you were a northern European or used to their ways, and luxurious by the standards of 1916. Ciara was sitting at the table, back amid her litter of plans and notes and her own sketch of the upper story of the house with what she intended to do drawn in, and she looked up with a smile as Luz kissed the top of her head.

"How did it go?" Ciara said.

"Excellently," Luz said, and gave the details. "I've gotten the nod of approval from Frau Blücher, and Sergeant Schultz is as putty in my hands. And I saw the light. That means some cold work later, but needs must when the devil drives. And how are you feeling, *Süsse?*"

Ciara chuckled. "Odd, darling, but certainly not *bad*. I'm sorry if I was a bit of a goose just now."

After a moment: "I've felt so alone since Da and Colm died."

"Not alone now!" Luz said lightly.

I did sort of catch her on the rebound, emotionally, she thought. *And I was starting to really, really want something . . . substantial, though I wasn't thinking of it with the top of my mind. Just the right moment for both of us, I suppose, and we were in a pressure cooker too there in Castle Rauenstein, or even more on the U-boat.*

"No, not alone anymore, never again. And that's been such a beautiful dream . . . but just now it felt so much more *real*, and that felt . . . I don't know, wonderful and . . . a bit painful at the same time. Like growing up. The difference between dreaming . . . dreaming vague dreams . . . and getting what you dream of and knowing what it is."

Ciara sighed and went on: "And I thought: how I wish I could introduce Luz to them! To Colm and Da. But I couldn't really, even if they were alive, could I? No matter how much I loved them, or they me."

Luz winced slightly; it didn't matter that they'd never have met if her brother hadn't died in the Dublin rising and her father of a stroke and grief, since that wasn't really the point.

"No, probably not, alas." She bent and put her arms around the other's neck, and Ciara leaned her head back against her. "But look at it this way; you *can* introduce me to your aunties . . . though that will be a bit nerve-racking for me. I just hope they approve of me!"

"They will when they see how happy you make me, and how good for me you are!"

Luz laughed into Ciara's hair, still smelling faintly of the medicinal scent of the hair dye. "When they see how I regularly get you into peril of your life? Though we can't actually tell them *that*, just some vague *we work for the government.*"

"I managed to get myself in peril of my life all on my own that first time, by listening to that . . . that *buinneachán* Sean McDuffy, not to mention having to stick Colonel Nicolai with a hatpin to teach him manners, and you got me out of it all, alive and with no more than a thump on the noggin!"

Then, sounding flatly serious: "And I'm here now by my own choice, my darling Luz. I'm here to fight for my country by the side of the one I love, and Auntie Colleen and Auntie Treinel would expect no less of me!"

Luz hugged harder. After a moment Ciara went on, with a different tone: "And how long before you must go out again?"

"Four and a half hours, a little more or less depending on how sleepy Schultz gets. And thirty minutes for preparation and limbering, though the climb's not anything like as bad as going over the roofs of Castle Rauenstein to get into Nicolai's office in that *pinche* cold rain that nearly killed me. Why?"

"I have to wait while the adhesive sets on what I put up, so there's nothing more I can do today . . . and war puts its hand on your shoulder and says *hurry*," Ciara said, standing and taking Luz by the hand with a determined grip. "Follow me!"

Luz found herself whistling *La Primavera* from Vivaldi softly as she finished slicing and buttering the four small loaves and packing the basket in the kitchen, and made herself stop. Then she took a series of slow deep breaths, making her feeling of relaxed contentment and benevolence toward the whole world go away, letting the cold seep into her soul. It would be too easy to drift into a mistake when feeling happy.

Baskets are wonderful things, she thought as she chopped the cheese into four equal parts. *So is the fact that nobody thinks anything of a woman carrying a basket. Even in a painting she's the background to the* important *things going on.*

Luz grinned. She remembered a night in Puebla three years ago, one that had ended with a Carranzista general by the name of Álvaro Obregón Salido and his staff and headquarters going skyward with forty-eight sticks of neatly placed dynamite in the cellar as the propulsive force, just before the Army and Marines swept into the town whose defenses she'd neatly decapitated. Nobody had looked in her basket then, either, except for a guard who'd grabbed a handful of the tortillas stacked on top of the explosives. She'd just been one more anonymous chattering female heading home with a fringed rebozo draped around her and a basket on her head, full of food for the family.

There were none so blind as those who would not see.

After which I made sure that the Black Chamber, at least, fears women bearing wicker containers! The Director listened, too . . . he said I saved us a thousand men dead and wounded with that bomb, like an artillery shell that could think . . . and he made sure Uncle Teddy heard all about it without my having to immodestly echarme flores. *I wouldn't be surprised if that made my career as a field operative.*

And if anyone took a look at the one on her arm tonight, all they'd see on top was several loaves of sliced bread and some cheese. They'd probably want to steal it too, but nobody would suspect a woman with a basket of food of anything but possible black-marketeering.

Also helpful is the fact that as a widow I'm expected to wear dark clothes, she thought. *Not exactly full mourning black, not with cloth so scarce and rationed, but dark. Virtually invisible now.*

She stuck her head through the bedroom door. "Four hours!" she said. "Starting from the moment you hear the door close!"

"Yes, teacher," Ciara said, her voice kept light by iron willpower. "I will remember."

That was the amount of time before Ciara ran for the escape route; they both had small bags of essentials packed, ready for a bunk-out. Luz didn't know the directions Ciara had received. She also didn't know if Ciara could make it to the location they contained, with her shaky German and lack of practical experience in Germany, but if she'd had to bet she'd have put her money on the younger operative pulling it off.

And I don't intend to be taken alive if I can avoid it. I know too much. I'm glad I took time to make that new will before we left, too, so my querida *won't have to worry about things if she gets back and I don't. Money won't heal grief, but the lack of it doesn't make you feel any better either.*

"And up! Dressed! Watching for anything that goes wrong!" Luz said with mock . . . or mostly mock . . . ferocity, shaking a finger until Ciara swung her legs out from under the duvet.

SIXTEEN

Siemensstadt (Northwest Berlin metropolitan area)
Königreich Preußen (Kingdom of Prussia)
Großdeutsches Kaiserreich (Empire of Greater Germany)
DECEMBER 1ST, 1916(B)

O ne of the tools included in the kit they'd been left was a little mirror on an extensible handle. She used that to look both ways from
a doorway held open a crack. Then she closed it again as she saw Sergeant Schultz's lantern heading down the street; he was just a hair
early, but he'd probably been frightened of falling asleep where he
stood. That would be potentially fatal in several different ways, of
which freezing to death would be only one.

Even with the sort of part-time superannuated ex-Reservist purely-
for-form's-sake token guard the elderly sergeant represented, the German armed forces took a very dim . . . pointed . . . fatally pointed and
dim . . . view of sentries sleeping on duty. German military discipline
wasn't nearly as brutal as most foreigners thought, nothing like the rain
of beatings and abuse enlisted men still got in, say, the Japanese Army
or had in the Russian, but it was very strict about essentials and didn't
accept excuses.

She waited until she was sure he wasn't just taking a turn around
the block to keep himself awake, checked again with the mirror, then
stepped out into the darkened street; with a heavy overcast sky and few
lights it was only slightly lighter than the inside of a closet with the
door shut, just barely relieved by a little reflected glow from the city on
the clouds overhead.

Her feet moved silently through the darkness, and she knew she was effectively invisible. The problem was that everything around her was, too . . .

It was also extremely quiet. Some parts of Berlin would have raucous hectic wartime nightlife, and the great factories were on multiple shifts, working every hour of the twenty-four, but in this area you could hear a pin drop, or more practically she could hear her own skirts and coat rustling softly.

Which is why I carefully walked this same route twice while there was light to see, she thought. *Four hundred thirty-two paces . . .*

The apartment building loomed in the darkness, a slightly more solid stretch of black against the dark sky; central Berlin was in that direction and it wasn't deliberately blacked out, being far too distant from any Entente base to worry about enemy aircraft. Her gloved hand brushed the heavy, crude bolt on the door.

Everyone inside had better pray they don't get a fire, she thought grimly. *Because it would make that one they had at the Triangle Shirtwaist Factory back a few years ago in New York look like . . .* ¡Una bagatela!

And the Party was *still* milking that one for electoral benefit; they'd used it to help roll up Tammany Hall in a series of very showy trials.

Everyone inside this deathtrap would die unless someone got here and opened the door very quickly indeed. Though to be fair, Sergeant Schultz certainly would, if he was here, even if it got him in trouble. I think Frau Blücher would, too, if she noticed in time.

Twenty more paces to the corner. She took off her right glove and took the three pieces of gravel out of her pocket. The corner window, three stories up . . .

Luz closed her eyes for a count of twenty, then opened them. That was the way to make your night sight as good as could be. Her right hand cocked back over her shoulder with the piece of gravel held between thumb and forefinger; she had to hit the glass without breaking it.

Click.

Impact on the glass, a sharp sound but no shattering. She made herself take three breaths of the cold damp air, slow and deep, before she tried again.

Tick.

Not glass, but probably the frame. The same interval of timed breaths. That was the right window, but the forced laborers might be too frightened to respond, or simply too tired to stay awake, which was why she'd come as soon as she could after Schultz left. He was good-hearted but also conscientious even stuffed and sleepy.

Or they might have informed on her, in which case she was about to die.

She lofted the last piece of gravel.

Click.

Silence again. Luz controlled her breathing, made herself relax, let things—the darkness, the discomfort of the cold wet air, the feel of the icy pavement beneath her feet—flow through her without thinking about them. Not thinking about anything, waiting that was just wait-ing, not trying to suppress the flickers of images and words that drifted through your mind, simply maintaining purpose. You were a lot less noticeable that way, for some reason.

There.

Someone had opened the window and was showing a white cloth; showing it *inside* the window, which argued very good sense. Luz took another deep breath. This was where danger started to multiply, by the cube of the number of people she talked to outside her cover identity. But the chance to get actual help inside the factory was simply too good to pass up.

We need to get this done, *we need to get this done fast and get out. I can* feel *Abteilung IIIb looking for us. They're terrible spies, but when it comes to fanatical attention to detail they're world beaters. They* will *find us eventually, by brute force and massive ignorance and looking under every rock no matter how many rocks they have to lift. The way to avoid a chat with Colonel Nicolai ... or—¡Dios no lo permita!—Horst ... is to be long gone when they turn over the right rock. Caution is folly here. So, Luz ... ¡vamonos!*

She pulled out the coil of knotted silk cord with the little folding grapnel on it, the one with the prongs coated in soft, rather sticky rub-ber. They went *whunk* as the spring pushed them open—a very quiet *whunk*, since unobtrusiveness was the whole point. Luz whirled the grapnel around her head twice, letting a bit more of the cord slip through her fingers to widen the circuit each time and pumping more energy into it as the air hummed in the wake of the silk. The hum built to a whine, and she let fly at a point just above the white cloth, hoping it wouldn't clout the cloth-waver in the face.

She almost went limp with relief when it didn't run into anything, but there was no time for that. Instead she let the cord rest for the count of twenty; someone on the other end pulled at it as if they were grabbing it, then gave three sharp deliberate tugs. She drew it in then, steadily but not too fast and hand over hand. When it went taut she added force to the pull, testing it; there was no give beyond the natural elasticity of the rope, and the tightness of the woven cord limited that.

It had hooked on something, or more likely someone on the other end had fastened it to something heavy or well-braced.

She slung the basket over her back, tucked the free end of the climbing cord through her belt, and went up the wall at a walk, fending off with her feet and pulling up hand over hand along the knotted cord until she was just below the third-floor windowsill, panting lightly at the heavy strain that drew the muscles of her arms and back taut.

Bless you, Flying Corelli Family, she thought. *And you had to do it smiling and waving at an audience, at that.*

This close she could see the window, gray on black, because it was white-painted against the darker stucco.

And this is the point where it's most likely that a grapnel will come undone. It's also a long way down! So . . .

"*J'arrive,*" she said quietly; she could feel the presence of other human beings in the room, perhaps sounds or sights below the level of conscious perception, perhaps something else. "*Tais-toi!*"

For a wonder, they *did* keep quiet, after a murmur of:

"*Une femme?*"

Without any other babble of words or clumsy interference intended to help; that might be worrying itself, because it showed more discipline than civilians usually had. A surprising share of people couldn't overcome that childish need to be involved.

So I'm either going in to recruit some informants, or into a fatal gunfight. How jolly . . .

She reached up and felt around. The sill was painted wood, rough beneath the fingers of her glove; Luz reached farther in, until her fingers could hook around the inner side. This was going to be a bit of a strain . . .

She brought her knees up, hooked her feet around one of the knots in the cord with an ankle-and-toes lock, and then surged up as she released the rope with her right hand and shot it out to catch the sill as she had with her left. Even with her leg muscles driving up and supporting part of her weight, the strain on wrists and forearms in the awkward position was painful, but she pulled, pushed, got a hip on the sill and pivoted over it into the room in one smooth wrench, panting slightly with the explosion of effort. Her right hand went inside her jacket at the same instant, fingers on the butt of the pistol.

"You *are* very truly a woman!" someone said in French.

Also a woman, and sounding mildly shocked. Luz let out a silent breath as she took her hand off the gun; she'd been ready to shoot the first round through the fabric, to kill anyone trying to immobilize her right arm. Then she took several more deep breaths, while reminding herself it was a temporary reprieve. Relief could make you careless.

"Vraiment, je suis une femme!" Luz said.

Putting a touch of wonder into the tone along with the very slight Provençal accent. Luz couldn't actually speak any of the many regional patois spoken in France—spoken more often than the supposedly national language in many places, at least at home—but she could be native-fluent in the standard tongue *as if* she'd grown up in four or five different parts of the country, based on girls she'd gone to school with and learned to imitate with a natural mimic's ease.

"Quelle surprise!" she added dryly. "What a surprise!"

At that, they might have expected a male agent to do the active part. Her lips quirked as she came to one knee, pulled the rope in, and coiled it with a quick deft circling motion. Men weren't always the only ones hypnotized by their own high opinion of themselves. The Frenchwoman snorted in acknowledgment.

Then she snapped: *"Ferme la fenêtre, qu'on discute."*

The window slid shut in response to her order, and there was the sound of a curtain being drawn across it.

"Is it safe to make a light?" Luz asked.

"Oui, madame."

There was a scraping clicking sound; Luz blinked in the darkness. That was someone using a flint and steel, the noise and the spray of sparks both unmistakable and familiar from her time in the more backwaterish type of Mexican backwaters, but it was odd to see it in one of Europe's great cities. More of what the Great War had wrought. She put in:

"I have matches."

She lit one, held between her cupped hands, and someone pushed a stub of tallow candle in to take the flame. Even in the dark Luz had known the room was small. With the low red flame of the candle—she thought it was homemade, with a wick teased from the hem of someone's blouse—she saw that it wasn't a room properly speaking at all; it had been something on the order of a really big closet, probably used for storing cleaning supplies. Now it had a set of crude bunkbeds knocked together from raw splintery lumber taking up most of the limited space, amid a feeling of crowding and smell of cold stale frowst.

Someone had taken the grapnel and put two turns of the rope around an upright of the bunk. The little space was barren save for two images; one a crudely hand-carved but forcefully made crucifix bearing a tormented-looking Jesus, and a Madonna and Child, done in low relief on a scrap-wood board.

There were four women staring at her as she came to her feet and rearranged her skirts, looking like the witches from *Macbeth* in the guttering light of the candle; three sitting on the bunks and one making sure the curtains of rough sacking with newspaper pinned to the inside were tight. That was the crop-haired, pregnant one she'd stumbled against.

Part of the sinister look was the lighting, and part was their gaunt, unwashed state; Luz discounted that. Part was an unnerving fixity of expression. Obsessive hatred and lust for revenge were states of mind with which she was intimately familiar, but here it was boiled down to its concentrated essence. Hardship and fear broke some people; with others it honed the entire personality into something like an obsidian razor.

She could imagine any of these sitting and knitting and glaring like that as they watched *Madame La Guillotine* do her work and the heads of aristocrats fall into the basket during the Terror.

There's an old saying that you should never do an enemy a small injury, she thought. *Here, the definition of small is leave alive.*

Luz held up a hand. "No questions! No names! What you don't know, you can't be made to tell; nor can I. *D'accord?*"

The bony-faced woman she'd picked as the most likely source nodded and spoke:

"Bon, madame. D'accord."

At close range and with better light than she'd had out on the street this morning, Luz revised her estimate of the woman's age downward, probably around thirty or even a bit less, and she'd probably been striking in a way when she was better-fed. One of the others was in her teens, all staring brown eyes in a thin pale face, the others in between. Looking at them, Luz decided to go a little further.

"Let's just say I've been in North Africa recently. I'm here to get information about something at the Siemens works because we know—"

They'd assume that by *we* she meant the French Deuxième Bureau, or at least the French government, but it would be better to let that go. They'd have heard only distorted rumors and German propaganda about what was happening in their homeland, both passed in turn through a filter of wishful thinking. Luz herself could easily be Provençal, or Gascon or Corsican, or a *colon* settler from Algeria, any of which would fit her looks better than German. She kept up the very slight southern accent in her French, too.

She wasn't here to give them a situation briefing. And it would be too depressing if she could, since the essence of it would be *France is dying on its feet.* Something new would come of these years of fire and blood and terror and call itself France, but it wouldn't be the nation they'd grown up in and might not even be in the same place on the map. In any event, the United States and France were allies and were fighting Germany together. Helping the Black Chamber was in effect working for France . . . and if they were interrogated, news about a *French* spy would muddy the waters nicely. Hiding a true answer among a stack of false ones was a very useful method for misdirection.

"—that another terrible secret weapon is being planned. But first, this."

She unslung the basket, opened it, and handed out the newspaper-wrapped loaves and cheese. A little to her surprise the Frenchwomen paused while the one at thc curtains, who seemed to be the leader here, clasped her hands and said softly:

"Benedíc nos Dómine et haec Túa dóna quae de Túa largitáte súmus sump-túri. Per Chrístum Dóminum nóstrum."

Then she crossed herself; Luz joined in the gesture, and they all murmured *"Ámen."*

At that point they did what she'd expected to happen right away: eating with intent ferocity.

"My God," one said. "Fresh bread! Butter! I haven't tasted this since before we were taken away!"

All except for the youngster, who stopped after her second bite when the other woman spoke. She wept, and it grew to enormous open-mouth soundless sobs that turned her face to something like a Greek tragic mask as she rocked back and forth, hugging herself.

"Maman!" she keened. "I want my maman, and Papa, I want François and Marie and my little Chouchou—"

Which was the sort of name you gave a cat.

"—I want to go *home!*"

Luz tensed, but the older woman shook her head; apparently this wasn't unusual enough to attract attention. The others gathered around the teenager and hugged her, patting her back and kissing her on the cheeks and head. After a while the fit of weeping cleared, and she lay down and began to continue eating, tearing small bits off the sliced loaf she clutched to herself and chewing them mechanically.

"I'm sorry," the older woman said to Luz. "Most of the time Simone . . . oh, name of a name, I shouldn't have, well, that *is* her name . . . most of the time she is all right, but sometimes . . . when things are too much, lately . . . she dreams she is home before the war, a waking dream, and then when something brings her back to things as they are . . ."

A very Gallic shrug. "It is as you see, quite bad. Even learning that we are not altogether forgotten can do it, it seems."

"*Pas de problem,*" Luz said, and reached into the bottom of the basket, hiding a slight inner wince since these people *had* been quite thoroughly forgotten. "I have here the plans of the various Siemens factories in this town. Which is the one at which you ladies work?"

She spread the papers on the floor—it was the only flat surface, because the beds were heaped with scraps of cloth and pieces of news-paper for insulation. After a good deal of back-and-forth—because the drawings were labeled in German, and the Frenchwomen spoke only enough pidgin to get by day-to-day and could read even less—she determined that they were all in the giant new Wernerwerk II build-ing, opened just a few months before the beginning of the war, and probably the best-equipped and laid-out factory of its type in the world as well as the largest.

That structure was listed on the helpful page attached to the map as producing *telegraphic, telephonic, wireless and other electrical equipment*.

"We . . . we here in this room . . . mostly work sweeping and clean-ing," the leader of the little group said.

Luz wasn't surprised. Total war meant chronic shortages of every-thing, including even the simplest forms of unskilled labor. A fair bit of routine cleaning had to be done if a factory was to remain efficient, or usable at all. It made more sense from the enemy's point of view to use foreigners for elementary work like that; even back home, with the drop-off in immigration from Europe you saw more and more Mexi-cans in that sort of job, or some of the Negroes who were leaving the South in such large numbers these days, both groups escaping a rural peonage that made even the most casual sort of town work look good.

And since cleaners' work required them to move around, they were likely to see more than someone confined to a bench.

"The others"—the Frenchwoman gestured to encompass the apart-ment block—"some the same, and also shifting carts of parts between places. And some at worktables fitting together parts, each doing one motion over and over. There are thousands of us from Lille altogether, but they keep us separated. We see—"

Luz frowned when she'd finished, and the others had made their interjections. They were as willing as could be wished; they described what she recognized as production of detonators and fuses and field telephones and possibly wireless transmitters. The problem was that they didn't understand much of what they moved around or saw assembled, and Luz herself didn't have any idea of what the thing she was really after *looked* like.

All she'd seen herself were huge rectangular shapes being riveted to the masts of warships in Wilhelmshaven; a single hurried glance in the dim light of a North Atlantic afternoon, and that was a glance at the outer housings rather than the equipment itself.

Which wouldn't have meant a thing to me and almost certainly hadn't arrived there yet anyway. If only there was a way for Ciara to look through my eyes! I may have to bring her in . . .

That didn't make her happy; the risk would be large. But the mission came first.

"What I am looking for will be very secret, or very secret until recently," she said. "It will have been shipped to the German Navy and possibly to the *Luftschiffe*, the Zeppelins, recently—in the past month or two. Large heavy electrical devices."

The forced laborers looked at each other. "Many things go to Wilhelmshaven from the works . . . many also to the airship base west of here. Staaken, they call it."

Luz nodded; there had been a Zeppelin base and construction yard there on the other side of Spandau since 1914, originally as part of the airship race with the United States but vastly expanded since.

"Have you heard of any such thing as an electrical rangefinder or viewing device mentioned?" she said. "Something that gives powers of sight? Sight in darkness or in cloud."

Silence and frowns and uncertain glances at each other. Then the teenager named Simone spoke.

"What is *Heimdall*?" she asked.

The older woman turned to shush her but halted when Luz touched her on the arm.

"Heimdall is a god, an old god of ancient days who could see everything, everything in the world even if it was hidden in darkness," Luz said, her voice firm but gentle.

Heimdall . . . could they really have been as careless about code names as that? Code names are supposed to conceal *what you're doing, not give you a dramatic*

Germanic mead-in-Valhalla-with-Wotan thrill! They might as well have put up a sign, Secret Experimental Range-Finding Device Here ... *Calling their horror-gas* the Breath of Loki *was bad enough, considering that the Trickster ended up under a drip of poison! Well, yes, so conceivably they could be that careless. The worst spies in the world,* verdaderamente ... *but if you're strong enough, you don't have to be subtle.*

"Where did you hear the name, Simone?"

"Two men ... one in a white coat, and one in a blue uniform. The one in the uniform, it was blue. He said *Heimdall* would see the English ships in the dark. And the one in the white coat said if he had a ... a something he could, Heimdall could see in the dark, if Valhalla had been electrified like Berlin. But I didn't understand that part. They were joking with each other, laughing. I didn't like the way they laughed."

Luz went over to the bunk where the girl lay and knelt, smiling. "That is very good, Simone," she said gently.

The girl flared up. "I'm not stupid! I'm just ... sad sometimes."

"Of course you're not stupid," Luz said—sincerely.

Perhaps un poco loca, *but not* stupid. *That was observant, and clever to link* seeing *with what I said. And she certainly has reason to be sad.* ¡Verdaderamente!

"It doesn't matter whether you understood the words," Luz said. "Just tell me what they *sound* like."

She kept her face relaxed and the tension out of her shoulders despite the primal urge to grab the girl and shake her; making people afraid had its uses, but getting them to think clearly wasn't one of them. It all depended on whether the girl had a talent for remembering the patterns of sounds. She waited, willing herself to be like a downhill slope, drawing information to her by force of gravity.

"He said ... Effa."

Which was just syllables. The girl's face knotted in thought.

Then the teenager's brow cleared. "And the one in the blue uniform said, in Valhalla they are ... *sair aldmoydish?*"

"*Sehr altmodisch,*" Luz said, and rendered it into French: "*Primitif ...* old-fashioned."

Simone nodded. "So *primitif* that they have, have no ... no power for a ... the word sounded like *one-eight ... fuuwrapffagung?*"

Luz closed her eyes and held out a hand for silence, not straining but letting the sounds sink into her mind and then pronouncing them there while she switched the interior flow of her thought from French into German and back over and over. For her, really *learning* a language as opposed to just being able to function in it had always turned around a moment when she sensed its rhythms with a swing and a sway, like dancing to a tune. After that the rest came quickly. Now it was as if some card file in her mind were flipping through thousands of alternatives, matching them against the *sounds*.

One-eight? she thought.

In the French they were using, Simone had said *un-huit*, and it didn't correspond to the way her language used numerals. But the girl was pronouncing them in a Picard way, *eune-'uit*, and then she paused and repeated it with the *h*-sound back in the second word: *eune-huit*.

Eune . . . could that be Eisen . . . Iron? No . . . ein, one. Huit . . . not a numeral in German, or anything like one. Heit . . . *quality of being. Einheit! Unit! Or* thing *or* device. *Talking about something scientific or technical, Einheit would definitely mean* device.

So, the Germans had been talking about a device. Now . . .

The beginning of the second word . . . that long u*-sound with a* wuh *at the end is an umlaut. But not a regular one! Isolate it from the rest:* fuuwr. *I think . . . yes, it's für. For.*

Luz O'Malley Aróstegui *did* have a talent for sounds; speech was like music to her . . . and she had perfect pitch.

Einheit für. *Apffagung. A device* for *something. And* ap, ab, *that's just the prefix for a verb in the indefinite form . . . so . . . we have a* device for *the-quality-of-doing-something-and-a-verb.*

Then her eyes flared open and she smiled, or at least showed her teeth. Simone flinched back, and Luz absently made a soothing, shushing sound and a pat-the-air gesture before she spoke.

"*Einheit für Abfragung,*" she said softly. "Device for . . . searching, seeking . . . detection! Or EfA, Effa, if you were using the letters as an abbreviation, an acronym. A device for detecting or seeing that requires an electrical power supply. Oh, loose lips *do* sink ships. Or keep them from being sunk."

The older woman shot her a keen glance; the others looked bewildered.

"Mesdames," Luz said seriously, catching the eye of each in turn. "You must not ask questions at your work concerning this! You must not!"

She pointed a finger to each face, one after the other. "You are not trained for it; you will be caught; then you will be tortured in terrible ways and killed, and perhaps me with you, and the *Boche* will succeed in their plot. You may *listen*, but that is all!"

She thought the point had gotten home, but . . .

Risks getting worse . . . what was that mathematical phrase Ciara used . . . exponentially. At this point, we need to get it done and get out *before the ceiling falls in. That's the problem with foreign operations; you can't shut things down by breaking cover and yelling for the cavalry the way I could sometimes in the Protectorate.*

The older woman spoke up. "Simone, where did you hear the men saying these things?"

Luz held up the map, and they settled on the spot. "What were you doing there?"

Simone shrugged. "Scrubbing the floors, dusting, emptying the wastebaskets."

"We clean in there," the older woman said. "And—"

She turned and scrambled through one of the beds, then handed Luz a sheet of paper. Luz glanced at it; the columns looked like accounting, or possibly a parts inventory using a lot of cryptic abbreviations. Nothing directly relevant, but then you couldn't expect lightning to strike twice in the same evening.

". . . we take paper to stuff inside our clothes and to add to our bedding, for warmth. It is against the regulations, all the paper is supposed to be set aside to be sent to be reused, but we do it anyway—they expect it! The pigs won't give us more clothes or blankets. And that place is where they make the . . . I think the word is *Tech . . . techni . . .*"

"*Technische Zeichnung?*"

"Oui."

"Working drawings," Luz translated; or rather she said *dessin technique*, which she assumed someone from a manufacturing town like Lille would at least recognize.

"Yes, the working drawings for the machine shops and fabrication benches."

"Ah," Luz said.

Working drawings were the final instructions for machinists, the ones that let you build or make something without further help.

"And nobody really pays attention to the cleaning staff . . ." Luz said thoughtfully.

Most of the discussion that followed was Luz hammering home the need for absolute caution. She thought she'd convinced them by the time she had to leave. The bread helped. When you were as hungry as these people, food became a symbol of magical significance, the essence of power and authority and belonging.

Then she put the grapnel in her basket, but unfastened the rope from it and put it around the upright of the bunk-bed in a loop.

"I'll leave this here," she said, tossing the end of the cord out as she peered past the curtain to make sure the street had the same deserted quiet.

"Keep it well hidden, and let it down if I make the same signal of three stones. *Bonne chance, mesdames!*"

Her mouth quirked as she slid down to the sidewalk; she took the basket in a normal grip as the rope whipped upward and began walking back to No. 27 at a steady pedestrian pace. She'd just found a new way to risk a terrible death.

Hurrah! she thought. *I'd much rather read about this than do it. I hope Uncle Teddy enjoys the report . . . and that he gets a chance to do just that.*

SEVENTEEN

Siemensstadt (Northwest Berlin metropolitan area)
Königreich Preußen (Kingdom of Prussia)
Großdeutsches Kaiserreich (Empire of Greater Germany)
December 3rd, 1916(b)

Luz chuckled as she read the latest edition of the *Kreuzzeitung* while she finished preparing their breakfast, at a story titled *The Hopak Is What Is to Be Done*, a little human-interest filler suitable for maniacs.

She was making *Bauernfrühstück*, which was as simple as cooking got, leaving ample attention to spare for the news. The name translated as *farmer's breakfast*, though she thought *hasty and hearty* would be just as appropriate. You basically did a series of things in the same skillet, one on top of the other starting with sautéing some onions in melted butter, then panfrying some diced cooked potato, then pouring on a mixture of beaten egg, milk, and a little salt and black pepper with some diced ham if you had it, which they did, all the while stirring vigorously and enjoying the mélange of meaty smells and earthy vegetable ones.

Laughter wasn't the usual response people had to this rag's contents. Even before the war their specialty had been narcissistic preening about the virtues of all things German (except, say, Social Democrats or modern art or stalwart women's rights campaigners or peace activists like Anita Augspurg) and bloodthirsty howls of demented rage directed at neighbors who outrageously threatened the *Reich* by existing. It was the sort of publication that gave xenophobic militarism a bad name and had been a haunt of Pan-Germanist geopoliticians for years.

Now it was the semiofficial organ of the semiofficial dictatorship of

Generals Hindenburg and Ludendorff, and it had become the voice of the new unofficially-officially-backed German Fatherland Party, which meant it was not just under Colonel Nicolai's thumb like all the German press these days but his main mouthpiece to the world. Many of the editorials came straight from his office. Several of them had made broad hints lately that it was rather wasteful and backward and self-indulgently unpatriotic for Germany to have more than *one* political party.

And guess which one should be the only one? Dumb-heads! she thought.

The thought was sincere; back home the Party knew that you needed some competition to keep you on your toes, in touch with the people. And that a credible outside enemy kept the Party's own inevitable factions under some restraint too, because nobody inside the movement was willing to do anything that gave the old order aid and comfort. Progressives had spent a long time in the wilderness, before Uncle Teddy and the Old Guard's own dimwittedness and bad luck led them into the Promised Land in 1912, and it would be a long time before anyone forgot how unpleasant that wait had been. But if you suppressed all opposition, a new opposition sprang up in your own ranks.

You can't use politics to take the politics out of politics, as Uncle Teddy put it.

That was basic Darwin, and Progressives were nothing if not Darwinist. There were still Democrats in America, and Socialists. The Democrats were really a regional party with rather pathetic national aspirations, now that the PRP had broken the northern urban bosses and supplanted them with the Party-affiliated unions of the American Labor Congress. Socialists elected the odd mayor or dog catcher and one solitary congresswoman named Flora Hamburger whose district included the Lower East Side. They both served the same purpose a good sparring partner (or punching bag) did for a boxer.

The German Fatherland Party evidently didn't look at things that way.

In fact, one of the headlines today boasted that the Fatherland Party now had two million members, which even if a little inflated wasn't bad for an organization only a few months old. Germans were as capable of grasping which side their bread was buttered on as anyone, not to mention that victory had a million—or in this case, between one and two million—fathers, while defeat was an orphan.

Apropos of which, another headline in massive, ominous-looking Fraktur type announced that shells from the heavy artillery of *Heeresgruppe Deutscher Kronprinz*—the Crown Prince's Army Group—were landing on the beach at Dunkirk, which meant that the last British toehold on the European mainland would follow Calais into surrender within days.

Still another read: *Tours in flames!*

She gave a melancholy sigh at that. Tours was a small city on the banks of the Loire in central France, set amid a countryside of lushly gentle splendor studded with the dreaming garden-embowered châteaux of a thousand years. It had ... or had had ... a beautiful medieval section that had given her endless pleasure on visits, with its half-timbered buildings on crooked cobbled streets and odd little bookshops and antique stores and tiny wonderful hole-in-the-wall places where a young visitor on a day excursion from Paris could have exquisite *rillettes de porc du Tours* on a fresh baguette and a bottle of red Chinon for a few francs and sit with a friend watching the setting sun lay its gold on the towers of the Gothic cathedral and the fleecy clouds of the Touraine sky.

Now she'd never be able to take Ciara there and watch her face as she saw it all ...

The Great War is indeed Moloch the Devourer come again. Still, this other bit is *rather funny*, Luz thought.

She filled two plates with the hearty *Bauernfrühstück* mixture and took the buttered toast she'd been keeping warm out of the oven to set between them. She smiled again, this time at herself and the happy glow of pleasure the little domestic ritual of feeding her partner gave her. Tumbling about in bed driving each other to ecstasy was utterly splendid, but the small everyday things counted too.

I've finally found someone I can contemplate seeing every day for the rest of my life without the very thought making me want to kill them, flee, or both.

Ciara reached out without really looking and took a bite of toast—very, very slowly. After a moment she swallowed, blinked back to the real world from her fog of Deep Thought, and raised her brown-dyed eyebrows.

"What's funny, darling?" she said. "Didn't you just laugh at something?"

"Oh, just an article here that proves Colonel Nicolai does have a sense of humor after all, sweetie," Luz said, tapping the newspaper she'd set beside her plate.

Ciara's face went hard and she scowled down at her fork for a moment before taking a mouthful; she'd had personal as well as political problems with the Abteilung IIIb chief during her brief and sincerely regretted spell as an Irish Republican Brotherhood liaison-courier. That she'd dealt with the problems in an exemplary fashion that involved stabbing a hatpin into a wandering hand and flourishing it near his eyes to . . . as it were . . . drive the point home hadn't made the process any more pleasant for her to recall.

I really must *remember to kill Nicolai someday*, Luz thought whimsically.

But also perfectly sincerely. Killing and facing death was part of a field operative's job, as it was for a soldier; she'd do her best to do the dirty to the other side right up to the end of the war, then stop and walk away with no particular hard feelings toward her German counterparts who'd been trying to do the same to her. Work was work; wars had beginnings and endings. But this was . . .

Personal, and personal never *ends. How shall I kill him? Let me count the ways . . . Dousing him in gasoline and setting him on fire would be the sort of memory you could warm your hands at, but it would upset* mi corazón's *gentle heart. Just knifing or shooting or blowing him up would do*, por falta de una solución mejor. *If it doesn't come up during the war, then afterward. Revenge is a dish best served cold. And premeditated murder is the easiest major crime to get away with, after all, if you're careful; far easier than robbing banks.*

"I'd bet it's a *nasty* sense of humor, at that," Ciara said.

Luz suspected that Ciara had just recently realized *how* brave she'd been to give the man a blunt set-down in his own lair in Castle Rauenstein . . . where an irritating foreigner might have simply disappeared, if Nicolai hadn't been basically too professional to act on impulse like that with an asset.

Then Ciara looked down again as she started to ply her fork. "This is delicious!"

"It's the Danish ham," Luz said modestly. "Back home I'd use that

Virginia ham Diehl's Grocery stocks, and add some fresh green peppers from the garden to lighten it a bit . . . And yes, an extremely unpleasant joke, but directed at a worthy target for once. There were a group of exiled Russian revolutionists in Switzerland—*Bolsheviki*, they were called, followers of Marx in a very wild and woolly way, assassins and bomb throwers and bank robbers and general bloody madmen."

"Still, the czars were bad," Ciara observed. "It's no wonder some wanted to get rid of them."

"True, but *this* gang would have made Ivan the Terrible look like George Washington if they'd ever come out on top. Or perhaps like St. Francis. They asked the Germans, specifically Abteilung IIIb, to help them to do it. The Germans agreed . . . or said they did."

Ciara frowned. "I can't see the German army *really* doing that. They're not exactly keen on revolutionaries of any sort! And they've got the Russian government in their pockets now, don't they? Why would they help these madmen overthrow it?"

"To be fair, this apparently happened a while ago, just about the time of the Czar's abdication and before the Grand Duke asked for an armistice, and they're only now letting the press know that Abteilung IIIb offered to send the *Bolsheviki* from Switzerland . . . where they couldn't be touched . . . not yet . . . to Russia in a sealed train in return for their promise to sow chaos and destruction, which they would have done gladly, and follow Germany's line against the Entente if they seized power, which they might have done just as long as it was in their interests and not a minute more. Forty-five of their top leaders duly boarded the train, but it was diverted to Moscow and there the Regent's men—"

"Grand Duke Nicolai?"

"Right. His men . . . Cossacks . . . had been tipped off by Abteilung IIIb and were waiting. And the Cossacks dragged them off the train and sabered them then and there and finished up by performing a Cossack dance called the Hopak around the bodies, one of those squatting and leaping and sword-flourishing ones that's even more primitive looking than *Schuhplattler*."

Which was a Bavarian dance done in lederhosen, one Luz considered very much what you'd get if you dressed spastic baboons in leather shorts and Tyrolean hats.

"There's a lot of that sort of thing going on in Russia just now . . . killing, not dancing, that is. Their leader . . . he went by the nom de guerre of Lenin . . . apparently was so surprised that he kept frantically shouting, 'What is to be done?' Until the sabers came down, which as the newspaper here says answered the question conclusively: the Hopak is to be done."

Luz chuckled again. "Colonel Nikolai's offer probably came under the heading of *seemed like a good idea at the time.* Even very suspicious people like spies and revolutionists are often oddly trusting—they sort of convince themselves that something's true because they want it so very badly. They end up distrusting everyone except the one person they *should* distrust. Nicolai took advantage of that for his little joke."

"That *is* a nasty sense of humor the man has . . . still, I suppose if the *Bolsheviki* were robbers and rogues and assassins themselves . . ." Ciara said dubiously, wincing a little.

"I speak from experience, sweetie: one of the Russian gentlemen tried to kill me back . . . let's see . . . just about three years ago, which may explain my *Schadenfreude.*"

Ciara's brow cleared and her eyes went wide. "Now, that shows they're wicked indeed, bad cess to them and a bad end! How on earth did that happen? Surely they weren't up to their evil games in *America,* were they?"

"A little group of them based out of New York were helping the *revolucionarios* in Mexico while I was there, just after the Intervention started. While pretending to be . . . no, they actually *were* war correspondents for European Socialist newspapers. But secret revolutionists as well, which was good cover I will admit, with the newspapers financing them both ways, as it were."

"But why?"

"Probably to keep their hands in at anarchy and subversion while they couldn't get into Russia," Luz said. "A thoroughly bad lot and attracted to chaos and destruction like flies to a dead rat. I was tasked in to investigate them under a local cover identity not long after we occupied Mexico City, because we'd picked up rumors that they'd contacted the Zapatista underground network, who were active there then when they weren't busy burning haciendas and chopping people up with machetes. One of the Russians realized I was an infiltrator and tried to knife me in the back . . . quite literally, but luckily I caught the motion in a plate hanging on the wall and dodged."

Ciara made a shocked sound, and Luz smiled.

"Things were . . . quite chaotic then and we were just getting organized. What was he called . . . Trotsky, that's it. Leon Trotsky. Quite a clever little man; he saw that I understood German, where my cover identity would not, though I swear I never gave any open sign. I was unlucky there, it turned out that this Zapatista sympathizer I'd cultivated . . . we started by chatting about embroidery at the Mercado de Coyoacán . . . had a *German* husband, of all things! And after all the trouble I went to . . . wearing those stupid huaraches and getting blisters on my feet . . . It was one of those beginner's mistakes. Trotsky was a false name too, we found that out later. It all ended badly for him."

That was in that ugly blue house in . . . not Mexico City, really, Coyoacán's more of a country suburb.

He'd been surprisingly quick and dangerous for such a rabbity little bookish fellow, with his goatee and glasses. And fearless as you could ask, but she'd gotten him right in the back of the head with something she'd snatched up—some sort of mattock, if memory served—after fifteen very trying midnight minutes of stalking each other through the rooms and courtyard of the sympathizer's house, where he'd gone to ground when he realized the Chamber was on his heels.

And which house, alas for him, I'd already spotted thanks to that embroidery discussion with Matilde Calderón.

It had just been the work of the day, though she regretted the fact that a little girl living there had woken up and stumbled into the room. The child had dashed out in understandable screaming hysteria while her mother ran through the house in the opposite direction crying: *Frieda! Frieda!* Killing was rarely as neat and tidy as books by the likes of Burroughs or Davis or Buchan would have you think, but that one had been more of a black horror-farce than usual.

"What do you have planned for today?" Luz asked, carefully not sounding impatient; some things just couldn't be hurried. "More breadboarding?"

Ciara finished off her *Bauernfrühstück* and wiped the plate with a piece of the rye toast.

"Well, that's the thing, my darling. I could refine things, but it turns out that they're using a set of patterns of different frequencies for the ... Heimdall device ... and I've already gotten the essentials. Hülsmeyer was using a spark-gap generator for the electromagnetic pulse—broad-frequency, you see—and a simple coherer to detect the echo, which was all they had available back then. He got distance by using two sets displaced horizontally and triangulating. The papers I got from ... N ... show that the Germans have been working on using thermionic value modulators and oscilloscopes, much more precise and powerful and very compact too. They have a very, very clever man, Professor Karl Braun, who developed the first Braun tube, he got the Nobel Prize for it in 1909, and he also made the first directional phased transmission antennae, I've read his papers and I mentioned him to, umm, N in my first report on Wilhelmshaven."

"And?"

"And N says he disappeared some time ago, and so did a lot of his students and colleagues. Not long after the war started, just before he was supposed to visit New York."

"*¡Ajá!*" Luz said. "Which means they've got him off somewhere working on something or things plural that's clandestine. We let ... N ... continue to publish the occasional innocuous paper and attend conferences just so people *wouldn't* notice that, and they'll just think he's finally gone completely crazy."

"And this Heimdall project is what Braun's been doing for the last two years, I think—it fits. We ... well, N's comments on my original notes ... thought that for more useful results, good enough for laying naval guns in the dark, they must be doing something less ... less scattershot than Hülsmeyer. What I've been picking up ... I think it's from standardized final tests they're running on each set as they finish it and before they pack it up for shipment. There are identical patterns of pulsed transmissions in the five-hundred-megahertz range and various levels around that. The power output is over two hundred kilowatts—very, very impressive! They must have developed something quite new in the way of a generator-modulator combination in those frequencies. If they're using a modified Braun tube receiver, say registering a wedge on a phosphor screen to give a distance scale and then—"

Luz cleared her throat. "This means, *querida*?"

Ciara looked unhappy. "Well, I'm guessing . . . but I've got information to inform the guess now, my darling . . . but I'd say from what I saw on *my* oscilloscope that our first thought—just counter-broadcasting on the right frequency to jam things up like a wireless radio broadcast—won't work well. The power requirements would be prohibitive and it would be too easy to switch frequencies unpredictably, and also you'd be lighting yourself up like a beacon in the dark for anyone with a receiver to aim at."

"Like trying to blind a sniper by shining a searchlight at them," Luz said thoughtfully. "The first thing you'd do then is just shoot out the searchlight."

Ciara nodded; she didn't have Luz's experience with both ends of sniping, but she grasped the concept quickly.

"*Just* like that. We have to interfere with the way the *reflection* works. Use the sender's own transmissions . . . make the reflection . . . make it *bounce* wrong. And . . . if they're making the sets and testing them here and shipping them out for installation . . . we don't have the time for a counter-broadcasting system."

"Well, that's all important knowledge in itself," Luz said.

Ciara perked up a little. "Yes, it is! With this information, we'll be able to make our own ranging Telemobiloscope much more quickly! There are all sorts of applications besides detecting ships. For aeroplanes, and for ships and aeroplanes and airships to navigate safely in bad weather, and—"

"And you should do up a summary and appreciation, right away, then," Luz said firmly, in what she thought of as her senior field operative voice. "I'll code it—"

In fact, she thought it would probably be better to use the invisible ink kit, underwriting coded messages about *other* information. She hadn't gathered anything absolutely crucial on this mission so far herself, but there had been any number of things that would be useful.

And Ciara's report would include mathematical notation that would be difficult or impossible in a book code.

Invisible ink is acceptable because even if intercepted, Ciara's analysis won't tell them anything they don't know. Though it would tell them what we know about what they know, bad enough, but considering how important the information is . . .

The invisible ink system was much more sophisticated than the old lemon-juice method, requiring specific chemicals rather than merely heat to show up. And she had a couple of mailing addresses—post office boxes—for Chamber undercover dropshops here in the *Reich*. It was important enough to send multiple copies. Even Germans couldn't examine every piece of domestic mail carefully; there would be millions of pieces per day in the Berlin area alone. How the dropshops would get the message out of Germany was their concern, not hers.

"I can do that," Ciara said. "The problem is that . . . well, darling, to come up with a really effective countermeasure . . . I have some ideas . . . I can't deduce enough about the receiving apparatus just from the transmission signals, or not without doing it for a very long time."

"We don't have a long time," Luz said flatly. "We have days, at most."

Ciara nodded. "So I have to *see* it. Or the plans, of course. A sample device would be perfect, or even just some parts of it. Now, if we get *that*, it would be worth the risk of using a radio transmitter."

Luz sighed and finished her toast; the electronic equipment could be repurposed for transmission, and there would be continuous monitoring on pre-agreed frequencies—precisely how or where or by whom was another thing she didn't need to know. The problem was that the *Germans* would be continuously monitoring for unauthorized transmissions too, and once detected a standard technique could be used to find the location almost immediately by triangulation; she didn't need to be a technical expert to understand that. Then they'd have to run for their lives. If they were caught, they'd die . . .

But not nearly as quickly as we'd want to die.

There were times when only her mother's language was good enough, though the word was one she'd first heard from old Pedro El Andaluz.

"Mierda," she said with feeling.

"Luz! *Language!"*

*D*u *Stück Müll!"* Luz muttered under her breath at the bicycle.

Which was a little unfair; the bicycle itself wasn't a piece of junk. But the steel wheels the Germans were using for want of rubber had more disadvantages than the rougher ride, though that was bone-jolting and you had to be careful not to bite your own tongue. Despite being grooved, the metal-shod tire also had terrible traction in this sort of weather because slush built up between the ridges and froze on the frigid metal, turning the ride into one of glassy-smooth iced steel on icy pavements. That made pedaling harder and unpredictable slips inevitable and it was the first time she'd ever used this contraption, unlike the people all around her.

Not being more physically competent than other people at an ordinary task was a rare experience for Luz O'Malley Aróstegui, and she found she didn't like it at all.

"Du schmutziges mieses Stück Müll!" she snarled much more loudly, after skidding across a pool of mostly frozen slush and nearly falling in front of a tram that loomed out of the snowy afternoon dimness with a clang of bells. Getting her legs cut off by its wheels and tons of weight would *really* handicap the mission.

The bicycle's front wheel rode onto the sidewalk and gave Luz a tooth-clicking jolt in the course of her recovering, stopping and bracing one foot against the curb. That brought her a glare as she came within an inch of a collision with a passing matron holding some sort of pre-Christmas bundle in her arms.

"He!" the woman said in alarm and anger, staggering back and nearly dropping her burden and saving it only by a scramble that nearly made her slip and fall. *"Ach du lieber Himmel!"*

Some of that was probably what Luz had just said; she'd called the bicycle a lousy, *filthy* piece of junk in a register that wasn't quite what a respectable woman would have used.

She's going to give me a piece of her mind, Luz thought, irritated still more at herself for the slip. *Can't have that.*

"*Na, und?*" she said dryly to the irate matron.

With a cool look and a gesture that involved putting a finger below one eye and drawing the lid down a bit.

The words meant: *So, and?* literally, but if you were translating colloquially and allowing for tone and the language of the body, something on the order of:

Do you have a problem you want to discuss . . . bitch?

The woman sniffed and marched on with her nose in the air. That was revenge enough, since it was snowing again—this was turning out to be a *terrible* winter, to match the wet, cold autumn that had left the whole continent hungry—and that posture let the wet flakes hit her smack in the elevated nostrils. Everyone else was walking with heads bowed into the weather, usually with their hands in their pockets because wartime made good gloves hard to get, mostly with that quick brisk Berlin walk that reminded her of New Yorkers.

Luz had a scarf holding on her low-crowned hat, which kept her face in entirely credible shade, and several layers under her long dark coat—with bicycle clips to protect the longish skirt and underskirt beneath from the gears. And bicycling was hard work with this machine in this weather; she was working up a sweat and then necessarily standing still . . .

Until I feel cold as a singing cat on a fence that catches a bucket of water in the face, she thought.

Not that it mattered. You got used to working while you were uncomfortable, and on the active misery scale you hadn't lived until you'd spent a solid day remaining absolutely quiet and still in a hide in the dripping Quintana Roo jungles, doing overwatch on a *revolucionario* camp . . . while getting bitten by swarms of half-inch *tabano* horseflies and army ants.

She'd been slowly making her way around the perimeter of the Siemens plant—a sprawling complex of plants, rather. Maps were wonderful, but you needed to match them to the actual ground if you could; otherwise you were more likely to make a bad call in an emergency. Putting your own eyes on things and traveling over them made the map in your head match the one you knew with your body better, which shaved fractions off the time you took to make an intuitive decision and made the results better too.

Common sense only works well in a familiar setting, she thought; it was part of what they called the home-field advantage in baseball. *There are times I think the human mind is like a clock made up of all sorts of little subclocks. You aren't really . . . really aware of what all the component clocks are doing until they chime or bong or set something else off.*

The problem with *casing the joint* . . . a term of art used by some of the Chamber's disreputable training consultants . . . was the danger of making yourself conspicuous while you were at it. There was a limit to the number of times you could pass a point in short order before someone noticed. If she'd had more time she would have arranged to get a room in a suitable tall building and then covered every inch for hours with a telescope, making notes and visualizing it over and over again in her head. Even on first acquaintance it was . . .

Impressive, she thought, glancing up at the redbrick tower of the administration building looming through the snowy dimness. *It's the size of a smallish city all by itself. Say, Schenectady or Pasadena; or Highland Park in Detroit. Well, let's see . . .*

There were a dozen of the giant brilliantly lit steel-framed brick structures, all five or more stories, not counting smaller structures and warehouses and the like, with a big low-slung powerhouse beneath towering chimneys; one road led her close enough to catch a hint of that endless rumbling whine that marked a large turbo-generator set. The factory complex spread out over scores of acres, with well-paved internal roadways, tramlines, and a maze of rail sidings and canal boat docks. Shunting engines were always at work, moving strings of cars into and out of loading docks, and there were many horse-drawn wagons and a fair number of motor-trucks and thousands upon thousands of people on foot.

Right, there's more of the prisoners, too, Luz thought. ¡Ay, Dios mío! *Germany's really at full stretch.*

Most of the push-and-pull, lift-and-carry work of loading and unloading and shoveling was being done by men in the tatters of foreign uniforms and greatcoats, the majority the olive-green khaki of the Russians, but some in Rumanian gray-green or French horizon-blue or even Serbian drab. *Landsturm* soldiers a little bit younger and much more alert-looking than the grandfatherly Sergeant Schultz were overseeing them, though civilian foremen were present also, and doing more of the shoving, shouting, and enthusiastic hitting with ax handles and riding whips and repurposed lengths of cable or hose.

There were fewer mechanical assists to reduce the amount of grunt-and-heave labor than there would have been in a factory complex of similar size in America. That was economics, not technical backwardness; before the war German wages had been far below U.S. levels, and it simply hadn't paid to install as many conveyor belts and ramps and powered hoists.

These days, factories were something a spy had to know about too. Where it counted, the plants here—and similar ones throughout Germany—were very modern indeed. Germany was a much older country than the United States, but that was most obvious if you got out into the countryside, where a folk-dancing, beer-quaffing world of peasants and lords and village craftsmen in funny hats lingered, atop an infinite layer cake of history stretching back to a dark pre-dawn past of wooden idols and human sacrifices. The urban-industrial parts of both countries were about the same age and a product of the same headlong growth over the past century, as the two great newcomers to the Industrial Age overtook the first entrants and stormed new heights.

Though I don't envy them trying to run a factory with thousands of men who don't speak German doing the heavy lifting, she thought. *Men who speak any number of* different *languages, come to that, and don't* want *to understand the one they're getting orders in. Management's probably substituting quantity for quality as much as they can, but that would be just the thing to drive a manager vindictively insane . . . especially a German one.*

Of course, as far as just languages went it wasn't much different in a lot of places in industrial America. There were plenty of big-city and manufacturing-town primary schools back home where a class of thirty or forty children might have fifteen or twenty different home languages, beginning with A for Adyghe and ending with Z for Záparo. Sometimes there wasn't one single native English speaker in the mix, not even the teacher.

Or not even the school principal, she thought. *The kids will grow up speaking English well and* their *children won't know anything else, but the first generation may limp along all their lives. Which creates difficulties but at least they're not actively* trying *to drag their feet at work. Not now that we've gotten rid of the Pinkertons and the Pennsylvania Coal and Iron Police and their ilk and brought the unions into the tent. But here . . .*

Even before the war the Germans had had an evil reputation as colonial overlords in Africa, worse than the Portuguese or the Boers. Luz suspected that the underlying reason wasn't so much ruthless greed like Leopold in his blood-soaked Congo Free State as it was sheer aggravated frustration. At people who didn't simply *fail* to measure up to their standards of punctuality and cleanliness and efficiency, but who'd never heard of or even *imagined* them.

And when *die Deutschen* got really, really frustrated that way, they tended to start clubbing and shooting the objects of their ire if they could. Deliberate passive resistance would do that here in spades.

Everyone talks about system and standardization and forward planning and bows down five times a day to the Golden Calf of efficiency these days, but these people . . . slacking enrages them on a moral *level.*

Luz finished making her mental notes and dropped the last letter with its book-indexed code and invisible ink version of Ciara's notes into a mailbox with the Prussian royal arms and the coachman's-horn symbol of the *Post-Briefkasten*.

Then she cycled away for a mile or two along the road that paralleled one of the railroad tracks that ran between Siemensstadt and Staaken, the giant new Zeppelin base a bit on the other side of Spandau. Huge hangars and building yards had been started there just before the war as the airship race with the United States went into full swing and both sides started shoveling money at it like coal into a furnace. They'd been expanded feverishly ever since and she could see from far out that it was a swarming construction camp even in weather this vile. There was a fair amount of traffic on it, including heavy trucks . . . which in Germany meant high-priority cargo, these days.

And most of the Zeppelins that destroyed Paris and London and Bordeaux were built here and started from there, even if they topped up their fuel at forward bases in Belgium or occupied France. Our sources talk about Area 17, which is so secret it's very conspicuous.

There was no point in trying to go anywhere near there openly, since the security would be much tighter. Her briefing papers said there was probably an Annihilation Gas production plant as well and certainly storage for the stuff, to keep from having to ship it in bulk over the railways—the consequences of a derailment would be ghastly.

¡Ay! she thought. *But* that *train* is *going there. It does always pay to look.*

The train from the Siemens factories was being pulled by a comical-looking little shunting engine perched on three pairs of small red-painted driving wheels . . . which meant that it wasn't going far, not far enough to be worth switching it to a mainline engine in these times of scarcity.

Definitely heading for Staaken, then, I think.

It was a short train, only two cars. The leading one was a slatted boxcar that held a set of four long rectangular shapes with the proportions of mattresses made for a giant's bunkbed, and as far as she could see made of riveted metal. Much like the casings being fastened to the masts of the warships in Wilhelmshaven, though a bit thinner in proportion to their length.

But that's not steel, she thought, carefully not staring directly, and wishing the light were better and that she dared to use binoculars. *The look's different, that dull sheen . . . aluminum! Or aluminum alloy. Metal on three sides, something else on the fourth—painted plywood or Bakelite. And Ciara said the actual transmission couldn't be through metal. Aluminum's expensive, you only use it where steel's too heavy . . . and airships need to be careful about weight. They're installing them on Zeppelins, then.*

German metallurgy was first-class, and they'd done a lot of work with new aluminum alloys for airships and aeroplanes. A possibility teased at her mind and was filed away.

That would be luridly spectacular . . . but these days, luridly spectacular things happen all the time. Ciara and I just saved millions after being pursued through the streets of Boston by U-boat sailors firing machine guns . . . and the sailors were on fire. *Edgar Rice Burroughs would have been embarrassed to use that! Keep it in the* possibles *drawer.*

The third railcar had unidentifiable boxes . . . but they were *absolutely* unmarked, which was bad tradecraft, because that singled them out themselves. Ordinary shipments had something written or stenciled on them, even if it was only a serial number. The way to disguise a bunch of crates was with *fake* signage of a carefully genuine standard appearance, while stashing them in a train that looked just like all the others.

Just as the best way to disguise a wisp of hay is in a haycart, and a needle in a box of needles.

The half-dozen soldiers riding guard were a giveaway too; they were *actual* soldiers, not older men stuffed back into mothballed uniforms, and they had a machine pistol and a Lewis gun as well as G98 carbines and potato-masher grenades stuck through loops on their belts, the weapons of frontline fighters rather than obsolete junk greased up and stored away a generation ago just in case.

You might as well put up a sign: something really worth fighting for here.

And they look quite alert, though also muy fríos, she thought. *They're wearing those new loose greatcoats cut shorter to knee length and with a hood and a changeable padded lining too, I think. Very modern, this year's issue for us and the* Deutsches Heer *too. Quite progressive.*

She didn't know who'd copied whom; possibly both sides had come up with the idea at the same time. The garments were based on an Eskimo model adapted and popularized by polar explorers, especially after Amundsen's triumphant combined South Pole and North Pole expeditions. Which Uncle Teddy—a hands-on explorer and genuine scientist himself—had followed with keen interest right down to the smallest detail, and with a good deal of envy. Sometimes he spoke wistfully of retiring and going into the wilderness he loved again himself, down some lost river in the Amazon jungles or into the mountains of Tibet with taxidermists in tow, massacring and cataloging rare birds and animals the way he had on his African expedition during the Taft interregnum.

She turned the bicycle around and—very carefully—cycled eastward through the gathering snow and the early darkness of a northern November from the outskirts of Spandau through patches of open ground and back into Siemensstadt. The great factories glowed like blurred cubes of light as the ceaseless shifts worked, and another locomotive passed her going westward in a blast of hot wet metallic odor. *That* train was perfectly conventional: freight cars, and boxes of whatever-they-were, fuses or field telephones or wireless transmitters, generators and electric motors to do any of a hundred things.

Or possibly aero engines for Albatross fighting scouts, or inter-rupter gear for their machine guns . . . No unmarked crates, no special guards, but a demonstration of power nonetheless.

We're fighting Germany at the end of a supply line that's much longer than theirs.

When two growing powers bumped into each other, they fought; that went back before Rome and Carthage . . . before Babylon and As-syria, for that matter. Another thing that wasn't going to change was that the consequences of losing a big fight were very, very bad. You could ask any of the ones in the ragged, tattered uniforms of shattered armies out there about that as they were beaten with sticks to make them work and fed on garbage, and get the drawbacks of defeat back chapter and verse in half a dozen different languages.

Or ask the ghosts of the newly dead who were about the only things left in central London or Paris. Or any of her Irish ancestors, or any of the Taíno Indians or the occasional Africans mixed with her Spanish ones, or the probable New Christians sweating with fear of the Holy Office of the Inquisition back before that. Or the people she'd be talk-ing to later tonight.

I'm standing between my people and destruction, she thought. *My life's nothing compared to that . . . or even Ciara's. I've been getting more happiness lately than I'm due on the odds anyway.*

EIGHTEEN

Siemensstadt (Northwest Berlin metropolitan area)
Königreich Preußen (Kingdom of Prussia)
Großdeutsches Kaiserreich (Empire of Greater Germany)
DECEMBER 4TH, 1916(B)

I should learn to climb and . . . and that sort of thing," Ciara said quietly, as they walked through the cold darkness toward the forced laborers' quarters. "It would be good for me, too. The *Strenuous Life* and all that."

Luz grinned despite the penetrating damp chill and the controlled tension of action to come. Her partner was naturally active, and fit from a life that had required a fair bit of scrubbing and hauling and shifting heavy boxes of books, and walking long distances because even a streetcar ticket's price had to be considered carefully. Not to mention the manual labor of workshops and her little home laboratory, which had given her strong hands and arms.

But she was a bit self-conscious about being fuller-figured than Luz, since the straight-up-and-down look of modern fashion was designed to flatter a boyish slimness.

"You look wonderful, my Gibson girl," Luz said quietly.

"Gibson girl? Then I'd have to wear one of those *horrid* swan-neck corsets they had back then," Ciara said lightly. "And they wore them even for mountain climbing!"

"When we get back home, we can start you on a bit of acrobatics, if you want," Luz said. "Sans corset; the Flying Corellis are fun, but hard taskmasters. And more riding, the way we did over at Los Olivos on the ranch."

"I loved that! It's beautiful there with the gold-colored grass on the hills, and I always wanted to ride, and the horses were so friendly, like great big pets and so eager for an apple. It reminded me of feeding cabbage leaves to the ice deliveryman's horse when I was a little girl."

The beasts were certainly friendly at the stable I picked, Luz thought. *Or like great big barely animate sofas. But you did very well for a beginner and you didn't flinch or complain when you fell off. Just laughed, in fact.* Dios mío, *but I'm lucky!*

Luz went on: "And maybe some cliff-climbing? Alpinism's great fun, with a friend. And jujitsu, judo; the Chamber has instructors."

She'd already done a little coaching in self-defense for the younger woman, though Ciara had winced when she demonstrated how to scoop out an eyeball with your thumb.

Which is a pity, it's extremely effective and relatively easy if your opponent underestimates you, she thought. *Granted it's a bit gruesome the first time even if the eyeball doesn't pop or leak.*

"This is it," Luz said.

Ciara's face was a pale patch in the darkness between her bell-shaped knit hat and the darkness of her dress and coat. More of the face showed as they halted at the corner of the building and looked up.

"I can barely tell the building's there at all!" she said. "It's like being in a cellar with no lamp!"

"Fortunately, because that means we're invisible," Luz said. "Nothing's as dark as an unlit city late at night; forests aren't in it by comparison. Shush, now."

Luz aligned herself with a memorized unevenness in the sidewalk, closed her eyes, opened them, and then tossed the three pebbles. This time all of them went *click!* against the glass, and the black rope tumbled down, more felt than seen. They sent up their baskets first, bumping lightly against the wall of the tenement block, and then the rope was tossed back down.

"I'll let down a loop," she told Ciara. "Your coat will pad it when you sit in it. Grip the rope firmly above the knot here with both hands, like this, and fend off—lightly! Very lightly!—with your feet. Don't try to climb—I'll pull you up."

Then Luz set herself, jumped, and went up the rope with a straight swarming hand-over-hand without bothering to use her feet; that was sustainable in a mere three-story rise, and she knew the rope was securely fastened up above. She pulled it up after her, whipped out the sheaf uplift pulley, clamped the little gadget to the windowsill, ran the cord through it, and tossed the looped end down. A three-tug signal showed that Ciara was ready, and Luz lay down on her back with her feet braced against the sill.

"Allons-y!" she said, set herself, and began to pull.

This was a straight hand-over-hand too, with the pulley set giving her mechanical advantage and its brake keeping the rope from slipping back; even so Ciara's hundred and thirty-eight pounds (plus ten of winter clothing and buttoned boots) were no joke, and she was already puffing a bit from hauling herself up.

A más prisa, menos velocidad, she thought, forcing herself not to snatch at it in self-defeating haste at the thought of Ciara exposed against the wall.

Nobody can see her! And how all the devils in hell would laugh if I put my back out, or dumped her on the street by setting it swinging.

Luz kept each pull smooth and regular, as much an effort of gut and back as arms and shoulders. Her father had given her the foundation—he had been an engineer to the core and delighted in shifting weights efficiently even when playing with his daughter—and the Chamber had brought in other instructors, not just the Flying Corellis but others who'd been everything from lumberjacks to firemen to construction workers. And some second-story men, passing on their skills in exchange for reduced sentences.

After a spell that felt long but wasn't, Ciara's cloche hat showed over the edge of the sill, which meant the knot of the carrying loop was just below it.

"L'aider!" Luz snapped.

The four occupants of the crowded room edged around forward; the two strongest reached down and grabbed Ciara under the armpits and hauled, the other two took handfuls of fabric when they could reach, and she tumbled into the room with a muffled squawk and landed on Luz.

"Well, hello! Do I know you, miss?" Luz murmured, then helped her up and packed away the rope and equipment. "You permit yourself strange liberties!"

"Oh, you!" Ciara said, relaxing . . . which had been the point.

Simone closed the window, and they lit a candle—this time a real one Luz had furnished, since the risk of error in bad light was greater than that of someone noticing. It was a German candle anyway, and the forced laborers understandably stole everything they could. The Germans punished that harshly whenever they caught someone, but they weren't surprised or suspicious when they found pilfered items, especially ones so accessible to cleaners.

The woman Luz had mentally tagged as Unfortunately Pregnant Lady looked at Ciara, whose cold-flushed freckled face looked even younger than it was.

"*This* is your American technical expert?" the Frenchwoman said.

Luz gave her a hard smile; the woman had been mightily heartened that an American agent was there too, a sign of the new weight thrown into the scales against Germany, but evidently this wasn't what she'd had in mind.

She had someone more like James *in mind, probably*, Luz thought, and went on:

"Yes, it's as absurd as a woman spying on an advanced scientific weapons project in the middle of Berlin, isn't it, madame?"

Unfortunately Pregnant stopped, visibly thought for a moment, then shrugged and laughed with a harsh chuckle; Simone smiled as well, while the remaining two looked blank.

"As you say, madame. And I suppose nobody . . ."

". . . will suspect her," Luz finished.

Simone spoke up: "You both look too . . . too . . . *dodou*."

Plump, Luz filled in; that was an unflattering slang term, and a telling sign of how standards in this little community of the starving had shifted. *Fortunately my darling's spoken French is elementary.*

"The young scientist very much. You, *madame avec cheveux noirs*, you are slimmer, but you are . . . you look . . ."

"*Comme une danseuse*," Unfortunately Pregnant said. "*Ou comme une acrobate.*"

Which was fair enough, and Simone nodded. As far as her physique went Luz *did* look like one of the Flying Corellis if you paid close attention, and rather like a ballerina too except that her upper body matched her legs instead of being a skinny torso with stick arms perched on long muscular gams. It was observant of them to notice it, since bundled up like this you had to deduce it from hints in the hands and wrists and neck and the way she moved.

Unfortunately Pregnant thought for a moment. "Not all of us are very thin. Some of us look puffy with the hunger instead of gaunt," she said, and then asked: "You have the cosmetics?"

When Luz nodded, the Frenchwoman went on: "I was employed at a theater for many years, managing costumes and hair and makeup. I will see what I can do."

Luz nodded again; she'd oversee that since makeup intended to actually deceive at close range was rather different from the theatrical variety, but she didn't want to waste any goodwill . . . or, quite possibly, talent. Just because you were better than most people at some things, it didn't do to assume you were better at everything than everyone. Making use of other people's talents for your own purposes was a basic skill of espionage.

Instead she told Ciara: "She says we look too healthy."

In English, which the Frenchwomen would recognize but didn't understand. And . . .

Talking to each other in German would be tactless and Spanish would seem odd.

"Too heavy, she means," Ciara said, with a wry twist of the lips.

¡Dios mío! *My love doesn't miss much!*

Ciara went on: "But the poor creatures are so thin, of course we must look overfed! And this is like a little closet!"

The younger woman was much more shocked by the underfeeding than the crowding; even after years of effort by the Party there were plenty of tenements just as bad back in America—and some, especially where people did piecework at home, were considerably *more* squalid, though those were far fewer now. Fixing all of that was going to take a generation at least, and the war would slow things down.

"Well, let's get to work," Ciara said.

Simone looked on fascinated as Ciara pulled out her notepad and a set of delicately precise sketches of what she thought various parts of the Heimdall device probably looked like—an informed guess, she'd said, based on the physical demands, on what she had observed and what she knew of Siemens practice and German electrical engineering in general.

"You are really a scientist!" Simone said admiringly, and Luz translated. "And so young!"

Ciara grinned at her, the leprechaun charm fairly blazing. Even in the press of business Luz reflected that Ciara could have cut quite a swath in the hothouse atmosphere of Bryn Mawr.

"A scientist?" Ciara said.

She thought for a moment, and came out slowly with: *"Scientifike? Neh pass. Sullymunt ingeeniur in . . . en preparation, possible."*

Which was ungrammatical and mangled the sounds but was a mostly understandable way of saying she was more of an engineer in training.

"But in the electrical field you have to have a good solid grounding in the theory and mathematics—it's not a matter for just tinkering about by rule of thumb like some areas still are," she added in English for Luz to relay. "You can't . . . you can't see the possibilities of things in your head unless you can see the . . . the structures in the fabric of things the numbers describe."

Simone nodded eagerly as Luz translated; meanwhile she and the others were looking over the drawings. Luz would have been more confident if one of the adults weren't solemnly examining them upside-down. She sighed silently. Simone frowned, and pointed to a portion of a drawing.

"Something like that?" she said.

That was something like a metal bedspring in a metal rectangle.

Ciara leaned forward eagerly and flipped through her drawings to one that concentrated on the antennae.

"Like . . . *come icy?*"

Simone nodded again despite the abomination of bad French by which the American woman attempted to say *like this.*

"But mounted in a turning base with a pivot at either side," the

French girl said. "Like a lady's dressing room mirror in its yoke, you see? With little levers, and then the whole thing pivots at the base—I have seen it moving in its test stand."

An enormous grin spread over Ciara's face as Luz translated and the young Frenchwoman put two fingers on either side of the drawing, then pointed in to represent two pivot pins.

"Yes! I should have thought of that!" Ciara said, quickly sketching in a modification.

"*Oui, exactement comme ça,*" Simone said.

To Luz, Ciara went on: "You'd need something like that so you could compensate for the movement of the ship and alter the focus point of the beam to scan large areas!"

She turned and hugged Luz even as the older agent was translating. "That's it! There's nothing else it could be!"

Luz sighed and reached into the basket again. "Time for makeup. First, this is boiled oatmeal broth."

Unfortunately Pregnant's eyes lit, and she almost smiled; probably, Luz judged, because using her skills was a reminder of the long-vanished time when she'd been someone and something else.

"Excellent! Just a little beneath the eyes, from the nose to the corner of the mouth, under the chin—it will age the appearance of skin, make it look softer and more wrinkled. Older, sicker."

Luz also produced a pair of scissors. Ciara winced, and Luz sighed inwardly a little herself.

"*Et une coiffure à la mode comme la tienne, madame,*" she said.

The Frenchwomen winced themselves in sympathy.

"You take your task seriously!" their leader said, and touched the kerchief that covered her bristle-cropped head.

"I take my life seriously," Luz replied. "Or rather, avoiding death as long as I can."

NINETEEN

Informers, Luz thought as they joined the crowd in the darkened corridor and trudged down the creaking stairs. *There are bound to be informers.*

She had had a splendid excuse for Frau Blücher and her informal neighborhood committee; she'd simply remarked yesterday that they'd be off early to see her injured brother-in-law in the burn ward of the Charité, and that she and the simpleton-maid would be staying late, taking instruction from the nurses in home care. Frau Blücher was a working woman and couldn't afford to waste sleep, and had just given her a sympathetic cluck. The secret to keeping a secret as a stranger in a tightly knit neighborhood was to provide a story in advance to someone whose word would be spread fast and accepted automatically. Then anything anyone saw would be molded seamlessly into the story in their heads.

There was an endless scuff of feet on the bare worn boards of the hall and stairs, a creaking of wood, and a chorus of coughs and sniffles. Luz suppressed an impulse to scratch at the ferocious itching of her cropped head because that might provoke an inspection once they got to the plant, where the Germans were evidently vigilant about lice. Even an inch long and dulled by strong soap, her hair simply didn't look much like that of someone underfed for two years, and the rest of her even less so at close range.

Occasionally someone would talk, or snap at someone else for stepping on their heels in the dark, but mostly there was silence under the brass *clang-clang-clang* of the bell and the shuffle of the damned.

Unfortunately Pregnant had a method for slipping them into the column of workers; two members of Unfortunately Pregnant's circle got a day off, and Luz and Ciara took their places, and most of their unpleasantly thin and dirty but not verminous clothes.

Unfortunately Pregnant probably doesn't think Schultz may be deliberately overlooking the occasional miscount, Luz thought. *I suspect he might be, though it's natural enough of her to assume the worst of every German. No way to be sure. At least there are more than enough people in this building that nobody can know everyone by sight and name. It's doable once . . . or twice if we absolutely have to.*

It was pitch-dark outside, which was natural enough in Berlin at five in the morning this time of year; darker still because it was snowing again. Schultz's lantern glowed through the flakes, but she wasn't worried that the *Landsturm* man would recognize her; people didn't see what they didn't expect, unless you shoved it in their faces. Dirt, rags, a little artfully applied makeup to hollow her cheeks and put dark circles under her eyes, and the kind and respectable young widow Frau Huber became the miserable and anonymous something-or-other forced laborer with *F* for *Französin* sewn on the back and front of her tattered dress.

"Shuffle," she said softly to Ciara. "Head down. Let your shoulders slump."

The younger woman's natural walk was a springy, forthright, head-up stride. Very American, in fact—in the Latin countries people kept their feet closer to the ground, and Germans stamped more. Ciara obediently ducked her head, clutched the ragged blanket around her shoulders, and shuffled on. It helped that the tattered clothing just didn't keep the cold out, and the wet snow cut visibility and put a slippery layer on top of the frozen slush beneath, which made it natural to walk with small steps. Someone among the hundreds was lurching or staggering at any given moment, usually caught by her neighbors and helped along for a step or two.

The best way to *act* miserable was to *be* miserable, though there was also the problem of duplicating the results of years of underfeeding on the way you moved, the stiffness of aching joints, and sheer lack of muscle; these women had all been on a gradually steepening downhill slope since about a week after the Germans marched into Lille in October 1914 after a ten-day siege. She was probably taking pains for nothing, but it didn't hurt. While most people simply saw what they expected, that wasn't true of *all* people.

She usually didn't herself, for example.

Luz could feel meltwater trickling through the rag-bound cracks in the shoes she was wearing.

Now, let's play spot-the-informer, so look for someone who's a bit less gaunt, since the payoff would be more food. Or perhaps they took hostages from family members back in Lille . . . though probably that's far too much trouble for a group like this. The Prussian Secret Police might be handling it, if not Siemens's own internal security. Fortunately, they'll probably focus most of their efforts on the male *prisoners.* Tontos. *Invisibility can be very convenient.*

Unfortunately Pregnant had said her little circle knew of two planted snitches, but those might just be the obvious ones; they walked together, with a slight bubble of space around them. One of the things *known* informers did was make everybody distrustful and suspicious because they'd assume there were others they hadn't found out, which in turn made any type of collective action hard. Any prison guard knew that trick. And one of the secondary but important purposes of spying was to make people see spies everywhere and waste effort and resources chasing their own tails and suspecting the blameless, who would look more suspicious precisely because they *were* so blameless. There was an old Russian saying:

When three men sit down at a table to talk politics, two are fools . . . and one is an informer for the secret police. They had another, too: *The one place where you don't fear being sent to Siberia is . . . Siberia.*

The trudge through icy, snowy darkness was about a mile; the column of women started out slow but kept about the same pace—Luz thought the prospect of being actually warm at the other end balanced the effort and kept them moving, like the proverbial carrot dangled in front of a donkey.

The five-story Wernerwerk II factory was a huge block divided within by courtyards; in the middle was a tall square office tower with four clock faces near the top, and then faux machicolations and a structure with square pillars surrounding it, rather like a secular minaret of industry. A series of entrances led to it, and a lot of the German workers were going in that way as the shift changed, but the *Französinnen* walked by them and around another quarter mile to a receiving and loading dock they reached by stairs along the wall, with Schultz grunting and sighing and putting a hand to his back as he climbed in the lead.

Luz blinked as they reached the top and seemed to walk into a rectangle of light like a door to another world; it was almost painfully bright by contrast with the inky, snowy gloom outside, and there was a bustle of work in the big concrete-floored chamber as crates and boxes were moved around with dollies and vanished into the interior of the factory, amid a smell of coal smoke, chemicals, and a generalized metallic scent. It wasn't much warmer than it was on the outside yet—it couldn't be, with a huge warehouse-style metal door open to where railroad cars were brought level with the floor—but at least it was dry and the light made them all *feel* a little warmer. Schultz walked up to a Siemens foreman and handed over a clipboard with a count of the laborers.

"All present and accounted for and four minutes early, Hans," he said.

"For what they're worth," the foreman said sourly.

He was fiftyish, skinny and dyspeptic-looking, with bifocals on his nose and his head emerging like a balding white sphere from a brown woolen scarf, and sounded disgusted as he went on:

"It takes nearly as much sweat to make them do anything as it would to do it yourself. I was getting more work out of twenty good German broads before the war than I am with a hundred of these and I didn't have to watch them like a cat at a mousehole to keep them from walking off with anything they could hide."

"*Eh, mach ma hia keenen auf Jraf Kacke, Hans,*" Schultz said easily, in Berliner-ese.

Which meant literally that Hans shouldn't act like Graf—Count—Shit, and was a working-class Berliner's equivalent of his American opposite number's: *Don't be more of an asshole than you can help, Mac.*

"When you think of what the poor bitches get fed, and don't get fed, they do well enough," Schultz added. "If you want more out of them, get the works to increase their ration a bit. I know food's short . . . don't I know it! But there must be something somewhere."

Luz leaned close and said very softly in Ciara's ear in the same jailhouse whisper the others were using: "He's telling the foreman not to be . . . ah . . . more of a jerk than he has to be."

"Zu Befehl, Herr General Engel von Gnade," the foreman said in a half-grumbling, half-bantering tone: *At your command, Lord General Angel of Mercy.*

He went on: "I will do just that. When they promote me to God, or at least to general manager. None of us are exactly stuffing our faces with mustard eggs and pig's knuckle and Königsberger meatballs with caper sauce and *Pfannkuchen* full of fruit jelly all the time nowadays, are we?"

Schultz sighed and smacked his lips at the thought of those vanished delights.

"How's your Karl?" he asked. "Any news?"

"Another letter yesterday—he writes more from hospital, more time I suppose. No more fragments in the leg according to the X-ray, and healing up well without much infection, thanks be to Almighty Lord God, his mother's happy about that, let me tell you, and I am too and happier still we've got three daughters to one boy. He tells us that the hospital rations are good, better than here, and they'll have him on limited duty in a month or two, probably there in Kiev. The doctors say in a year he won't even be limping."

"That's good news, by Almighty Lord God!"

Hans signed the clipboard with a flourish and presented one for Schultz to sign in turn.

"At least you're not getting me into a shitstorm by being short a couple this time, you old fraud," the foreman went on, giving the column a quick once-over and obviously doing a mental count.

Luz kept her head down like the rest of the women; listening without looking was another knack she'd picked up.

The foreman's voice was bitter: "Have you any idea what it's like trying to keep this place from getting buried in crap with the scraps they give me to work with? The brooms and scrubbing brushes are all worn out, the mops are just string, I haven't seen a sponge in a year, there aren't any rags, and half the time we can't even get *soap*! *And* we have to sort all the rubbish for reuse. *So ein Misthaufen!* They'll give us reusable asswipes next. Made out of some scratchy Ersatz rubbish that falls apart in your hand, too."

"*Ja*, well, it's the war, and war is a world carved out of shit," Schultz said. "Unless you're a general."

"You're telling the truth there, for once. We're all *beschissen*."

"Amen, brother. At least *our* generals know their trade—that Ludendorff is a real hammer on the enemy's head, eh? So it looks like this bastard of a war may finally be over soon, and then everything can be normal again. Or better—Alfons writes me he's been promoted to *Oberfeldwebel*—"

Hans snorted. "They'll make just about anyone a sergeant these days," he said, pointedly looking at the tabs on the collar of Schultz's greatcoat.

Schultz made a rude local gesture, flipping his hand in front of his face to suggest that his friend was a bit short in the wits department.

"Nonsense, it's a rank that only goes to true heroes, and ones with brains too. Anyway, that'll get him two hundred hectares with the new law—it's good black dirt around that Rostov place, he says. Rich, rich—if you plant shoelaces they'll sprout. Enough land to live like a lord, with meat and white bread every day and a Martinmas goose for Sunday dinner whenever he wants instead of once a year . . . you know, apple-stuffed roasted goose, with red cabbage and potato dumplings and chestnut sauce on the side. Ah, his Katrina does it a treat, the whole flat smells like heaven all day, let me tell you!"

"You *have* told me. Many times, with details. It's *just* what I like to hear when I'm cold and hungry, so I can spend the whole *day* thinking about it."

Under her tension, Luz hid a slight smile at the sarcasm and the way it bounced off the sergeant's beaming face. The way to Schultz's heart was *definitely* through his stomach. Everyone here in Germany was obsessed with food in these days of grinding shortages, and terrible quality in what little was available, but she strongly suspected the old *Landsturm* man had always been the type who lived for his belly. There were far worse faults, of course.

"So here's to victory and booty, eh?" Schultz finished. "Can't say we haven't earned it, by God!"

"From you *to* God. But that's what the newspapers are saying so *warte gar nicht erst darauf dass es passiert* and don't hold your breath or try to eat that roast goose just yet. Yes, we're winning battles, but that's not the same thing," Hans said pessimistically.

Schultz grinned at him. "Me, I'm not doing so badly now anyway," he said as he started loading his pipe. "A young widow has moved into the neighborhood near my duty station, and she's been bringing me fine hot soup and good bread in the evenings, real pre-war style bread, that she bakes herself. With fresh farm butter on it! And farm cheese. *Ja*, I have to eat it while I'm freezing my arse off standing in front of that door like a statue in a winter graveyard with snow on my nose, but it makes the waiting a lot better. My boys will never believe it."

"*I* don't believe it! Fresh butter and real bread! She must be a *rich* widow!"

"Even better: relatives in the country with a fair-sized farm. It's not as much fun as pea soup and rolls at Aschinger's, but that's only because it's colder and there's no beer. It's still plenty good."

Hans chuckled and punched him on the shoulder. "Bringing you *soup*, eh, you dog! Ah, these pretty lonely widows, fond of sausage!"

Schultz laughed in turn, shaking his head ruefully.

"I wish! She treats me like her own granddad, which is fine with me. I *do* wish I was forty years younger, or even thirty—I'd marry her for her cooking in a minute, let me tell you!"

He smacked his lips again. "Hardworking and clever, even if she is Bavarian and *eine Katholische*, and a real looker too—she used to be a schoolteacher and talks like one, a proper lady but not stuck up at all. And kindhearted. She's here to look after her brother-in-law when he gets out of the hospital, he was in the Navy and got bad burns at the *Skagerrakschlacht* back in the spring when his ship was hit by an English shell. Steam-burns from a ruptured high-pressure line she says, all over, his whole body and face and in his throat and lungs."

"Christ!" Hans said, and shivered at the thought like a man who'd worked in factories all his life and seen his full share of industrial accidents. "Like being flayed alive inside and out with red-hot razors. That's as bad as it gets."

"Well, he's not dead," Schultz pointed out.

Hans shook his head, his features twisting at some memory, as if at a bad taste.

"It won't be much of a life for him, or for her, and he'll probably be wishing he'd died every day until he *does* die, and I hope for his sake it's soon. God damn the English and God damn the war! Though at least he has someone willing to look after him."

Schultz nodded. "Good-hearted, like I said. Ah, her husband was one lucky swine!"

"Except he's just another *dead* swine rotting in the mud now," Hans said dryly. "With lots of company."

"Well, lucky until he stopped a bullet, of course, poor fellow. Maybe I can introduce her to my boy Ulrich when he gets home and they'll have me over to dinner three days a week for Bavarian *Tafelspitz* and such. Or even you now and then, you sour old *Kerl*, if I put in a good word for you."

"Those Bavarian cannibals in leather pants will eat anything, every organ the calf's got and then they boil the dying squeal it gave for its momma and serve it to you done up with liver dumplings. And all that sweet and sour they use gives me a bellyache."

"*Nein, nein*, I like southern cooking," Schultz said, and slapped his own obviously much-shrunken belly. "And their baking is great! You know, *Dampfnudel* and *Gugelhupf* and stuff. Not that anyone's seen treats like those for a while."

"Go get your breakfast, then, if you'll still deign to eat lousy *Kriegsbrot* and margarine with the rest of us unfortunate starving bastards," Hans said. "Stop hanging around beating your gums and get going, I've got work to do."

"Better *war* bread than *no* bread," Schultz said cheerfully as he walked off yawning and puffing on the pipe.

Hans turned to the women and pointed to a doorway: *"Werkskantine!"* he bellowed; that meant *factory canteen*.

Then: *"Wo-la, mes dammen!"*

It took Luz a moment to realize he was taking a stab at saying *over there, ladies* in vile pseudo-French. The forced laborers had come to quivering intentness at the words, knowing they meant food; the expressions reminded Luz of pilgrims she'd seen on a visit to Lourdes before the war. They remained absolutely silent and walked forward in a column of fours with an almost military precision, through a tall set of metal doors and into another large barren room, this time one with benches and trestle tables. Once the doors rattled and clanged behind them it was blessedly warm for a change, and there was a long collective sigh and a rank odor as their none-too-clean rags began to dry out and added their steam to the air.

"We miss the meal if there's any confusion," Unfortunately Pregnant muttered to Luz in a jailhouse whisper.

Luz nodded to herself; that would be an *incentive*. Really hungry people developed a focus on food of almost religious intensity.

The feeding was organized in what Americans would call cafeteria-style; everyone picked up a tin bowl and spoon and a cup from a stack, walked past tubs of soup to get a ladleful, and then was handed a small-ish chunk of black bread as they walked out to the tables. She suspected that each lump was *precisely* two hundred fifty grams. They also all got the cup poured full of some lukewarm nameless mouth-puckering herbal thing that smelled of spruce or pine needles, probably because it *was* made by steeping spruce or pine needles, and was meant to safeguard against scurvy without wasting any actual fresh food on them. The Ranger-Scout wilderness survival course she'd gone through at Fred Burnham's Yaqui Valley school had taught that an infusion of spruce buds would in fact work as an emergency antiscorbutic.

Someone in the line ahead of Luz was whimpering slightly and wiping at her mouth with her sleeve, but the group as a whole was very quiet and moved steadily without jostling. The rustle and scrape of shoes on the concrete floor was the loudest sound.

The galvanized-metal bowls and utensils were battered-looking but quite clean; dysentery would run through a place like the worker's barracks as swiftly as fire, so the management was taking precautions. The apron-clad attendants by the cauldrons were obviously foreigners here too; all youngish women, better clothed and slightly but definitely

better fed than the French laborers—people who handled food all day
were harder to starve. There was a local supervisor, also a woman and
in her fifties, with the barrel-like build Germans often got about that
age, who watched them closely. From the way they flinched when she
moved, the hardwood billy club she carried fastened to her wrist with
a thong wasn't just for show.

Slavs of some sort? Luz thought; the cooks were very fair-skinned and
several were ash-blondes where their hair showed under plain kerchiefs
tied at the napes of their necks.

In the aggregate, you could sometimes tell a large crowd of Poles or
Ruthenians or Russians from Germans even if they were dressed alike,
or sometimes not; but individually it was nearly impossible without
some other clue than sight alone.

One of them putting soup into Luz's bowl wobbled a bit with the
ladle at an awkward angle, and her companion called:

"Būkite atsargūs, Jadvyga!" in something unknown and mellifluous,
with a nervous look at the forewoman. *"Nepamirškite sriubos!"*

Or maybe not *Slavs,* Luz thought.

She could speak a little Russian in an elementary sort of way, albeit
with a strong German accent, and understood a little more. There had
been a few Russians at the *Reichsgräfin's* school a decade ago, but they'd all
been from aristocratic families and had already spoken good German
and better French and regarded Russian as a slightly comical patois you
used with peasants and servants; when they spoke to her in anything *but*
German and French it was usually to improve their own English.

*And a lot of them are probably dead now, poor silly girls, alas. They were
mostly harmless in a Marie Antoinette let-them-eat-cake sort of way.*

In Russian soup was *sup* and in Polish she thought it was something
like that, perhaps *zupa,* and none of those words had been even close.
The rhythm and sounds she'd just heard didn't ring quite true either;
she'd learned enough at school to produce a convincing Russian accent
in her own German and French when she wanted to, just for the fun of
it and to make friends laugh when they were playing charades back
then. Though it might come in useful now . . . but what the girl with the
ladle had said lacked that back-of-the-throatiness and rounded, almost
spitty sound on the vowels she associated with Russian.

"Danke," she murmured as the others had, and again when the eight-ounce lump of black bread was handed to her.

Unfortunately Pregnant and her clique had an established section of the tables, though they muttered at a few stains left by another shift. The routines of this place had worn deep into their minds; Luz could see several of them blink a little in surprise as they looked at her because they didn't associate her face with this part of the day, and she remembered not to start in until they'd all said grace and crossed themselves. A lot of the others around them didn't bother, but very few gobbled their food. Instead they ate quickly but efficiently, breaking the crust of their bread into the soup in small pieces and carefully spooning the softened, soaked chunks up last, then tilting the bowls to their lips to drain the final drops, tearing the rest of the bread into scraps and using it to polish the inside before eating it, and picking up crumbs with their fingertips and licking the bowls and spoons.

Luz kept the corner of her eye on Ciara as she followed suit, and nodded to herself in approval; if you were watching *very* carefully you might see that she wasn't eating with the same enthusiasm as the majority . . . but then, nobody had any reason to study her expressions and blank neutrality would do. A few of the forced laborers were making themselves eat, probably because of stomach problems.

A little to her surprise the soup didn't actually taste nauseatingly bad or rotten, though it certainly wasn't good. It was watery and bland and mealy instead, with barely enough salt to taste at all, and the base of the vegetable mush had probably started out as potato, mostly peels, with chunks of turnip and a few beans and odd scraps of greens that were probably trimmings. The bits of cabbage in it managed to be consistently mushy and stringy at the same time, which meant they were discards. At a guess the basic ingredients were the peelings and leftovers from the canteen that served the actual German workers and made them actual soup, and they weren't discarding much there either. Though potato skins were actually quite nutritious.

The bread was fresh, which made it less intolerable than it would be stale, but it managed to be both soggy and hard at the same time and the burned crust would have broken hunger-weakened teeth if there hadn't been something to soak it in; there was more potato in it, probably added as extracted starch, and husks, but as far as she could tell neither straw nor sawdust.

The main problem with all of it was that there just wasn't *enough*, nor enough protein and fat in what there was. From what the French-women had told her there would be exactly the same quantity of exactly the same mushy soup and black bread and spruce-needle pseudo-tea at midday and again after they knocked off, before they were marched back to their quarters.

Like most Progressives Luz was familiar with the modern nutrition-ist jargon of protein and carbohydrates and calories and the mysterious, newly discovered vital-amines or vitamines, though she didn't make a gospel of the *scientific diet* as some of the more self-punishingly puritani-cal and, in her opinion, deeply stupid ones did. The new science *mostly* didn't tell you much that common sense and rule of thumb wouldn't, but the exceptions were useful—it had helped the Department of Public Health and Eugenics make a real start on eliminating pellagra and rick-ets in the more backward parts of the United States, for instance, simply by giving all the schoolchildren a spoonful of brewer's yeast and an-other of cod-liver oil every day along with their pint of milk. And if Scott had known about it before he went to the Antarctic, he could have avoided the scurvy that plagued his expedition.

This so-called meal three times a day couldn't be more than fifteen hundred calories or so total, probably a bit less.

For hard work and in cold weather . . . what they're giving these women is a slow-motion death sentence. But just enough and just well-balanced enough to keep you sinking on an even keel, more or less functioning right up until you col-lapse and quietly, quickly, economically die of heart failure or get carried off over-night by a sudden fever. I don't think that's an accident or just *because they're short on everything here. Someone fairly nasty with access to medical experts put a lot of thought into this . . . I suspect one reason for handling it this way was not to shock their own people too badly.*

"Now at least I won't feel so hungry . . . for an hour or two," one of the women said.

The German woman supervising the cooks began beating on an empty kettle with her length of doweling. Everyone handed their dishes to their right immediately, where the last recipients piled them up at the end of the table and the kitchen team collected them in sacks and carried them off to be washed. Then they put their clasped hands on the table and sat still and silent, looking down at them.

Another reason to eat quickly, Luz thought.

"Sanitary inspection!" a voice called in German.

Luz could hear a rumble of wheels on the concrete floor—casters, in fact. A little while later she could see it coming near, a large sheet-metal bucket on wheels. Pushing it were two more of the not-really-Slavic young women in white kerchiefs and a sort of bib overall-apron, accompanied by a severe-looking older female in a white coat and stethoscope, and a hefty supervisor with a length of stout wooden dowel in her hand.

"You," the one with the stethoscope said.

She used the *du* of familiarity; not the way you did it with friends, but in the alternative tone directed at servants, misbehaving children, and dogs.

The dowel wielder prodded a worker, who stood, turned, sat again, and bent her neck. The woman in the white coat efficiently parted the hair on her head and examined her scalp with a magnifying glass. Luz recognized the technique, one used to check for lice and nits by the National Health nurses in slum schools back home these days.

"This one is clean," she said after a moment; her German had a rather odd accent, an educated woman's but sounding as if she'd spent time in Switzerland.

She moved on to another, apparently picking a set proportion of the total, each individual chosen at random.

"You," she said, and then after the examination: "Nits."

The team went into a practiced routine as everyone else politely looked away. The worker found to be infested stripped and stood on a cloth, and one of the helpers clipped the hair on her head and body down to a bristly stubble with a pair of shears. The first pusher pulled a nozzle on a hose out of the bucket and worked a lever; that produced a fine mist of something with a sharp chemical smell rather like turpentine. The clothes were sprayed too, and wrapped and pinned into a bundle; the worker was given a long, shapeless—and chilly-looking—canvas shift, wooden clogs, and a kerchief from the bucket on wheels, and a chit for reclaiming the clothing in the evening after it came back from being deloused. A broom carefully gathered the clippings, which went into a separate bag with another spritz of the disinfectant. Hair had a number of industrial uses.

The whole thing took only moments, though the team then checked the people on either side; it was repeated half a dozen times, and then four more workers held up their hands to show that they'd spotted lice themselves. Luz let out a slight, almost soundless sigh, and she and Ciara looked at each other out of the corners of their eyes. Being lost in an anonymous mass was one thing, but having a medical professional examine them at close range—literally with a magnifying glass—was another.

"Well, at least they're doing that," Ciara murmured.

"You can starve people selectively, but typhus is no respecter of persons at close quarters," Luz told her, and she winced.

Ciara was pale but looked calm enough, if you weren't close and couldn't see the pulse beating in her throat. Luz kept her eyes on her hands and her mind on controlling her breathing; this was the single point of failure and there was absolutely nothing they could do about it but continue to imitate passive resignation. Seconds crawled by . . .

"Los alle zur Arbeit!"

The bellow of *get to work* had everyone rising in unison, turning, and trooping out a set of doors; evidently everyone knew where they'd be going.

Uncle Teddy will love this part of the report! Luz thought, following Unfortunately Pregnant and her group. *I'll cap any of Fred Burnham's stories about fighting the Matabele and the Boers!*

Simone was walking beside Ciara as they left the canteen, talking quietly but with animation, and looking less haunted. Luz smiled to herself.

My darling's a likeable sort and people do like her, she thought fondly; it ran below the animal wariness and the cinema camera that was recording everything as they passed. *She should have friends of her own—and not have to wait until the war's over and we can get her into Stanford, either.*

She could introduce her to her own friends in the Chamber, though they tended to be slightly older, and a trip to the Technical Section's upstate HQ was a good idea, not just to let Ciara fall worshipfully at Tesla's feet but to let her meet with some peers, youngsters with similar talents and interests just starting on their careers.

The cleaners walked through vast halls shaking to the clamor of machines, or filled with workbenches and the clatter of tools, with parties dropping off as directed and beginning the eternally recurring labor of picking up and sweeping and mopping. The rest, including Unfortunately Pregnant's group, trooped up a set of iron staircases. Luz nudged Ciara, who'd been so intent on the production machinery that she'd started to trot up the stairs with an enthusiasm beyond her supposed status as a depressed, starving forced laborer.

"Pardon," Ciara said, trying—and failing—to pronounce it in the French fashion.

Then Luz looked over her shoulder, and caught one of the women following them staring at Ciara; when she saw Luz glancing her way her head went down again with an exaggerated snap, the unmistakable guilty attempt to convey: *no, I'm not looking that way, not at all* that amateurs always used.

Luz called up her glance at the woman's face without repeating it. *Is it my imagination, or is she just a bit less skinny than she should be?*

There was some variation in the laborers; some people just stored fat more efficiently than others—Uncle Teddy was an example, and it took something like walking across a thousand miles of African savannah to trim him down despite a robust appetite for physical effort that almost matched his intake of food. She nudged slightly at Unfortunately Pregnant and said quietly:

"When we reach the landing, look at the one on the left, four rows back. Do you know her?"

The Frenchwoman did; the need to turn at right angles on the landing to take the next set of steps made it easy to do so casually, and evidently she hadn't wasted her time around the theater and kept it very casual with an actor's skill.

"That one? Hélène Carpentier? *Une pute*," she said contemptuously. "She goes with Germans for food. And not even very much food."

Which would explain her being not quite so thin, but then why would she stare at Ciara?

"Un pute?" Luz said. *"Ou peut-être une mouche?"*

A *mouche* was a fly, literally, but it meant *snitch* in the everyday tongue, or at least to that part of it that included the theater and similar louche quarters.

"No, don't stare at her—but keep an eye on her and pass the word."

Though of course there may be other informers too, Luz thought, grinning behind the mask of her downcast face. *Isn't this fun? Well, no, not really.*

They turned down a corridor on the fifth floor, and paused a little while one of the party went into a helpless coughing fit, sounding as if she were retching up bits of her lungs. Two friends moved in to support her on either side, and the coughs were muffled by a rag.

"There is an infirmary," Unfortunately Pregnant said quietly, in response to a glance that held an unspoken question. "You go there to die. Better die among friends, if die you must."

A supervisor, yet another of the barrel-shaped German women of indeterminate age, in a mourning armband and with a length of dowel stuck through her belt, was waiting by the elevator and oversaw handing out the cleaning supplies; evidently trotting up four flights of stairs was beneath her, and it certainly wasn't very practical when it came to heavy gear. Luz took a very worn mop and a bucket of water with a few suds floating on the surface. This floor of the building had some offices, but most of it was open-plan rooms with draughtsman's tables, big windows, and banks of overhead lights that turned them from gloom to eye-blinking brightness when they were turned on. The group the two Americans were with turned into one of those and everyone went to work; the first chore was gathering the wastebaskets and dumping them into a larger container, which helpfully made quiet conversation easier.

"The chief supervisor . . . the man you saw talking with Schultz at the entrance . . . checks our progress twice a day," Unfortunately Pregnant said. "We clean these offices and workrooms before the staff arrive . . . many of them work late . . . then move down through the day."

Luz nodded. The way to get work out of people who didn't want to give it wasn't to stand over them prodding; doing that didn't get you much but the ruin of your own digestion and a long post-graduate-level course of fieldwork in the higher forms of shirking and evasion. Instead you divided them into groups, pointed each of the groups at the work you wanted done, and assigned so-and-so much to each. That way you only had to check that it *had* been done on time and passably well. With a threat of punishment for the whole group if it hadn't, which meant they watched each other to make sure nobody was doing less than their share and did it far more efficiently and far, far more constantly than you or any possible number of overseers could; that way you only needed enough supervision to make sure they didn't run away or steal the furniture or set the place on fire.

"We're docked food if we don't meet our quota," Unfortunately Pregnant said, and confirmed her guess. "And we can only do that much if we push ourselves."

And that is a very *effective threat*, Luz thought.

Ciara edged closer. "Simone can take me to the assembly room for the antennae," she said softly. "That's the thing I most need to know."

"You're absolutely sure you don't need to take notes?" Luz said. "That would be risky, but less so than coming back tomorrow."

"No," Ciara said earnestly. "No, I can deduce all that I need from the measurements."

"Then go for it, sweetie," Luz said, keeping her face calm, and nodded to the Frenchwoman.

Unfortunately Pregnant escorted the two of them to the door, and then said in a loud hectoring tone as she waved to the German woman at the elevator:

"And be quick about it! It had better be clean!" before repeating in pidgin-German: *"Die Jauch'grub."*

Which meant roughly *the crapper.* Luz could see the German nod as Ciara and Simone scurried by her, with heads down and mops clutched in their hands. Even a setup like this couldn't eliminate calls of nature, and ill health often led to digestive problems. The price for using the toilets was a spell spent cleaning them, and the German supervisor would check that it was done well.

That left the team in this room short. Luz pitched in herself with a will; she had less experience than the rest, but did more simply because she was healthy. She and Unfortunately Pregnant took turns moving desks and draughtsman's tables so that the mop-wielders could get at the linoleum beneath, which was the hardest part of the job.

"My God, but you're strong!" the Frenchwoman said. "It's not just that you're not starving."

"My occupation requires climbing and running and lifting," Luz said, and continued to herself: *Not to mention occasionally stabbing and shooting and hitting.*

One of Unfortunately Pregnant's confederates came over and whispered to her. Luz made no effort to overhear; they knew and trusted their own leader and didn't have any reason to trust someone they didn't know from Adam.

Or from Eve. Or possibly from Lilith.

She turned to Luz, her eyes going wide in the gaunt face.

"Hélène Carpentier—she is gone!"

TWENTY

I must go after her, and now," Luz said flatly.

Unfortunately Pregnant hesitated for all of five seconds, then said: *"Bon."*

Luz picked up a mop and a bucket of water that smelled of disinfectant, as the Frenchwoman called out:

"Die Jauch'grub!"

She sidled out of the door, scurrying past the watcher at the elevator with her head down. The German woman grumbled under her breath:

"Warum haben die französischen Sauweiber nur alle den Dünnpfiff?"

And sat down again on a folding stool with a groan that bespoke arthritic knees and hips gained in forty years or so of scrubbing floors, sighing and taking a nip from a bottle she tucked back into skirts that from their length and volume looked to have seen their best years before about 1897. Luckily the poor state of the laborers' health *did* explain why they all had the thin whistle—galloping shits—today, which was what she had, rhetorically speaking, asked.

The corridors were brightly lit now, but still vacant except for the cleaning staff, and they were mostly busy in the larger rooms where the teams of technical draughtsmen worked. A few of the offices for higher-ranking staff were locked; those probably had safes in them, something that always made a spy prick up her ears.

Luz could open doors like that in a few seconds, and most safes, though German ones were often very well made. But while there were quiet methods of opening a safe, and there were quick methods . . . contrary to what some of the adventure stories would have you believe there were no quick *and* quiet ones for high-quality safes. Even if you were a real specialist, which she wasn't; her instructors had said she had a talent for it, and with five or six years of concentrated practice could be first-rate and make a very good living at that specialized variety of second-story work or being the type of locksmith who rescued people who'd lost or forgotten their combinations. Or both, as some enterprising souls did. One of the ones from the wrong side of the law had even offered to take her on as an apprentice, when he completed the reduced sentence he'd gotten in return for passing on his skills, saying he'd been caught because he was getting too stiff for the climbing part. Luz had declined with thanks, and had to settle for being at competent-journeyman safecracker level. And in any case, the truly secret papers here were probably collected every evening, taken to a central location with a *really* good safe, and kept under constant armed guard.

What was more important was that most of the offices had telephones, as you'd expect in a Siemens factory. She went down the hallway, turned . . . and the bigger office just past the corner was lit, and the door was half-open. She'd been counting on that distance; the informer wouldn't want the German supervisor to see what she was doing and interfere. If she had any sense she'd be shaking with terror right now and in a hurry.

Most people couldn't hurry without forgetting things and making mistakes, especially when they were afraid, any more than they could fly by flapping their arms.

Luz put down the mop and bucket . . . carefully and very softly. Her right hand went inside the jacket and closed on something smooth and cool and rather heavy, a short bar of lead of the perfect size to be clenched in a fist and used as what their jujitsu instructors had called a *yawara*; unremarkable in a factory setting . . . and not a weapon, to most people's way of thinking.

The thing about most people is that most people *are idiots,* Luz thought, with a slight carnivorous smile as she walked forward with swift precision, her weight cast forward on the balls of her feet.

For example, they forget to close and lock doors behind themselves. And they turn on the lights and mark themselves out; you don't need a light to talk, and it's much safer in the dark. As well as metaphorically more appropriate when you're ratting someone out.

She could hear a woman's voice speaking very bad French-accented German inside, stumbling over itself:

"What say Herr Bladis not there? I say only Herr Bladis! Who you?"

Then faintly, as if she was echoing something just said by the person at the other end of the line, and with a bit of a squeak in it:

"Preußische Geheimpolizei?"

So, the *Prussian Secret Police* had somebody in the factory. It was an organization the Chamber had studied in detail. It had originally been mostly tasked with spying on political dissidents—their surveillance dossier on Karl Marx's exile in London from the 1850s was a masterpiece of unintentional comedy—but lately it had been modernized and had become much larger and more proactive, and closely linked with Abteilung IIIb and the military *Feldgendarmerie.* The latest rumor said it was about to be renamed the *Reichsgeheimdienst des Großdeutschen Reiches,* the Imperial Secret Police of Greater Germany, and formally transferred from the Kingdom of Prussia to the central imperial government of the now vastly enlarged realm run from Berlin. It wasn't a bad institutional arc for what had started out in 1849 as a seedy collection of down-at-the-heel sheet-sniffers, freelance blackmailers, and the underemployed, overbred second cousins of the moderately influential.

The French laborer went on in an appropriately shocked, faint voice as she realized who she was talking to:

"Yes, sir. I understand, sir. But—"

The thin, big-nosed young woman took a deep breath. "Sir, I will tell you when you come and take me out, not over the telephone. They'll kill me in my sleep if they find out I was the one who told you about it! You must protect me! Please, quickly!"

Then, in a considerable display of courage, she set the modern one-piece telephone handset down in its cradle to keep from hearing any more commands or threats until she got the face-to-face she wanted.

Which was fairly clever; it was much more difficult to turn someone down when they were right in front of you than it was to deny a disembodied voice on a telephone line, though a disembodied voice couldn't punch your face in either. Changing the informer's contact wasn't clever at all on the Germans' part, though. Sources like this tended to be understandably nervous, and needed coaxing and patting. Threats were more effective when they were unspoken. Carpentier *knew* she was under threat from the other French workers, and it was easy to develop a sincere dislike of people who were always watching you with bad intent. The Germans were passing up a golden opportunity to *really* turn her rather than just buying bits and pieces of information.

The receiver clicked down. Luz stepped through the half-open door, twisting as she did to avoid touching it. Hélène Carpentier was leaning her palms on the broad executive desk, taking deep shuddering breaths as the terror she'd suppressed while she spoke with the secret policeman flooded through her.

A whisper alerted her, perhaps of sound or just of moving air. She had just begun to turn when the fingers of Luz's left hand drove into the back of her neck like slender steel rods, clamping shut as if they were a mechanical grab in a wrecking yard. Luz punched with her right fist, twisting her body to put weight behind the lead-weighted knuckles as they slammed into the small of Carpentier's back below the lowest rib and to one side of the spine . . . directly above the right kidney.

Thump.

A boned canvas corset muffled the blow slightly, and Luz repeated it twice with blurring speed: *thump-thump*, feeling the shock run up her wrist and forearm, worse for the body being braced against the rigid surface of the desk.

The Frenchwoman collapsed forward onto the top, only a slight breathy keening escaping her lips; that was one of the most intense pains the human body could suffer, enough to make your lungs seize up for a few seconds and very effective at preventing a scream. You struck first to disable and only then to kill, since it was much easier if there was no resistance. Luz took a sideways step and hit again, this time a whipping blow downward with the side of her fist, where the lead bar protruded slightly. It made a dull thumping sound as it hit the base of the skull right at the junction with the spine, and the informer's body slumped to the ground, twitched a few times, and went utterly limp. Luz tucked the lead rod away again and moved quickly, gathering the woman's skirts up, tying them and the underskirt up like a giant diaper, leaving the pale stick-thin lower legs like pipesteps against the carpet beneath the desk.

The bowels and bladder didn't always let go with a sudden death, but they often did, particularly with severe pain and a head injury. She couldn't afford to leave traces. With that in mind she tore off a scrap and carefully wiped up the desk, where a few spatters of blood from the final blow had landed.

Then she touched the neck with two fingers. The slack feeling of the skin told its own story of instant death, but she waited a few seconds to be absolutely sure she'd completely severed the brain stem and stopped the heart—human beings could be amazingly, unpredictably resilient, and a moan at the wrong moment could ruin everything. Then she dragged the body behind the desk and shoved it folded up into the leg well; fortunately it was a large double-pedestal model with a full front modesty panel, and you'd have to get down on the floor and peer underneath to see anything. After that she cautiously peeked outside and fetched her abandoned bucket and mop.

Breathe, she thought as that odd distanced feeling swept over her, the sensation of not being quite *there* somehow. *Breathe.*

Hélène Carpentier probably hadn't been a notably bad person back in Lille. No worse than most, at least—as that English writer said, Original Sin was the only religious dogma for which there was plenty of hard evidence—until the pressures she was under had reached the point where she buckled. Impossible circumstances and the choices they'd driven her to had put her in a position where her death was necessary for Luz's mission. Not to mention her survival, and Ciara's.

The Great War killed her. And I did too, of course. It's odd; we're at war with Germany but so far I've been killing far more French people. C'est la guerre.

Luz closed the office door and made the brief blaze of violence fade into the blur of memory. She opened herself to the world around her as she drew deep breaths; the stark electrical illumination, the smell of metal and ozone and coal smoke in the air, the creak of boards under-foot and the hiss of the mop on wet wood, the leather-and-paper scent of the banks of technical references and bound journals with titles like *Zeitschrift für Elektrochemie* in the bookcases.

There was another bit of work coming, and this would be a much more serious threat physically. Waiting was just waiting, a long-perfected habit—there was no point in coiling the spring any tighter than the spot marked *ready*. She had an hour and a half until the man who worked here arrived, probably. But the secret policeman who'd been on the other end of that telephone thought that all he had to do was intimidate one hapless forced laborer . . . and a woman at that . . . to score a coup that could make his career; he'd be here quickly. She considered impersonating Carpentier, but the man probably had a description and possibly a photograph of her on file, and they looked nothing alike. More importantly, they *sounded* nothing alike, and he'd just been talking to the real Carpentier over a clear connection. It wasn't a good balance of risk and reward to assume that he was a totally oblivious idiot; that would *reduce* the chance of taking him by surprise.

You stake out the goat to draw el puma, she thought. *And information gets our goat, we pantherish spies.*

Instead she concentrated on rolling up the carpet in front of the door, giving it a dose of the mop and wiping the wet floor with a scrap of soap, blessing her *mima*'s thoroughness in teaching her the hands-on details of the domestic arts the while. She'd learned the risks of housekeeping—such as slippery floors—and what *not* to do as well; right now she was making a deliberate mistake, one few men would spot.

You don't always have to fool someone, she thought, as hard brisk heel clicks sounded in the corridor outside and she suppressed a murderous snarl that would be badly out of character for a hungry, depressed foreign worker. *Just confusing them will do, short-term. And then you kill them before they get their balance back.*

The door opened. Luz gave a start—which was *in* character—and then grounded her mop and bent her head, giving a convincing impression of fear. The man who stepped with the same confident stamp was burly, the type who'd be heavy in middle age if he didn't work hard at it but was just a knot of muscle now. Not much taller than her five-foot-six but thick through the chest and shoulders and arms, in a dark-gray sack suit and matching waistcoat and low dark shoes, with a narrow tie and modern turned-over collar.

The secret police eat well. ¡Qué sorpresa! *I'm shocked, shocked!*

One foot slipped a little and he automatically adjusted his stance in a way that immediately suggested athletics to Luz's eye—gymnastics or boxing, at a guess. His face was square and clean-shaven, and he appeared to be around thirty, brown hair cropped close at the sides and only a little longer on top, blue eyes darting around the room and making her thankful she'd been thorough about hiding the body.

"Who are you, woman?" he barked, in accented but fluent French, standing with his hands in his pockets. "What are you doing here?"

"I am Marie Lecomte, sir," she said meekly, giving the name of one of Unfortunately Pregnant's group who was getting a holiday, and rattled off her identification number. "I am a cleaner, sir."

"I can see *that*, you stupid slut," he snapped. "Where is Hélène Carpentier? She called from this office less than ten minutes ago."

"I know nothing of any Mme. Carpentier, sir," she said, calculating distances and chances with cold detachment behind the surface that was playing a part.

Don't get into a punching match with this one, chica; *a solid right would rip your jaw off and I doubt he's enough of an idiot to be chivalrously inhibited about hitting women—that type generally don't join the secret police. He's thick-boned, too, with lots of muscle over it. You'll have to get to the vulnerable parts to take him.*

The human body, especially a strong one, could stand an amazing amount of general battering and keep right on functioning; it was an exquisitely designed and very robust machine. There were a number of points, though . . .

"I only clean the rooms I am assigned, sir," she quavered; it was still possible he'd just go somewhere else in a futile search for the woman lying dead behind the desk. "I have been here for more than half an hour, all alone, sir."

"That is impossible—" he began.

The man started, visibly remembered something, and barked:

"Look at me!"

When she did he actually *looked* at her for the first time, a trained observer's feature-by-feature examination rather than the swift dismissive glance he'd used the first time, the non-attention that the socially invisible got. It was belated, but still very dangerous.

He's not just trying to contact his snitch, he's looking for someone and that's what he was hoping she could tell him. Looking for a specific woman . . . working from a picture or a description . . . ¡Huy! *He's looking for* me, *somehow!*

Luz kept herself from tensing . . . but the man's eyes flared wider, and his right hand whipped out of his pocket in a motion that would end under the front of his jacket on the left.

"Stand back! Hands up!" he barked as he started to step back and halted as his foot began to slip again.

Luz dropped the mop and stepped forward instead, planting her feet carefully. In the same moment she slapped her left palm under his right elbow, shoving hard *with* the direction of his motion toward his shoulder-holster, upward and forward in a motion like a shot put with a hard, fast twist of her body and hips behind it. It was smooth enough that the motion felt almost cooperative, as if they were dancing.

Her arms were quite strong, strong enough to haul her own weight up a rope at speed for several stories. His were much stronger . . . but it was extremely difficult to halt a motion once you were already committed to it. The reflex when you felt someone pushing was to snatch the limb away from the contact, and a man's center of gravity would be much higher than hers. She'd long ago learned how to use that.

The German instinctively stepped away as the motion levered at his balance and pushed his upper body backward. The smooth leather soles of his shoes skidded on the soap-slick boards, and he twisted for a single brief moment on the edge of toppling. Luz's reflexes told her not to try to use her knee, not on this uncertain footing she'd manufactured and not against someone who'd probably had that move played on him before. Men often kicked or used their knees on that target, but rarely their hands. So . . .

Instead she shot her right hand downward toward his crotch, with the heel of the palm hammering into the man's pubic bone in a solid jolt that ran back up into her shoulders. Then her fingers gripped with savage strength and twisted. The thick wool of his trousers and underdrawers resisted her, but she clenched her hand into a fist and ripped it backward hard with a crouch and twist.

The secret policeman's eyes bulged and he jackknifed forward with a thin shriek, trying to clutch at his groin. Luz snapped her arms wide in a parody of an embrace and then swung them inward, fast and hard, keeping her wrists loose until the instant her cupped palms landed over both the man's ears with a simultaneous double *smack* sound, hollow but loud. That stung her hands and wrists and jarred her elbows... but ruptured both his eardrums and smashed dense slugs of compressed air into the delicate, nerve-rich structures of the middle and inner ears. The pain was even greater than his savaged groin and paralyzed him for an instant, long enough for her to drive paired thumbs into his eyes just to either side of the nose, scooping outward. His feet scrabbled, but his sense of balance had been destroyed as well as his hearing and eyesight. He crashed down on his back, arms and legs jerking like a beetle.

Luz stepped closer, raised a knee high, and drove the heel of her right foot down into his throat above the Adam's apple with clinical precision. The sensation was familiar, rather like stamping on a bunch of celery stalks wrapped in a piece of veal, and she repeated the blow three times as hard as she could. The man's breathy attempt to scream ended in a gurgle as blood and shattered, collapsed tissue filled his throat. His back arched and he tried to scrabble at his neck for a few moments; then he slumped and went limp.

Luz wiped her thumbs on the man's jacket and then stayed bent over for a moment, wheezing, with her hands on her knees and spots swimming before her eyes. The explosion of total effort was grossly draining, as much a matter of mind as body.

"You should... have had... your gun... in your hand... when you came through the door," she panted. "You died of... arrogance, *cabrón*."

Then she flogged herself into motion, going to one knee by the door before opening it a crack and checking in either direction. The corridor remained silent and empty, with that desolate early-morning feel and only an occasional distant clunk or murmur from the cleaners. Apparently there hadn't been enough noise to attract attention, but then it was surprising what people could ignore or misinterpret. And often extremely useful.

Luz drew the office door softly closed, locked it, and dragged the secret policeman's body behind the desk. She swiftly went through the dead man's pockets, laid the spoil on the blotter, and then tied him in a fetal position with strips torn from his jacket and the rest of it wrapped around his face and neck to absorb the leakage before she shoved him into the leg-well with the equally dead informer. Then she sorted the documentary prizes.

Oh, that's so German, she thought, methodically examining his wallet.

He actually had a card identifying him as a *Preußische Geheimpolizei* agent!

Though to be fair, the FBS carry theirs far too often too. I think it makes them feel chic and powerful. This would be more useful if the Germans were Progressive enough to have women as secret police agents, but I don't think anyone would believe I'm him.

A certificate folded in the wallet stated that *Vizefeldwebel*—sergeant first class, roughly—Arno Batz, born April 10, 1886, in Neurode, was discharged honorably from the 11th Silesian Grenadier Regiment in December 1914, after recovering from wounds and on detection of a heart murmur, with the award of the Iron Cross Second Class; that accounted for why someone his age and built like a bull wasn't in uniform. You could stop exercising in a gymnasium when the warning signs hit you, but not in the field when you were trying to drag a wounded comrade to shelter or sprint over broken ground raked by Hotchkiss fire with twenty-five pounds of Lewis gun in your arms. Six years of *Realschule* made him a natural for the *Geheimpolizei*. And all German police forces favored veterans as recruits—American ones did too these days, for that matter.

She regretfully left his Luger in its shoulder holster.

Too easy to detect. I'm not going to take a real risk for the imaginary comfort of having a gun on me.

Much of the rest was the junk of daily life: small change, keys, tramway tokens, a cigarette case with *Love From Your Darling Erika* engraved in one corner in curlicue script with wings and hearts around it, pictures including one of him standing grinning between six other soldiers, muddy and grubby, and another of him in a 1914 *Pickelhaube* and the uniform he'd marched off with that lost hot August, with an older woman who was probably his mother trying to look stoic beside him.

The documents, however . . .

Luz hissed to herself as she unfolded a bulletin. Her description and Ciara's, and quite accurate physical descriptions—including the small white scar beneath her right ear that was the fruit of a sniper's duel in the Sierra Madre Occidental—were included, and an instruction: *Extremely dangerous, shoot on sight.* And a signature. Captain Horst von Dückler.

"Well, *that's* flattering! Oh, Horst, *mi güey,* I see you have been busy," she murmured to herself.

He was the only man in Germany who could have given that detailed a description and was probably going mad trying to get people to take Luz seriously as a threat. The only comforting factor was that the descriptions listed Ciara as titian-blond, and herself as having shoulder-length hair of a striking raven color; neither was true anymore, but it was just the sort of thing people would look for first. It wouldn't make much difference to someone—maybe a confidence man, or a spy, a policeman—who was really used to looking at *faces* and not just a few markers, and who took the time, but it would help.

But that just shot our escape plan through the head. With copies of these up in every train station and post office, traveling is going to be insanely risky. Maybe Staaken is the best idea after all . . . and it's an idea that's absolutamente pésimo, *the only reason it* could *work is that nobody would expect it.*

And the inside pocket of his jacket held various authorizations directed at the Siemens management, including an extremely general one for commandeering labor and supplies for government purposes.

"Now, that may be useful," she murmured, as plans stirred in her mind. "But I have to buy us some time."

First she used the mop, carefully going over the floor to eliminate any spots of blood from the brief savage assault that had killed the *Geheimpolizei* man and removing the excess soap and water before she unrolled the carpet. Then she went back to the elevator. As you would expect from someone who took a nip of schnapps for pain control at six in the morning, the supervisor was dozing a bit.

"Excuse," Luz said humbly.

With luck, the German would have trouble remembering her own name when she ended up answering *Geheimpolizei* questions, much less the details of personal interactions she profoundly wished would just go away so she could get more sleep, but it never hurt to be careful and consistent.

"*Ja?*" came a mumbled response.

"*Die Haushaltswagen, bitte?*"

A *Haushaltswagen* was a housekeeping cart, a bag or basket on wheels; she knew the factory used them, because she'd seen one at the forced laborers' vile breakfast during the sanitary inspection.

"*Da drüben, da drüben,*" she said vaguely, which meant *over there*, while waving in the other direction.

Luz bobbed a half curtsey and went past her at a scurrying pace. *Over there* turned out to be a storage room, gratifyingly large and lined with deep shelves but, when she flicked on the light, looking rather bare with wartime shortages. But it *did* have several housekeeping carts, all about chest-high on her, with side panels of rather worn canvas. She poured the water in her bucket down the drain, refilled it, hung it on a hook on the side of the cart, slid her mop into the helpful loops, and pushed the empty cart back to the office.

"This . . . should . . . just . . . about . . . fit," she grunted, hauling the secret policeman's body—he weighed at least a hundred and seventy pounds, or seventy-eight kilos to be local—up and tipping it into the cart.

The informer's much lighter corpse followed; a sniff made clear that she had to scrub under the desk as well. That was only to be expected, but . . .

Me cago en esta soplona, me cago en la policía secreta prusiana, y me cago muchas veces en toda esta ciudad fría y fea de Berlin, she thought sourly. *I shit upon this snitch, I shit upon the Prussian Secret Police, and I shit many times upon the whole cold and ugly city of Berlin.*

A spy had to be versatile; sometimes you had to be a chambermaid. Then she pushed the cart back to the storage room, considered thoughtfully for a few seconds, and rearranged the shelves so that there was a suitable space at the left rear, dumped the bodies out and shoved them in with a layer of curtains beneath in case they leaked, dumped half a bottle of some disinfectant that smelled strongly of coal-tar and something that was like, but was probably not, wintergreen on them. She poured the rest of it into her bucket, and then stacked the oldest—and hence least likely to be disturbed—supplies around them. She followed up by washing herself, and inspected the ragged dress Marie Lecomte had donated for anything that couldn't be explained by her work . . . though that had provided dirt and stains enough.

The factory also had plenty of wall-mounted clocks. Luz was mildly shocked to see that she'd only been gone twenty minutes. Better still, Ciara and her new assistant-friend Simone were back. Luz glanced at her and got a short nod, albeit with an anxious, preoccupied expression. Simone was fairly dancing with poorly suppressed excitement, and Luz flicked her eyes that way. Ciara nodded, and began to whisper urgently in her ear to calm her down. Joyous excitement was rather conspicuous for people in their position.

Unfortunately Pregnant raised an eyebrow as they went back to work. Luz murmured softly:

"Carpentier won't be a problem anymore, and neither will her secret police contact."

Unfortunately Pregnant smiled unpleasantly, and then her eyes went wide as she went beyond the pleasures of revenge to possible consequences. Luz continued:

"The . . . remains won't be found for a while, hopefully for a day or so. Yes, I know that will implicate you, but I have a plan for that. I'll give you the details later."

That amounted to saying *trust me*, and when someone said that it was usually a very strong hint that you shouldn't, but Unfortunately Pregnant seemed to be ready to wait, even if she wasn't very satisfied. Luz let the matter rest; what she had planned was half-formed. Still . . .

We have the information. Now all we have to do is get the information out . . .

Which they could do quickly, if they didn't mind giving themselves away.

. . . and hopefully get ourselves *out of the enemy capital with legions of*

intelligence agents and secret policemen and the regular police after us, our descriptions and probably our pictures being posted everywhere . . .

Which was going to be much more tricky. The original idea had been simply to travel to Hamburg under yet another identity, and then make contact at a Chamber safe house there and be smuggled across the Danish border. That was a *really bad* plan now.

TWENTY-ONE

Siemensstadt (Northwest Berlin metropolitan area)
Königreich Preußen (Kingdom of Prussia)
Großdeutsches Kaiserreich (Empire of Greater Germany)
DECEMBER 4TH, 1916(B)

S hit," Horst von Dückler said with conviction as the factory doctor pulled back the sheet.

The Siemens plant was big enough and paternalistic enough to hold its own well-equipped clinic, now doubling as a morgue; it was brightly lit, electrics gleaming off polished enamel and wood and the glass of cabinets, and smelled of medicine and disinfectant . . . and now slightly but detectably of dead meat if you knew the odor well.

The doctor was a woman, oddly enough, a dry middle-aged stick with a strange part-Swiss accent, but she seemed competent and she was keeping doggedly at the work despite the late hour. The room was big but fairly crowded, with Röhm and his stormtroopers present, Gustav Diehl from the *Geheimpolizei*, Kurschat of the regular police, and a nervous-looking rabbity fellow with an East Prussian accent named Bladis, who was in charge of security for the Siemens plant and effectively head of the Siemensstadt police as well. Before the war he'd been a glorified night watchman mainly concerned with petty pilfering, and he was obviously out of his depth here.

The centerpiece was two canvas-draped tables with the bodies. The doctor drew the sheet down to the female body's knees; she was resting on her front, with the face turned away from Horst. He was just as happy that it was. There was something about the empty slackness of the faces of the newly dead that disturbed him in a way that the results of smashing and ripping by bullets or explosives or cold steel did not. It gave the bodies an oddly childlike look that felt obscurely accusing.

"This was done very quickly," the doctor said. "I believe it was a surprise assault. First these multiple blows with a fist to the kidney area, with the deceased immobilized by the assailant's left hand. The bruises on the back of her neck are compatible with a handgrip."

Kurschat scowled; he'd wanted to wait until a *real doctor* from the regular police force could be called in. The company medic had *almost* smiled when Horst told Kurschat what he thought of that. Why was it that civilians couldn't understand the importance of *time* in a fight? Handing an opponent a single minute was like giving them ammunition to shoot you with.

Horst did raise an eyebrow himself; that was a very detailed account. She gave a very slight, very chilly smile and said:

"I worked as an assistant to a student of Dr. Virchow for several years, performing autopsies at a charity hospital. One saw a good deal."

She moved the dull dark-brown hair aside with her pencil and placed her left hand in the air above the marks on the thin neck, showing that they corresponded to four fingers and a thumb, of a left hand and one much the same size as hers. Then she moved the pencil down to the massive discoloration below the too-visible ribs and just right of the spine. All the men winced slightly, whether they showed it or not. They knew by experience or firsthand observation how that sort of injury *hurt*. And it would have you pissing blood for a week, at least, even if you healed eventually.

"These are the marks of a fist, though I cannot be absolutely certain because the corset acted to spread the force slightly. Then a blow to the base of the skull with a hard object, I think held tightly in the right hand—one strike, very precise. You see the small size of the depressed impact wound, about five or six millimeters? A smooth piece of metal, perhaps a short rod, perhaps iron, perhaps lead. The medulla oblongata was severed here where it connects with the spinal cord. The medulla controls heart rate, breathing, and blood pressure. Instant death. The whole thing probably took no more than fifteen or twenty seconds, perhaps as little as ten."

Bladis spoke, rather obviously fighting to keep his voice neutral. "She . . . she was an informant of mine among the Frenchwomen employed here, helping me to control petty sabotage and the like. Hélène Carpentier. We were going to shift her to individual employment soon; I think they suspected her and that would mean . . . an accident, something of that sort. Batz insisted on taking over dealing with her when he arrived."

Horst looked at him as he swallowed and mopped at his balding head with a handkerchief, judging the reaction. Part of it was simply a civilian's unease around a body, and the sort of nervousness a timid man would feel in the same room with so many specialists in violence, like a rodent among great killer cats, but . . . Horst's eyes went back to the stark-white, skinny corpse.

Some sort of personal link. No accounting for tastes, he thought.

"Herr Bladis," he said dryly. "Bear in mind that if Batz had not taken over contact with your informant—which I admit was . . . hasty— it would very likely be *him* looking at *you* lying on that table right now."

Bladis apparently hadn't thought of that and went pale and put a hand to his mouth.

The doctor covered the body and drew down the sheet on the male. Diehl, the *Geheimpolizei* captain, spoke first in a carefully controlled voice that covered a cold rage:

"Arno Batz. Former sergeant in the 11th Silesian Grenadiers before he joined our service, and a first-rate man, tough and clever and unsentimental."

Horst mentally translated that as *smart ruthless bastard*, which was his judgment of Diehl as well . . . and of himself, for that matter.

"Incidentally, an amateur boxer and wrestler and a good one."

Horst grunted thoughtfully. Batz's corpse, resting faceup, *looked* formidable, muscled like an athlete and without any spare flesh—though these days that latter didn't mean as much. There were what he recognized as old bullet or shrapnel scars on the muscular hairy torso as well. The damage was what attracted the eye, though.

The doctor used the pencil as a pointer again. "Note the distortion of the testicles and penis. Yet not excessively engorged, which indicates blood pressure dropped very soon after the damage was inflicted; otherwise there would be gross swelling."

This time all the males *really* winced, with all of them feeling an instinctive desire to cup their groins; Horst did himself, and Röhm looked positively appalled, under a stone face. Both of them were men who'd seen other men screaming for death, or gutted like hogs or blown into random bits of viscera and shattered bone spattered widely by the mechanical, industrial-scale modern violence of projectiles and explosives. Seen it so often it had become routine, like living amid the rotting bodies in the frontline trenches and the bloated rats that feasted on them and the flies and maggots that did the same in summer.

But some things you *couldn't* get used to.

Horst was reminded of something his older brother Karl had said on his return from German East Africa a decade ago: that in cold fact a fanatical Maji-Maji rebel tribesman with a musket or spear hiding behind a bush was far, far more dangerous than a lion . . . but when you heard a lion roar in the night, something deep, something older than the days of caves and stone axes, whispered to your soul: *This eats men.* The damage to the dead man's crotch was objectively nothing much compared to gutting or blowing off limbs or cutting a man in half . . . but it spoke to the same ancient part of your brain.

"And the ears. I think this was done with a slapping or clapping stroke—but to both ears at exactly the same time. I have never seen anything quite like it, but I don't see any other possibility. It resembles pressure injuries to deep-sea divers that I have read of in the *Virchows Archiv für pathologische Anatomie und Physiologie.* Fascinating!"

The pencil indicated the trails of dried blood and matter from both ears.

"And much more destructive than it appears. Massive rupturing of the internal structures. And then there are the eyes."

Both had come out on their fleshy pink-and-white stalks, turning a bit gray now. They gave the body an inhuman look, like a pop-eyed doll ruined by a careless child, emphasized by the thick tongue sticking out between the swollen lips and the dusky color under the brown of dried blood.

"See here at the inner side of the left eye, the mark of a fingernail? Again, both were gouged at the same time."

She illustrated by jabbing her own thumbs forward, with the nails facing each other only a few inches apart. Then the pencil moved to the throat.

"This is the proximate cause of death. The other injuries would be crippling and extremely painful—"

"*Kein Scheiss!*" someone muttered in the background, the precise equivalent of the English slang term: *No shit!*

"But not necessarily fatal. As you can see, the injuries to the throat are immediately fatal. Here, and here, overlapping horseshoe-shaped impressions; definitely the heel of a boot or shoe, and not a very large one."

A frown. "I would even say a woman's shoe, if . . . The damage is extreme—multiple blows, delivered downward after the subject had collapsed—"

"Collapsed?" Horst said. "Not *been knocked down?*"

The doctor shook her head. "The injury to the ears . . . the inner ear . . . would destroy the subject's sense of balance immediately."

She went on, moving the pencil in slight exact increments to show the overlapping strikes:

"A series of stamping blows, delivered very quickly and with great force to the upper throat, at a slight angle to avoid the jaw, with the subject's head firmly against the ground. The result was complete separation of the larynx and trachea, multiple severe fractures of the cricoid cartilage, and collapse of neck tissues into the airway. Death followed quickly by asphyxiation; hence the dark discoloration of the face and the swelling of the mouth and tongue."

The doctor pursed her lips. "Both killings were done by the same individual; the pattern is unmistakable."

She paused, frowning. "I have seen the bodies of murder victims before. They usually show evidence of . . . of frenzy. Many unnecessary blows as well as the fatal ones."

Horst and the stormtroopers nodded. The same was true in hand-to-hand combat, usually.

"Not here," the doctor said. "This was an attack of the utmost savagery, but done with calculation: swift, brutal, precisely administered force, by someone with great knowledge of human anatomy and vulnerabilities—almost surgical, in fact. I think the sequence was, first the twisting and ripping damage to the testicles and penis, the clap to the ears immediately following, then the eyes, and then the victim collapsed after which the assailant immediately stamped on the throat. All done in . . . perhaps half a minute? Less? Scarcely more time than for the first victim despite the difference in size and strength. In both cases the victim was rendered helpless by pain and severe traumatic injury, then killed in a way that was very quick but would have been difficult unless they *had* been rendered helpless."

"Like a leopard with a human mind," Horst said softly. "And she didn't even bother to take his pistol. And then she mopped up the mess . . . quite literally mopped up . . . the mess, put both bodies in a *Haushaltswagen*, wheeled them down the corridor *past a witness*, and tucked them away in a storage room where they weren't discovered until just now! And might have gone undiscovered for *days* if someone hadn't gone looking for a bottle of ethyl alcohol for a mimeograph machine!"

He looked around at the policemen and soldiers.

"Does anyone wish to make another joke about kissing the spy before shooting her?" he asked dryly. "Well?"

There was silence, heads shaking in negation and a sound of shuffling feet.

"Good. I am glad to see you are taking this matter seriously"—*at last*—"comrades."

Diehl's eyes narrowed. "It will be difficult for them to escape from Berlin, now that the posters are being widely distributed and the civilian police are on the alert as well as we of the secret police and the *Feldgendarmerie.*"

"But not to go to ground and wait us out," Horst said grimly. "And we must assume that they have the information they came for and will try to communicate it to enemy intelligence. Every moment they breathe increases the danger of that. Time is crucial here if our Navy is to maintain the advantage of surprise. Meanwhile—"

The door burst open, and a bespectacled young man in his vest and shirtsleeves ran in, waving a piece of paper.

"Herr Bladis! Herr Bladis! The wireless transmissions monitoring stations have sent us a warning!"

TWENTY-TWO

Siemensstadt (Northwest Berlin metropolitan area)
Königreich Preußen (Kingdom of Prussia)
Großdeutsches Kaiserreich (Empire of Greater Germany)
DECEMBER 4TH, 1916(B)

The upper loft of the house on No. 27 Rapsstrasse was cold and dim as Luz finished coding the sequence; the glow of the thermionic valves in their glass tubes underlit their faces, still looking drawn where the makeup had been scrubbed off. The paper lay on the pebbled surface of the trunk; Luz's imagination turned it into a death sentence . . . which it very well might be.

At least it's short, she thought. *Shorter is better. Sending this is like lighting a fuse . . . while you're holding the stick of dynamite in your hand.*

Which was something she'd actually done, though she'd dropped it out of the window onto someone's head immediately and ducked back to cover.

"Strips of aluminum foil?" she said, looking down at the page. "Half the wavelength long and wide?"

"Yes, I think that will work, darling, given the frequencies," Ciara said, with that slight frown of concentration; it made Luz's lips quirk even now. "And it can be done quickly—in a day or two, in any base machine shop—including opening and refilling the shells. Everything's easily available. Anything else would take a *long* time and many tests to get ready. This will work at least once. The Germans are far ahead of us; we can't compete on their terms."

"They're beginning operational deployment and we're just doing proof of concept," Luz said. "So this will blind them?"

Ciara paused for a moment to put it in nontechnical terms, then went on: "Remember we talked about searchlights and snipers? This . . . this would be like shining a searchlight into a fog, a dense fog."

"Or like generating smoke around a target," Luz said, and gave her a quick double thumbs-up gesture. "That's my girl! I'd say that was too sensational if I read a tale about it in *Argosy All-Story*!"

Ciara hesitated. "Darling . . . will they pay attention? To us? To me? There isn't much time, probably."

Luz smiled and rested a hand on her shoulder; it was clean, but there was still a little black under the nails from an hour spent lifting the coal out of the cellar and spreading it all over the lower floor of the house, along with anything else easily flammable, while Ciara put the transmitter together from dual-purpose parts no longer needed to record the Heimdall transmissions. Luckily Luz could just discard the clothes she'd worn to heave the fuel around; they'd gone on the coal with everything else, and then she'd wiped herself down and put on the set she'd be wearing to get out of here.

"*Mi amor valiente*, anything under the mission code for this will go right to the top, and Uncle Teddy and the Director will most *certainly* pay attention to it. Think of what we did the last time! And everyone else will pay attention to *them*, most certainly including Admiral Sims."

And the Royal Navy will pay attention to him, *but let's not mention that right now.*

Ciara laid a hand on hers where it rested on her shoulder. "I'm, well, *not* used to *not* being ignored when I say something!"

"Things have changed. You're not Ciara Whelan, anonymous eccentric girl, not anymore. You're Black Chamber *Operative* Ciara Whelan, and you were fifty percent of saving the world. And this will go right to N, too, even if they have to drag him away from putting bits of cracked corn between his lips and feeding his pigeon bride."

"N will understand right away," Ciara said, and suddenly grinned despite the situation. "It'll . . . it'll explode in his head, the way it did for me when I saw the antennae and measured everything! And *everyone* will listen to him, too!"

"Even the ones who think he's mad," Luz agreed.

"Mad? He's the greatest scientific genius of his generation!" Ciara said.

"*Verdaderamente*. But yes, he *is* a bit mad, *solo un poco*. Still, he's *our* madman."

"Then let's go," Ciara said, her full lips firming. "And give him something to think about!"

She turned back to the mass of exposed components and methodically checked it over, flipped a switch, and then stood and waved Luz forward. The older woman sat, put her fingers on the key, and held the paper down in a puddle of light with her left. The letter-number combinations were as easy as reading plain text, and as easy to transfer to Morse, if you had as much experience as she did with using field telegraphs and the newer wireless variety.

The key was smooth and somehow crisp-feeling beneath her fingertips, pregnant with meaning. Pressing it would send consequences rolling down the years, for her, for Ciara, for the world. Choice was illusion here; the fingers wouldn't work unless her mind and will told them to, but it wasn't . . . within the realm of possibility . . . that she wouldn't give them that command. She'd made that choice many years ago, and it had been technically more real, more of a *choice*. She'd had to push hard to get into the Chamber, push very hard indeed, ignore thoughts of giving up, but it hadn't *felt* any more real back then. You couldn't *not* do something you wanted so badly. Luz O'Malley Aróstegui smiled slightly at the way that choice alternated with necessity, and the illusion of each blended into the other.

Then she began: identifier, message, through to the end, over, repeat, repeat, repeat. While she did Ciara tapped her notes together and stowed them in a pocket. It took barely enough time to do that, and she knew from the way she tilted her head that her partner followed the Morse as if it were a piece of music.

"That's it," Luz said. "Now we move!"

Because we've just put up a big sign reading: ¡Hola, Horst, mi viejo cariño! ¡Aquí estamos! Por favor, mátennos ahora! *And I don't think Horst will have to be asked to kill us twice.*

She hung the cut-down Winchester shotgun inside her coat through the loops, and then picked up the Springfield in its container like a suitcase . . . which was what it looked like. They were already in the clothes they'd leave in, outwardly another set of the plain respectable garb appropriate for Frau Huber and her charity-case quasi-moronic ward. In reality they were warmer, with special linings, had grommets that allowed freer movement and an interesting array of pockets. They were accompanied by stout shoes suitable for rough work, and via concealed steel toecaps for dealing with the inconveniently nosy.

Ciara sighed as she looked around at the circuitry she'd assembled and improved.

"It seems like a shame to leave all this beautiful equipment . . . and you know, it's been fun here, part of the time. Almost like home!"

"Home is where you are, *querida*," Luz said.

It must be a little odd for her; she lived all her life until the spring in the same house, the one where she was born. And then all that vanished, her family, the bookstore, the bed she'd slept in for twenty years . . . off to Germany, and then me.

"And my home is you . . . so yes, that's why I felt that way about this cottage. But the *Casa* is better! That'll be our real home, the place we make together."

"And better still, once we rig you up a laboratory and get Papá's workshop back into commission!"

They moved down the stairs quickly, and Luz trailed a finger along the line of detonation cord she'd rigged in the little eyebolts along the base of the wall and out to the front door, making sure everything ran smoothly one last time. She'd been tempted to put the tripwire a dozen feet in, to get two or even three eager searchers, but that would be greedy and relying on them being extremely careless. Ordinary civil German policemen probably *would* be that careless—they hadn't had the experience with planted bombs that their American equivalents did over the past few years—but she knew Horst was involved in this, and she respected him enough to know he'd get better help if he could. And his own sense of animal wariness combined with keen wits would have him stopping ten feet from the door at a minimum.

That was why she had put the last six packets of the new malleable explosive on the inside of the door, fastened there with rubber cement and linked with detonation cord like a daisy chain. Luz blessed the Technical Section's habit of justifying their existence by throwing in anything they thought *might* be useful as she ran the end of the cord through the loop of the explosive pencil and then through the hole she'd drilled right down at the bottom. Sometimes it was annoying that you were deluged with just-in-case junk that had to be inconveniently disposed of. Other times . . .

Most of the force will go back down the corridor along the line of least resistance, but most *is not* all. *That's more explosive than the filling of a six-inch howitzer shell,* she thought happily. *Flame for an old flame . . . Absolutely nothing personal, Horst, but I really do want you taken off the board of this game, so* please *be the one that opens the door. We can compare notes in Spy Valhalla over Wotan's mead someday.*

Outside she quickly checked that nobody was in sight, then closed the door very carefully, took up the cord until there was no slack but it wasn't twanging-tight, secured it with a dab of putty that would look very much like the surface of the door, and snicked off the extra with her knife.

Then they were out into the cold darkness, lit only by the lights behind them at the intersection and walking toward the forced laborers' barracks. Luz smiled at Frau Blücher's silent, darkened house; she and her children would be sleeping the sleep of the very tired and underfed now, and they would be profoundly shocked when the police questioned them about the pair who'd very briefly been their neighbors. If the boom didn't wake them up first. Either way, it would give her something to talk about the rest of her life, too.

"Frau Blücher and her neighbors won't be in any great trouble with the authorities, even here, and I'm glad of that," Luz said. "Enough of the little people everywhere get caught in the avalanche as it is. Sometimes it can't be helped, but not this time."

Ciara nodded and Luz thought she smiled. Then she said, her voice carefully controlled: "We're putting Simone and her friends at risk, aren't we?"

Luz shook her head; there was just enough sky-glow from the factories reflected off the clouds above to make it visible.

"No, we're giving them a chance at life, sweetie," she said, truthfully; though truth wasn't much of a consolation sometimes. "It isn't a very *good* chance, not even as good as ours, but if they stay here they're dead. They're being killed, just as surely as if they were lined up in front of a wall looking at a Maxim gun, except that it's slower and more painful."

Ciara sighed. "I suppose you're right. It's just . . . so nasty."

"It's war, sweetie, and a bad one at that, a lot worse than the Intervention and I saw enough bad things there to last me a lifetime. Even Uncle Teddy knows this one is *muy mal*, and *he* enjoyed going up San Juan Hill like nothing else he's ever done in all his life."

"And they *want* to do it," Ciara said, as if convincing herself. "You can tell."

Luz gave a wry chuckle. "My beloved, woman who holds my heart . . . think how you feel about the English in your worst moments."

"When I heard that Colm had died in Dublin, and Da fell down like he'd been hit with a hammer, and I knew they'd killed half the people I loved in all the world?" she said, her voice harder, with a little shake to it.

Then she firmed it back. "I've made my peace with it now. The English have paid a thousandfold, and that's enough. Much more than enough, when the women and little children and the common poor folk who'd never harmed anyone died in London with the titled landlords and the generals and politicians. And I'm glad, very glad I had no part in *that*. That I fought against it! But what I might have done, if I'd been a bit more angry, or I hadn't met you at the castle . . . and . . . and . . . I'm still angry, sometimes . . . it makes me feel as if what I *am* is . . . sort of accidental. That I might have gone places and become things that I don't want to think about if just a few things had been different."

Luz nodded again.

"You wouldn't be human if you didn't feel angry in a situation like that, or if you weren't haunted by might-have-beens. Now imagine on top of all that . . . that you'd actually been *there* for every story you heard from your father or his friends about . . . well, everything from Strongbow to Cromwell and King Billy and the Men of '98, and then the famine to boot. And it had all happened in the last two years, not stretched out over eight hundred. *That's* how they feel. Yes, they want to do this."

Ciara pursed her lips and whistled a little; she was good at putting herself in someone else's place, when she actually thought about it.

"Looking at it that way . . . yes, I see."

Sergeant Schultz was trying to warm his hands over his lantern when they appeared out of the night, and a broad grin lit his face.

"Frau Huber!" he said in delight. "And this must be that pretty little miss you care for! You are out late tonight . . . and with a suitcase?"

"We will be at the Charité tomorrow, perhaps late, perhaps into the night, so I thought we could go there now and help the nurses and sleep there—I do not like sitting idle."

He nodded; the Charité was just across a canal from the Lehrter station, a redbrick mass with alpine-style wooden loggias and a distinctive corner clock tower. It was still a long way from here.

She went on: "But first we have a little something for you . . . girl!"

Ciara made an inarticulate stammering sound and smiled and ducked her head. Then she put a hand in the pocket of her overcoat and brought out something wrapped in a cloth.

"S . . . ssss . . . *Splitterbrotchen!*" she said.

Besides the stammer, she gave it an *s*-swallowing Upper Bavarian accent that sounded as if it came from an Alpine yokel who'd been asleep for the past sixty years, which was about when her Auntie Treinel's parents had left their mountain village for the New World.

Splitterbrotchen was a variety of local Berliner pastry; you folded chilled butter into the risen dough, making a ragged, splintery crust and soft crumb; the top was lightly brushed with honey and sprinkled with sugar, and baked until the outermost layer was slightly fried.

Luz caught Schultz's eye; he was nobody's fool and knew the dish was specifically of this city, not something you'd expect a Bavarian to whip up.

"I got the recipe from Frau Blücher," she said. "Living here, I should be less of a stranger."

She *had* gotten the recipe that way, though she'd known it already. Shortly now her cover story wouldn't matter at all, but there was a certain pleasure to the sheer artistry of it, and consistency was a habit it was just as well to maintain. Good habits kept you alive when you were too busy to think things through in advance, and this was something the Frau Huber she'd constructed in her head and woven around the Documents Section's artistry like a vine around a tree trunk would have done. It also gave her an excuse to tell Frau Blücher that she'd be giving the sergeant his treat that night. Blücher felt genuine concern for the elderly man, but she also had three children to feed in this hungry city on an absent husband's meager military pay, eked out only by what she could pick up from odd jobs and a top-up from Siemens, and few of her neighbors were any better off. That lowered the chance of someone sticking their nose out of doors when they could stay inside and not share and do it with a good conscience because someone with priceless rural connections was doing it for them.

Schultz leaned his rifle against the wall beside the door and took the *Splitterbrotchen* eagerly; it crunched beneath his teeth as the still-warm softer center steamed in the cold chill, and he almost groaned with pleasure, holding his left hand beneath his mouth to catch any crumbs.

"Ah, my sweet Luise made it just like this in the good old days," he said through a mouthful. "Have I told you about my youngest son, Ulrich? He's a very steady young man, about your age—well, a little older—reliable, a *Gefreiter* now with a good job waiting for him as a fitter at the Borsig-Werke when the war's over. He writes to me every week, and before his mother passed away he wrote to her every *day*, or nearly. And he reads books, as you do. All sorts of books! Why, he must have a dozen, or even more, that he bought himself! He even keeps a book with him in his knapsack at the front! And he has a good heart. He adopted a puppy he found abandoned in a French house and carried it about and shared his rations with it, and now Max—that's the name he gave it—follows him everywhere and all the men in his *Zug* look after him. They even rigged him a gas mask and Ulrich says he can smell gas before any alarm goes off and comes running to have it put on, barking to wake everyone."

Luz forced herself not to laugh; she suspected that the real Frau Huber, if there had been such a person, could do much worse than Corporal Ulrich Schultz and his steady habits and faithful dog Max and love of reading, and a father-in-law who adored her cooking and would spoil his grandchildren with treats and stories and snore by the stove after a heavy Sunday dinner and a mug or two.

Or maybe I'm just being a typical newlywed and wishing everyone *could find that special someone,* she thought. *Even imaginary people I'm pretending to be.*

"From the bottom of my heart I regret any trouble I may have caused for you, Mr. Sergeant," she said as she inconspicuously worked her feet to test that there was nothing slippery on the pavement and nodded at Ciara.

"Why, Frau Huber, you have done me nothing but—no, Fraulein! You will hurt yourself!"

Ciara giggled as she picked up his bayonetted rifle and shook it tentatively, then raised it over her head in both hands, doing a little dance. Luz gave a gasp, and he said without looking around, "Don't worry, there's no round in the chamber."

Which was kind of him, but the old rifle had an even older-style two-foot bayonet from about 1870, which Schultz, either from dutiful-ness or habit or sheer boredom, had kept good and sharp. If this had been the situation he thought it was, Ciara would be in considerable danger of a nasty gash, and so would he be if he got close to her.

"Now, young miss, you give that to me! Don't be such a naughty bad girl!" he said, in the voice of a man who'd spent considerable time around young children.

He put his big left hand with its prominent veins and knobby knuckles on Ciara's shoulder, firmly but not roughly, and stretched his right up toward the antique Gewehr 88 to snatch it out of her grip. Luz sprang instantly, precise as a cat at a bird, and her right arm went under his and snaked up across his thick wattled neck. The odor of stale wool and tobacco was rank in her nostrils; the feel of his once-rugged, once-fat body was bony and ropy as it surged under her impact. Her left hand slapped onto her right wrist and dug that knuckle into his neck over the carotid in a *sime-waza*. He gave a choked grunt, started to hunch to throw her off in a display of creaking ancient reflex that showed he really had been a fighting man once, and then slumped limp. Luz went down with him, crouching over him to keep the hold on for a few more seconds, then released him and caught him by the shoulders to keep his head from thumping on the doorstep of the apartment.

Ciara leaned the rifle against the doorway where Schultz had put it. "He isn't . . ." she said anxiously.

Luz chuckled and shook her head, though she held two fingers against his neck and her other hand in front of his nose to make sure from pulse and breath. You couldn't always tell with old people; sometimes hearts just gave out with a little nudge that most would take without harm. This time everything was fine, though the sergeant wouldn't be happy when he woke up, for a whole clutch of reasons.

"No, he's just out for a little while; twenty minutes, maybe a little longer. He'll have the tequila hangover from hell, though. *Absolutamente crudo*. Give me a hand here, *querida*."

They gripped Schultz by the back of his greatcoat and pulled him along the side of the building. There was still nobody in sight; several nights of observation had convinced her that this place was deader than an abandoned cemetery at this time of night. The irony of it was that if anyone *did* see them, they'd think they were helping the man; unless the women involved were obvious prostitutes, that was the assumption most people would make. A false buttress on the building's front provided a little shelter, and they propped him in it, tucking his hands into his pockets and leaving his rifle leaned against the wall and pulling the scarf he wore around his head up to shelter his face. It was cold, but not raining or snowing.

Searching Schultz's pockets took a few instants. She found what she needed quickly, what she'd been expecting based on what she knew about German bureaucratic procedure, military and civilian.

"This is an authorization from the Abteilung für Kriegsrohstoffe und Industrielle Gleichschaltung," she said. "I *thought* there would be one."

"Some sort of war board?"

"It got started by a man named Walter Rathenau—"

"The industrialist? AEG?"

"The same. It's more or less like our War Industries Board and War Trade Board rolled together; it's grown like Topsy but originally it was set up to tap the resources of the occupied territories for the German war effort. Add in that they're allocating raw materials, and it was a natural to take over the forced labor program when Ludendorff expanded it in the spring with his *absoluter Krieg* policy—the military rounds them up and provides guards from their fourth-line formations, and the Abteilung für Kriegsrohstoffe und Industrielle Gleichschaltung distributes and supervises and farms them out to member firms. And this, my darling, is an authorization to transport French female workers to their place of employment. Which place is not actually specified."

Ciara grinned. "And transport them we will!"

Schultz had the key to the padlock, too. When Luz unfastened it and pulled the doors open, Simone was there looking like a huge-eyed deer with a grin, and Unfortunately Pregnant looking grim as she usually did, but more alive around the eyes. Behind them were about twelve others, the core of her circle.

"This way, ladies, in a column of fours, as if you were going to work," Luz said.

They fell into line—literally—and Ciara went down it handing out everything immediately edible they'd had in the house, from boiled potatoes to open cans of wartime mystery meat. It all went down quickly, and by the time they were finished more faces showed in the door, blinking back the sleep of exhaustion and weakness, showing instinctive fear at the break in routine. Other pale, drawn faces showed in the hallway entrances and stairwells as Luz stepped into the foyer.

"Mesdames," she said in clear French, pitched to carry and keeping the slight southern accent she'd decided on with Unfortunately Pregnant in the first place. "The door is open, but the German soldiers and secret police are coming. They will be looking for spies and sabo-teurs. The *Boche* will not believe you when you tell them you know nothing."

There was a moment of stunned silence, then a stifled shriek from someone quick-witted, and a rising hum of voices as the clear-thinking ones filled everyone else in. The worst possible situation for an inter-rogation subject was to be genuinely innocent in the hands of people who wouldn't believe you, or didn't care. After all, the guilty would deny everything too . . . as long as they could. Truth and trust became very elusive things, in the secret world.

"I suggest you all get out of here and run as far as you can," she said. "I very strongly urge you to do that. *Run away! Now!*"

It probably wouldn't help, but it wouldn't hurt, and at least it might delay the onset of the questioning. Berlin was a very large city—in America only New York was larger—and a few might actually find someplace to hide. And in any case, looking for them and questioning them would tie up German resources, hopefully for days or weeks after Luz and Ciara were gone. At the very least it would cause massive con-fusion, always a good thing when it was inflicted on the other side.

The news poured through the building quickly, doubtless growing as it spread—one of the training exercises she'd done was playing tele-phone, a children's game made more serious, where you repeated a message down a line from mouth to ear and then compared the first rendition to what came out the other end. The distortions could be startling, even with grown-ups trying to be as accurate as they could, and here you had to throw in the effects of terror operating on words conveyed in half-heard shrieks.

Even the shout of *The Germans are coming to kill us all!* she heard wasn't really necessarily inaccurate, when you thought about it.

Luz stepped out of the apartment-house door into the cold darkness; the column of workers was already a half block away. As she moved to follow there was another shriek, this time from above her. She looked up and saw someone—she thought she recognized one of the women her contacts had identified as informers, despite the meager flickering candle-light within—being shoved relentlessly out a second-story window by half a dozen pairs of hands, despite her frantic writhing and clutching at everything from the frame of the window to someone's hair. Luz stepped out briskly as there was a last scream and thump behind her, and the scurry of many feet. Lights were coming on up and down the street at the noise and commotion.

She grinned as she caught up with the head of the column. Unfortunately Pregnant spoke:

"Staaken is to the west of here, no? Quite a distance?"

"Several kilometers," Luz said. "Madame . . . what is your name? It doesn't matter now, one way or another."

"Yvonne Perrin," she said with surprise.

Luz went on: "But it's a well-traveled road, even at night, and I don't think we'll have to walk all the way."

She looked up; the stars were visible through wisps of cloud, but there was a deeper dark to the northeast.

"That's weather building up," she said, taking off a glove and holding her hand up; the wind was definitely from the northeast, and blowing harder. "I hope it holds off for a while . . . but not too long."

You imbecile! You toad! You utter dumb-head!" Horst von Dückler barked in his best *Uradel* Prussian officer's tone.

The elderly *Landsturm* sergeant braced to full attention, stone-faced despite an involuntary wince at his throbbing head. He was brightly lit, showing every wrinkle and crag; one of the *Geheimpolizei* trucks had a swivel-mounted light that was shining in his face. There were six of them, and a few more Siemens vehicles, and they'd emptied of their cargos of *Sturmtruppen* and policemen quickly. Outside the puddle of light, policemen were running up and down the street telling people to stay inside until they were contacted; luckily, in Berlin they'd probably be obeyed without question.

"*Jawohl, Herr Hauptmann! Zum Befehl, Herr Hauptmann!*" the man said, his white-mustached face the stolid mask that soldiers and peasants put on while a superior was yelling at them.

"Why were you wandering around calling: *Ladies! Please! Ladies!*" Horst asked.

"It is my assigned duty to keep these foreign laborers under guard, Herr Hauptmann, and they had mostly run off by the time I woke up. But there was only one of me, and they scattered so, like chickens or cats . . ."

Horst bit off the rant he could feel building; it wouldn't serve any useful purpose, and the man was already probably frightened enough for all practical purposes. Even allowing for the ragged-edges effects of being choked unconscious, he looked as if he was old enough to have fought in the Wars of Unification; back then it wouldn't have been anything out of the ordinary for a sufficiently annoyed Prussian officer of the old school to have an enlisted man stand at attention while he cut the soldier's face to the bone with blows from a steel-cored riding crop. Or for a noble to do the same to a peasant, of course, though that still happened occasionally. In the background he could hear irritated shouts and terrified squeals as—some of—the forced laborers were rounded up again, or rousted out of places they'd tried to hide in the building; Diehl's men were setting up a questioning room somewhere in there, but that was just going through the motions.

Horst lit a cigarette and pulled ferociously on it as he thought until the coal glowed white-red in the dimness. A snowflake touched his face just below the brim of his peaked officer's cap, and he looked up; the storm coming in from the Baltic had just started, making a *perfect* end to the day. The flakes started to dance in the beams of light from the vehicles, only a few but with the promise of more to come. The sergeant spoke again from his ramrod brace:

"Sir, Frau Huber—"

"There is no Frau Huber, you dimwit! Those were American spies!"

"Yes, Herr Hauptmann. The spies were at number twenty-seven, and they pretended to be Bavarians, not Americans, and that is all I know. They fooled me completely, sir. I make no excuses, sir."

"Fooling you probably wasn't hard," Horst said in disgust. "You are dismissed! But don't go far, you may be needed again. We have a doctor with us; get her to look at your injury when there's time."

"Jawohl, Herr Hauptmann! Zum Befehl, Herr Hauptmann!"

Diehl looked at his retreating back as he marched off in parade-ground style and shook his head.

"At least the triangulation system got us to the right road, combined with knowing they hid among the laborers at the plant. That's the only lead we're going to get," he said. "This old man Schultz is an honest fool; we'll check, but that's my professional judgment. I don't think we're going to get more than: *A woman opened the door and told us to run, then walked away*, from the Frenchwomen, either. You don't think they had any other actual Americans working with them here? Just the two women?"

Horst took another draw on the cigarette and shook his head. "No, more agents would be bad procedure, multiplying the possibilities of detection and making cover stories more difficult to maintain; we will check when we have time, but no. The Black Chamber usually don't make mistakes of that sort, and anyway they don't have all that many agents who can pass convincingly as Germans; they must economize on them. Those two almost certainly developed contacts among the forced laborers, but those would have been the first to run when they left."

The doctor rose from the bodies on the sidewalk and came over to join them.

"*Meine Herren*, one of these was thrown out of the window and landed on her head," she said. "The blood, missing fingernails, and hair under others indicate the . . . the defenestration . . . was done by mob action."

Horst smiled thinly; his Silesian home had been part of Austria once, and memories of the Bohemian custom of expressing dissatisfaction by defenestration—throwing people out of an upper-story window—persisted. From his orderly's subdued chuckle, he caught the reference too; but then he was Austrian-born, and not far from the Bohemian part of the Dual Monarchy at that.

"When?" Horst asked the doctor.

"Hard to be precise with these low temperatures, but I would say not more than an hour. The other one was punched and kicked to death—slowly and inefficiently, not by the person responsible for the bodies we examined earlier at the Siemens factory."

The Siemens man, Bladis, was holding a handkerchief to his mouth. "Those are Marie and Chantelle," he said. "My other informants. They said they were under suspicion."

Ernst Röhm chuckled. "There seems to be very little job security in working for *you*, Herr Bladis!" he said. "Not a solid position like being a *Kruppianer*, eh? No twenty-five years and a pension in a company cottage!"

Horst was mentally composing a coded telegraph to Colonel Nicolai:

ENEMY AGENTS ALREADY IN PLACE AT SIEMENS WHEN I ARRIVED
STOP CONFIRM AGENTS INDIVIDUALS IDENTIFIED IN TRANSIT
RECIFE TUNIS STOP NAVAL INTELLIGENCE ENTIRELY UNAWARE
STOP HEIMDAL PROBABLY COMPROMISED NO LATER/POSSIBLY
EARLIER THAN THIS DATE STOP HAVE LOCATED ENEMY SAFE
HOUSE STOP ENEMY AGENTS FLED ONE HOUR+- 0100 STOP AM IN
ACTIVE PURSUIT OF ENEMY AGENTS STOP NAVY MUST REPEAT
MUST IMPLEMENT OPERATION HAMMERFALL SOONEST STOP

Röhm rubbed his hands together. "Well, let's get started on their house, eh?"

The Berlin policeman, Kurschat, cut in: "My men have experience in that, Herr Hauptmann. Let them go first. We must be careful not to destroy any evidence."

He added that with a glare at the soldiers, as if to accuse them of being vandals and smashing things up by reflex, like so many bulls in a china shop. Some of the Berlin police were making the rounds of the neighboring houses; plainclothes detectives took the preliminary statements, which was a good thing. It was important to get testimony immediately, before people had a chance to amend their memories or talk things over with each other. Others had put sawhorse barriers in place outside No. 27, painted in police colors. Four waited with a door-knocker, a heavy length of steel pipe with a mushroom head and handles riveted onto it.

"Fusch," Röhm said to his lieutenant. "You've got three men out back?"

"Ja, Herr Hauptmann," the lieutenant said. "The nest may be empty, but then again maybe not, no reason not to be thorough. With the assault rifles they can cut anyone trying to get out into dog meat."

"Yes, better to do more than enough rather than less," Röhm said. "All is ready, Hauptmann von Dückler."

The rest of the *Stoßtruppen* were waiting in their teams, assault rifles in their hands and grenades in their belts; several had fixed their bayonets, and their eyes were ferally alert under the beetling brows of their *Stahlhelms*.

"Right, look alive, boys," Röhm said jovially.

Horst and his aide stood well back, but they both clicked the safeties off their own weapons, carefully keeping the fingers outside the trigger guards. The policemen gripped the doorknocker, lifted it with a unified grunt, and trotted forward, pausing before the single step up and swinging it back. Horst felt himself frowning.

The operation was all very clean so far, just what he'd have expected of . . . *her*. In, get the information, broadcast it to the waiting American monitors—probably in neutral Denmark, possibly undercover here in Berlin—and then get out, no tracks except what was essential to preserve her cover for just long enough. But something nagged at him—the field experience she'd had in Mexico. It had been on the other side than the one he'd believed when she was passing herself off as Elisa the Mexican revolutionary, but still . . . what you did when you were retreating, if you had time . . . and the sly grin she'd had as she handled one of the French grenades they'd captured in Amsterdam, and the way she'd lured the Deuxième Bureau agents into throwing range by playing dead, making them feel very very safe . . .

"*Scheisse!*" he exclaimed, as it all came together. "You with the battering ram! Stop!"

Horst went flat with the speed of conditioned reflex; those who'd been where he had and hadn't developed it were dead or crippled for life.

"Do not touch the door! Get away!"

"*Deckung!*" his scar-faced little orderly screamed: *Cover!*

And threw himself flat with weasel speed and the assault rifle springing to his shoulder. "*Kattun! Kattun!*"

That meant *calico*, literally. In front-pig slang it meant that hell was about to drop on your head.

The words blended together, and the soldiers all instantly threw themselves flat, the ones with really finely honed instincts landing before Horst did. The policemen with the doorknocker didn't pause, but a couple of the others looked over their shoulders, trying to understand what they were saying and looking with puzzlement at the *Stoßtruppen* all flat on their bellies. You could tell which of the policemen had seen frontline service themselves. They were the ones who saw what Röhm's men were doing, and then threw themselves down too with varying degrees of speed. Another thing you learned under fire was that it was much, much better to take cover when you didn't need to do it than to hesitate when you did.

WHUMP!

The blast picked Horst up and thumped him back on the ground; he had his mouth open to equalize the pressure inside and out to keep it from damaging his ears, but his head still rang and he tasted blood. He was back in a place where you could see three or four different things happen at exactly the same time as if you were concentrating exclusively on each. The door blasted outward in a gout of flame six feet long and the policemen with the doorknocker seemed to burn into his eyes as silhouettes against it. That was a trick of light and perception, because in the same instant the doorknocker came flipping back in a whirling blur and decapitated Diehl as neatly as a guillotine, splashing blood and matter in a fan thirty feet long and leaving his corpse upright and spouting blood for an instant before it slumped to the ground like a sack of rye.

The door and its frame smashed out in fragments of shrapnel moving too fast to be visible in the poor light. All the windows in the little house did likewise, stabbing the street with glass like the obsidian knives of savages. At almost the same instant another series of explosions rippled around the join between the walls and the roofline. As if in a slow-moving dream the roof collapsed downward while the walls fell in, and gouts of flame speared upward through the wreckage. In seconds the fire was like something out of a metalworking forge, and getting hotter fast enough to feel the difference from moment to moment.

He got to his feet and helped some of the injured move back and did some quick field-bandaging; luckily there was enough morphine in the stormtroopers' field kits to go around. Kurschat was upright, bleeding from cuts on his face but yelling for men to run to the nearest call

box and summon ambulances and fire engines and for others to evacuate the houses on either side. There was nothing wrong with his guts
and instincts, at least, even if he was a bit stodgy and defensive about
his organization's tribal territory.

Horst had an eye for the consequences of explosions and fires,
honed by years of experience both in making them happen and in having them drop on him unexpectedly. No. 27 was going to end up as a
heap of smoldering ash that would take days to cool enough to sift
through, and there would be nothing to find when it did. But the fire
was remarkably contained, since the charges—they were of a type of
explosive unfamiliar to him, from the sound and color—had dropped
everything neatly inward, and it would all fall into the cellar quite
soon. Even the houses to either side with common walls weren't much
damaged, and probably wouldn't burn—if the fire engines got here
quickly. If they did catch, it wouldn't be fast enough to endanger the
people stumbling out in their nightclothes even now.

The whole thing was a mockery, like dangling meat before a
chained dog and then snatching it away.

"I lost one of my best men!" Röhm said; almost raved, in fact. "Two
more are wounded!"

"You'd have lost more if they hadn't known enough to hit the
ground when someone yelled *kattun*," Horst said. "That was my man
and me."

Then he put his hand to his face, wiping off blood that was partly
his own, partly from Diehl, and the rest from who-knew-where. He
held the palm up before Röhm's distorted face.

"And I didn't ask you along on this to pick flowers. I didn't tell you we
would be having tea with the *Gräfin*, either. I spent all of a train ride between Warsaw and here trying to convince a cocky Bavarian asshole it
was serious business, killing business. Do you believe me now? And if
you do, are you going to give up and crawl away?"

Röhm stopped in midrant, froze for a moment, and then smiled . . .
or at least showed his teeth.

"You have a point there . . . you cocky Silesian baronial asshole.
This makes it personal."

He slapped the assault rifle slung across his belly. "And you did help me with that General Staff fuckwit and that too-smart Jewboy. That was good work and I'd have lost my temper and my chance if you hadn't."

A policeman ran up to Kurschat, a detective with a bald head and a walrus mustache, looming out of the darkness.

"Captain Kurschat! We have a witness who says that an organized group left the foreign laborers' quarters before midnight, going north, just before all the *Französinen* escaped!"

TWENTY-THREE

Siemensstadt (Northwest Berlin metropolitan area)
Königreich Preußen (Kingdom of Prussia)
Großdeutsches Kaiserreich (Empire of Greater Germany)
DECEMBER 5TH, 1916(B)

"Halt!" Luz cried, running into the roadway and waving her arms.
The blocky Stoewer three-ton truck in army field gray halted . . . eventually, when the driver realized she wasn't getting out of the way, skidding first and turning at an angle in darkness relieved by the slow flicker of beginning snow through the beams of the headlights. They were very modern electric ones, but the steel wheels had the same terrible traction she'd noted before. The radiator was five feet from her chest when it did slither to a halt; it had only been doing twenty miles an hour, but that was more than enough to leave her a smear on the pavement with that much weight behind it, and she heard Ciara give a muffled bitten-off gasp just before the end. Only when the truck was nearly on her could she smell the hot metal of the engine and the harsh low-octane exhaust; the weather was muffling sound and scent in that northern European way that made you feel as if you were locked in a damp barn.

"I could have killed you, you stupid twat!" the young soldier driving the Stoewer screamed in a strong Bavarian—specifically, Franconian—accent as he leaned out to shout and shake his fist. "You could have killed *me*, you crazy sow! What the devil do you think you're doing?"

He was wearing a greatcoat and something bulky underneath it, and a knit scarf wrapped around his neck and head beneath the round, brimless field cap with its red band. She didn't blame him for that, since in wartime style the truck dispensed with effete luxuries like a windscreen or doors and had only a meager canvas hood above him, and he'd been traveling into the teeth of the gathering weather and had streaks and clumps of snow on his coat and scarf and dripping from his scraggly semi-mustache. She'd picked it to flag down because this model had about a three-ton capacity and a long body, more than ample for what she needed, and because it was coming eastward empty, which meant it had almost certainly come from the Staaken base itself and had enough fuel to get back there. And because it had only the driver in the cab; two men were far more difficult to manipulate than one, much more than twice as hard.

Luz had to fight down a slight smile at the *I could have killed you* remark, considering some of the ways this could have played out, or might yet.

The soldier was probably Ciara's age or younger—driving an automobile of any sort wasn't a common skill anywhere, rarer here than it was in America, and rarer still among older people. He looked cold and grumpy and genuinely frightened at the near-accident, but otherwise unremarkable except for a very unfortunate attempt at a mustache that would better have been delayed until he was shaving more than twice a week and didn't have pimples. The mustache's conspicuous failure to flourish took place under a big aquiline nose amid heavy peasant features; he was unarmed except for a carbine slung over the seat behind him, the short weapon with the turned-down bolt issued to gunners and horsemen and truck drivers. His expression melted a bit as he saw Luz's face under the hat; she was smiling at him, her face framed by strands from the dark-brown wig she'd selected. Luz was *good* at charming smiles, if she did say so herself. Ciara was looking grave but added to the effect just by existing.

"Sorry, miss, but I nearly did run you down, the way you jumped out at me in this lousy weather," he said; then his china-blue eyes went wider as he saw the dim forms of the Frenchwomen farther back. "What's going on here?"

"I'm sorry to stop you, but I'm at my wits' end, Mr. Corporal."

Meaning, this is the alternative to shooting you and hiding your body. For your own sake, listen carefully and believe everything. It'll be much better for me at the entrance to the base if I have someone they know driving, and much better for you if I don't kill you.

"I'm in charge of these foreign laborers; they are Frenchwomen, employed in cleaning up . . . difficult situations with . . . factory spillages. I supervise them."

It was reasonably credible that a German woman would have that job; women had been taking over many positions, with mobilization and huge losses making men more and more scarce, concentrated more and more on the things only they could do . . . or that they thought only they could do . . . and that was an ever-shifting barrier, even here. Some psychological quirk made supervising cleaning crews seem like an extension of housework, perhaps.

She could see the ambiguous wording of *difficult situations* and *spillages* working its way through the soldier's mind, translating it to *deadly chemicals that make you sick or kill you.*

"*Ach, so,*" he said, which was an equivalent of an American's *Umm, yeah.*

"I received an emergency message as I was bringing them back from the Siemens factory that a cleanup crew is needed, needed urgently, at the Staaken base. Here is my authorization—you will see, it refers to the Siemens factories over there."

Luz pointed off to the southeast toward a barely seen glow; the Siemens plant was only a few miles away, and everyone in this part of Berlin would know about it. She handed him two pieces of paper, one from the *Geheimpolizei* agent she'd killed and the other taken from Schultz.

"I was *supposed* to be getting transport laid on as well, but apparently not. Something seems to be going on there in Staaken, and I didn't want to wait anymore."

He put the papers close to an illuminated dial on the truck's control panel to read the small smudgy print, and pursed his lips in recognition at the headings.

"This appears to be in order, miss," he said respectfully.

Anyone with papers from the Abteilung für Kriegsrohstoffe und Industrielle Gleichschaltung and the Prussian Secret Police as well had authorization of a heavy-duty variety, even a woman. Then his face changed:

"A . . . difficult spillage at . . . Staaken."

Aha, Luz thought.

She kept the same smile—one that invited him to share in her exasperation with superiors who managed to foul up such a simple task. With a German that would be coupled with indignation; they tended to have a low tolerance for ordinary organizational incompetence. Not that it didn't happen here, just rather less often than in some places.

Those rumors about horror-gas production or storage at Staaken in the briefing papers were right. He knows, or suspects, and it's scaring him green, and he knows that expendable foreigners would be just the people picked to clean things up if there was *an accident and he's wondering if he should warn* me. *But by the same token he doesn't want to be uncooperative, because everything associated with the horror-gas project has the highest priorities. And the* Geheimpolizei *make everyone nervous, especially these days now that they've gotten so much more . . . proactive . . . than they were before the war.*

"Well, I'm sorry your transport didn't arrive, miss, but what can I do for you?" he said, his eyes moving as if he already knew the answer and knew he wouldn't like it, either, whether he did what she wanted or not.

"I'm afraid I'm going to have to ask you to take me and my workers to Staaken, Gefreiter . . ."

"Gefreiter Rudolf Dassler, miss. But I have orders to return this truck to the vehicle park so it can be ready for shipments in the morning; I can't stop for civilians!"

"Captain Diehl of the *Geheimpolizei* will be glad to record that you were asked to assist him and did so," Luz said persuasively. "He gave me my orders, and as soon as I get to a telephone, I can clear it with him and he will speak to your commanding officer. It will all take only a few minutes, and then you can drive to the vehicle park again."

And you will have to explain why you didn't help if you don't, went unspoken.

Dassler sighed. "Sergeant Kuhn is not an easy man to convince, I think not even by the secret police."

Luz knew she'd won the little tussle and that Dassler's short existence wouldn't end this minute with a blast from her shotgun into a very surprised face.

"Very well, miss."

Luz and Ciara shepherded the Frenchwomen into the back of the truck; it had a canvas hoop cover, and there were wooden benches along the sides. Since Dassler couldn't see them well, they were able to give the weaker ones a boost as well and a few murmured words of reassurance. Unfortunately Pregnant . . .

Yvonne Perrin. I must remember to think of her that way; it's not a risk now, and it would be very unpleasant if I slipped and actually said the nickname aloud.

. . . and Simone had given them a rundown. Several of them were crying with the pain of awakening hope. Luz hoped it wasn't premature, but it was better to die hoping than despairing, anyway.

The driver's seat of the big truck was bench-style, with ample room for the three of them; Luz took the middle position, folding her skirts aside to keep from interfering with the gear-shift lever, and giving the controls a quick once-over in case she had to drive. She introduced herself to Dassler under the Frau Huber schoolteacher-watchmaker's-widow identity, slightly modified and simplified.

"Ah, I thought you were from around München, Frau Huber, from the way you speak, and so precise and scholarly, that's like a teacher," he said cheerfully; if he was going to drive two attractive women and get to do it with the wind and snow at his back rather than spitting frigidly into his face, he apparently wanted to make the most of it.

Then in a mumble: "I am sorry I . . . called you a bad name."

She smiled. "I startled you. And you're from the northeast, *Herr Gefreiter*? Nuremberg or somewhere near it?"

"Ah, you've got a good ear! Yes, from Herzogenaurach," he said. "My family makes shoes in a plant there."

Luz hid a smile this time; he'd pronounced *Schuhe*, the German for *shoes*, as if it were the English word *show*, which was almost comically regional, like someone from Mississippi calling a guitar a *gii-tai-uh*. The *Reichsgräfin* would have fainted dead away if any of her girls had said it that way. Ciara was looking over her shoulder at the Frenchwomen fairly often, which was in character if they were supposed to be shepherding them; and she was doing it because she was concerned for them ... which was in character for *her*. Luz herself would prefer that the women from Lille came through this alive, and would be regretful in a mild, abstract way if they didn't, but Ciara was genuinely anxious. At least it helped distract her from the thought that their own chances were about one in four, if that ... though their odds on escaping capture and hideous torture were rather better than they had been at No. 27 Rapsstrasse.

And they'd gotten the information and gotten it out, together.

¡Ay, Dios mío! *And I always thought that if I really fell in love it would be with someone who was like* me. *I was so wrong!*

Fear dropped away from her, leaving only taut purpose.

I am going to do this. I'm going to save her. And it's going to be legendary!

A few years ago Staaken had been a village in the flat, sandy Brandenburger countryside a little west of Spandau and Greater Berlin's ever-growing tentacles, the beginnings of a garden suburb, and plans. The plans had been given the equivalent of a goose with high-voltage electric cables combined with a hefty injection of Benzedrine into the heart when Kaiser Wilhelm heard Roosevelt's public pledge to outdo everyone—and specifically, Germany—in airship construction.

He'd responded with the German equivalent of *the hell you say, Herr Roosevelt.*

Thereafter Count Zeppelin hadn't had to hold any more charity drives, lotteries, and pledgings of his wife's estates to keep his enterprise going. One of the strings attached to the rain of golden marks and military contracts that followed was putting the big new Zeppelin yards here, close to Berlin and as far north from Friedrichshafen as you could get in Germany without getting your toes wet in the Baltic's brackish water. Then the war came ...

And now if you're insane enough to try to hijack an airship, this is the place!

The gateway at which the truck stopped was flanked by concrete bunkers; the snouts of Maxim machine guns showed dimly within. Twelve-strand barbed-wire fences showed to either side, with more coils of wire on top and—just visible through the growing murk—guard towers, probably with more machine guns in them and certainly with searchlights, because she could see them spearing in fuzzy columns through the darkness now and then. Despite the snow and the fact that it was one in the morning, bright lights were visible inside, many mounted on tall standards, each a point surrounded with a diffuse glow, and moving dots must be the headlights of many vehicles. A guard hut flanked the overlapping twin portals of metal framing wound in more barbed wire, and a noncom came out with a lantern in one hand and a machine pistol slung over his shoulder.

"Dassler?" he said, in a Berliner accent; the Fliegertruppen des deutschen Kaiserreiches recruited nationally rather than locally. "What the hell are you doing here? You just left, and the transport people should have gotten that piece of junk you're driving at the vehicle park by now—they'll need it in the morning when the next shipment comes through . . . wait, is that *women* in the cab with you?"

He looked more closely, and his voice took on a dangerous edge. "And more women in the back? You gone into the brothel business, Dassler? If you're picking up tarts, I'll have your backside on report and on punishment detail for the rest of eternity and three weeks more—no, I'll have you in the infantry and on your way to the Western Front—"

"Sergeant Kuhn, these ladies here"—he pointed to Luz and Ciara—"are in charge of a cleaning detail—"

"You're carting *charwomen* around in a *Fliegertruppen* truck, you idiot? *Was für Quatsch ist das?*"

"Excuse me, Mr. Sergeant," Luz said, letting her Bavarian-flavored German creep a little up the social scale. "We have orders to bring a cleaning detail of foreign workers to deal with a chemical spill in Area 17."

The sergeant's beefy face, ruddy and much more abundantly mustachioed than Dassler's, went a little pale.

Well, the Chamber definitely guessed right: Area 17 is where they make and/or store the Annihilation Gas. If you're not afraid of that stuff, you're dead—at least from the neck up.

She handed over the documents again; Sergeant Kuhn frowned at them, scanning them much more thoroughly than Dassler had, with one foot on the running board of the truck by the driver's side and his lantern raised.

"Well, these aren't very specific—" he began.

Luz's mind traced a series of actions; bring the shotgun out, shoot Dassler with the weapon concealed behind his body, shoot the sergeant in the face, throw two grenades through the door of the guard hut—she was inside the arc of the machine guns in the bunkers and could ignore them—then shove the body out from behind the wheel and crash the barricade . . .

And then fly to the moon by putting my head between my knees and spitting very very hard . . .

Instead a man came out of the guard hut and virtually tugged on the sergeant's arm.

"Sergeant! Emergency!" he said. "From the Herr Hauptmann—prepare to evacuate the base! Emergency in Area 17! Emergency evacuation!"

The noncom froze.

Ciara's lips moved silently: *Jesus, Mary, and Joseph*. Luz decided that perhaps there was a God after all . . . but one with a very nasty sense of humor, who'd gotten them into the base by flooding it with horror-gas. Which couldn't be seen or smelled and was deadly in inconceivably small amounts.

She leaned forward and plucked the documents out of his hand. "That will be what Captain Diehl of the *Geheimpolizei* was talking about," she said brightly. "Let us through now, please, Sergeant Kuhn."

Just then the unmistakable muffled thudding *whump* of an explosion in the distance forced its way through the night's cold, wet air. Everyone's heads pivoted, as if pulled on strings. The report came from the north and slightly to the east. As they looked there was another *whump*, and a flash of reddish-white light reflecting through the snow and off the low clouds above. That was the direction of Area 17. A whimpering sound came from the enlisted man who'd dashed out with the news, and Kuhn fairly bristled.

"Turn out!" he growled. "Everyone out! Open the gates! Get moving, Schmidt, you gutless wonder! We're going to keep this gate clear and guide traffic so that things don't clog up. We'll have to push things off the road too, if there are collisions—and there will be. Merkel, Sussman, Brandt, come on, get the winches and jacks and come-alongs ready! Time enough to run when we've done our jobs."

The guard detail came tumbling out of their hut, some of them still yawning and blinking and buttoning their greatcoats. Under the lash of Kuhn's tongue they cranked the gates open quickly—the structures were mounted on wheels and slid back and forth rather than swinging like doors mounted on hinges, and they overlapped for about three-quarters of their length. As they did, the rising-falling-warbling moan of sirens began to sound, starting in the north of the base and spreading southward; some were loud and sounded like the hand-cranked variety, and some were *very* loud, the electropneumatic type. Luz put on an anxious look over a strictly hidden death's-head grin. Sirens were certainly a way of getting people's attention, but she thought they tended to encourage panic by drowning out thought and conversation.

And there's never a time when panic improves your chances.

"Well, get moving, Dassler!" Kuhn bawled, waving his right arm forward. "Get out of the fucking way, drop off your charwomen, and get out of here; you're not home in godforsaken fucking Franconia making shoes now!"

Dassler crossed himself and put the truck in gear; Luz distinctly heard him mutter under his breath: "And how I wish I were back in Herziaura bending over my bench, by God and the Virgin!"

Luz glanced at Ciara, who inclined her head to the left and quietly mouthed: *The airship sheds and docking towers and launching fields are* that *way.*

So they were; but Dassler was doggedly heading toward Area 17, despite a dread that was enough to give him a white-knuckled clench on the wheel and made him clench his teeth, doubtless against an impulse to chatter.

Brave man, Luz thought.

Then she excluded all consciousness of the invisible death drifting on the wind from the northeast with a practiced effort of will; it would kill them or it wouldn't, but there was nothing she could do that she wasn't doing already.

The gas may kill me; *getting distracted will* certainly *kill me.*

They bounced over the frozen ruts of a graveled dirt road between faceless, almost identical frame buildings, now disgorging their night-shift inhabitants in a dashing-back-and-forth manner that resolved into an outward motion: on foot and in and on everything that had wheels, down to bicycles. She suspected that the confusion would have been much worse if this had been daytime, when there were probably three or four times as many people about. Once they had to stop at a level crossing, to let a train of flatcars piled with people clutching each other and throwing themselves down to grip the edges of the cars go by, in a blast of steam and a shrill whistle.

Then they went through a darker section where most of the buildings were skeletons under construction and the finished ones still unoccupied. Then someone jumped out into the roadway, waving his hands. Dassler stood on the brakes, and Luz braced herself with a foot and reached across Ciara's waist to grip the frame and hold her against the forward surge.

"Almighty Lord God, what have I done to deserve this?" the driver screamed.

Once again the truck had slowed just in time, though the rougher surface made it quicker; Dassler really was quite a good driver, considering the road conditions and the tires he had to work with. The man waving had a *Feldgendarmerie* gorget on the chest of his greatcoat, a gray-painted coalscuttle steel helmet, and an *Oberleutant*'s one-pip shoulder boards. Two more of the military police were behind him, and those two had a fourth man between them, gripping him tightly by the arms. He was in the uniform of a German major but *without* a greatcoat, a tall lean man with black hair and a bandage on his right hand, and as they hauled him out into the roadway and into the cones of light the truck cast Luz could see that his left leg was bleeding freely from a wound on the outside of his thigh not far below the hip.

The headlights picked them all out with pitiless clarity. Ciara stiffened:

"Isn't that—" she began incredulously, startled all the way into English.

"Yes, it's James," Luz replied in the same language. "Senior Field Operative James Cheine, wounded, bleeding, and captured by the enemy in *la maldita ciudad de Berlín*."

As she spoke Luz pulled the shotgun from under her coat and slammed the steel cap on the rounded cut-down butt into Dassler's head just behind the ear with a hard stiff-armed thump. A boost from her hip sent the groaning half-conscious man slithering down to the ground, clutching feebly at things as he went. She leveled the weapon over his slumping body before it got halfway out of the cab of the truck, and before the man standing there could do more than start his hand toward his pistol.

BAM!

And the charge of double-ought buckshot went into the *Ober-leutnant's* face, along with a foot-long spear of flame.

The weapon bucked against her hands, and she let the recoil point the muzzle up. Darkness and snow were merciful as the body fell backward in the track of the gout of red; at three feet all of the pea-sized buckshot slammed directly into the man's face and throat and the soft tissue *splashed* away from the bone. Bits spattered onto her, shockingly warm for an instant in the cold air.

Crack-crack-crack.

The sound of a nine-millimeter pistol was curiously muffled. The wounded man had wrenched his arms free as the two military policemen reacted to the sudden violence that they couldn't see quite clearly by reaching for their weapons—a carbine and a machine pistol. That let the suddenly ex-prisoner snatch the Luger from the belt of one, jam it against that man's coat, and pull the trigger three times before his wounded leg gave way and he dropped to the ground. The last German quite sensibly turned and ran to report and get help.

Luz half rose in the seat; it was a straight no-deflection shot at only thirty feet, but she'd only get one chance, with the weather and the night and the availability of cover close by. She kept the trigger pulled, leveled the weapon, and worked the slide action—

*Shikk-shack-*BAM!

—with just enough of a fractional second to bring the muzzle level back down—

*Shikk-shack-*BAM!

—the cut-down shotgun wasn't intended for precise aiming from the shoulder anyway—

Shikk-shack-BAM!

Snow flew out of the running man's coat, like dust beaten out of a carpet; he dropped his carbine and fell forward on his face, holes blown in his back, his legs and arms briefly twitching. Luz reloaded, thumbing four more of the fat shells into the magazine of the shotgun, pushed it back through the loops inside her coat, and jumped down from the truck, her feet making a gritty *chuck* sound in the wet snow as she landed. Dassler was stirring slightly; she pulled the belt out of the trousers of the dead *Feldgendarmerie* officer and used it to bind his hands behind him before dragging him out of the roadway. Then she went around to the front; Perrin had hopped out of the truck and was already there, flanked by Simone as they knelt by the injured man—

. . . who is undoubtedly alive only because they wanted to question him . . .

—cutting the trouser-leg with a bayonet and applying the antiseptic powder and wound-bandage packages from one of the *Feldgendarmerie* men's webbing gear.

Ciara had picked up a dead man's carbine and was standing guard; she was visibly shock-white, but her hands were steady as she looked around.

"Oh, now this is embarrassing, Luz," James Cheine of New York City and the Black Chamber said, in English, before switching to French: "Thank you very much, Madame . . . ?"

"Yvonne Perrin, Monsieur . . . ?"

"Cheine, James Cheine. *Et vous, mademoiselle?*"

"Simone Chaix, monsieur," she replied in a small voice.

"James, James," Luz said. "If I keep having to rescue you like this, people will begin to talk! Are you trying to ruin my reputation as a wholesome, innocent all-American girl who's pure in thought, word, and deed?"

The rest of the Frenchwomen were sticking their heads out to the sides of the truck and they began to gabble as Simone and Perrin brought James around with his arms over their shoulders, hissing slightly as his foot touched the ground and the injured thigh muscle flexed. The wound was a simple in-and-out through the outer flesh from a pistol round and hadn't hit any major blood vessels, but it would certainly be damnably painful and it meant he couldn't use the leg.

Perrin looked inquiringly at Luz and inclined her head toward her countrywomen. She'd obviously figured out what was going on, but the rest needed to hear it.

"Madame Perrin, this man is an American secret agent, impersonating a German," Luz said.

James managed to grin and spoke in French, in the accentless accent a professor or senior civil servant would use, conveying a polite bow without making one:

"That is the truth, mesdames. Though at present not a very mobile American agent."

Perrin looked at Luz again, and she could see things going click in the woman's mind as bits and pieces aligned into a new whole. Luz had never thought she was stupid, and nodded slightly:

Yes, I'm American too . . . and I never told you differently, did I?

Perrin glanced at the body of the last German lying and accumulating snow by the side of the road. She gave a brief wintry smile at that, and a nod of her own. Things were going *much* better from her point of view since Luz arrived, regardless of the spy's identity. And much worse for the Germans, which was probably more important to her.

"Get down and help," she said to the others.

"Put him in the cab," Luz said. "And if several of you could drag the bodies—and the living one, do not kill him—into that vacant building over there," she went on. "Quickly, please."

Half a dozen of them slid down to do so, several spitting on the corpses—and on the unfortunate semiconscious Dassler and giving him a covert kick or two—as they did. The snow would cover the blood and the drag marks quickly, and other little indicators like spent casings, and the sharp smell of nitro powder was already gone. Luz quickly secured all the weapons; the last thing she needed was fourteen excited, hate-filled, and desperate people with no firearms experience at all sitting behind her waving loaded guns around. If she was going to be shot, she would prefer it was not by an ally and not by accident.

"Are you fit for purpose, *mi camarada*?"

Cheine nodded. "As long as the purpose doesn't involve walking."

"Morphine?"

He shook his head as she handed him the MP's machine pistol and the two extra fifty-round drums in their webbing carriers.

"Not until we're safe; if I'm going to die, I want to be able to do my dying scream coherently."

Luz nodded and checked the Mauser carbine Ciara had picked up; she'd given her a little basic instruction on rifles back at the *Casa*. The younger woman touched the safety tab behind the bolt handle, which was all the way to the right.

"Push this left to fire?" she said.

"Right. It's loaded and cocked. Don't . . ."

"Try to use it from very far away, yes, darling. I'll be careful. No dying of stupid, as you say." A smile. "And it's just a piece of machinery. I'm *good* at machinery."

Cheine cut in: "Speaking of which, I evidently didn't do nearly as much damage to the Annihilation Gas facility as I planned, but this still isn't going to be a healthy location for long."

"Don't worry," Luz said. "We're going to be leaving soon and you're going to help. In point of fact, you already have. *Más o menos*, and assuming that the gas leak creates confusion we can use without actually killing us."

H err Privatdozent," Horst said.
       "Hauptmann von Dückler," the thin, white-haired old man said.

Privatdozent von Bülow hadn't looked quite so old the last time Horst had seen him, back before Boston . . . back before the gas codenamed the Breath of Loki had fallen on the cities, which had been as much von Bülow's doing as anyone's.

Since he invented the stuff, and convinced Colonel Nicolai . . . who convinced the High Command . . . that we could use it. The Army broke the Russians, but it was the Breath of Loki that ripped the heart out of France and let us drive the English into the sea.

Von Bülow had been a young *Fähnrich*, an officer-cadet, in the Wars of Unification against Denmark and Austria back in the sixties of the last century, before his academic career as a chemist got going. Now he looked as if he'd aged twenty years since the spring, and that wasn't counting the slick of blood that covered half his face from a wound where a bullet had taken off half his ear and had come within a few millimeters of spattering his brains. It had dripped onto his white lab coat in a thick spatter.

"I look better than my colleagues," he said.

Horst eyed them; there were six of them and they were all dead amid a litter of papers and overturned chairs, before the banks of brass-rimmed dials and pipes and gauges and levers of the glassed-in room that controlled the poison-gas plant. It had been designed to be operated from a distance as much as possible—large parts of the actual factory had to be decontaminated by men in rubber suits or expendable laborers every day it was used.

One of the dead was a *Feldgendarmerie* officer on his back with his pistol still lying by his outstretched hand, and a single spent cartridge in a pool of blood not far away; there was a bullet hole just over his left eyebrow, and a much larger one in the back of his head. Horst's mind reconstructed that—the man had come rushing in when he heard something, had fired one shot . . . and then taken one that was better-placed. He wasn't surprised. A secret agent on a sabotage mission was much more likely to be a really good shot than a random military policeman, for whom the automatic at his waist was more a symbol of rank than a real weapon.

The rest of the bodies were in lab coats like von Bülow or in workman's overalls. One middle-aged bald man had a small round puncture wound leaking a trickling dribble of blood and clear matter on the back of his neck, the sort you'd get by driving a thin stiletto in between the upper end of the spine and the opening where the cord entered the skull. Another had a similar wound at the angle of his jaw, a back-handed strike upward into the brain from that angle that argued for a long thin blade too. The others had been shot like the military policeman.

All single bullets to the head.

And all fatal, except for the creasing shot that had put von Bülow down but not quite out.

Perhaps the Black Chamber has a house style. This was not her, *but there is a likeness.*

Under the blood and the death reek there was a chemical tang in the air combined with a rotten-egg taste that made the skin between his shoulder blades tighten, and his scrotum. He knew that was foolish, at least with the front part of his head. Annihilation Gas had no scent, and if you were in contact with it you were already dead. The feeling persisted nonetheless. Sweat gleamed in the electric light on Röhm's face, and some of his stormtroopers were looking uneasy too.

"He was most convincing, with excellent documents," von Bülow said. "Almost as convincing as the woman was, back in September, when she fooled the both of us. And he was passing himself as a German, which is more difficult for a foreigner. Even a Brandenburger accent like mine! A tall man—about your height, but slimmer, blue-gray eyes and black hair, in the uniform of a staff major. The first warning we had was when the telephones stopped working . . . that must have been him, but we didn't suspect until he killed poor Fritz Haber . . . he's the bald man over there. A very capable fellow, even if he was a Jew."

"Losing this base will be a severe blow," Horst said.

The scientist started to laugh, then put a hand to the side of his head. "No, fortunately he did not kill me—this wound looks worse than it is, and I am a dry old stick. And I was able to—"

The explanation faded off into technical jargon. Von Bülow saw that, and simplified it:

"We do not store the *Vernichtungsgas* here except just before an operation. It is unstable in metal containers . . . impurities . . . and the dispersant . . . Instead we store the two precursors, which must be combined together with a sulfur compound under certain conditions of temperature and pressure to produce the final product; neither is toxic to any extent by itself. That is what you smell now, the catalyzing sulfur compound. I regained consciousness and managed to set the precursors to purge themselves just as the explosions ruptured the line to final storage; otherwise it would have sprayed many tons of the material. And the wind is blowing away from Berlin. Still, there will be much damage in this base. This area here will not be safe for long. You were lucky that you approached it from upwind."

Horst bared his teeth; they'd only come in that way because it was closest. Then he put the heel of one hand to his forehead and squeezed the fingers on his short-cropped scalp, as if to force thought. This must be a different operation from the one *she* had overseen at the Siemens plant—more lurid but less important in the larger scheme of things. It would have been terrible tradecraft to let two operatives know about each other.

So why did she come this way? he thought. *Not to sabotage the gas facility; that was coincidence. Think, you dumb-head, think!*

Then he grunted as if belly-punched. "She was trying to get out information on the Heimdall device. She may have gotten the data. But how could you get a *working* device out of Germany? If she conducted thorough surveillance, she'd have known they were being shipped here to Staaken to be mounted on patrol airships!"

Horst's eyes went wide. "Quickly!" he snapped to von Bülow. "Come along, we must get to the hangars and docking towers!"

The old man shook his head. "I would be useless there. And I must stay here near the controls as long as I can, to keep the damage to a minimum."

That means death, Horst did not say aloud.

The scientist did smile at the unspoken words. "I did my major service for the Fatherland when I saw what the Breath of Loki could do, and pushed through the project. I am an old man; I have grandchildren; now my last service is here and there is a certain ironic fitness to it. Go!"

He waved a hand. "Go now!"

Horst saluted before he left at a run.

TWENTY-FOUR

B lack Flag?" James Cheine said. "We're a bit shorthanded."

Luz nodded as she drove. *Black Flag* was the way the Chamber usually operated in situations like this. Unlike soldiers in the uniform of their country, secret agents didn't have even a theoretical claim to surrender on terms; like rebel guerillas or revolutionaries they had no rights if taken, not even to a quick execution unless a captor showed an unlikely degree of mercy.

"Black Flag it is," she said. "It would be nice to be able to force some of the crew of the airship to man their stations for us, but it's too risky with just the three of us, and your wound."

Ciara was sitting between them on the bench front seat of the truck, and she made a slight puzzled sound. Luz explained, as she fished in her pockets with her left hand and gave two of her grenades to Cheine:

"*Black Flag* means no prisoners," she said. "We go in hard and fast and we kill them all."

Ciara's face was in shadow, but her nod was decisive and her voice grave but steady.

"No more mercy than their airships gave London or Paris," she said; her second stay here hadn't elevated the low opinion of Germany she'd gained on the first trip. "And those they killed there weren't fighting men in uniform."

"Sound thinking, Miss Whelan," Cheine said. "I do wish I could be of more use!"

Luz grinned. "You're a German major or a convincing imitation thereof, James," she said. "With all my talents I would still find *that* hard to carry off. And you're a qualified pilot. I'm not going to turn down the gifts of fortune."

"*Aeroplane* pilot, though I've done a little training on airships," he said. "Still, better than nothing. You should have done the course too."

"I would have been *much* more conspicuous than you on an Army base pretending to be a trainee pilot for the Air Corps, James," Luz said dryly. "Even in these progressive times."

"Oh, yes, hadn't thought, sorry . . . *Jesus!*" he said, and then hissed again as they went over a rut and she braked hard to avoid colliding with a staff car making a sharp turn in front of them.

"I do wish they were panicking more here . . . And Ciara will be very useful too when we get to the airship we pirate away," she went on. "If it's mechanical or electrical, she can generally figure it out. I'll go in first, clean out the crew, and then the Frenchwomen will bring you in, James. Ciara, you follow me, but give me a minute or so."

"I'm . . . I'm sure you'll come through all right, Luz," Ciara said, hope transparent in her voice.

"Once you've seen her going in hot a few times, you'll save your concern for the enemy, Miss Whelan," Cheine said lightly. "They're the ones who need it."

Then Luz concentrated on driving through the semi-chaos of the evacuation, to the endless rising and falling of the sirens. James's major's uniform and an occasional barked order cleared them through obstacles, until they were into the southwestern part of the base, where huge cleared and leveled fields rested billiard-table flat beneath the snow. Rows of high-powered lights marked the ventilating clerestory on the curved roofs of the immense hangars, each a thousand feet long and two hundred high. Those held—or since the heavy losses in the horror-gas attacks of October, didn't hold—the big zeppelins, and were used to assemble them too. More lights clustered on tall light standards.

Then something huge and barely seen went by overhead with a roar of engines. Just in front of their truck a torrent of water fell out of the sky, hundreds of gallons turning the snow-covered roadway ahead into an instant puddle of slippery half-liquid slush that had Luz braced and cursing as she wrestled with the wheel and the already miserable traction of the steel tires on snow suddenly vanished altogether. The wheel bucked against her; she came half-erect as she hauled frantically, steering against the direction of the skid as the vehicle came up on two wheels to a chorus of shrieks from the rear, then crashed down again. Something snapped with a metallic *pinnnnggggg!* that she felt through her backside as much as heard with her ears, and she feared the suspension would never be the same again, but the Stoewer pressed onward with a pronounced list to the left and a growing grinding sound somewhere in the power train.

"Give me another four minutes, you *pedazo de basura!*" she snarled at the machine. "*Then* you can go to motor truck Valhalla!"

"There!" Ciara said, pointing.

Through the darkness and slanting lines of snow that flickered in and out of patches of light loomed a long row of squat docking towers running north and south, the powerful electrics on top of each glowing. Ten of them were occupied that Luz could see, fading off into the night on either side despite searchlights and the internal and external lights of the flying machines themselves. They were surrounded by swarms of ground crew making a frantic effort to get the airships ready for irregular and highly risky launches into the night and into bad weather, though if they could get aloft and above the cloud layer they'd be safe enough until dawn; this class was designed to stay up for eighty hours at a time. The grinding roar of radial engines sounded as truck-mounted machines spun up the airship propellers.

Each craft had a number on the bows, preceded by the initials *HL*—for *halbstarres Luftschiff*, semi-rigid airship, what enlisted men in the U.S. Navy jocularly called half-hards. These weren't metal-framed monsters like the *Battle*-class ships Luz and Ciara had ridden from Los Angeles to Tunis or the bombers that had destroyed the capitals of Britain and France, but they were big enough to loom huge once you were close: a hundred meters long, around three hundred thirty feet, and plumper in outline than even the most modern teardrop-shaped rigids.

"Those are very like our antisubmarine patrol airships," Ciara said, peering to catch details as they approached. "I read an article on them a year ago in *Popular Mechanics*."

Luz chuckled. "It's a natural resemblance; they copied the design wholesale, the way we did for their rigids, probably starting with that article in *Popular Mechanics*," she said. "Everyone steals everything instantly these days, and nobody much cares where it comes from if it works. I'm going to head for the southernmost one."

Cheine and Ciara both nodded, and began to speak simultaneously. She stopped, and he made a polite *go ahead* gesture.

"With the wind out of the northeast, that one has the best chance of a clean launch," Ciara said.

"Exactly," he added.

It was impossible to tell, but even under the wolf-tension of approaching action, Luz smiled a little at what she was certain was Ciara's flush of pleasure.

"And look! Those two rectangular box-things up at the top of the gondola at either side, they all have them! Those are new—they're the antennae for the Telemobiloscope system, I swear they are. They must have just had it installed! From an airship you'd have a *really* good reach, sending the broadcast frequencies out and down. If we get the whole thing . . . that would be *wonderful*!"

Ciara bounced in her seat a little, transported out of their grim situation for a moment by shining technical possibilities and by the glory of presenting the president . . . or more probably in her mind, Tesla . . . with an intact example of the enemy's secret weapon that could be reverse-engineered for American use.

"Those would have to be German *Navy* airships, then, wouldn't they?" she added thoughtfully.

"Probably," Luz said. "This Heimdall thing is naval in general. Probably they flew them in from Wilhelmshaven or Kiel to be fitted out here because it's close to the Siemens plant. The Zeppelin company builds for both services."

As they approached, the ground crew scattered backward from the southernmost airship. It cast loose from the docking tower and seemed to move backward as if jerked by invisible wires as the wind caught it. Then it slowed slightly as the engines roared to put way on it and give purchase to the control surfaces, turned and curved upward into the snow and the low cloud above. It was a bravura display of skill and nerve, and as Luz steered toward the next airship, now become the southernmost, she only hoped they could duplicate it by blind luck and overconfidence.

If we can't . . . well, the crashing and burning will be fairly quick, at least.

Luz steered toward the HL-22; the snow was growing thicker, and the wind was gradually picking up. She drove as close as she could to the lowered ramp at the rear of the gondola and was only a few paces away when someone noticed and came trotting over waving frantically.

"Who the hell are you and what do you think—"

The man in charge of the ground crew was a senior NCO in his forties with an upswept mustache losing some of its waxed perfection as it soaked through; he sheltered his eyes against the flakes with a palm and peered upward at the cab of the truck, then stiffened to attention and saluted.

"Oh, sorry, sir!"

"That's all right, *Feldwebel*," James said crisply, returning his salute. "We'll be boarding now. You're about ready to launch, correct?"

"Ah . . . launching now, sir, just about to raise the gangway and cast off, we're doing it from south to north . . . it's all naval personnel . . ."

The sergeant was visibly wondering how to tell a superior officer—and one with General Staff piping too!—that he was being a panicky idiot without putting his own sensitive parts in the wringer and without wasting precious time on soothing an exalted dimwit in a dangerous situation when he should be doing his job. The way Cheine's face was drawn with pain would pass for fear in bad light, which added to the impression. Luz hit the ignition button to turn off the motor truck's engine, and as she did she took three deep slow breaths, letting go of everything but a focus like the point of a knife. Her hand went into the right pocket of her jacket and closed on the mother-of-pearl and brass of the *navaja*'s hilt, like the touch of a childhood friend.

"Sir, we're launching these airships with minimal naval crews as fast as we can get them back from their transient barracks, it's not safe, you'd be better off just driving out the gate . . . is that a bunch of *women* you have in that truck, sir?" the German sergeant said.

"Yes, *Feldwebel*, it is," James said, as he raised the machine pistol and shot him in the head at four feet distance.

Crack.

"But you shouldn't have noticed," he added mildly.

He put the Thompson back down by his feet and looked around to check if anyone *else* had noticed. Nobody had turned to look, being far too busy and the night too dark and the backfires, clangs, and whirring of machinery too loud; the snow didn't help either.

Now. For the mission, for the country, for my life, for my beloved. Kill!

Luz launched herself out of the truck's cab before the *Feldwebel*'s body hit the ground or the thought was complete.

"Damn but I hate being wounded, it's so rotten *inconvenient*," Cheine added behind her.

He jerked the pin out of one of the grenades and threw it at the outline of a vehicle moving through the murk fifty feet away. The little bomb landed just aft of the driver's seat and went off with a brief snapping red spark in the darkness and a moderate *whamp!* sound. It was a mostly empty fuel tanker truck, and the remainder of its load exploded in a ball of fire a few seconds later as hot fragments ripped through the thin sheet metal into the enclosed space filled with a mixture of fumes and air.

WHUMP!

Gasoline by itself wasn't really explosive. Fuel-air mixtures certainly were.

Not many people had noticed Luz's vehicle drive up in the confusion, except the late *Feldwebel*. *Everyone* noticed the shower of fire, and the way the truck slid into another loaded with boxes and splashed burning fuel over that. They ran to drag the flaming tanker away and beat out swatches of flame wherever they had landed. You didn't ignore fires when giant bags of hydrogen were floating over your head. The ground crews were brave men and very well trained, but that training had had certain priorities. Ones that didn't include how to deal with infiltration by secret operatives.

Luz was running for the stair ramp up into the HL-22's gondola when the grenade hit the truck; she staggered at the blast, recovered without having to think about it, and kept going. The man at the top of the ramp had turned around and ducked down to see what had happened, thick and bulky in his warm fur-lined flight suit of glazed leather.

The sailor-airman certainly didn't have a front-pig's reflexes. Military airships were deadly weapons, and deadly dangerous to their crews, but it was a different sort of danger than face-to-face killing.

"Help me!" Luz shrieked in artfully hysterical German, making her eyes bulge and mouth go wide. "We're all going to die from the gas—help! Take me away, take me away!"

The man looked puzzled but not in a way likely to make him suspicious, or to expect anything but a woman crazy with fear who'd managed to get through the airfield's perimeter, one last straw in an overburdened day. He straightened and spread his arms to stop her from getting into the gondola's body. That presented him like a target dummy as the *navaja* snicked open and Luz closed the last three feet in a running lunge that ended with the point slamming up under his jaw just in front of the throat, driven by all the strength of her arm and her momentum as well. Luz wrenched it free with desperate haste—there was always a risk of sticking in bone, even the thin bone that guarded the brain pan behind the palate. Then she put the knife in her teeth and pulled the shotgun out of her open coat.

"Erich?" someone said. "Erich, what in the name of God is—"

A man coming down the central corridor of the gondola gaped. Presumably-Erich fell backward and landed at the man's feet in a thrashing tangle as his damaged brain sent random signals that arched his body and made his heels drum on the stamped aluminum planks and his arms flail like an epileptic fit even as blood pumped out of his neck. The second man's mouth and eyes went very round and wide as his hands rose in an ineffectual warding gesture toward Luz and the muzzle of the shotgun rose faster still, and with tiger precision.

BAM.

She kept the trigger down. Motion and targets were all she saw, the rest of the world vanishing with the past and the future and all thought.

She leapt over the bodies in a brief billow of skirts. Past them, and a man sat with earphones on his head in a side cubicle, in front of the dials and switches of a wireless set. Pivot, aim between his shoulder blades, and work the slide as he sensed something and began to turn . . .

Shikk-shack-BAM!

Into the cramped control cabin. Aluminum and brass and wicker and exposed conduits and wires. Five more men. An officer in his thirties, turning and scrabbling at the symbolic pistol in the buttoned-flap holster at his waist as he saw what was coming his way, blood-spattered face and knife clenched between snarling teeth, eyes like pools of night and the shotgun aimed at his chest . . .

Shikk-shack-BAM!

Another two, trapped between their chairs and the helm wheels. Aim for the junction of neck and shoulders.

Shikk-shack-BAM! *Shikk-shack*-BAM!

The fourth lunged at her, hands outstretched. They had almost touched her when she stuck the muzzle of the shotgun under his chin.

Shikk-shack-BAM!

Shikk-shack, and a round in the chamber as she began to turn.

Then arms seized her from behind, a big man and bear-strong, lifting her right off her feet. She stuck the shotgun down at the floor—the only position she could, with his grip on her—and fired.

BAM!

Something bit her calf as the recoil twisted the weapon in her awkward grip. A shout of pain from behind her, but the German sailor kept his grip and bellowed and pushed her forward, aiming to crush her between his body and the steel and brass of the horizontal helm wheel. Luz whipped up both her legs and jammed them against the wheel, springs to swallow the impetus of his charge. The grip on her slackened just enough to wrench one arm free. She spat her knife into that palm and stabbed blindly backward, feeling the point score through cloth and leather and the unmistakable soft heavy resistance of *finding flesh*. Then the hard tick of the point jamming into bone.

Another bellow, earsplittingly loud this time, and she flipped her legs up and then down, sinking into a shoulder-shrugging squat that stripped her out of the bear hug. That left the empty shotgun to fall.

Luz abandoned the grip on her knife and caught the stubby gun instead, holding it by the hot barrel with both hands as she pivoted, striking like a baseball player up at the plate. The squat thick-bodied blond-bearded man behind her was half bent over to grab at the knife with its point buried in his thigh bone, and the steel-sheathed hardwood knob of the cut-down butt chunked into his temple with a *thock* that was hard and wet at the same time. She hit him twice more as he went down, straight overarm blows like swinging an axe to split wood but blurring-fast, *thock-thock*, and cracking bone crunched each time as she screamed, a high keening shriek of elemental rage.

Then she was bent over with her hands on her knees, wheezing in the cold bloody fecal reek. The blood steamed in the frigid air.

¡Otra vez la misma historia! she thought, as her mind started to function again and she pulled the knife free, wiped it on the man's fur collar, and ran a finger through the locking ring to snap it closed. *Back in business at the same old stand!*

"Darling! I heard you—are you hurt? *Are you all right?*"

Ciara's hands were on her shoulders. Luz sucked another breath down into the bottom of her lungs and straightened, looking into the anxious turquoise-and-green eyes. Her partner gave a horrified gasp of dismay, and Luz realized what the problem was.

She wiped a hand over her face, looked at it, and said:

"I'm fine, sweetie. It's not mine."

A line of hot fire along her calf made her add:

"Well, not much of it is, and what there is I shed myself. And here I thought *shooting yourself in the foot* was just a metaphor."

She stood and smiled and thumped a hand on her partner's shoulder, and got a valiant smile in reply.

"Now get us in the air, *mi querida!*"

Ciara was already scanning the controls, blanking the bodies out of her mind with commendable quickness. Focus kept you alive, and that meant excluding the irrelevant . . . until your mind brought it up in your sleep later, of course.

"This must be the emergency internal release for the bow connection," she said, touching a lever. "The engines are running on idle, fuel is at full, ballast at full . . . I think, I can't tell for certain, there's . . .

urrrg . . . stuff . . . on the dials . . . but this is definitely the emergency ballast vent control."

"I'll see about keeping the pursuit on the back foot, then."

The Frenchwomen had poured into the airship in her wake, making it sink down on its single under-gondola wheel. Two of Perrin's band were helping James along toward the control cabin while she directed the rest on board and set them to stripping the bodies and dragging them to the ramp.

His lean face grinned like a skull as he overrode his body's urgent messages of *damage damage damage.*

"And now, let us abjure the gloom of Germany for the sunlit slopes of France," he said, biting off the last word as they eased him into the pilot's chair.

Simone had Luz's suitcase, hanging on like grim death and then smiling after a blink and a gulp when Luz gave her an approving nod and took it with a word of thanks. If Luz recalled correctly this class of airship had a normal crew of fifteen; there had been seven on board, but German naval crewmen averaged considerably heavier than the starved women of the forced-labor gang. Speaking of which . . .

"Madame Perrin!" Luz called.

She had James settled into the helm seat in the control cabin and had checked the bandage. At Luz's call she stuck her head back into the corridor.

"There will be a galley on this airship, supplied for a patrol of several days for fifteen men. Please, put one of your reliable friends . . . no, two . . . to minding it. A light meal would be a good idea when we are underway, and more later, but some of your party might injure themselves if they eat too much too soon."

"Bon, d'accord," Perrin said.

The laborers had been hungry a long, long time; Luz judged Perrin herself to have iron willpower and to spare, but people varied, and some might drop everything to stuff themselves. They were going to have to nurse their stomachs and guts back to healthy function . . . if they lived that long, of course.

"I shall see to it," Perrin added with a grim nod.

The rear ramp was still lowered, and the French laborers pitched the bodies off its sides, looking oddly doll-like in their stained long underwear. The semirigid rose on its single wheel, rocking with a greasy motion. A quick look out as Luz opened the rifle case showed that most of the men in sight were still dealing with the result of Cheine's lucky hit with the grenade, and nobody had actually run over to find out what was going on here; visibility was poor and getting worse. She found a length of line fastened to an eyebolt and ran it through the back of her belt just in case, opened the case, and brought out the rifle, opening the bolt with an upward shove of the palm and pulling it back with a smooth oiled double *snick* sound.

"Bueno, gusto verte aquí, viejo amigo," she said to the weapon. *Well, it's nice to meet you again here, old friend.*

She thumbed five of the rounds from the box marked *Incendiary Tracer Armor Piercing* into the magazine and slid another into the breech. The bolt went *snick-snack* again as she closed it with the heel of her hand, and she tightened a loop of the sling around her left bicep as she sank to a sitting position at the head of the ramp and braced her heels against fittings to either side.

Then a buzzer sounded through the airship; probably an automatic take-off alarm rigged to the release at the nose. From here she could see the control surfaces in the horizontal tail fins reverse. There was a slight shiver as the connection to the docking tower cut loose and then the ground began to fall away, an elevator surge as the ballast released and they bounced a hundred feet into the air and a swooping feeling like the downward part of a roller-coaster ride at a fun fair as the wind pushed them backward. The motion slowed and a surge pulled at her as the engines thuttered and roared to put headway on the HL-22 as it rose.

Then it banked and turned, and the line of docked airships came back into sight. Or as many as she could see through the snow that was now falling hard and thick—the running lights helped with that, the more so as someone up front cut their own, so that the HL-22 was in darkness itself. From the ground they would have disappeared completely, and the people down there had enough to deal with anyway. One semirigid was on fire where bits of the fuel truck had hit, and the ground crew had turned it loose to head west across the open field; it got about a thousand yards before the main fuel cells caught with a huge soft *WHUMP* and it crashed to the ground in a towering pyre. Most of the men probably thought the HL-22 was just making a break for it, and that all the trouble around them was a natural result of the clustered disasters that happened when you tried to do things fast and dirty.

Confusion was a wonderful thing, when it was the other side's and you were riding its crest.

Another airship was getting underway, the HL-25; it cast off and rose and pivoted to run with the wind behind them as she watched.

Can't have that, Luz thought.

These airships all had machine-gun mounts in the chin turret below the control car and the stern above the ramp, twin light air-cooled Maxims, and she very much didn't want one chasing her and shooting, even if she could shoot back. It would be entirely too much like a duel with flamethrowers in a room ankle-deep in kerosene. There was always talk of substituting helium for hydrogen in airships, but it was too scarce and expensive.

She brought the scope-sighted rifle to her shoulder, left elbow braced against left knee, the sling keeping it steadier still as she snuggled her face into the chamois-covered cheekpiece.

Experience in this war had shown that it took multiple hits with incendiary bullets to set an airship on fire; hydrogen burned, but only when it was mixed with air. You had to make rips in the envelope to create that mixture and then keep shooting. That wasn't really practical for her with a bolt-action rifle, even firing tracer-incendiary ... but the great big orca-shaped balloon wasn't the only thing to shoot at either. She moved the sight across the airship's bow and out to the motor; there was one on either side, radials mounted on short winglike struts jutting out from the body of the gondola, illuminated by the cabin lights and the glow of their own exhaust. Radials had their pistons in a circle around the crankshaft, which made the view like a bull's-eye at a beginner's firing range, before they moved you up to man-shaped targets.

Distance about six hundred yards and steady ... take a deep breath and slowly let it out ... stop ... squeeze gently with the ball of the index finger against the trigger-pull ... a click as the first stage was tripped ... take up the slack ... a ghost of pressure on the hair-set second stage ...

Crack!

The recoil that swayed her shoulder and torso back was a surprise, the way it always was when you were shooting well, and less than it would have been with a standard-issue Springfield since the sniper weapon weighed several pounds more. The tracer showed like a curved line of red fire through the night and made a distinct blue spark that she could see easily through the 6X scope, striking right on one of the connecting rods. The engine sputtered to a halt with a screech of tortured metal clearly audible despite the distance and almost immediately began to trail black smoke.

"You're not flying anywhere with that," she said.

Then she worked the bolt and resisted the temptation to put a few through the control gondola. Shooting *people* would just make them finally realize they were under attack. Instead she scanned for something else worth hitting before they were out of range. She thought she saw the distinctive rounded outline of a fuel truck through the snow and gave it the remaining four rounds as fast as she could, four more curving lines of fire in the night:

Crack! Crack! Crack! Crack!

She was rewarded by a blurred blossom of yellow-red flame, chuckled, and called out as the airfield dwindled:

"Me encantó verte, ciudad fría y fea de Berlín, pero me tengo que ir. ¡Hasta la vista!"

"What does that mean?" Yvonne Perrin's voice asked. "It's Spanish, isn't it?"

Luz rose and turned the crank that closed the entranceway; the noise of the airship's passage and the drone of the engines both grew more muffled, and though their breaths still showed in white puffs it didn't seem quite as cold without the buffeting wind drawn in by their increasing speed.

"Yes. It means: *I loved seeing you, cold and ugly city of Berlin, but I have to go now. Bye-bye!*"

Perrin's mouth gave a glacial twist. "So you speak Spanish too?"

Luz nodded. "My mother taught me; it was her birth tongue. And I spent time at school in France and Germany before the war."

"And I thought you were Provençale!"

Luz shrugged, and let her French revert to her upper-middle-class Parisian default. "In truth, I'm Californian . . . but we have olive groves and vineyards in California, and hillsides that smell like spice, and a beautiful blue ocean, too."

Perrin hesitated. "How much were the *Boche* lying? Is there a France to return to?"

"They weren't lying much, not about that. About half of France is still holding out, but not for long," Luz said honestly. "It's a bloody slaughterhouse all around."

"I thought the Americans were helping us?"

"We are, and our troops are on the Loire now—that's why the *Boche* aren't on the shores of the Mediterranean already. But there isn't enough shipping or harbor capacity to move enough of our army across the Atlantic and *into* France, now that the Channel and Atlantic ports are in German hands."

"What is left for us to do, then?"

"There's North Africa—they're calling it the National Redoubt of Overseas France now. That will hold, I think."

If *we managed to alert our navy and the British in time about Project Heimdall, but you don't need to know that.* Aloud she went on:

"If we survive this trip, I can arrange passage for you and your friends—many millions from France are heading that way. It'll be a rough life, though: work and hardship and danger, and little else but building everything from nothing for many years. Or you could go to America."

Perrin's bitter, wary eyes searched hers. "You would *arrange* that, too?"

"Yes. You helped us, and we owe you a debt for it: The United States does, and the . . . organization I work for. We pay what we owe and we don't forget friends."

Granted, as much for policy's sake as anything, but it is *good policy . . . and Uncle Teddy's iron principle.*

"We can't give you back your homes, or the people you've lost. But we can offer refuge for you in America, and a chance for a future there if you want one—houses, and schooling in English, and work. Most of our people have ancestors who fled war or plague or persecution or simple poverty."

"I will talk with the others about this," Perrin said, then hesitated and added: "Thank you."

Luz rose and stretched. "You're welcome. But we're not watching the Statue of Liberty come up on the horizon yet."

"A *French* statue!" Perrin said over her shoulder.

Luz didn't have much doubt that Perrin's followers would fall in with whatever she decided.

There was water enough to scrub her face and arms in the little lavatory, and some soap—blood was surprisingly like glue in some respects if you let it dry hard. Airships usually had plenty of water since they used it as ballast; it was even lukewarm, from the hot exhaust routed around the ballast tanks to keep them from freezing at high altitudes in winter, which would be a deadly hazard. When she opened the door Simone was waiting, with a flight suit that was only a little too big for Luz; and it was clean. The one *she* had on was so oversized that she'd had to roll up and pin the sleeves and pant legs a third of their length, and it had had bits and pieces of the former wearer all over the front of it where Luz and her shotgun had left them. Someone had tried hard and skillfully to wipe them off, and the glazed surface helped, but it left stains.

"They had some extra ones in lockers, madame," the girl said; she looked even younger than her midteens in the too-big garments.

"Merci beaucoup, Simone," Luz said gratefully.

As she shed her outer garments, switched various items into the multiple buttoned pockets, and donned the flight suit, Simone's eyes got wider and wider.

Here's another one acquiring romantic illusions about the secret world, Luz thought. *Still, she's spent a very nasty spell being powerless in the hands of malignant enemies. It's natural enough that anyone fighting them acquires a bit of a halo. Hmmm . . . perhaps a scholarship from the Chamber?*

"Is it true that we may go to America?" she asked.

"Well, yes," Luz said. "You'll all be welcome."

If we make it out of Germany, which we haven't yet—I don't think we're even out of Brandenburg.

"But we're not there yet," she cautioned, trying to be realistic without raining on the understandable elation the Frenchwomen felt at escaping their ghastly situation.

"What's America like?" Simone said eagerly.

"It's not *like* any one thing, it's too big—bigger than all of Europe together," Luz said. "Beautiful and ugly, hot and cold, wet and dry, mountains and forests and deserts and plains—heaven and hell. It's a *world* as much as a country."

"Are there cowboys, and Indians?"

Luz had met plenty of Europeans before the war, including otherwise well-educated ones, who expected Californians to live in forts and risk getting scalped on their way to pan for gold in the mountains or wrestle with bears or fight pistol duels with bandits at the gallop amid herds of stampeding longhorns with Indians in warbonnets somewhere in the background. To be fair, *some* of those things were only a generation or two in the past, and less in places like New Mexico or the Dakotas.

"Yes, there are cowboys and Indians. And these days some of the Indians *are* cowboys," she said, and Simone went off with visions of exotic adventures in her head.

When Luz had completed the complex business of fastening the flying suit, she went into the dimly lit control cabin. Ciara was in a flight suit, and James was too except for his left leg, where some cunning soul had slit the trouser up from the bottom so that he could get it on over the wound without too much pain and then bound it back up with strips of blanket to keep him warm. Perrin had just handed James a big tin mug full of nondescript canned soup with cabbage and beans and a hint of some nameless meat in it, which was filling and salty and hot at least; more came out for the rest of them. The view out the windows was black where the airship's riding lights didn't shine and gray where they did, and snow was still hitting the glass. Occasionally a gust of wind would make the craft rock, and the vibration of the engines was a subliminal thrum, but mostly the flight was very smooth.

Though the fact that they were flying *literally* blind was a bit nerve-racking, when you thought about it.

"We're navigating by dead reckoning, darling," Ciara said. "I think our ground speed is about eighty miles an hour—better than an express train! With the tail wind, you see. And we're a thousand meters up, which is fine for now."

"I'm having the devil of a time keeping her west of due south," James said, his voice a little thin. "It's a good thing we don't have to economize on fuel, or we'd end up ramming into the Swiss Alps. Do you think you could spell me for a little?"

Luz called for two of the Frenchwomen, and between them they got Cheine out of his straight position and on his way back to one of the seven bunks; he swore sulfurously as the stiffening wound was jarred, but in liquid-staccato Mayan profanities he'd picked up in Quintana Roo and Yucatán, and he would probably be better for the rest. The broad horizontal wheel bucked against her hands, and she grinned—she *was* flying this thing, and gradually bringing it back around to the compass heading Ciara indicated.

"Just tell me what to do, *mi corazón*, and I'll be delighted to give it a try," she said.

Ciara chuckled unexpectedly. "Well, that's a switch from the beginning of the honeymoon, but all right," she said, and they both laughed.

There was a map on the console between her and Ciara; it showed Germany, the Low Countries, France, and Switzerland, and bits and pieces of other places. Someone—she suspected Ciara—had drawn a line from Berlin, swooping south of Frankfurt and then from there over the Rhine and into unoccupied France.

"But we could be north or south of that line," Ciara said over her shoulder. "It's an . . . approximation."

She pronounced *approximation* as if it were a mildly naughty word; she preferred precision.

"Well, if we don't know exactly where we are, neither does anyone else," Luz said cheerfully. "If I know Horst, and I do, he'll never give up while we've got a working example of the Telemobiloscope to hand over to our wise men, not if there's any prospect of catching us at all. I wouldn't, in his place! But he can scarcely comb the skies in this weather."

Ciara made a slightly embarrassed sound and pointed to one of the vacant positions in the banks of instruments that surrounded three sides of the control chamber like a horseshoe.

"Darling . . . I think that's the receiving apparatus. There's a modified Braun tube in there—really, I wish I had more time to study it! And the display is an oscilloscope. And . . ."

Luz leaned back and to the side for a moment to see past the vacant operator's chair. Someone had given the banks of dials and switches a thorough going-over, because the blood and the bits of hair and skin were gone. The small round screen of the oscilloscope glowed green, and a blurry white dot pulsed on it.

"That's . . . I really think that's someone using the transmission apparatus on *us*," Ciara said. "I think it was designed to look for ships on the surface, but it'll work for this, too. So they'd be able to track us."

Luz reviewed her own last sentence, and gave the only possible response. *"Joder."*

"Luz! *Language!*"

Yes, Hauptmann von Dückler, we have acquired the target," the commander of the HL-27 said, turning from where he'd been leaning over the man operating the Telemobiloscope.

"Thank you, Herr Korvettenkapitän," Horst said.

With malice aforethought, he knew perfectly well that in the Kaiserlich Marine it was customary to address any ship's commander as *Kapitän* plain and simple on the bridge. Röhm knew it too, which was probably why he gave his grating troll-chuckle.

The airship captain turned beet-red, as far as Horst could tell in the odd light of the instruments, then swallowed and went on:

"You understand, Herr Hauptmann, I too wish to find and punish the swine who butchered my comrades on the HL-22."

He'd been standing over the knifed and shot-ripped bodies cursing when Horst and the *Stoßtruppen* pulled up.

"I simply did not think the risk of losing another vessel was appropriate without orders from my chain of command after you told me that the escape of Annihilation Gas was more limited than originally thought. I was wrong: I admit this, and I offer my apology as an officer and a gentleman."

"Apology accepted, Kapitän," Horst said mildly.

The bruises where Horst had grabbed the naval officer by the throat were still roughening his voice, and there was a slight fleck of blood in his seal-brown mustache; the muzzle of the Luger rammed up his nose had made him bleed a little. One look into Horst's single gray eye had convinced him that it was all absolutely serious. More than the pain, probably, but there hadn't been time for an extended conversation and as the Americans said it didn't hurt to wear belt and suspenders both. The Navy man wasn't a coward and seemed to know his job; he'd just been falling back on bureaucratic procedure in a situation where improvisation was necessary.

I'm a little sorry I let the rage out. I must be more careful with that, he thought, and added aloud:

"But any hazard is worthwhile if there is any chance at all to keep the Hülsmeyer-Braun apparatus out of the enemy's hands."

Another telegram had gone out to Colonel Nicolai from the HL-29's wireless:

ENEMY AGENTS PENETRATED STAAKEN BASE STOP AGENTS
SABOTAGED ANNIHILATION GAS PRODUCTION FACILITY STOP
SEIZED NAVAL-CREWED SEMIRIGID HL-22 EQUIPPED WITH
AIR-SURVEILLANCE TELEMOBILOSCOPE AND ARE ATTEMPTING
TO ESCAPE TO ENTENTE TERRITORY STOP DETAILS AVAILABLE
KURSCHAT OF BERLIN POLICE AND PRUSSIAN SECRET POLICE STOP
PLEASE ALERT ARMY FLIGHT TROOP BASES FOR INTERCEPTION BY
FIGHTING SCOUTS IF AT ALL REPEAT AT ALL POSSIBLE STOP HAVE
COMMANDEERED NAVAL HL-29 AND AM IN PURSUIT STOP

"When will we catch them?"

The *Korvettenkapitän* shrugged slightly. "Impossible to say. These are identical vessels and we are both running before the same strong following wind and trying to make way a little across it. This sort of circumstance is precisely why *a stern chase is a long chase* is a proverb. We have an experienced crew—"

More experienced than a bunch of French charwomen, two spies, and a technical prodigy barely out of her teens, Horst thought dryly.

"—and so we should make a slightly better speed. Certainly not before dawn. Which is around oh-eight-hundred this time of year."

Horst hissed; they were doing nearly a hundred and forty kilometers per hour, counting the tail-wind and with engines full ahead. It was six hours until dawn; they would have traveled something like eight hundred kilometers by then . . . and that would put them in France, on this heading. Not necessarily in *unoccupied* France, and there were a lot more *Fliegertruppen* fighting-scouts available close to the front, of course.

"I still say you should let my men man the machine guns, Horst," Röhm grumbled. "I have a score to pay with the unnatural bitches too."

Horst shook his head. "The Navy personnel have more experience with air firing," he said. "I have a little experience with *Luftschiffe* combat—"

Specifically he'd been aboard ZL-209 in the trial-run gas attack on Paris back in May.

"—and that was enough to know that it's specialized gunnery, shooting from an object moving in three dimensions at another one that is doing the same."

He bared his teeth, and even the stormtroop officer blinked a little at the expression.

"I'm not going to be manning the forward guns myself . . . and that, Ernst, is a *real* personal sacrifice."

TWENTY-FIVE

That's too close," Luz said, looking out the portside windows of the HL-22's control cabin at the airship trailing them. "They're a little south of us now. If we try to cut the cord and turn farther south, they'll get within firing range."

As if to illustrate the point, both the machine-gun positions on the other airship—it had *HL 29* on the bows—showed blinking-winking muzzle flashes. It was futile . . . but the angles meant the gunners knew their business. Luz thought she might be passible on the HL-22's own guns, but no more than that; Cheine was injured, and their only real pilot besides.

"Why is the bloody man so set on having a machine-gun duel with us?" Cheine said from the helm, and gave a murmur of thanks as Perrin handed him another cup of hot not-really-much-coffee-in-it; those two had been chatting off and on all night, when he wasn't sleeping. "Damned suicidal in these flying bombs."

The world outside the cabin glowed in shades of white and pale gray an hour after dawn; white from the snow-covered, crumpled landscape below, palest pearl from the uniform bank of cloud a few thousand feet above with the sun only a brighter spot to the southeast, and a subdued gray ambience that seemed to drift like fog in through the glass. The silver-gray of the HL-29 was almost lost against it.

Ciara answered, surprising Luz a little. "Because if we both blow up and burn and crash, he wins, because then we don't get the Tele-mobiloscope," she said. "And Captain von Dückler will do anything to win."

"But you got your information out," Cheine said. "He's already lost, on the main point."

"He doesn't know that; he knows we got *something* out, but it was a very short message, and he probably won't suspect it was a counter method. A working Telemobiloscope would be much more important if . . . well, it *is* important, anyway, it'll cut six months, maybe more, on making our own. And he hates us, Luz particularly, and she's been ahead of him these last few days, always just out of reach, and it must torment him like an itch he just can't scratch," Ciara said.

Cheine looked back at Luz. "This one is smart," he said. "Alarmingly so."

"Why, Mr. Cheine, you say the sweetest things!" Ciara said.

She's not as naïve about people as she was, Luz thought, and met her smile with one of her own. *Fast learner, my girl! And she absolutely nailed Horst there.*

Perrin and Simone and one of her other followers brought in thick slices of pumpernickel with bad cheese toasted on it, and slices of nameless sausage on that. It all tasted dreadful—the sausage was about as much breadstuff as the bread, and the bread had potato as well as rye and was stale—but they all ate every scrap; they weren't in any danger of freezing in the thick flying suits, but the body still craved everything it could get in this cold, and made you long for things like greasy fried potatoes and honey-glazed ham and sugary pastries. The French-women were making heavy inroads on the supplies, though Perrin policed it rigorously.

Luz closed her eyes and drew lines in her head. "We need to get down; we need to land, and right now. They're trying to nudge us back north behind the German lines and we don't have a counter while we're in the air—they have a full trained crew and we don't."

Saying so made it seem more real, and she was sick with rage at the thought, the more so when she looked at Ciara.

"They'll get over us and shoot," James warned; how risky that was didn't need much comment.

Here I am on something that can do sixty miles an hour, fast as a good motor-car, and we're going to have to walk *through snow.*

"Still better than the alternative. There's no good ending if we kick the can down the road. Any luck on the receiver?" Luz said.

The wireless set's receiving apparatus had had an unfortunate encounter with some of the buckshot that had spattered bits of the operator across it.

"No, we just don't have the parts, but I'm absolutely sure we're getting our transmissions *out,*" Ciara said.

"We will be landing, yes?" Perrin said.

Luz nodded, a little surprised; she hadn't followed the English conversation, but she'd gotten the essential point.

"And we will be on foot, through snow?" At Luz's second nod she said, "I have an idea," and turned and walked rapidly out of the cabin.

"Let's keep on this heading as long as we're making any headway south," Luz said. "Then we dive for the deck."

Tense silence reigned for a little while. Then:

"Here comes proof that messages are getting out," James said. "Or that the HL-29's are."

Luz's head came up quickly, warned by his flatly neutral tone. On the other side of the airship from the barely visible HL-29 a series of black dots had appeared, flying in loose gaggles of four. They swelled as she watched.

"Fighting scouts!" she said.

"*German* fighting scouts," he confirmed grimly, then picked up a pair of binoculars and leveled them. "Albatross DV-5's. Twin Maxims—"

"High speed, very maneuverable," Ciara completed. "Monocoque plywood fuselages, excellent fighting scouts, especially since they solved the wing-spar problem and with the new two-hundred-sixty-horsepower high-compression engine."

Ciara's eyes met Luz's, and they exchanged something wordless. Then James said softly: "Well, I'll be damned. You *did* get through to the right people, Miss Whelan."

He had turned and was looking south. "SPAD Vs and Curtiss Pumas," he said; those were the French and American equivalents, and they were higher, just under the cloud cover.

Those dots swelled as well, and then faster, formations stretching out as they dove. The *jasta* marked with the Maltese cross of the German Empire climbed to meet them, and faintly through the thin air came the *tackatackatacka* of aerial combat. Luz nodded once.

"Take us down, you two. Now, and fast. It's less risky than staying up here."

She paused to shout down the corridor in French: "Brace yourselves! We will be landing and it may be rough!"

Would be rough, but at least she'd given them some warning.

Then she strapped into one of the crew positions. Perrin and Simone came back in, and several of the others, and fastened themselves into the seats as well.

The HL-22 curved westward as James turned his wheel. Ciara hauled on hers, and the nose went down. Her hand went out and tripped a lever, and there was a distant hissing sound; almost immediately a sinking feeling in the stomach accompanied it, a floating lightness like an express elevator in a New York skyscraper going down.

"Negative buoyancy!" Ciara said crisply. "It'll keep venting until it's all gone. The less there, the less to burn if they shoot at us."

The ground swelled ahead of them; they'd just passed over a broad area of forest, and Luz could see a long irregular field white with snow, the dark line of some trees along a creek, more trees planted on either side of a country road in the French fashion, and then a farm and more fields. Or what had been a farm; wisps of smoke still rose from it, and there was a black circle in the whiteness otherwise all around. She thought they'd get just past the ruined buildings and not far from another clump of woods.

"Put her nose up and dump ballast when I tell you," Cheine snapped.

"Aye-aye, sir!" Ciara replied.

Luz felt her heart turn over; Cheine snorted acknowledgment, his eyes fixed on the ground ahead. Something trailing smoke went by them very fast, then plowed into the ground and went up in a ball of flame and a thudding sound felt deep in the chest. It was too quick to see what country the young man who'd just died had served; or that of the pursuing aeroplane that did a victory roll as it climbed out of their view, but it didn't pause to strafe the HL-22. The snowy ground was coming up fast, and looking less smooth all the time—there were plow marks beneath it, she thought.

"Now!" Cheine screamed, and cut the throttles back to their rest position.

The engines coughed and went silent, for the first time since they'd stormed the airship back in Staaken, and the HL-22 slowed; a balloon a hundred meters long had a lot of surface to catch the air. Ciara's hand slapped the emergency vents for the water ballast, and a rumbling waterfall sound came from below, and a sudden perceptible slowing of their descent as well as they shed weight faster than lifting power. The nose of the airship turned upward with ponderous speed as she wrestled with the vertical controls, the horizon dropping in the forward view until for a moment all they could see was sky.

Luz braced her legs, bent forward, and wrapped her arms around her head.

Whump.

Impact flexed the gondola like a whip as the stern fin struck the ground and dug in, and the straps drove her breath out with a bruising grunt. Metal ripped and tore with screams of mechanical anguish, a blow hard enough to snap her clenched teeth open and shut with a painful click and give her a sharp stabbing pain in the side.

The collision scrubbed more of the speed off the airship, and as it slowed it fell forward with a ponderous motion like falling in a dream. The gondola struck the ground instants later; the body of the HL-22 pivoted on that point with another long scream of sheet aluminum crumpling and tearing. The envelope of the lifting body tore too, and the last of the hydrogen whistled free; the airship fell onto its side, and the fragile interior latticework of triangles and keels and supporting cords snapped and failed.

Silence fell, except for the ongoing snap and crunch of structures collapsing under stresses they were never meant to bear and the pop and tinkle of the windows going . . . and a chorus of shrieks from the French forced laborers farther back; it must have been even harder for them, not having anything to do but wait blindly. Luz shook her head, but the darkness wasn't her, it was sheets of the outer pressure fabric falling over the shattered windows. The emergency lights came on, dim and red.

"Out, out, out!" Luz shouted, ignoring the second stab of pain in the left side of her chest.

"Leave me," Cheine croaked. "I'll only slow you—"

"Ne sois pas stupide!" Perrin snapped.

She and Simone moved according to some prearranged plan, though they both had blood running down their faces from minor cuts or a smacked nose. Perrin cut the webbing straps of Cheine's harness with a very sharp knife she must have gotten from the galley, and she and the girl dragged him out—ignoring a smothered yelp as his leg was jarred; there was fresh blood on the bandage—put him on an improvised sled, and pulled it down the slanted corridor. Ciara groaned and put her hands to her head.

"Why do I always get a thump on the noggin when I fight Germans with you, Luz, my darling?" she said, but her voice was strong, without the threadiness it had had after she was pistol-whipped in Boston.

Luz got free of her straps, flicked open the protective case, and took out the Sharpshooter, slinging it across her back with the muzzle down and to the left.

"Let's vacate this lemonade stand, business prospects are terrible here, *mi corazón*," she said, offering a hand.

Ciara staggered up; there was a trickle of red from a cut over one eyebrow, but she moved faster after the first few steps. She was alert enough to see that Luz was favoring one side.

"What's wrong?" she said quietly.

"The strap of the harness caught me hard when we hit. I think it sprang a rib—not a bad crack but a thin fracture."

"Arm around my shoulder and take some of the weight off," Ciara said, and Luz obeyed gratefully; it still hurt, but she could move faster.

The corridor was slanted, but light poured in where the exit ramp had been torn away. They pushed through under a huge flap of torn envelope, which was surprisingly difficult, and looked around.

The fighting scouts were still mixing it up above, in a wheeling scramble that gradually moved away northeastward. The HL-29's colors made it difficult to see for a moment, but it was there a few thousand yards to the east. Luz scooped Cheine's binoculars up and cursed softly as she leveled them. The German craft was hovering most of a mile away with its engines barely turning over—she couldn't hear them, though the fighting scouts buzzed overhead like great audible dragon-flies as they fought—and men were coming down ropes from it; as she watched the last of them slid to the ground . . .

Fifteen, she thought automatically. *Sixteen.*

. . . the ropes were reeled up and a torrent of water ballast was released, as the airship turned and rose, heading north at low altitude to get away from possible Entente fighting scouts with twice its speed. Horst was getting it and its Telemobiloscope out of reach of any Entente ground troops in the area . . . and heading over to destroy the HL-22 and *its* precious Telemobiloscope, and not-so-incidentally to kill her and Ciara and the others. The pursuers would be all soldiers and all fit; they couldn't possibly stay ahead of them for long through this unknown snowy desolation.

They don't even need to hurry, and they probably won't, Luz thought; a chill settled around her chest, but she ignored it.

¡Sigo viviendo! *As John Carter says*, she thought, breathing carefully against the stabbing in her chest. *I still live!*

She looked around. "Over there," she snapped. "The ruined farmhouse! We can hold out better there, maybe keep them from the wreck until help arrives."

And maybe John Carter and Tarzan will show up, she thought.

Luz led the way with her arm over Ciara's shoulder; even so they made enough speed that the others didn't crowd them. Perrin and Simone and several others pulled Cheine on his sled, and still others drew several more with gear and food. There was no sound but the panting of breath and the creak and crunch of snow underfoot . . . except for a dull intermittent rumbling in the distance to the northwest, waxing and waning but never entirely going away.

"The front. Artillery," Luz said at Ciara's inquiring look.

As they got closer to the snagged ruins Luz frowned. The building had been nothing remarkable before it took something like a field-gun shell through one wall and burned down—two stories, symmetrical stucco with ragstone underneath and ashlar-block quoining at the corners, four windows up and down and a bigger one over the door. That made it the farmhouse of a very prosperous farm, or the chateau of a very modest estate; the same incident had wrecked the stables and barns behind it even more thoroughly, and it was impossible to see how much of a garden there had been around it. Most of the walls were down to chest height all around, or less, but by one of the usual freaks of destruction a section next to where the front door had been stood up about sixteen feet. From the smell of the smoke it had been burned about a day or two ago, and the bulk of the flames put out by snow since then.

But there was something about it . . .

She froze an instant before a voice from inside the ruins said: "*Hande Hoche*, ya Kraut bastids!"

The voice was speaking English, and Nu Yawk Brooklynese at that, of the *Toity-toid an' Toid Street* variety. Luz did put her hands up, as she spotted a very slight movement . . . like a gray Parkerized-steel barrel zeroing in on her. She didn't dive for the ground; an instant calculation told her that fingers were on triggers, eyes glued to sights, and any rapid movement would bring a storm of fire.

Which spares my abused torso, at least. And it looks as if we ran into some help all unawares.

"I'm American!" she called back, in her natural neutral General American accent; it would show she was a woman, too, which wasn't obvious at this distance while she was wearing a flight suit. "From California."

Ciara spoke up: "And I'm from South Boston, I am!"

"Jesus!" the voice said, and there was a murmur of conversation just too soft to catch behind the gaping hole where a window had been.

"What were you two broads doing on a German airship?" the Brooklynite called out suspiciously.

"We stole the airship in Berlin," Luz said crisply. "We're American secret agents, except for these French ladies we rescued."

"And who's da Kraut on dat sled? 'Cause that's a Kraut uniform."

"And actually . . . Sergeant, is it? I'm from Manhattan myself, and not Yorkville, either," Cheine said in his best patrician drawl.

Yorkville was the city's most heavily German district, though these days it was draped in enough starry flags and red-white-and-blue bunting that every day looked like the Fourth.

He went on: "Thirty-six Gramercy Park, to be precise—corner of Gramercy Park and East Twenty-first Street."

"Well, fuck me," the voice said wonderingly. "Yeah, Sergeant . . . ah, pardon my French, Sergeant Eddie Capra, 106th Regiment, 27th Division. Look, come forward, and keep your hands where we can see 'em."

Luz called back over her shoulder in French, and the whole party came forward slowly. Sergeant Capra came out, a skinny dark young man in a U.S. Army parka and an improvised white cloth cover on his turtle helmet, with a Colt-Browning semiauto rifle in his hands and a mostly smoked Camel dangling from his lower lip.

"Well, f . . . foolish me," he said wonderingly, after looking them over.

Following him out was another soldier, this one in a very tattered and very grubby French horizon-blue uniform with greatcoat and a dark beard spilling down his chest to show why the nickname for soldiers in this country was *poilu*—"hairy one."

He began talking to Perrin and the others in French that was fluent but made it obvious his first language was Breton, and then turned to the American:

"Eet is . . . 'ow you say . . . de trut, Edeee," he said, and noticing her, said in French: "I am a sailor before the war. *Harponneur de baleines.* I sail with men from New Bedford sometimes."

Then in English of a sort again. "No shit!"

"There are actual Germans after us, Sergeant, and they're coming on quickly," Luz said. "And I don't think they're going to be at all pleased with what we've done."

"Yeah, well, lady, misery loves company. Come on in; it ain't much, but it ain't home either. We just got here a couple hours ago."

There were seven soldiers inside the ruined farmhouse, not counting the three dead laid out with their coats over their faces; two were French, ragged stragglers from a unit that had been retreating since the horror-gas attacks broke the old Western Front. Five were Americans, and all were lightly wounded in ways they would have taken more seriously in less desperate circumstances.

The American noncom was voluble but not very informative. That wasn't a surprise; enlisted men often had no coherent idea of what was going on in a fight, outside what they could see for themselves. That went double when things were going badly.

"Divisional HQ's down in Nevers," he said. "That's about fifteen miles. I think. We went into the line two weeks ago, right off the boats, and we hit the Krauts a good one, had 'em moving back fast . . . then, Christ, I don't think even the brass knew what hit us. All of a sudden it was raining gas—regular gas, not horror-gas, our masks worked—and HE and den dey were all over us like flies on . . . manure. *Behind* us even, and we kept moving back. My squad got cut off on a forward patrol, two days ago, lost some men, and when we got back the company had pulled out. Hell, da whole battalion. I don't know crap about what's happening. We was going to keep going tonight and move back, try and find our lines."

Then he turned his head. "Hey, miss, don't touch—ah, da hell wid it, it's busted bad anyway."

Ciara was bent over a partly disassembled Lewis gun, with the maintenance manual and toolkit both open beside her. Her fingers began to move, while Capra explained:

"McGillicudy was our Lewis man, but he and his team"—he nodded toward the bodies farther back in the next roofless room—"didn't make it. Caught some fragments from a mortar, same one dat f . . . fuddled up da gun. This was far as we could get them and they all croaked right after we stopped. Damn his Irish ass, I needed him, that's better 'n half the squad's firepower."

The two Frenchmen had Lebel rifles, slow-loading and slow-firing anachronisms, and not much ammunition for them. Capra and the remains of his squad had Colt-Browning rifles, five or six magazines each, and some grenades, and not much else including food, having eaten their iron rations; the Frenchwomen had taken everything edible from the HL-22 and were moving around so that the soldiers could eat at their positions, to emphatic gratitude.

"You know how to use that Sharpshooter, ma'am?" Capra said, nodding at the rifle over her back.

Cheine laughed. "Sergeant," he said. "You don't know the half of it."

"Yeah, if there's . . . fifteen, you said, miss?"

"Fifteen or sixteen including their commander, who is very bad news," Luz said crisply.

"Fifteen, maybe sixteen bad *Boche* coming, we ought to get set up, and I'll be glad to have ya. Christ and His Mother—"

He crossed himself.

"—I'd take Teddy with his fff . . . full-bore cowboy six-shooters right now. Or Carrie Nation and her ax!"

"There!" Ciara said with satisfaction, coming out of her brown study of concentration. "It was the return spring, Sergeant Capra. There's a spare here in the tool case . . . there . . ."

There were a series of *snicks* and *snacks*. "There, it ought to be working right and proper now. Just like the manual says!"

Capra glanced at the newcomers again; the Frenchwomen had a small fire of wood scraps going already and were heating soup in a battered sooty pot they'd salvaged from the shattered kitchen.

"Youse guys is strange," he said.

Cheine laughed again. "Sergeant," he said. "You don't know the half of it."

L uz carefully scanned across the field through the telescopic sight. "Sergeant," she called downstairs . . .

Not that there was much of the second-story floor left, just a piece of the wall that supported the remains of the staircase and about twelve feet of joists and floorboards that still clung to the wall.

"Ma'am?"

"I make it eight of them coming at us across that field to the east. That means half of them missing, and they'll be infiltrating through those woods to the north and trying to get around us. They're making very good use of cover and they're carrying some new type of rifle I don't recognize, definitely not Mausers."

"Right you are, ma'am," he said, then raised his voice. "Winock, Yannik—"

Evidently the Frenchmen were *both* Bretons; the French army had always been regionally recruited.

"Youse guys get back where da kitchen used to be, but careful dat nobody sneaks up using what's left of the barn for cover."

Winock looked doubtful, and Luz called a translation, at which point Capra blew out his cheeks and their thick black stubble in a gesture of relief and waved a hand in thanks.

"Miss," he went on to Ciara, "you take that Lewis back wid 'em."

Luz gave a quick nod when Ciara looked up at her; that was the right tactical decision. The enemy could get closer there under cover and so it was the right spot for a mass of portable firepower.

Capra went on: "One of youse tell them French broads to get low and stay dat way. All of youse back there in the kitchen hold fire until they're close, right? Everyone else, we got trouble knocking at the front door. Lefkowitz, how many rifle grenades you got left?"

"Two, Sarge."

"Ahhhh, *shit*. Make 'em count. Look, you get your ass back there in the kitchen too with the frogs and the Lewis—I swear to God they're gonna use the wrecked barn for cover, you can pop 'em behind it, maybe catch a bunch. Got it?"

"Right, Sarge," Lefkowitz said, pushing his helmet down on kinky reddish hair and folding his gangly length as he moved, careful not to let anything show over the remains of the walls.

"Short bursts, sweetie," Luz called down to Ciara. "Keep the butt tight against your shoulder and aim low."

"I read the manual, darling," she replied with calm cheerfulness in her voice, carefully laying the spare barrel on her right by its carrying handle.

¡Dios mío, *but I love that woman! I wish I could say so.*

Luz forced fear for her partner out of her mind, along with the nagging pain in her side and the wish that there were time to strap it up. The only way they had a chance of coming out of this alive was to win, and to do that they had to concentrate on each doing her part of the job. Cheine murmured to Perrin and Simone, and they helped him crawl over to a position where he could see over a section of rubble where a window had been, tumbled ruin just high enough to give him cover. He lay there with a charred chair cushion under his stomach to take pressure off his leg and the two drums of ammunition ready to hand.

Luz looked down the section of second-story wall that remained intact; it was about twelve feet long, there were three good firing positions, and the wall's stone construction would stop rifle rounds. Which made her thankful it wasn't wood or brick—people tended to underestimate how much material bullets could punch through. She took out a strip of cloth that had started out as bedding in the HL-22, rubbed it on the charred surface of the wall to dirty it, and wrapped it around the barrel of the rifle to break the outline. Then she eased it over the edge of the stone and began scanning, alternating between her binoculars and the more powerful but narrower view through the scope. Some people preferred to work with a spotter, but she never had . . .

The field was about twelve hundred yards across from the forest to the farmhouse, with the little stream and its brush and trees about two-thirds of the way toward the house. The problem was that it was rolling land and had patches of dead ground. On the good side the Germans were all in standard field-gray, which was actually more like a dull gray-green, highly effective at any time *except* winter but only a little better than black against snow. She saw a flicker of movement, half glimpsed and then disappearing behind a ridge of snow piled up against a furrow. She worked her hands to limber them, then stripped off the right glove with her teeth. The .30-06 boattail could punch through several sandbags or a foot of hardwood quite a ways out . . .

Luz had to guess where a man *might* be lying behind that ridge. Arm in the loop, breathe in, ignore the pain from the sprung rib, let most of it out, *squeeze*—

Crack!

And fire stabbed through her side.

"¡Ay! That *hurt!*"

A perceptible fraction of a second later there was an upward spurt of dirt and snow from the ridge she'd fired at. *Something* heaved up and fell back behind it.

"Surprise, Fritzie!" she muttered. "It's the worst day of your life."

The bolt went *snick-snack* as she reloaded, fast and smooth, but in the interval seven or eight men picked themselves up, dashed forward, and went to ground behind good cover picked out in advance. They were down before she was ready to shoot again, and she couldn't be absolutely sure where several of them were. And now they knew they were within the killing range of a good sniper.

"Oh, this is bad," she murmured to herself.

Aloud: "Sergeant Capra! I got one but there are eight more out there, and they've all been to school. And they're all carrying some sort of stubby rifle with a large-capacity magazine, twenty or thirty rounds. They're all automatics. That leaves six or seven unaccounted for somewhere around us. The ones in front were waiting until their friends had time to come at us from the rear, behind the barn."

"Ah, *shit!* Thanks, lady, dat's what I figured."

Capra was working his rosary as he lay and waited for naked-eye targets. Luz felt a certain sympathy for the young man pitchforked into responsibility in a situation where there weren't any good answers. At least the weapons the Germans were carrying didn't seem to be very long-range, which meant they couldn't keep her head down with covering fire . . . not yet . . . but she suspected that they'd be difficult to . . .

Two more broke cover in a short zigzagging dash.

Crack!

A miss, though it kicked up snow and dirt not far from the feet of one man, making him leap aside; the rib was putting her off.

And those are Stoßtruppen, *I think—I recognize the description of their tactics, and the Germans use them to deploy new weapons. Trust Horst to lay his hands on the best.*

Another pair dashed forward. She worked the bolt, fast and smooth, readjusted . . .

Crack!

A wailing scream in the distance that faded quickly; everyone except possibly the Frenchwomen knew what that meant.

The rest of the *Stoßtruppen* had all made it farther forward. The four American riflemen below began firing, slamming out the contents of their twenty-round magazines, but at least six of the Germans made it to the banks of the little stream. A rasping stutter, and chips flew off the stonework ahead of her position in a peening, sparking clamor of high-velocity metal on stone. She ducked down; whatever the Germans were shooting could be used like a machine pistol, but it had a *lot* more range and those bullets were hitting much harder than nine-millimeter parabellum. They still had to be four hundred yards out at least, and now they were moving forward again with some firing to keep her head down while the rest moved.

A gurgling shriek came from below as one of the American soldiers was hit. She rolled onto her back and pushed herself along to her next firing position, wriggling like a snake to stay low with the rifle lying down her body, panting and curling her lips away from her teeth so she wouldn't bite them as the movement made the injury worse. If the ends of the rib were severed, they might work their way into a lung . . .

So not *good.*

"Les Boches! Les Boches!"

A yell in French from the kitchen of the wrecked house, and the slow *bang . . . bang . . .* of the clumsy tube-magazine Lebel rifles firing. Then a *whunk . . . BAM*, as Lefkowitz expended one of his precious rifle grenades, and a chattering rattlesnake *brrrttt-brrrrttt* from the Lewis gun, precisely the short bursts the manual specified. The chance that Ciara would actually *hit* anything except the landscape in general was low; that wasn't a skill you could get out of a book, but she wasn't getting upset and burning out the barrel by keeping her finger clenched on the trigger either and the mere sound would make experienced soldiers wary. Everyone who'd been up against them hated and feared machine guns.

The firing was getting more intense on both sides. A man sprang up from the stream bank and began to run forward, a stick-grenade in his right hand with the priming button dangling on its string and the odd-looking rifle held at the balance in his left. She happened to be pointed in his direction when he jumped up.

Crack!

"¡Ay! ¡Coño!" she snarled; the pain from the recoil was definitely getting worse.

This time there wasn't any doubt; through the scope she could see the round punch into the German's chest just at the top of the breastbone, and his handsome smooth face flexed like a rubber mask as he pitched over backward. She ducked down again immediately, smelling her own sweat despite the damp cold as a storm of the automatic-rifle fire chewed into the stone above her head. It would chew *her* into bloody rags in an instant if she showed herself.

And I've got no cover at all from behind. Whatever those weapons are, they're a menace!

It was time to get out of there, and the peening of the bullets seemed to be producing a clanking iron clamor in her head. She worked the bolt, slung the rifle again, let herself slide backward until her legs were over the place where the floor wasn't anymore, then slid back and caught a beam that creaked ominously to break her fall.

Luz landed on the rubble, one foot slipping a little on the broken panels of a door, half a scream escaping her. White fire flashed across her vision for a second. She fell to her knees with clenched teeth bared, fighting against the nausea of agony that made her mouth fill with saliva, clutching at her side and hissing. Then she spat to one side—at least she couldn't see or taste any blood in it.

Firing was a ceaseless hammer now and definitely from both sides of the ruined house: the Thompson firing burst after burst, the Lewis gun rattling, American egg grenades exploding in a vicious whine of cast-iron fragments, and German stick grenades going off with that distinctive *bamp* sound—fortunately they relied more on blast, and it hammered at her eardrums without anything biting her flesh. More automatic fire, like half a dozen machine guns firing at the same time. Bits and pieces of stone stung the back of her neck. Whatever weapon the Germans were using was a killer at close range, *un verdadero asesino.*

Her attention split, as if two moving pictures were playing in her mind at the same time:

Lefkowitz was cursing sulfurously in Yiddish, rising up to fire another rifle grenade and then falling backward, four exit wounds stitching across his back and flopping him down like a rag doll. Ciara lying white-faced, putting another drum on the Lewis behind the tumbled cast-iron stove, her breath panting and eyes wide but fingers steady with the complex task. One of the Breton soldiers slumped limply, the back of his head gone and leaking red and pink. In the front room of the ruined house Capra was yelling and clutching at his calf, blood welling between his fingers.

And Horst sprang over the ruined wall of the farmhouse, his one-eyed face not handsome at all as it contorted like a wolf.

Oh, how I wish I'd guessed wrong about it being him!

He smashed an American away, blood flying as the butt of the German weapon cracked across his face. That turned smoothly into a wheel with his stubby bayoneted rifle raised as Cheine's Thompson clicked empty, ready to drive the point through the fallen man's body.

Ciara struggled to raise the heavy Lewis as a German came at her in a limping but snake-fast rush, with a sharpened entrenching tool raised, his hideously scarred face contorted and pale blue eyes staring . . . and some distant part of Luz's mind recognized him, from when she'd crashed over the Dutch border into Germany last September in the car with Horst and von Bülow . . .

Luz fired the Sharpshooter from the hip.

Crack!

The little German's body snapped sideways as the bullet hit the blade of his entrenching shovel, punching through it and at a slant into his belly, the distorted shape of the bullet pinwheeling like a tiny buzz saw. He screamed and staggered right into a last burst from Ciara's Lewis gun that sent him flopping backward with most of his torso smashed into fragments of meat and bone. Ciara froze, her eyes wide as she stared at the body. Nobody else was on their feet there. Two of the Frenchwomen crawled into the kitchen; one of the Bretons was still breathing, but unconscious, and they started to bandage him.

And out in the burned remnants of barn behind the house a brief savage firefight was raging, American Thompsons against the German whatever-they-were, a couple of grenades, and then a shout in an unmistakable hillbilly rasp:

"All daid, Loo-tenant! Ever'thang clar here!"

A shell exploded, fifty or sixty yards away in front of the house. She didn't have time to wonder where it came from, but none of those fighting here in the beginning had brought artillery with them.

Ciara's safe there now. Move, Luz, move! Horst's still alive!

Luz came up and whirled, dropping the empty sniper rifle, the *navaja* clicking open in her hand, moving forward with the blade ready but her left hand pressed to her side and face twisted in a rictus of effort. Horst pulled his rifle free; the point had stuck in the boards of the floor when Cheine hammered it aside with the empty Thompson gun. The German began another lunge that would be impossible for the wounded man to block.

Then Horst saw Luz. Their eyes met, and the motion stopped; his flared wide open, white showing all around the iris.

"*¡Híjole!*" she blurted, shocked even then at the sheer fury in the gaunt one-eyed man's face.

Then he screamed, an endless racking snarl, weapon leveled as he charged in a blur of motion. She left it until the last second, until not even someone as agile as the big German could swerve, and twisted to her right, sweeping the knife at the rifle. Steel clanged on steel and Horst went past her, dodging her backhand cut at his face by going under it with cat-quick grace.

That's not going to work twice, she thought, bent over and gasping as he came erect; the point of the knife wavered as she struggled to keep it between them. *He's got six feet of reach on me.*

Crack!

Horst jerked and fell, his foot turning on a loose piece of rock as the impact of the pistol bullet hammered into his shoulder. Cheine started to laugh, looking at Yvonne Perrin where she lay flat two paces away with Cheine's Luger in a clumsy two-handed grip that had been good enough. Simone half dropped, half flung the head-sized chunk of rock she was carrying down on Horst's wound and slumped backward herself, collapsed against a snag of wall. Even then Luz thought Horst might have stood again, but she managed to hobble over and kicked him behind the ear, hard, gasping again as it jarred her rib.

"*¡Ay!* But I bet that hurt you worse than it did me," she panted.

Ciara came up beside her, and Luz leaned a hand on her shoulder as she hobbled to the doorway.

A machine was sitting outside the farmhouse, a machine of angular armor plates riveted together, smoke curling up from the muzzle of the six-pounder cannon in its turret. She remembered what she'd seen on the flatcar outside Los Angeles; the first wave had been on their way to Europe then, just as she'd thought. Four more like it were crawling forward, lurching as the endless treads that bore them ground obstacles into dust, their engines roaring with mechanical ferocity, and behind them were others of the same general make but with a boxy compartment for a squad of infantry instead of a turret.

One of the . . .

Tanks, she reminded herself.

. . . fired its gun at a cluster of Germans running for the shelter of the creek and bodies flew, though she thought one squat man managed to dive into cover in time.

Luz started to smile. Ciara buried her head in Luz's neck and sighed, sliding an arm around her waist, and they helped each other out into the open.

"*Hola,*" Luz said to the man who stood in the hatch of the vehicle . . .

She closed her *navaja* and slipped it into the pocket of the flight suit. *Remember to call it a tank.*

He was in a dark uniform like a mechanic's overalls stained with use and grease, a padded leather helmet on his head and goggles over his eyes, a knit scarf wound about his neck and a bandaged left arm in a sling. Despite that she felt a tug of recognition.

"Ted?" she said; once she realized who it was, the frog-wide Roosevelt mouth and grin were unmistakable, especially in his narrower face, despite the goggles and leather helmet he was wearing. "*Ted?*"

Theodore Roosevelt Jr. spoke into the cone of the speaking tube in front of him and the engine noise dropped to a ratcheting idle amid a cloud of blackish acrid-smelling exhaust fumes. Then he pushed up the goggles and gave her a long look.

"Luz?" he said equally incredulously, looking past the flight suit, and the scrapes and dirt and blood. "What the hell are *you* doing here?"

"Spy work," she said.

Memory clicked, and she pointed to the wreck of the airship to the northeast.

"Secure that, would you? Important ultra-secret German machinery in there. We need to get it back to our lines, *pronto*, and shipped home."

Then, after he'd called and waved and sent a squad to guard it:

"And what are *you* doing here, Ted? Not that I'm not grateful, but . . ."

He looked around at the wreckage of the farmhouse and signaled several men with Red Cross armbands forward.

Then he slapped the side of the turret, where the 2nd Cavalry's palmetto leaf and eight-pointed shield were painted in white.

"I'm doing what the cavalry always does, Luz—ride to the rescue!" he said.

She laughed, and it hurt.

But in a good *way*, she thought.

EPILOGUE I

North Sea
HMS *Queen Elizabeth*
Flagship, Grand Allied Fleet
DECEMBER 20TH, 1916(B)

"That was too bloody close," Grand Admiral Beatty said, as the German shells sent icy seawater slopping nearly as high as the great ship's conning tower. "The intelligence report was right, for once; they *can* see in the dark."

They couldn't see the German ships at all from the superdreadnought *Queen Elizabeth I*'s bridge despite its height; it was four on a winter's afternoon, near sunset this far north, and there was rain mixed with snow. They *could* see the muzzle flashes of the High Seas Fleet, lighting the eastern horizon from north to south, like a flickering illusion of sunrise. They could also see the sea of fire where HMS *Bellerophon* was ablaze from stem to stern behind them. *Temeraire* had just gone skyward in a volcano of flame and sunk with all hands, and the flagship's thirty thousand tons had staggered to the blast.

"Sir!"

The rating came through from the wireless room behind the bridge. "Sir, another urgent message from USS *Lexington*. The same as the last: *Imperative fire Santa Shell immediately.*"

"Bloody Yanks," Beatty said sourly.

Part of the tone was sheer envy; those were lovely, lovely ships, and well-manned; their gunnery was particularly good. He was *less* glum than many of the men on the bridge, and unlike some he didn't have a burning personal resentment that the horror-gas attacks on America had been thwarted when London and Paris were destroyed. Nor was he half-mad, which was nearly as common as not, now.

His fury at the Germans was collective and cold, rather than a near-disabling mass of personal grief. He'd been in the middle of a disastrous, in fact truly vicious, quarrel with his wife when she died in London during the October attacks that gutted the city, and in his innermost heart he regretted her much less than a number of chance acquaintances, club friends, and for that matter the deaf-and-dumb flower seller in St. James he'd been in the habit of buying a boutonnière from when he was in town.

His predecessor, Jellicoe, had simply gone silent and refused to talk to anyone since the fall of London, and for the last week had refused to eat or drink. Self-proclaimed Lord Protector Milner had stepped in and appointed Beatty from his new headquarters in, of all places, Birmingham. Nobody had objected; nobody knew what was and wasn't legal anymore except that Princess Mary was now Victoria II, and Milner was effectively dictator by common consent. Maybe that was what the Empire needed. It was certainly what they *had*, and he'd done wonders keeping the supplies coming and getting what he could of the British Army out of Europe through Dunkirk and Calais.

"Santa Shell? Why do they call it that?" he said. "What sort of code name is that?"

"I believe it's a reference to Father Christmas, sir," his flag captain, Ernle Chatfield, said. "They call him Santa Claus, and the shells are stuffed with something very like tinsel and it *is* nearly Christmas, so . . ."

"Bloody Yanks," Beatty said again.

People in England weren't laughing much these days.

Then: "Signal all ships, fire Santa Shell, and maintain at rate of one shell for every five minutes."

He smiled, very slightly; that was what the Yank technical wizards said would work, and they did appear to have a thumb on the enemy's pulse this time. God alone knew how; perhaps they had a suave, sinister master-spy like the ones Buchan wrote about. It was humiliating, and he didn't want to acknowledge it, but better the Yanks than *nobody* doing it. And since he wasn't going to repeat his mistake at the Battle of Jutland—

No, the First *Battle of Jutland*, he thought.

—and fail to push the action . . .

"And signal, *All ships, engage the enemy more closely.* Time to give London a memorial, and I can't think of a bloody thing more fitting than a lot of German ships on the bottom of the bloody sea."

A growl went around the bridge, just as the *Queen Elizabeth*'s forward turrets slammed out a quartet of fifteen-inch shells eastward. Even through the thick armor, it was a sound like the hammer of doom.

EPILOGUE II

Casa de los Amantes
Santa Barbara, California
JANUARY 1ST, 1917(B)

U ncle Teddy!" Luz said in delight and surprise, walking quickly
down to the big Pierce-Arrow limousine, taking his hand, and
kissing his cheek. "Good to see you at the *Casa* again!"

"I heard you were laying on a roast for New Year's and couldn't
resist," he said.

Then, into her ear as he gave her a cautious hug, though the thin
fracture in the rib was more or less knit by now:

"The miscreant is safe behind bars once again."

She chuckled. That was taken from a well-known summation of the
First Battle of Jutland, when the High Seas Fleet had sortied, given
rather better than it got in a confused scuffle, and then scuttled back to
Wilhelmshaven and Kiel to avoid being ground under by superior
numbers. The witty remark then had been that the German Navy had
assaulted its jailors and then returned to its prison cell. Apparently the
Second Battle of Jutland had turned out the same way, with the Germans bottled up by the blockade of the Royal Navy and its U.S.
counterparts.

"Aunt Edith!"

"Darling Luz!"

Kisses on both cheeks this time.

"And Director Wilkie!"

He got a firm handshake.

"John, please, Executive Field Operative, on a social occasion," the head of the Black Chamber said.

"Well, I'm Luz, then, John," she said.

She signaled the temporary staff forward to take coats and hats and wraps as they went up the stairs and under the tall arched entranceway into the hallway. Everything was bright, the lights inside blazing and Japanese paper lanterns scattered through the grounds, amid laughter and chatter and the sprightly sound of dance music in the middle distance. The scent of the Mexicali Rose flowers mingled with the pleasant odors of the barbecue.

The president, in a fit of nostalgia and Westerner-ism, was in rancher's BBQ-going gear, down to Stetson and string tie. The two Secret Service bodyguards behind him wore evening dress, which made them a little conspicuous in easygoing California's even more easygoing Santa Barbara. Aunt Edith was, of course, in exactly the same elegantly conservative evening gown she'd have worn to a garden party on Long Island, one with a surplice drapery of Brussels net embroidered in gold and pastel colored threads, more gold embroidered net for the sleeves, a cluster of rosebuds at the waist, and a ruffle of gold embroidered net at the bottom of the full folds of the dress. It made Luz feel very radical and perhaps just a trifle démodé in hers, which was a low-cut maroon number that had a skirt that was open-sided over a lace underskirt.

"Come in, come in!" she said, as the presidential limousines crunched away.

Though the party was as much outside as indoors, with tables and chairs scattered among the lawns and flower banks. It was a fine evening by the standards of January in Santa Barbara; a bit over sixty degrees, with a post-sunset sky clear and showing only a few trails of high cloud among the first twinkle of stars. The lanterns glowed along the second-story balustrade around the courtyard, casting light colored by their paper and hand-painted designs, and outside more led down the pathways in the garden toward the sea and the beach. A band was playing something lively in the pavilion next to the retaining wall overlooking the beach; she'd managed to get Morton's Red-Hot Ragtime Band away from American National Airways for the evening by a ruthless exercise in pull—and a dozen couples were dancing, including one Ted Roosevelt Jr., who was about to ship out again and who'd probably been the one who betrayed the date of the party to his father.

People were strolling around, or milling about the bar and buffet set up in the court, with its centerpiece of pit-roasted whole pig scenting the air and a rented carver leading the servers behind it in white aprons and hats. Uncle Teddy perked up at the sight; it appealed to his Viking-chieftain-McHearty-frontiersman instincts, and also to his lifelong fondness for large solid platefuls of roast beast. Josh Taguchi was over by the punch bowl and its flanking barrel of red wine, in his new-minted Army captain's uniform—Engineers, of course—with his parents and sisters looking fit to burst with pride, and an extremely pretty red-headed girl he'd met at Stanford on his arm looking terminally shy while Ciara grilled him on something technical. James Cheine had been listening to them; as he saw who was at the entrance he began to drift over, walking fairly well but leaning on his cane and assisted by the woman at his side. The leg wound would heal eventually, but hadn't quite yet.

"Mr. President!" he said, and got a broad smile; a wounded hero could rely on that from Theodore Roosevelt.

"Madame President," he added.

And got a lively smile in return; the Cheines were part of the Knickerbocker world Edith Roosevelt, née Carow, had been raised in and where she'd always been most comfortable.

He gave a polite and discreet nod to Wilkie; now that they were inside there were too many people without clearance in earshot to mention the Director's name. Then he brought forward the woman on his arm.

"And may I introduce my fiancée, Madame Perrin, formerly of Lille, Mr. President?"

Teddy Roosevelt's eyebrows went up as he bent over her hand, something she accepted with regal calm betrayed only by a flicker of eyes toward Cheine; the official story was that she was a widow . . . which was true . . . and that her pregnancy somehow dated to before her deportation from Lille . . . which wasn't and which violated the laws of arithmetic and biology.

"Congratulations!" he said, shifting into fluent but not particularly grammatical French. "America can always use more good French blood." A toothy grin: "Like my own!"

Perrin's eyes went wider. "You . . . you are of French descent, *Monsieur Le President*?"

Teddy Roosevelt laughed. "One of my ancestors was a lady named de Veaux!" he said. "I'm a purebred American mongrel—Dutch, French of two varieties including Huguenot refugees on my mother's side, English, Scots . . . everything under the sun!"

The fiancée part hadn't been in the reports at all; it had surprised Luz and she still wasn't sure she understood the emotional dynamics. Perrin was looking less gaunt than she had, and much younger; the pregnancy was more advanced, now, of course, under an empire-style gown. And she was much calmer, too; her still-short hair had been formed into a Brutus-style ring of curls. Luz was still wearing a wig, a black shoulder-length one this time, so she could segue back to her own hair painlessly.

"I'm helpless in the hands of women who save my life, Mr. President," Cheine said easily. "And speaking of which, here is Simone—to be Simone Cheine, as soon as the adoption papers come through, which we expect shortly after the wedding."

"Bully! And delighted to meet you, Madame Perrin, and young Miss Cheine-to-be," Roosevelt said; both staggered under the impact of the famous presidential charm. "I've read of your exploits, and America will be the better for two such new citizens, and their children and grandchildren."

Luz stepped aside ruefully as the president swept into the court, leaving a trail of *bully* and *delighted* and handshakes and dropped-jaw astonishment as he went, not least when he returned Josh Taguchi's snap to attention and salute with a hearty handshake. Her family had been friends of the Roosevelts for a long time and it wasn't in the least out of character for him to attend a party here, though he hadn't since her parents died. It still wasn't what anyone expected, or what she had either until the telephone call a few moments ago.

And if Uncle Teddy was there, he'd be the center of attention; he couldn't help it, any more than he could stop breathing.

Ciara came up beside her in an emerald-and-silver outfit as the president began genially grilling young Captain Taguchi on technical subjects about which he was alarmingly well-informed, and they linked hands.

"I'm having *such* a good time, darling!" she said. "I'm so glad I finally got to meet Josh, and it's lovely that Madame Perrin and Simone will be close by . . . well, San Francisco is fairly close . . ."

There was a discreet cough from Director Wilkie, who'd drifted over from the presidential comet tail, unnoticed in the blaze of Rooseveltian charisma.

"John?" Luz said.

The Director sighed. "I'm sorry I have to throw a shadow on your party, Luz, Miss Whelan. But I'm afraid I have bad news . . . that came in while we were en route here, an express message to the *Saratoga* in flight, no less."

Officially the president was on a tour to meet the governors of the Western states, and doing it via a *Battle*-class airship to show how Progressive he was. Unofficially he just needed to get out of Washington occasionally, and had a childlike fascination with airships. At Luz's raised eyebrow the Director went on:

"Horst von Dückler has escaped from the Army prisoner-of-war camp at El Paso. Two men dead, both with their necks broken with a single twist. Apparently, the Army didn't quite believe our warnings."

Ciara's fingers tightened on hers almost painfully. Luz sighed. "He'll head down into Mexico," she said. "His Spanish is very good, better than his English."

"He'll be conspicuous there," Wilkie said hopefully.

"No more than I was in Germany; there are blond Mexicans. And there are plenty of gringos living in the Protectorate nowadays."

"Hundreds of thousands and more all the time," the Director confirmed. "Plus the garrison."

"The *revolucionarios* are quiet but we didn't get all of them. He'll make contact, and when he does . . ."

"We'll be hearing from him," Wilkie confirmed. "But not for a while. Enjoy yourselves in the meantime, but I thought you'd want to know."

Because that is a very dangerous and very vengeful man, Luz thought. *I can't even really disagree; we* did *need to know right away.*

"How are we supposed to do that?" Ciara asked indignantly, after he'd moved away. "Enjoy ourselves in the meantime?"

"Well, for now, we'll mingle, chat, and sip wine and nibble and then go do some dancing to Jelly Roll and his band," Luz said. "Though I suspect the president will cut in—he does like to cut a rug. And later—"

Ciara threw back her head and laughed. "This isn't quite happy ever after," she said. "But I think we can manage the happy."

For a while, Luz thought, smiling back. *The longer, the better.*

Photo by Anton Brkic

S. M. Stirling is the author of many science fiction and fantasy novels. A former lawyer and an amateur historian, he lives with his wife, Jan.